PRAISE FOR THE
SCHOOL FOR BRIDES

A Convenient Bride

"Cheryl Ann Smith surprises readers with a multilayered storyline. Beautifully romantic with a touch of mystery, *A Convenient Bride* is a rare gem among historical romance novels."   —*Fresh Fiction*

"I enjoyed reading it very much and found it hard to put down."   —*Night Owl Reviews*

The Scarlet Bride

"The School for Brides has a new resident, allowing Smith to add another strong, resilient heroine to her feminist series. It's wonderful to get reacquainted with past characters, and the connection between them, as the plot—complete with suspense, murder, and passion—unfolds."   —*RT Book Reviews*

"A very well-written novel and one that is full of the realities of life in that time period . . . Both a very good love story as well as a well-written mystery."   —*The Book Binge*

"The heroine is a courageous person who suffered terrible abuse but never lost her spirit, while the lead male is a strong person . . . Fans will appreciate this investigative historical thriller."   —*Genre Go Round Reviews*

continued . . .

The Accidental Courtesan

"A fast-paced, amusing, romantic historical filled with fun, and a delight to read." —*Fresh Fiction*

"With a dash of humor, plenty of sensuality, and a fast pace, Smith's second School for Brides novel is a pure delight. Readers will enjoy the charming cast of secondary characters and the mystery." —*RT Book Reviews*

"A charming story with characters that engage you from the first sentence. Truly a joy!" —*Night Owl Reviews*

The School for Brides

"Chockablock with plot twists . . . Plenty of passion and intrigue." —*Publishers Weekly*

"Smith makes a dazzling entrance to the romance community with a charming, sexy, innovative tale that sparks the imagination. There's a bright future ahead of Smith." —*RT Book Reviews*

"An unusual premise and an interesting story . . . Readers are in for a treat . . . It has . . . everything readers want in a romance." —*Romance Reviews Today*

"Delightful . . . And I loved the twists." —*The Romance Dish*

"A warm gender-war historical romance . . . Fans will cheer." —*Midwest Book Review*

The Wife He Always Wanted

CHERYL ANN SMITH

BERKLEY SENSATION, NEW YORK

THE BERKLEY PUBLISHING GROUP
Published by the Penguin Group
Penguin Group (USA)
375 Hudson Street, New York, New York 10014, USA

USA I Canada I UK I Ireland I Australia I New Zealand I India I South Africa I China

Penguin Books Ltd., Registered Offices: 80 Strand, London WC2R 0RL, England
For more information about the Penguin Group, visit penguin.com.

THE WIFE HE ALWAYS WANTED

A Berkley Sensation Book / published by arrangement with the author

Copyright © 2013 by Cheryl Ann Smith.
All rights reserved. No part of this book may be reproduced, scanned, or distributed in any
printed or electronic form without permission. Please do not participate in or encourage piracy
of copyrighted materials in violation of the author's rights. Purchase only authorized editions.

Berkley Sensation Books are published by The Berkley Publishing Group.
BERKLEY SENSATION® is a registered trademark of Penguin Group (USA)
The "B" design is a trademark of Penguin Group (USA)

For information, address: The Berkley Publishing Group,
a division of Penguin Group (USA)
375 Hudson Street, New York, New York 10014.

ISBN: 978-0-425-26066-1

PUBLISHING HISTORY
Berkley Sensation mass-market edition / September 2013

PRINTED IN THE UNITED STATES OF AMERICA

10 9 8 7 6 5 4 3 2 1

Cover art by Jim Griffin.
Cover design by George Long.
Interior text design by Laura K. Corless.

This is a work of fiction. Names, characters, places, and incidents either are the product
of the author's imagination or are used fictitiously, and any resemblance to actual persons,
living or dead, business establishments, events, or locales is entirely coincidental.
The publisher does not have any control over and does not assume any responsibility for
author or third-party websites or their content.

If you purchased this book without a cover, you should be aware that this book is
stolen property. It was reported as "unsold and destroyed" to the publisher, and neither
the author nor the publisher has received any payment for this "stripped book."

ALWAYS LEARNING   **PEARSON**

For Ethan.
The only twelve-year-old boy who actually wants
to see his name in a romance novel.

Chapter One

Sarah dropped the scrawny chicken into the pot, atop the few chunks of floating parsnips, and then sighed as she rubbed her hands off on her apron. To stretch the stew out for several days, she added more water, well knowing that the thin broth would be barely palatable and not enough to satisfy the emptiness in her rumbling stomach.

Still, it was something, and she silently thanked Mrs. Croswell for her generous gift of the chicken.

While the pot steamed over the fire, she took a seat at the table. Weary under the weight of the desperate desire to survive, her back ached and she twisted this way and that to ease the pressure on her spine.

"Who knew nineteen would feel like ninety," she said to the empty room. Even her cat had gone off weeks ago to seek out better accommodations and more plentiful scraps.

Once the stew began to boil, she covered the pot and tidied the kitchen. Once upon a time, she'd had her aunt for company. After her death two years previous, her visitors were mostly limited to Mrs. Croswell, and occasionally the parson's wife, whom Sarah thought dutifully visited to make certain she was still among the living.

She gave the stew one last stir, collected a basket filled with damp sheets, and went outside. She'd just begun to hang them to dry when the hairs on the back of her neck prickled and she whirled around to the sound of boot steps stopping behind her.

Standing a few paces away was The Widower, Jasper Campbell, his dark, intense eyes staring at her from beneath his hat with a less than casual bent.

Her stomach soured. His pursuit was becoming worrisome. He refused to consider that she did not want to wed him.

"Miss Palmer."

"Mister Campbell."

Almost thrice her age and three times her girth, his penchant for fighting, his six unruly children, and a thorough avoidance of soap and water made him an unacceptable suitor. All these, added to the unsettling feeling she had when he looked at her, solidified her determination to free herself of his unwanted presence.

Just yesterday morning she'd chased him off again, when the anger and impatience in his eyes had sent a shiver of alarm through her. How long would he allow her refusals before he took what he wanted by force?

He snatched the dusty hat off his head. "I have come to see if ye've given further consideration to me proposal."

How could she not? He was relentless. "As I have said previously, we would never suit, Mister Campbell. I think it best if you turn your attention elsewhere."

His heavy lids narrowed. "Ye think ye are too good to be a smithy's wife."

With her gaze unwavering and locked onto his, she picked up the basket and clutched it to her chest. "I think it's time for you to leave." Without hesitation, she walked briskly toward the door and hurried inside, throwing the bolt behind her and falling back against the panel.

"Oh dear." The palatable rage she'd seen in the instant of her refusal caused her heart to race. She pushed away from the panel and ran through the house to lock the front door. Once the cottage was secure, she hurried back through it to the kitchen window then peeked outside between the curtains. He stood in the same spot, watching the house for several minutes, before returning to his horse and riding away.

Relief flooded through her. Deep inside she knew he'd be back for her, and next time the choice to wed him or not would no longer be hers to make.

What to do? She had no means, no family to shelter her, no way to escape. For a woman in her situation, her choices were limited, and had been so for a very long time.

If she accepted Mister Campbell's proposal and wed him, she'd have food, clothing, and a life of abject misery. If she stayed here, she would likely starve. Unfortunately, she saw the latter as the more palatable option to bedding the beast.

Sarah slumped against the wall and closed her eyes. Certainly a life of suffering and loss had earned her one favor from above. So she dropped her head into her hands and said a little prayer for guidance.

A knock on the front door brought her head up and a twist in her stomach. Certainly Mister Campbell had not returned so quickly?

With a second pass through the cottage, she tiptoed to the front window. Careful to keep hidden, she glanced out in the direction of the stoop to see the back of a man loitering outside the door. From the angle and limited view, she could tell he was not the blacksmith. Thank goodness.

But who was he? She glanced around the overgrown yard and spotted his horse filling its belly on weeds and grass. By the looks of the fine chestnut steed, the stranger was no common vagrant. This eased her concerns a bit.

"There is only one way to find out what he wants," she muttered. She tugged off her apron as she crossed to the door, swept a stray lock behind her ear, and opened the panel. Her eyes opened wide and she squelched the shriek racing up the back of her throat.

The man standing before her in the open doorway was unshaven, dressed in some sort of fringed garment, and was so dusty that he looked as if bathing was an unknown concept for him. However, what truly made her knees knock and her body tremble with terror was his size and menacing scowl.

The man could easily crush her with his two hands alone. What a mistake to have opened the door without serious contemplation of the consequences!

Unfortunately, it was too late for regrets. She instinctively knew to show no fear. Alone in the cottage with neighbors too distant for help-summoning, she'd be vulnerable should he attempt something nefarious. So, as calmly as she could manage, Sarah reached to the hook beside the door, where she'd hung her hat, and fingered the item until she found the hatpin. Then very carefully, to not give away her intention, she clasped it between her thumb and forefinger. She was about to slide the weapon free, when he spoke again.

"*Are you* Sarah Louise Palmer?" he asked, the harsh timbre of his voice giving her no ease. When she did not, or rather, could not, answer, he stared. "Albert did not tell me you were mute."

Albert? Her lips parted and what came out was a breathless gasp. Knowing that she'd just all but confirmed his assessment that she *was* mute, she shook her head to clear her mind and regain some control of herself.

"How do you know my brother?" she asked, slowly releasing the hatpin. She could not imagine that any circles of Albert's and this man's would ever converge.

He pulled off his rumpled hat and ran a hand through his abused brown locks. "We are, were, friends." He twisted the hat in his hands. "It is sad tidings I bring you, Miss Palmer. Your brother is dead."

Sarah frowned and her heart lurched painfully. "You are a bit late with the news, sir." She tried to picture her brother being friendly with this unkempt savage. The idea was absurd. "I have known of his death for over a year."

"How? I came here straightaway."

"By way of the moon?" she asked, sharper than she intended. The pain of her brother's death was still fresh, despite the passage of so many months. "He has been dead since a year ago last January." She scanned his bearded face. "I thank you for coming to tell me this, and I do not mean to be rude, sir, but I have a pot of stew on the stove and I fear it may be burning."

She intended to close and lock the door, but a scuffed boot stopped the panel in mid-swing.

"Your stew will wait. I have come a long way," he said and placed a hand flat on the wood. With a firm push, he slowly eased the door wide open.

Heart thudding, Sarah stepped back and darted a quick glance at the hatpin. It was still within reach.

Thankfully, he remained planted on the stoop.

"There is more for us to discuss than Albert's death. You see, as he lay dying, he made me promise to take care of you. That is a vow I intend to keep."

Sarah stared. "My brother has been away for ten years, with only a few letters to assure me he was alive. Now he decides on his deathbed that he should show me some brotherly concern?" Her sadness dissipated and a fire burned in her chest. She'd loved her brother dearly, but he had not been the best caretaker for her. "I release you from your vow, Mister—?"

"Harrington. Gabriel Harrington."

"Mister Harrington." She stepped fully into the opening, lest he see how shabby her living conditions were. After her aunt died two years ago and her tiny pension ended, Sarah's funds had dwindled down to an alarming degree. She was within weeks of being penniless. Still, her pride would not accept assistance from this stranger. "I am quite capable of seeing to my own needs."

"As I can see," he said, peering over her head.

Sarah's spine straightened and her neck prickled. "I do

not care if you and Albert were as close as brothers; I do not need your help. Please go."

He grumbled under his breath and his face became a blank mask, as if he was pondering his next argument. He took half a step forward, his expression one of defeat. "I am more than Albert's friend." He sighed deeply. "I am your fiancé."

Gabriel watched her pretty mouth pop open. As quickly as he'd spoken the lie, he wished he could take it back. He'd impulsively offered to forever shackle himself to Albert's sister. What in the hell was he thinking?

The image of Albert's face as he lay dying, a fever ravaging his body, and the partial responsibility Gabe felt over his death were surely what caused this misstep. Or perhaps it was the desperation in her violet eyes that changed him from irresponsible rogue to damsel-saving warrior.

Guilt raced through his bones, and he felt the thickness of the mire he'd just stepped into on his boots. He *had* promised to take care of the chit. He had not promised to marry her.

Find her a vicar or farmer to marry her, Gabe, Albert had said. *Give her a life that keeps her safe and hidden from the danger that I fear still haunts our family. She deserves a far better life than what I have provided.*

A second wave of guilt followed. Albert had been correct. Gabe *was* a woman-loving, adventure-seeking, irresponsible rogue without the stability to care for a wife. He was wrong to offer to marry Sarah just to keep her from kicking him out on his arse. Albert would never allow the wedding if he were alive. In fact, he was probably cursing from the heavens.

Hell, if she'd not been so eager to see him gone, he'd have asked her to come with him to London and leave her in the care of his mother. However, the girl appeared to teeter on the edge of desperation, and from the looks of her, starvation. He could not leave Albert's beloved and prideful sister to such a fate.

Gabe could not save Albert, but he could save Sarah.

He bit back a curse as his freedom vanished and an invisible and weighted chain circled his neck. All he could do now was make the best of his situation.

Perhaps she'd refuse him and free them both. One could hope.

"We are betrothed?" Her face went white. He reached to take her arm, fearful she'd faint at his feet, but she brushed him away and whispered, "I cannot believe Albert would marry me off to a barbarian." She turned and wobbled toward the nearest chair, dropping down onto the frayed surface.

Taken aback by her insult, Gabe stepped into the cottage. The top of his head brushed the doorframe of the low door.

"A barbarian?" He looked down. His shirt and buckskin breeches were dirty, streaked with salt and dust and who-knows-what from his trip from America. He'd intended to change into suitable clothing after he boarded the London-bound ship in New York, but his trunk had disappeared somewhere between the wharf and the *Lady Hope*. By the time he noticed it missing, they had left port.

This left him in buckskin, a second shirt from his pack, and the kindness of a fellow traveler, Mrs. Johnson, and her lye washing soap to keep him from smelling most foul.

No wonder Sarah though him barbaric. He did look rather fierce. "Sadly, I spent all but my last few coins on the horse. The journey here was long, and I thought a sturdy gelding a more worthy purchase than clothing."

Clearly, she did not share the same notion. She could not pull her eyes away from the colorful beaded necklace that dangled to the middle of his chest.

Chuckling softly under his breath, he examined her from her frayed gray hem up to her stricken face. The girl was not unpleasant to look at, somewhat pretty, really, albeit too thin for his taste. She was dressed in the severe manner of a spinster, though he knew she wasn't yet old enough to wear that title. Still, he could do worse in a wife. And since it was too late to withdraw the lie and the damage already done, he

silently vowed to do his best to give her the comfortable life
his wealth could provide. And once they tired of each other,
he could always take a mistress.

Men still did take mistresses, did they not?

Hell. He'd been away from society so long that he wasn't
entirely certain of the rules. Until a few minutes ago, he'd
carefully avoided the marriage trap.

The chain tightened around his throat. He urgently needed
a brandy. He doubted her meager stores included that spirit.

"I assure you, Miss Palmer, I do not usually look so savage. My purse is rather light at present to allow the purchase of a razor and soap." His attempt to reassure her did
not stop her lower lip from trembling. "I will shave and
change as soon as we reach London."

The effort to calm her worries failed. Sarah lifted her
sad eyes to his. There was hopelessness in the violet depths.
She'd lost the flicker of spirit he'd first glimpsed when she'd
tried to run him off.

Truthfully, he couldn't fault her dismay, or her tears.
She'd lived for the last ten years in this small village. And
according to Albert, she had never traveled far outside its
boundaries once she'd been secreted away here as a girl,
thus limiting her experiences with strangers. He could understand her dismay over his clothing and appearance.

"Chin up, Miss Palmer. With a careful grooming, some
women find me quite pleasing to look at."

The attempt to lighten the moment gained him no quarter. Her shoulders slumped forward. He tried again. "Would
it help if I told you that my father is an earl and my family is
well respected throughout England?" She remained as she
was. "That we have more money than the Prince Regent?"
He paused. "When we wed, we will live in a fine house in
London with servants aplenty. You will never again have to
make your own bed."

The mention of London and servants seemed to rouse her
a bit. She rubbed her eyes with her palms then lifted her gaze
to peer around the dismal room. He could almost see the
effort it took for her to hang on to the last of a fighting spirit.

Even the poorest citizen would find the sparse accommodations somewhat lacking. He was certain she'd sold off whatever she could to survive, leaving behind only that which had no monetary worth.

"How do I know you are who you claim?" She met and held his gaze. "You could be a bounder out to take advantage of my plight. Give me proof of your connection to my brother or this conversation is finished."

The flash of resistance, and the question, took him aback. In that moment, he saw a bit of her strong-willed brother in her. The lass wasn't as meek as she first seemed. If she wanted proof, proof she would have.

"I have a letter." He reached into his pocket and withdrew the missive. "It is unfinished, but it is in Albert's hand."

He handed over the single sheet of parchment. She took the item in a calloused yet delicate hand. "He began it before he died. The fever came fast—" He let his words fade behind the lump in his throat as she unfolded the slightly crumpled note and read the two simple paragraphs. "He would want you to have it, even unfinished."

Her eyes welled. For a moment she silently stared at the page then blinked the tears away. Then, "We are strangers. How can a marriage between us work?"

"Marriages have begun with little more than financial gain," he offered. "And we are not truly strangers. Albert told me many stories about you, and I'm certain he wrote to you about me. There is much we know about each other already."

She lowered the letter and nodded. "Yes. Enough stories to warrant my refusal of a marriage to you."

It took a moment for her words to sink into his brain. He snorted. "On that we both agree. You should flee from me." He ran a hand through his unruly hair. "All I can promise you at the moment is security. The future is yet to be settled. As you said, we are strangers. We may grow to despise each other."

"What a grim notion," she said.

"I can make you no promises of love," he replied. "Only a life of ease. If you can accept that then we will wed."

For a long moment, he waited for her answer. Finally, he read her acceptance in the slump of her thin shoulders before she spoke. Their fate was set.

"I suppose I can do no worse," she said softly.

She could do no worse? He bit back a grin. At the very least, a wife would keep the society matrons and their giggling daughters at bay. At best, his mother would be pleased he'd given up wandering the world and come home settled with a bride. That alone made the idea of the unwanted marriage palatable. He'd been a terribly neglectful son. Anything to assuage Mother's ruffled feathers was worth the price paid.

Sarah's eyes drifted over him, taking his measure. Was she weighing her choices? Did she already have a suitor? This was something he'd not considered.

Before he could inquire about another man, she puffed out a breath. "I accept. I will marry you."

Half of him wished she'd said no. The other half knew it was too late for regrets. He nodded. "We'll take care of the deed when we are settled at Harrington House."

Something flashed in her eyes. Worry? Desperation? "You promise we will live in London?"

"Of course." He watched her eyes light up. Something about the city intrigued her. This was the first time he saw some hope in the girl. Perhaps she was weary of living in the center of nowhere. Even the smog-choked city was better than this desolate dirt patch. "My family is from there. It is where we will make our home."

She drew her bottom lip between her teeth and pondered the idea for almost a full minute. When she finally lifted her eyes to his, gone was the defeat in the violet depths, and in its place, acceptance. Or was it eagerness?

Her next words surprised him.

"We might as well get the deed completed today. There is no reason for waiting," she said in a rush. She straightened in the chair. "Parson Morse is just down the road. I shall ready myself for our wedding."

She pushed up from her seat. Then, without acknowledging him, she walked with a stiff gait from the room.

The speed of her surrender left him speechless. What was her hurry? A few minutes previous, she looked at him like he was horse droppings on the bottom of her shoe. Now she wanted to rush the wedding?

Something was amiss. Could she be with child?

Looking at her, the notion did not fit. Her narrow frame showed no signs of that condition.

Then what? Maybe the chit saw him as preferable to starvation, or bedding men for coin. Perhaps she'd become infatuated with his weighted purse. He had told her his family was wealthy. This alone would be enough to lift him up, even in his current condition, in the eyes of most women. Was Sarah any different?

Whatever her reason, she would soon be his wife. He glanced around and discovered a mirror over a small table. He walked toward it and bent to stare at his reflection. He smirked. He was truly surprised Miss Palmer had not shrieked at the sight of him. She was much sturdier than he'd thought at first glance.

Unfortunately, there was nothing he could do about his appearance. Even if she still possessed some of Albert's clothing, he'd been a head shorter than Gabe and thinner of frame. All he could do was marry the girl and get to London. A good valet and tailor would set him to rights.

He stared out the window and a rush of excitement filled him. The idea of seeing his family again brought happiness into his heart. The last five years of his life had been a wild adventure. Now it was time to go home.

What would Mother think of his surprise return? She'd been displeased when he'd left, calling him irresponsible, and worrying for his safety. As a married man, he would be the picture of responsibility. Mother would be pleased.

The idea solidified the rushed wedding. If Sarah wanted to marry today, he would see the deed done.

A sound brought him around. Sarah had returned, stuffed

into a featureless black gown with a high black lace collar and matching lace at the sleeves. The grim gown hung on her and did nothing to uplift the somber mood of their wedding day.

If this was an omen to their marriage, he'd have a rough path ahead.

"It was the gown I wore when mourning my father and brother," she said in way of an apology and explanation. "It is the best I have."

She was indeed in a dire condition if her best gown was a mourning gown. He'd not shame her by asking her to change.

However, he could not marry her like this. He stepped forward. "Please allow me some consideration. I am as unprepared for my wedding day as you are for yours. Certainly we can make a few small changes to your gown to make it more wedding-like?"

She shrugged. "Do what you must."

With her permission in place, he slid his fingertips into the collar. He felt her stiffen, but she did not shrink away. With a few tugs, the inexpensive lace gave way with a soft tear. Once the seam loosened, he managed to remove the rest quite easily and without making intimate contact.

Though not perfect, the gown looked much improved. At least Sarah could breathe. Then, giving thought to the heat of the day, he turned his attention to the long sleeves. He discovered the best place to detach the sleeve was just below the puffed part. Using a good amount of creativity, and his short-bladed knife, he separated the remaining sleeves from the puff. He slid the fabric down, first one arm and then the other, to free her. Gabe tossed the sleeves on a table nearby.

The alterations did make the gown appear less mourning and more bridal. Well, as bridal as a black gown could be.

"Better," he said. Sarah took the desecration of her best gown stoically. He supposed she was holding her emotions by a tenuous thread.

Smiling encouragement, he rubbed his hands together and held out his elbow. "Ready?"

She nodded and gingerly took his arm. She held him back as he took a step toward the door. "What will your family think of our hurried vows?"

He looked into her worried face. "I cannot say for certain, but my mother will be satisfied that I have given up my wandering ways." He squeezed her fingers. "Do not worry. I will spin a tale so grand that they will see ours as a love match. That should be enough to quell any speculation."

The gelding stood where he'd left him, half asleep and chasing off flies with his tail. Gabe frowned. "I apologize for not bringing a carriage. Thieves stole my trunk and most of my funds."

"I can ride," she said, sighing.

Gabe rolled his eyes upward, mounted the horse, and pulled her up behind him. Despite her wish to wed, the girl acted like she was headed to her hanging. He wanted to ease her worry, but there was nothing he could do. They'd known each other for little over an hour. He was still surprised that she'd actually agreed to marry him, though he suspected it was the lie over Albert's last wishes that had ultimately led to her agreement.

It certainly hadn't been his charm.

"I hope that once you've gotten over the surprise of our betrothal, you'll see that becoming Mrs. Gabriel Harrington is not as grim as, say, a beheading."

She frowned. "I'd rather think not."

The ride was short, and just a few minutes later they met the parson, who was clearly shocked at the sight of Gabe squiring Sarah into the tidy church. His eyes were owl-round behind his spectacles. When Gabe explained the reason for their visit, the parson took Sarah aside and began what Gabe suspected were several minutes of the elderly man begging Sarah to reconsider.

Sarah won the argument and they married before God and two flabbergasted middle-aged women that the parson had shuffled in off the road to act as witnesses. Gabe brushed a kiss on Sarah's cheek and the deed was finished.

"Chin up, love," he said. "You are now Mrs. Gabriel Harrington, Lord help you." Gabe paid the parson, thanked the still-startled witnesses for their kindness, and took her back to her cottage.

A second look over the property did not change his first impression. The cottage *was* positively ramshackle. He'd done his wife a service by marrying her.

"I shall warm the stew," Sarah said as they crossed the threshold. She hurried away.

He dropped into the nearest chair and rubbed his eyes. The last few hours had been impulsive and reckless. Clearly, he'd not shed these impulses with maturity. He only hoped he'd not done Sarah a grave injustice by tying them together for eternity.

The evening slogged on in silence, but for the few times he struggled to engage her in conversation. Where Albert had been a man known to charm everyone around him, his sister was clearly content to keep her own company.

Perhaps desperate measures were needed. "I am wanted in Texas for murdering a pair of marshals, a school teacher, and a herd of goats."

"Hmmm." She stared down and pushed the thin stew around her bowl with her spoon.

"And I hope you don't mind sharing my affections with other women. I have eight more wives and forty-seven children that will be living with us, once we get settled in a permanent home of our own."

"Hmmm." She reached for her teacup, sipped the bitter brew, and made a face. Without funds for sugar, the tea was unpleasant to the tongue.

Gabe gave up. He let the clock break the silence.

When dusk settled and bedtime approached, Sarah stood from the settee where she'd been sewing and twisted her fingers together. "I shall ready myself for bed, Mister Harrington."

"Gabe, please," he urged, but she was already out of her chair and halfway across the small room.

Gabe watched her vanish into the hallway, still wearing her dreadful black gown. He'd prepared to offer to delay the bedding until she became used to him, but she'd not given him a chance to do so. She was as skittish as a filly. However, he suspected she'd resigned herself to completing the task and would see his offer as a rejection.

This marriage had been a dismal mistake. Sadly, there was nothing he could do about it now.

S arah paced the small bedroom, her thoughts jumbled. She was Mrs. Gabriel Harrington, whatever that meant, and her wedding night was upon her. Remembering his kindness thus far, she supposed, if she asked, he would allow her a few days to settle herself into the marriage before pressing upon her his marital rights. But something had changed in the moment he'd pledged himself to her. He'd looked deeply into her eyes and a small shiver had gone down her spine.

And the shiver had not been from fear or panic, but from realizing for the first time that he wasn't entirely unattractive, her husband. The feminine side of her had noticed this despite his untamed whiskers and odd clothing.

From that moment forth, she'd noticed everything about him: his hands, his voice, his manners. Even as she all but ignored him through supper, woolgathering about him certainly, he'd been unfailingly polite, acting as the gentleman he'd claimed to be.

A gentleman, and her husband.

Her heart beat a little faster. If she did not refuse him tonight she might get her very first kiss. She'd never been kissed. Were kisses pleasant? Was she ready to be kissed?

She glanced in the small mirror. Her nondescript brown hair tumbled around her and down over the white night-dress that even nuns would consider prim. Her violet eyes reflected her apprehension, her fears, her dismay over having accepted and married Mister Harrington with little more than an unfinished letter as proof he was who he said he was.

Could she let him kiss her, bed her, just to solidify her place as his wife?

Her stomach grumbled. No, that was not her only reason. He was, in truth, a way out of this desperate life. That he was a friend of her brother, and a gentleman of sorts, had moved him to the head of her very short list of suitors.

A great sigh escaped her. "Having accepted him as my choice, I will see this through."

Lud. There was no woman of age in all of England more innocent than she. Her one suitor was the brutish smithy, and even he had not tried to steal a kiss. Now she was married and unprepared for all that it entailed.

The sound of his knock swung her about. The moment was upon her to decide the course of the evening. She closed her eyes and inhaled deeply for strength.

"Enter," she called out, and the decision was made. Her future was set by the parson's words. There was no use delaying the inevitable.

She clasped her hands together as the door swung open. Mister Harrington dipped his head to step inside. Pausing to glance around the sparse space, he finally turned back to her. His expression was unreadable, but his eyes showed his hesitation.

"I almost did not come," he said.

"I thought about locking the door," she admitted. He smiled. She dropped her gaze to his mouth. A second shiver went through her. Would she enjoy his kisses? Would his breath be sweet or foul?

His full set of white teeth gave her confidence of the former. Thankfully, he had none of the blackened and broken teeth of Mister Campbell.

She shook her head to dispel her scattered thoughts and returned her attention to Mister Harrington. She watched her husband shuck out of his fringed coat and place it over the chair. His shirt stretched across his wide back and muscled arms. Despite her nonexistent experience with men, she suspected most women would believe he cut a fine figure.

Her bear of a husband was no mincing fop.

"It is not too late for me to make use of the bedroom across the way," he said softly as their eyes met.

Did he find her that unappealing?

She crossed her arms to hide the outline of her small breasts from view. She had lost weight, and her curves had all but vanished, but to have him see her in her nightdress, and reject her, was too much to bear. Her lower lip trembled.

"Sarah." He closed the distance between them and took her chin in his large hand. "I meant nothing by the offer. You've gone through much on this day. I thought you would fare better with time to become used to the marriage before we consummated our union."

The roughness of his fingers on her face infused her with warmth. In the years after her aunt's death, she'd ached for someone to care for and to care for her. Now she had her unexpected husband under this roof, and she discovered that she did not want to be left alone, again.

She twisted her fingers into the worn fabric of the night-dress and stared down at her toes.

"I have never been kissed," she whispered, her honesty laid bare. Her face burned with the admission.

His soft chuckle made her humiliation worse. "My innocent Mrs. Harrington. How neglected you've been." He tipped up her face and peered at her from beneath unruly dark hair. "If nothing else, I can do that for you."

He lowered his head until their breathing mingled. She stood frozen in place as his lips pressed gently against hers. Then he slid the tip of his tongue between her lips, just enough to shock her but not enough to make the kiss unpleasant.

In fact, the kiss was rather . . . interesting. Her body flushed with the intimacy of the moment. He tipped his head slightly to the right and his tongue touched her clenched teeth.

Lud! Was a tongue part of kissing?

From the back of her throat, she was certain she moaned involuntarily. He must have taken the sound as encouragement.

Slowly, he walked her back to the bed, never losing contact with her mouth. From some distant place, she felt herself lowered onto the coverlet.

When he lifted his head, he asked, "Are you certain this is what you want?"

Thinking he meant kisses, she nodded eagerly. "Yes."

He reclaimed her mouth and his hand went to caress her thigh. Suddenly, she understood his question, and it was not about kisses but consummation.

Remembering what Aunt said about men and beddings, she ended the kiss, turned her face away, closed her eyes, and braced herself for entry.

"If you please, I would like to keep my nightdress on," she said and gripped the item at her hips.

Above her, Mister Harrington went still, his breath still brushing the side of her face. After a moment, she opened one eye and looked askance at him. Puzzlement etched his features.

"You are not ready," he said softly.

"I am," she replied, her voice quivering.

Mister Harrington pushed up from the bed, stealing the warmth of his body from her. She shivered. He raked his hands over his head, further mussing the locks, and let his gaze move down to where her fingers still tightly gripped the nightdress. Quickly, she unlocked her hold and smoothed the fabric. He chuckled and shook his head.

"I think it better for us to wait until we are both ready." His voice was low, rich, and confident. "We have a lifetime to figure out exactly when that will be."

Sarah wanted to protest, but the words did not come. He was correct. She wasn't ready to be a wife, not in the least. So instead, she slid over to the far edge of the bed to offer him room. "Will you stay with me?" She glanced to the empty hearth and rubbed her arms. The cold night air was already creeping through the cracks in the windowpanes. "I have only enough wood to cook with. Perhaps we can share our warmth?"

Frowning at the lack of fire, he turned back to her and nodded. "I agree. I fear I am too weary to start a blaze anyway." A yawn followed.

He sat on the bed and pulled off his boots. Sarah resisted the urge to touch the muscles on his back or ask him to kiss her again. After the dismal end to his attempt at seduction, she thought it wise not to tempt the man to change his mind about completing the bedding.

The mattress moved as he finally joined her still wearing his fringed trousers and white shirt, lay back, and closed his eyes. "Good night, Sarah."

"Good night, Mister Harrington." He opened an eye. She smiled sheepishly. "Gabriel," she corrected.

Despite the suggestion of shared body warmth, he remained on his side of the bed, and she, hers. The intimate kisses and his compassion had not been enough to completely settle the unease she felt with her husband. And for a moment, she considered asking him to take the other bedroom, cold night or not. She would certainly rest better without him sprawled on her mattress.

A soft rumble in his chest showed that she was too late to make the case for separate sleeping quarters. He'd fallen into an exhausted slumber.

She reached out and turned off the lamp. She might as well get used to sharing the bed. They were married after all.

There was just enough moonlight to see him framed in the darkness. His bearded face, his long body, the way his feet hung off the end of her bed all drew her curiosity.

He was not anywhere close to what she'd pictured when she'd dreamed of a husband. Yet, he was kind and not without humor.

Truthfully, it wasn't as if men were knocking on her door to court her, Mister Campbell aside. All but penniless, she had nothing to offer a man; no dowry, no influence. All she owned was a ramshackle cottage and the few shabby furnishings that she hadn't yet bartered for food or coin. The scrawny chicken in tonight's stew was gifted out of pity by her neighbor, and her garden was nearing the end of its offerings. No, Mister Harrington had been God-sent and perfectly timed when she needed him most.

But as she lay there beside him, it was not Gabriel or marriage that held her thoughts. No, her mind was on London, a place she barely remembered from her childhood and the city she never expected to see again.

The city where her father was murdered.

One night, on a quiet street, an assassin had ruined her family. Yet, the city held all of the answers to Father's last days if she chose to seek them out.

When Gabriel mentioned living there, all of her long-buried desires to see her father's death avenged came to the fore. In that moment, she accepted her betrothal. In fact, she'd hurried things along, lest he change his mind and leave her behind.

Marrying Mister Harrington had been a fated step toward solving the long-forgotten mystery, and the marriage would be the price to save herself and unlock her history.

Ever sensible and exceedingly practical, she vowed to make a success of her marriage despite its bumpy start, and to find Father's killer, no matter what lay ahead.

Chapter Two

Sarah kept her eyes averted from Gabriel as if the mere sight of his face was enough to send her into hysterics.

Was Sarah prone to hysterics? She'd shown no sign of a predilection to that emotion thus far. Still, it was impossible to know her true nature with an acquaintance of only twenty-seven hours and thirty-six minutes in which to base his conclusion.

This time frame included attempting to inform her that her brother was dead, mankind's shortest courtship, and a hurried wedding that was her idea, in fact. She certainly could not hold that, or his dismal attempt at seduction, against him. He'd wanted to wait. She'd asked for his kiss. What man, after months of celibacy, would ignore the invitation to kiss a willing woman? Why then was she ignoring him now?

Could she have been hiding her true nature yesterday? She might be shrewish, mentally unstable, or worse.

Still, if anyone should be in hysterics, it was he. She'd done nothing since he appeared on her stoop but morosely agree to the marriage with the enthusiasm of a woman who was about to die a slow, painful death, rush him to the parson, and then respond with some surprising passion to his kisses.

Certainly, she'd not be angry over a few small liberties taken on their wedding night?

He'd awoken this morning to find her valise packed and Sarah dressed for traveling. After offering a small heel of dry bread for his breakfast, she'd coolly shooed him off to arrange their passage to London and spent the rest of the morning pointedly ignoring him.

He wasn't certain he could recognize his own wife's voice with his eyes closed.

Bound together forever, and he couldn't make it through one day without wishing he could rewrite everything from the moment he knocked on her door.

Worse, the guilt over betraying his friend did not soothe his conscience. Unfortunately, it was too late for regrets. He had to make the best of the situation.

"There is an inn up ahead," he said amiably, fighting to hide his impatience. "We can stop there for rest and food."

She lifted her deep violet eyes above the rim of her book and shrugged. "Whatever is your pleasure." As soon as the sentence was out, she flushed crimson, as if remembering last evening's ill-fated attempt at lovemaking with the poorly chosen words.

The book snapped back up and covered all but the top of her forehead and a bit of light brown hair.

He bristled. She was put out. Why, he could not fathom. If he lived another fifty years with this puzzling woman, and spent the majority of those looking at her, or rather, the cover of some book, he'd go mad.

He'd thought marriage was the simplest way to keep her protected from whatever had caused Albert to flee England. As he looked at his wife, he knew plots were often made complicated when moved from mind into practice.

Though Gabe only knew pieces of the story, he understood enough to realize Sarah could be in danger now that

Albert was dead. It was the details of that danger that were murky.

Their father had served the Crown early in the Peninsular War and had died mysteriously. Albert had feared his father's past and knew a secret that could endanger Sarah. So he'd dropped her at the cottage with an elderly aunt and broke off almost all contact with his sister, hoping the distance between them would protect her from harm.

No amount of cajoling ever convinced Albert to share his secret. On his deathbed from a fever, he'd been adamant that Gabe find and protect her from an unknown foe. Any secrets were taken to the grave.

Albert expressed the hope that his death would set Sarah free. Gabe was not entirely certain that the deaths of both men ended the matter. When he was in New York awaiting the ship, he was convinced he was being followed. Then his trunk, including Albert's few possessions, was stolen. Coincidence? He couldn't be sure.

The longer he considered everything he did know, the more he realized that marrying Sarah *would* best serve the man who'd saved his life. Unfortunately, he wasn't convinced Albert would feel the same.

All he could do now was remain vigilant and hope to learn the mysteries of both men. For now, he had to familiarize himself with his wife.

"According to the coachman, this inn serves a magnificent lamb stew," Gabe continued, searching for a way to get her out from behind her book. As the only coach passengers, he was bored and tired and longed for conversation to pass the time.

"How nice," she said politely, book unmoving. "I'm certain I will enjoy a pleasant repast."

Gabriel Harrington, world traveler and adventurer, glared at the damned book and the prim figure that was his wife, and growled low in his throat. With the swiftness of a lioness running down an antelope, he leaned forward, snatched the book out of her hand, and tossed it out the open window.

Sarah gasped; her eyes went wide. "Oh!"

He brushed his hands together, satisfied he'd finally gotten her attention, and slumped back against the well-worn squabs. Stretching out a long and dusty buckskin-covered leg, he grinned wickedly as her pink-hued lips vanished into a thin line of disapproval.

"I do apologize, Wife, but I grew weary of talking to your book."

She frowned. "You could have asked me to put it away. I am now out one of my few remaining possessions. And it was a very interesting book."

"I shall buy you a new one when we get to London. In fact, I'll buy you an entire library full of books." He ran his gaze from her expressive eyes to her downturned mouth. "Until then, I intend for us to converse during the rest of this journey like civilized people."

She let his words settle before lowering her attention to his buckskin breeches. "Civilized?" One brow went up. "I have lived a sheltered life and have never had the chance to move in London society. However, I am quite certain that no gentleman, from baron to duke, wears breeches made from fringed animal hide."

He snorted at her tart comment. Finally, he'd wrung some emotion from her. Well, unless one considered the horror on her face when he arrived at her small and tumbledown cottage, announced he was her fiancé, and hauled her onto the back of his big black horse before dragging her to the nearest parson.

The tightly held emotions he suspected were buried deep beneath her blank façade would come out eventually. She'd lost her mother, father, aunt, brother, home, and freedom. This was a heavy weight for anyone to carry.

He hoped they'd be home at the Harrington town house before the dam released. His mother was better skilled at handling female tears than he.

"I do like to shock," Gabe said. Now that he was stuck with her, he wanted to make the best of the marriage. "I think I shall make my societal debut in these. I'll be gossiped about for years hence."

Sarah gaped, clearly mortified. "You would not dare."

He'd certainly chosen a prissy and humorless wife. She didn't understand teasing. "Perhaps not. We Harringtons are already known as a wild bunch. Socializing dressed as an American woodsman would only serve to confirm the fact." He glanced out the window. The coach was nearing the inn. "The surprise of my unexpected return will be enough to set the gossips twittering. My arrival with a wife in tow will notch up the news to a feverish level without adding buckskin breeches to the mix."

She relaxed, a bit. "Thank you for your consideration."

The coach stopped and Gabe helped Sarah down. Her cool hand was small in his as he led her into the inn.

They ate the stew, served with bread and butter. Both turned out to be quite good. After her fifth suppressed yawn, Gabe decided they should spend the evening there and use the last of his funds to procure seats on the morning coach to London. He'd put off their travel for one more night to give Sarah a few extra hours to settle into the idea of her new life.

"We will arrive rested and ready to face my family," he said as he guided her into a small but tidy chamber. "I fear my letters were clipped and far between. They know of Albert from my letters but nothing about his death, or our marriage. It will be a jolt."

Sarah moved to the window.

He stepped aside as a pair of servants carried in a hip bath and set it before the fire. Buckets of water followed. Soon the tub was filled with steaming water. A maid set out a pair of towels and soap and withdrew.

Gabe reached above his head to stretch then scratched the sides of his face. Several weeks of beard growth covered his skin and added to the heathenish first impression he'd left on Sarah. Bathing aside, it had been years since he'd worried about proper grooming. When traveling across the plains of America or stomping through jungles along

the Amazon River, no one cared if he'd missed a few days
of shaving or had a decent haircut.

Mother would be appalled.

He smiled.

"Would you care to have the first bath?" He planned to
see her settled, bathe himself, and spend the rest of the
evening partaking of ale in the tavern room below.

A sniff followed his question. A quick examination and
he could see her visibly trembling.

"Sarah?" He crossed the room to her. She stood, stiff,
peering out the glass. A light rain had started to fall. Gently, he turned her around. Tears were flowing unchecked
down her face when she looked into his eyes.

"My brother is dead. I have no more family," she whispered.

His heart dropped. "I know, dearest, I know." He eased
her into his arms and drew her to his chest. She resisted
only for a moment before she slumped against him with a
soft sob.

Rain pattered against the window while Sarah cried for
the brother she'd never see again. "I'd hoped the author of
the letter I received about his death was mistaken and Albert
was not truly gone. Your arrival took that hope away."

"He was a good man and loyal friend," Gabe said, hoping to give her comfort. "He loved you very much."

"Why then did he never come back?" Sarah said with a
catch in her voice. "I was left alone with my aunt after Father
died and my brother sent very few letters. Auntie did her
best by me, but life wasn't the same without Albert."

Gabe knew her mother died in childbirth and their
father had a shadowy past. Sarah deserved a sensible explanation to a mystery for which he had no answers.

"I believe he thought he was protecting you."

Sarah lifted her head. "Protecting me from what?"

Her red face and swollen eyes tugged at his heart. She
looked so fragile and wounded. "That, I do not know. What
I do know is Albert was hiding a secret that he thought

would endanger you. He thought keeping away from England was best and hoped that when he left, any danger would be drawn away from you. He never spoke of the reason for his fears to me."

Sarah sniffed and stepped away. "And yet, you were his closest friend. If he trusted anyone, it was you."

Gabe shook his head. "We drank, got into mischief, and shared many adventures that almost killed us. Still, there was always something in his eyes, sadness and worry he didn't share." Gabe moved to take Sarah's hands. "However, I do know one thing as truth. Leaving you broke his heart."

Sarah pressed her hands to her mouth and her tears began anew. Gabe eased her back into his arms.

S arah cried for her brother, the man she only knew from memories. He'd been just nineteen when he'd left, and she only nine. Yet, she remembered his smile, the way he teased her, and those last grim days after their father was killed. Upon hearing the details of the murder, that jovial boy had changed into a man overnight.

She remembered he'd vanished for a week or two after the funeral. When he returned with their elderly aunt in tow, he'd packed a few possessions, made her say good-bye to Nanny, the only mother she'd ever known, and fled into the night. He deposited Sarah and their aunt deep in the countryside in the tiny cottage that became her home for the next decade. Then he'd kissed her on the forehead and left with nary a satisfactory explanation.

It was impossible to know then that he'd never return.

Even after his death, she'd lived the last year in denial, hoping the letter from the missionaries had been mistaken. Although she'd worn black, it was Gabriel's arrival that confirmed that Albert was indeed gone . . . forever.

While the memories rushed through her mind, she held tight to her husband, the man who'd swooped in and married her without warning, the man who was now legally bound to her, a man she knew nothing about.

He smelled of earth and exotic spice. His soft white cotton shirt was open at the neck, and she could feel the warmth of his skin against her cheek. A stranger, yes, but at the moment he was also the one solid object she could cling to in an effort to keep upright when her legs wanted to fail her.

In his solid embrace, she felt safe for the first time since her aunt passed and her life became untenable. So she held on to him for as long as he allowed, taking from his strength.

Once her tears were all shed, he lifted her face and brushed the last tears away with a fingertip. "Come, you will feel better after a bath."

Numb and exhausted, Sarah offered only a weak protest when he undressed her and led her to the tub. She was half asleep when he bathed her from head to toe, rinsed her off, and dried her with a thin towel. She barely felt him slide her nightdress over her head or put her in bed. All she remembered after was a soft kiss pressed to her brow as she drifted off to sleep.

Gabe bathed then carried a rickety chair to the bedside and gingerly lowered himself onto the scarred surface. Sarah's breathing evened in sleep as he watched her in the dim light, trying to forget the image of her thin and naked body cast in firelight.

He felt like a cad for experiencing lust while she grieved. His arrival had opened the wound of her loss, and all he could think about, as he assisted her with her bath, was how her long hair had draped over her breasts, tempting him to look at places on her body where he ought not to look.

Despite a valiant attempt to keep his gaze positioned from the neck up, he'd failed to control his baser thoughts, as men often do when confronted with a flash of creamy bosom. The fact that she'd been fully unclothed had been his downfall.

His wife was painfully thin. The hint of her rib cage showed beneath her skin. He imagined her dying of starvation in that dreadful cottage, and buried without a family to grieve her passing.

Anger burned in him for all she'd suffered.

Yet, despite his misgivings over whether the marriage would work, there was something about her that drew him to her. Perhaps it was the desire to be her savior. Perhaps it was something more primal. When she looked at him with those lovely eyes of hers, something deep inside him tugged at his emotions.

When bathing her, his cock had stirred under the buckskin. For a woman so tightly bound up in prim propriety, who'd not even wanted to remove her gown on their wedding night, he'd realized over the last hour that she had the makings of an innocent temptress, with her white skin and perfect breasts.

If he could get her fed and in decent clothing.

A grin broke through his sober musings. Seeing her in her altogether had changed everything. She was no longer just Albert's young sister. She was his *wife*.

He'd find a way to shake her free of those years of misfortune and teach her that life was not always grim. That fun could be discovered outside of her overgrown patch of land and her dreadful cottage.

Hell, there were many things he wanted to discover about his wife. Did she have a long-buried sense of humor? Truthfully, he wasn't entirely convinced she had all the teeth required for a proper smile. He'd only seen a hint of them as she chewed.

Did she dance? Flirt? Have any article of clothing that did not strangle her about the neck?

The first matter to contend with once arriving home would be to burn her wardrobe and give his mother the task of refitting Sarah with gowns that did not offend his eyes when he looked upon them.

It would be a large step forward in breaking through the protective layer surrounding his too-proper bride.

Gabe drew his eyes down her covered form and back up to focus on the hint of exposed skin just above the high lace of her gown, and just below her left ear. She'd likely die of fright if he dared nibble the spot.

Grinning, he decided to forgo a trip down to the tavern below and instead sat in the chair, closed his eyes, and fell asleep with visions of her delightful breasts dancing across his thoughts.

Chapter Three

Sarah awoke with tear-swollen eyes and a defeated disposition. A glance confirmed Gabriel was still sleeping, so she forced herself from the bed, taking the reprieve to right her appearance. She had to look a fright.

Pressing a tepid washcloth to her face, she looked back at the bed. Sometime during the night, her bear of a husband had joined her, dressed in his breeches, on the lumpy mattress.

Her life had taken a downward spiral since the death of her father all those many years ago. With Gabriel's arrival, her tenuous hold on her emotions had finally broken, and she'd cried for her losses all over his dusty white shirt.

Despite having married, she had no one. Not really. She knew nothing of this man, or his family. He'd told her the Harringtons were wealthy, but it could be the ramblings of a braggart. The family might well be pickpockets or house-breakers. Despite the note, was he truly a friend of her brother, or a stranger taking advantage of her plight? Dressed as he was, it was impossible to tell what sort of man was this Gabriel Harrington.

Uncertainties weighed on this the third day of her marriage that had not been there the day before yesterday when she'd gone willingly off to the parson. Was solving the mystery of her father's death worth the sacrifice of tying herself forever to this stranger?

Perhaps once she had her answers, he could be convinced to send her back to the cottage, with a small income, enough to let her live comfortably for the rest of her life.

"You will wear down your skin with so much scrubbing," came Gabriel's voice from the bed. "Perhaps you should cease before you hit bone."

Sarah frowned and dropped the cloth in the basin. "I thought you were sleeping."

"I find sleep less appealing than watching my wife complete her morning toilet."

A flush warmed her skin. She ignored the comment.

"Hmm." Despite her concerns about pickpockets and thieves, his voice bore the aristocratic tone of many generations of good breeding. This was a good sign. She'd rather not be married to a thief. "How many hours until we reach London?"

While awaiting his answer, she pulled her second-nicest dress from her valise. She'd done her best to keep her clothing well tended. Still the cloth of this faded blue day dress bordered on threadbare, and she could do nothing about it except hope it did not tear when she bent over.

She prayed Gabriel's family would not judge her too harshly when she arrived at their door dressed as a peasant.

"Three hours if the roads are decent." He rolled from the bed and padded over to her, his odd breeches hung low on his hips. His eyes skimmed over the dress. "You need a new wardrobe."

Jerking her eyes from the thin trail of dark hair that ran from his navel to disappear a short distance below, she scowled.

"I barely had food enough to eat. New gowns were a luxury I could not afford." She handed him the dress and he helped her pull it down over her head. The intimacy of the act was not lost on her when his fingertips brushed along her skin. This stranger was her husband. Forever and always.

Gabriel laced the gown. "Tending to you will be my first act once I have regained access to my allowance."

Scanning his face, she wrinkled her nose. "Your first act should be finding a valet with a razor."

He reached to tug at his beard and smirked. "My own mother won't recognize me." He looked down at his clothing. "It's been years since I was a dandy. I'm no longer certain what's considered fashionable. Mother will be charged with dressing us both from the skin out."

A lump formed in her stomach. "What will your mother think of me? You've gone off on your adventures and returned with a shabby bride in tow. She certainly will not be happy."

In her mind, she pictured his mother as a judgmental and sour-faced society matron who would live to make Sarah miserable.

He met her eyes in the mirror. "My mother will be both thrilled to have me home and pleased that I am settled. You could be a Mayan high priestess straight from the jungle of the Amazon and she'd find something about you that she liked."

"I am not convinced of that." Sarah stepped away and picked up her brush. She knew that any mother of lofty stature would want a wellborn wife for her son.

"We shall see," he said.

Gabriel whistled as he cleaned his teeth. In half an hour, they were ready. After a quick breakfast, they climbed into the mail coach and began the last three hours of their journey.

L ondon was all Sarah expected . . . and worse. It was dirty and loud and crowded as people hawked their wares from carts parked on the streets, or from baskets hanging from elbows. She leaned for a better look out of the window of the hackney Gabriel had hired to take them from the last coach stop into the city. She watched in horror as a woman dumped the contents of a small chamber pot out a second-story window onto the street below.

She shuddered. "Lord, save me," she muttered. London was a horrible, horrid place.

Gabriel chuckled. "Before you leap from the coach and race back to your cottage, please note that in Mayfair servants do not dump their chamber pots into the streets."

"And you expect me to be grateful for that one small consideration?" She glanced at him. "How can you breathe here? There is soot everywhere."

"We are passing through Whitechapel, love," he said. "I promise cleaner air the closer we get to my home."

Gabriel was correct. The last part of the drive changed from dirty air and unwashed everything to tree-lined streets and houses big enough to engulf her tiny cottage.

Sarah watched in awe as they passed a house so large that it had to rival a palace. She gawked. "I have never seen the like," she said as she leaned forward for a better view. Hope rose for the first time since they began this journey. This neighborhood was much improved from that awful Whitechapel.

"That is Collingwood House, home of the Duke and Duchess of Stanfield." He peered out his window to admire the huge stone façade. "From my mother's letters, I understand I am now kin to the duke through a long-lost cousin."

Dropping back on her seat, Sarah stared aghast. "Please tell me you are jesting." She ran her hands over her faded skirt. She was a country mouse, married into a family that included a duke. Could her life get any more worrisome?

"I am not. It's true." He took her hand. "Breathe, Sarah. You are turning blue."

Within minutes, the hackney stopped and the driver descended to open the door. He leveled a second disbelieving glance at Gabriel and his odd attire. "The home of Lord and Lady Seymour, sir."

"Thank you, good man." Gabriel climbed down and

turned to help Sarah alight. Though not as grand as Collingwood House, the property was lovely. Too lovely. If not for
Gabriel's hand on her arm, she might have finally suc-
cumbed to her anxiety and fled into hiding.

Gabriel paid the driver and led her toward the door. Her
scuffed slippers were lead filled.

"I cannot do this. I cannot," she said weakly as her throat
closed up. Her world tilted in a rush of panic.

Gabriel squeezed her fingers tightly, enough to cause
some discomfort, and her eyes cleared. He hadn't realized just how intimidated she was about meeting his family
until this moment. "I can carry you in, dearest, if you
please," he offered and was rewarded with a frown.

"You will not." She lifted her chin, righted her bonnet,
and squared her shoulders. "I will meet my mother-in-law
while standing, thank you."

For a timid young woman, she did occasionally show a
bit of pluck. Pluck that did not extend to the trembling hand
clutched tightly to his arm like a vise.

Further comments were left unsaid as the door opened
after a single rap. Busby stood in the opening, the butler a
bit older and grayer than Gabe remembered. As he looked
down his nose, it took just a blink before the servant's eyes
widened when he looked Gabe over.

Gabe kept his face bland as the man raked a bemused
gaze over his scruffy face and woodsman's clothing.

The normally unruffled butler was clearly put off his
feet. He stood and stared, appearing unsure of how to proceed when the town house was besieged by a ruffian.

"Deliveries are made in the back." He pointed in that
direction. "You can find your way."

"I cannot believe you don't recognize me, Busby. Have
I been away that long?"

The butler's eyes widened further until they nearly
popped out of his head. "Master Gabriel?"

"None other."

The butler let out a funny sound and grabbed Gabe by the shoulders. "I cannot believe it's true." Hazel eyes scanned Gabe's face before the butler pulled him into his arms.

Gabe thumped the older man on the back. "It is grand to be home, Busby. I've missed your scowls and scolds." He released the butler and lifted his eyes to the staircase when the sound of skirts swished from above.

Kathleen Harrington, Lady Seymour, stood at the railing, peering curiously down at the commotion. She was as he remembered. Gabe's heart danced. Lud, he'd missed his mother. More than he'd imagined possible.

"Busby, call for the footman and chase this vermin off the stoop before he infests our pantry with lice."

Gabe heard Sarah gasp behind him, but his eyes were on his beautiful mother. She hadn't aged a day since he saw her last.

"I should have known the beard would not keep you from recognizing me," he said, grinning.

"A mother knows her son, even when he's dressed as a savage." With that, Mother lifted her hem and raced down the stairs. "Gabriel." She threw herself into his open arms and laughed joyously. "I missed you so, my errant son." Gabe lifted her up and spun her around.

"I've missed you, Mama."

For the next minute or two, his mother went from happy to exasperated to happy again as she groused over his long absence and thanked the Lord that he was home. It was only when Busby cleared his throat that Gabe remembered Sarah standing quietly in the still-open doorway.

"Mother, there is someone you need to meet." He took his mother by the hand and led her to Sarah. "Lady Kathleen Seymour, this is Mrs. Sarah Harrington. My wife."

A flicker of surprise crossed Lady Seymour's lovely— and not at all dour or pinched—face. Still, the woman managed not to shriek out her disbelief, lament her son's poor judgment, or faint. Instead she calmly took Sarah's measure with her eyes and then nodded stiffly.

"I see."

I see? That was all? Sarah wasn't entirely convinced that she wouldn't prefer at least a small bit of shrieking from the countess. The calmness portrayed by the Lady was unnerving. She gave no hint of her thoughts. This terrified Sarah more than the railing of an outraged mother would.

Sarah curtsied. "A pleasure, My Lady."

A second reserved nod followed. Clearly Lady Seymour was in stunned disbelief. There was no other plausible explanation for her lack of emotion.

Gabriel stood silently, offering no help from his quarter, though he did appear amused by the exchange, or lack thereof. Obviously the Lady was dumbstruck by the arrival of both her long-missing son and his tattered new wife.

Sarah watched for signs of a faint in the making, but the Lady did not look like a fainter.

If not for a small frown settled upon her wayward son, she was a stone.

Finally, Lady Seymour reached out a hand. "Welcome, Mrs. Harrington. Come, I will show you to your room."

With slight hesitation, Sarah took the offered hand and the countess tucked it under her arm. Side by side, Sarah suspected they resembled a queen and a pauper.

Sarah glanced back at Gabriel, silently beseeching him to intervene. Instead, he smiled and said nothing. At that moment, she despised her husband. He'd thrown her under a carriage and would not offer rescue.

"How did you meet my son?" the Lady asked softly. She'd finally found her voice and the inquisition had begun.

"He was a friend of my brother, Albert. They met during their travels, as I believe Gabriel wrote to you in his letters," Sarah answered honestly. "Albert died in America, and Gabriel felt the need to inform me personally of his passing. The information came a bit late, for I already knew. What I didn't know was that my brother had betrothed me to

Gabriel. His arrival at my cottage with *that* news took me by surprise."

"When did you wed?" They started up the marble staircase.

"Three days ago."

"And how long have you known Gabriel?" The Lady turned them right at the top of the stairs.

"Three days." She briefly explained to the countess about her home, her situation, and their nonexistent court-ship.

Lady Seymour's steps faltered and she stopped. She quickly caught herself and turned to face Sarah. Her eyes were troubled but not unkind. "Do you love my son?"

Sarah had a choice. The truth or a lie. The truth was eas-ier to manage. If Gabriel had wanted her to fib about their grand love affair, he should not have left her alone with his mother. "I do not know your son well enough to form an opinion one way or another."

This brought a small smile. "You are honest, Sarah. May I call you Sarah? We stand on a shocking lack of for-mality in this household."

"Please." Sarah was beginning to suspect that Lady Sey-mour was more than just a wealthy woman in a very expen-sive gown. Either she was as warm as Sarah had seen when she greeted her son, or a spider waiting to pounce on an unsuspecting fly.

Her.

At the moment, she thought the latter. Time would tell if her observation proved correct.

They stopped in front of a door in the middle of a long hallway. Lady Seymour frowned. Then she stepped across the hallway, opened a second door, and led Sarah inside.

The room was tastefully decorated in shades of pale blue and white, with just enough frills to give it a feminine feel.

"This is not Gabriel's room," Sarah said.

"It is not. His is across the hall."

Puzzled, Sarah set her valise on the floor. "I assumed

we would share a room. I believe that my parents shared theirs."

Lady Seymour walked to the window and pushed open the curtains. "My son married you without warning and dragged you here, without preparing you for this life. You were denied a proper courtship and a chance to marry for love. I find the situation appalling." She walked back to Sarah. "When, and if, you choose to share a room with my son, it will be your choice, not his."

The countess moved to the open doorway. "If I were you, my dear Sarah, I would make him work for that right."

The Lady left her.

Stunned, Sarah reflected on the countess's words. Had she already made an unlikely ally here in the town house? Unless she'd mistaken the meaning, Lady Seymour expected Gabriel to court her as if they had not already spoken their vows.

This was an interesting thought. Courted by her husband? She wondered what Gabriel would think of such a notion.

Sarah set her valise on the bed and began unpacking when a maid arrived. The woman was well into her twenties with a round, pleasant face and a stout frame.

"Good afternoon, Mrs. Harrington. I am Flora. I will be your lady's maid." She curtsied. "My Lady asked me to make your stay pleasant." She glanced at the contents laid out on the bed. After a cursory examination, and several "oh dear's," the maid took matters into her capable hands.

The next hour was met with a flurry of activity as two other maids arrived to assist Flora. Sarah was stripped and put into a hot bath. The soap had the scent of oranges and exotic flowers. It was delightful, a decadent treat. Sarah sighed loudly, in a most unladylike way. This caused the younger maids to giggle.

Flora leveled on them a scolding glare. They went back to work, placing an array of womanly items out on the dressing table. A silver brush, perfume, creams, everything made to pamper. Flora placed a dress on the bed, a fetching concoction of yellow and lace.

"Lady Seymour found this in Lady Brenna's old room," the woman explained. "There are several dresses for you to use until your new wardrobe has been ordered and delivered. I hope you like yellow?"

"I do like yellow." At this moment, the dress could be a ghastly mix of orange, blue, and pink, and she'd find it more palatable than the gowns she'd brought with her.

With the bath concluded, the maids helped her from the tub, dried and fluffed her. Flora trimmed her hair and put the brown mass into an attractive twist at her nape. Once dressed, Flora turned her toward the mirror. Sarah's breath caught.

"You have made a miracle, Flora," Sarah said. She almost did not recognize herself. Though no grand beauty, she did look rather pretty.

"You must not doubt yourself, Mrs. Harrington," the maid replied. "You just needed a bit of help."

Sarah laughed and Flora flushed, as if suddenly realizing she'd both insulted and complimented Sarah in the same breath.

"Oh, Mrs. Harrington. I did not mean—"

Sarah cut her off with a wave of her hand. "No insult was taken. I did look a bit of a fright. I am unused to dressing for anything. My appearance was dull indeed."

The maids smoothed the dress and declared her fit for a late lunch with the family. Sarah pulled in a deep breath for courage as Flora led her to the staircase where Lady Seymour was waiting below. Sarah joined her on the landing. The countess smiled.

"My, don't you look lovely," the Lady said and took her arm. "Gabriel will be pleased."

Sarah put her free hand over her fluttering stomach. This was the first challenge to her mettle.

"You need not worry about being overwhelmed by family," Lady Seymour said. "Simon and Brenna are married and gone, and Lord Seymour is out of town until tomorrow. It is just us three for lunch."

The words gave her some comfort. They entered the dining room and the maid brought tea. Unable to think of a single topic on which to converse with the countess, Sarah walked to the buffet and examined the food. There was enough to feed a family for a full week.

Her stomach rumbled. She hadn't realized how hungry she was until this moment.

"There you are, darling," Lady Seymour said from behind her.

Turning, Sarah expected to see her burly husband in animal hide. Instead, a man, a very, very, handsome man, stood in the open doorway, bedecked in black but for a crisp white shirt and cravat. Her breath caught.

Dumbstruck by his male beauty, Sarah scanned her eyes down his tailored clothing to his polished boots, and back up again. His face was clean-shaven and his hair trimmed neatly, if not a bit long at the collar. Whoever he was, Sarah was certain that he could give her husband tips on proper grooming.

She did not realize she'd been staring like a ninny until she heard Lady Seymour laugh. The man smiled at Sarah's discomfiture, showing a set of very nice teeth. Her heart fluttered and her face warmed.

The countess cleared her throat and stepped toward the man to take him by the hand. She led him to where Sarah stood. The scent of sandalwood and spice teased her senses.

"Sarah, I'd like to introduce you to my son, Gabriel Alexander Harrington."

Chapter Four

At first, Sarah thought Lady Seymour was playing a prank at her expense. However, when he reached out and took her hand, and she looked into his familiar green eyes, she knew this perfect male specimen was indeed her husband.

Her knees knocked and her mind went blank. He kissed her hand and the crinkles around his eyes deepened with his smile.

"The shock of seeing me thus has overwhelmed my wife," he teased. "I fear she might swoon."

Sarah's spine stiffened. "I do not swoon," she said quite breathlessly, and not entirely certain that swooning *was not* in her future. Who would not swoon under his attention?

If she'd thought herself married well above her station before, when he was a scruffy barbarian, his perfect manly perfection served to confirm the notion. Not only was he wealthy and noble, but he was so handsome that beside him, she faded into the background like ancient sun-damaged wallpaper.

Composure, Sarah, *composure*, she silently scolded. It

would not do to present herself as a silly and besotted girl in front of Gabriel. A handsome face did not a man of sterling character make. He could be a gambler, a drunkard, a libertine.

"I am surprised to see you do possess cheeks," she said, fighting to untangle her tongue.

His chuckle was rich and deep. "Mother found me a razor."

"I see." Lud. Why couldn't he be average? He was much easier to accept as the bear-man. Now she suspected were she to be introduced to society on his arm, everyone would wonder why Gabriel had chosen her, when he could have had his pick among the Ton beauties.

"You look pretty, Sarah," he said, breaking through her woolgathering.

Sarah blinked. "Pardon?"

"I said, you look pretty. The gown suits you." He kissed her knuckles again. Her hand tingled where he'd pressed his lips. She had to bite back a ridiculous sigh.

Proper, drab, and shy Sarah Palmer was taken with a man. Everyone she knew from home would find the notion quite amusing. She'd never had a *real* suitor before. Now she was married to the prince of the castle. No one would believe her good fortune.

If this was indeed good fortune. She wasn't convinced. However, it would be nice to stare at his handsome face over the dinner table. She'd grown tired of the beard.

"Thank you," she managed. She knew he was being polite but liked the compliment anyway. When he released her hand, it was all she could do not to fan herself with her fingertips.

Focus, Sarah, she thought. She'd come to London for one reason and it wasn't to become taken with her husband.

Hoping to hide her flush, she turned back to the buffet as Lady Seymour's mouth quirked. "Now that you two have properly met, let us eat," the countess said. "I am famished."

Sarah made her selection, careful to keep her eyes averted from Gabriel, and spent the meal pushing her food around on her plate. Her fluttering stomach made eating difficult. Thankfully, neither her husband nor Lady Seymour seemed to notice as Gabriel regaled them with stories of his travels.

"You really rode a camel?" the countess asked.

"I did," Gabriel answered. "He was a humorless beast. And he smelled like you'd expect a camel to smell. Unpleasant. I also rode a donkey and was almost eaten by a crocodile, if not for the quick thinking of our guide who snatched me from the beast's great jaws."

"Oh dear," Lady Seymour said, aghast. "Perhaps you should tell me no more. I do not think I want to hear that story."

"Then you will probably not want to hear about the tribe of Amazon natives that wanted to eat Albert and me for dinner?"

Lady Seymour paled. "Can you not come up with a story that does not involve you almost getting consumed?"

Gabriel laughed. "Most of my best stories revolve around peril. There are many places in the world where the citizens are less than civilized." He winked at Sarah. She flushed. "And if I remember correctly, there are society matrons here in London who would certainly fit that description."

"That is why I am thankful that you are no longer dressed like a savage," his mother countered. "I cannot imagine the stir that would cause. We have enough scandal in our history without adding to the whispers."

"I thought you spent all your time in America," Sarah said.

"There and farther south. The camel belonged to a merchant in San Francisco and the crocodile lived in the Amazon River. You should be happy I did not make a trip to Africa. I hear the crocodiles are much larger there."

"Please, no more," his mother begged with a laugh.

Lady Seymour spent the next hour telling him all about the family news. Sarah learned the story of their newly discovered cousin Eva, her duke, and their baby; Simon and his Laura; and Brenna and her husband and son. Added to the tale were the adventures of cousin Lady Noelle and her American husband to complete the picture. By the time the storytelling ended, Sarah was exhausted.

"Your family is very colorful," she said during a lull.

"They are," Gabriel replied. "Though I cannot vouch for the spouses, as I have not yet met any of them, I can assure you that the Harringtons are all a lively bunch. They will keep you endlessly entertained."

She imagined being overwhelmed, most likely. Had her family been alive, she could count them on one hand. And since her aunt died, she'd been alone for two years with only a few neighboring acquaintances to keep her company.

Most people thought her odd, and some thought her too poor to befriend. The rest were just too kind not to offer her a chicken, a bucket of milk, or an occasional conversation.

Never social, now she'd been thrust into a world so unlike what she knew. The whole was simply overwhelming to contemplate. And so far she'd only met Lady Seymour.

Lud, she was a Harrington now, with all the expectations behind the name.

Her hands began to shake. What little food she'd ingested turned to stone in her belly. Fearing the rising rush of panic, she quickly excused herself and hurried to her room, crossed the space, and stared out the window to the street below.

It was not acceptable to break in front of the countess. Showing weakness would be the ultimate humiliation.

From what she'd learned about the family thus far, Harrington women had to be strong, confident, and charming! Could she meet those lofty standards? Not in fifty years!

The marriage would never be successful. Perhaps she could convince Gabriel to return her to the cottage with a small monthly stipend before they grew to hate each other.

They simply did not suit.

Unfortunately, the countess followed her up before she could gather the courage to go off in search of her husband

and make the offer to leave London. With a knock on the door, Lady Seymour broke her privacy. Sarah brushed tears from her cheeks and turned away from the window.

"Come sit with me." Gabriel's mother sat on the bed. Sarah joined her. The Lady peered into her face for a moment then spoke. "Gabriel told me a few things about your life. After your father's death and your brother's disappearance, you spent years trying to survive. According to Gabriel, you were clinging to your existence by the tips of your fingernails."

"I was." Sarah straightened. "I suspect that had my brother realized the condition I was in, he would have returned home straightaway."

"Perhaps. Still, he never should have left you to fend for yourself with only an elderly aunt to watch over you. You've been terribly neglected."

The Lady did have a point. "My aunt had meager funds, and my brother sent some money, though not nearly enough for my upkeep. And our village was so small that prospects for marriage were nearly nonexistent." She decided to keep her worries about Mister Campbell and his intentions to herself. "Had Gabriel not come for me, I truly do not know how much longer I could have survived."

Both women knew what may have happened to Sarah in that situation. Women without prospects often met grim fates.

"How old are you, Sarah?" Lady Seymour asked.

"Nineteen." She felt so much older.

"I did not realize you were so young." The countess sighed. "Have you ever been to a ball, hosted a party, or danced?" Sarah shook her head. "The Ton will gobble you up should we foist you upon them in this condition. There is much work to do."

Lady Seymour patted her hand. "First, we shop. Tomorrow afternoon we will head to Bond Street and see you refitted from the skin out. Then there will be lessons and more lessons until you have the skills to navigate society."

Sarah's hands shook again. The countess took them both in her warm grip. The Lady's eyes showed good humor. "Do not worry, Sarah. We will take one tiny step at a time."

After the countess excused herself, Sarah slumped back on the bed and stared up at the ceiling. Lud. Society? Lessons?

What if Gabriel did not agree to send her back to the cottage? What if he wanted her here, at his side, forever?

She could be trapped in this marriage for eternity.

Was she ready to be a Harrington? The idea of being launched on society terrified her. Yet, the idea of cowering in her cottage, rather than facing the challenges ahead of her, was worse. When had she become so fearful of life?

There was something about changing herself from country mouse to Lady that appealed to the feminine side of her.

Gabriel appealed to the feminine side of her.

Dare she imagine he could someday become fond of her? Was there a chance she might both solve the mystery of Father's death and remain in London, with him?

She ran her hand over the borrowed dress. The fabric was kitten-soft under her touch. Her mind went to balls, parties, and dancing in Gabriel's arms.

When she'd seen him as a way to get to London, she'd not considered the marriage further than the vows. If her future was that of Mrs. Gabriel Harrington, then she'd have to accept him as her husband and play the part of amiable wife.

Could she settle into that role?

Gabriel would be part of everything in her life from now forward. But what if she fell in love with him? The idea, though difficult to believe, was not an impossibility. He was a charming rogue. The question was, could he fall in love with a church mouse like her?

Not ever, most likely. She was a duty, nothing more.

Her father held her here for now. If she asked to leave London after his case was solved, what would he say?

Perhaps Lady Seymour had been right. Gabriel had done nothing thus far to earn her affection or made any attempt to play attentive husband. She'd followed along like a pup, without questioning most of his directives, ever since the moment she'd found him on her stoop and he'd dragged her off to the parson.

With Lady Seymour's help, that could change.

Could they be happy together or was she a foolish woman with a silly dream of happiness with a handsome prince? Would she be an adored wife or forever trapped in a marriage of tolerance, and little else?

Their wedding night had been unsettling. She knew deep in her heart that it had been her fault. He'd tried to show her some affection, but her nerves had overwhelmed her and she'd begged for a rushed consummation. Still, her virginal fears *were* understandable. They'd only just met and she was innocent.

Her mind went to the Gabriel who'd entertained her at lunch, the man with the laughing eyes and sculpted face. Even now, her skin tingled with the memories of his eyes on hers. He'd spoken with such passion about his adventures. Could that passion be directed at her in the same way? Would the bold Gabriel Harrington ever find her exciting, too?

"Gads. You are already smitten with the man," she muttered. "Foolish chit." Then the truth pressed into her mind. "He's too prideful to allow me to leave him. I am trapped here forever. Accept this fate."

She stood, went to the mirror, and considered herself with a critical eye. She was too thin, too pale, and too drab. Even wearing the pretty dress, she was colorless, humorless, not the kind of woman that drove men to passion.

"I have to make this marriage work." Her shoulders slumped. "But how can I when he hardly notices me?"

Lud. She could live with him but not under these conditions. If she wanted to make this marriage acceptable for both of them, she needed to change, wanted to change. Starting tomorrow, she'd make it her mission to be the kind of wife that befitted a Harrington. Gabriel Harrington.

Somehow she'd learn how to intrigue her husband.

* * *

Bond Street was crowded and noisy. "Are you not afraid of being crushed beneath coach wheels?" Sarah asked the countess with a quivering voice. She hesitated to climb down from the open carriage and into the madness.

Lady Seymour smiled. "You must learn to step lively." She smoothed her gloves and waited for the driver to help Sarah alight. "It is all about timing."

After waiting for a carriage to pass, they hurried across the street, hand in hand, toward a shop where a lovely young woman waited on the walk. Sarah felt the intensity of her gaze from beneath her bonnet as the stranger assessed her as they neared.

"There you are," Lady Seymour said. The woman and the countess exchanged cheek kisses and then Lady Seymour introduced them. Above an amber-colored eye a brow cocked at the news of Gabriel's marriage.

Sarah managed a brief curtsy. "Lady Noelle."

"I cannot believe Gabriel is home and with a wife in hand," cousin Lady Noelle said by way of greeting. She openly stared at Sarah like she was a curiosity at a fair. "I expected him to meet his demise at the end of a pistol wielded by an outraged husband. I am pleased to see he has curbed his wild ways and finally settled his life."

Sarah was not certain what to say about the comment. She did not know her husband well enough to form an opinion about his character, nor did she know how, or if, she should defend him to his cousin. The Harrington family was still a confusing puzzle.

"Thank you. I think." Sarah stared back. Lady Noelle was pretty and lively, impeccably clad in blue from her feathered hat to her lacy hem.

A touch of envy welled inside her as she touched her borrowed gown with her gloved hand.

Noelle took her arm. "Let us go inside away from prying eyes and you can tell me all about yourself, Mrs. Harrington. I am truly dying to know how you managed to snag Gabriel. I never thought he'd fall into the marriage trap."

Sarah glanced at Lady Seymour, who shrugged.

Within an hour, Sarah had made her first friend in London. Noelle was charming and funny, and she had a way about her that set Sarah at ease. She knew fashion, as no one else could, and had an eye for color. Soon Sarah was weighted down with packages filled with pretty undergarments and silky nightdresses. Added to the purchases were one green gown and a plum day dress. And they were still at the first shop.

"I should not spend so much," Sarah said, overwhelmed by the cost of each gown. "Gabriel will be displeased."

"Posh," Lady Seymour said and reached for a pair of lacy black gloves. "My son has an allowance and investments that will more than cover a new wardrobe."

Noelle stepped forward. "Do not take this as an insult, but if anyone needs new clothing, it is you, Sarah. From what I understand, your gowns are nearly worn through. You are one curtsy away from splitting a seam."

"You have been talking to Gabriel." He'd used the same words last evening when he came to her room to say a brief goodnight. She grinned. "I did marry him in a mourning gown. Perhaps I *should* spend some of his allowance."

"You married Gabriel in black?" Noelle asked and her lips parted. She and Lady Seymour gaped.

"I did, after he'd altered it with his knife." She laughed lightly and told the story. "You should have seen his face when he saw me in that gown. I thought he'd drop from apoplexy to the floor."

The three women laughed.

"I wasn't entirely certain at first that you and Gabe were a match," Noelle admitted and crossed her arms. "He is quite bold. However, a woman who can get him to agree to wed her in a mourning gown is capable of bringing him to heel. But it will take work. Are you up to the task?"

"I hope so," Sarah said. At Noelle's frown, she nodded and stood a bit straighter. "I am."

Despite her attempt at confidence, and her hope to entice her husband with her charms, she did not truly think she could ever lead Gabriel on a merry chase. Her sheltered life had taken a toll. She knew nothing about men. Nothing. And there was so much to learn.

As if reading her face, Noelle casually drew her away from Lady Seymour under the guise of looking at stockings.

"You look so glum, Sarah." Sarah looked at her toes. Noelle lifted her chin. "Is there something wrong? Something you'd like to share?"

Sarah shook her head, unwilling to unburden herself to her new friend. Noelle peered into her eyes. "Has Gabriel been unkind? If he has, I will flog him myself."

"No, Gabriel has been kind. He is more than I ever dreamed in a husband. It's just that—" She stopped; the shame of her situation warmed her cheeks.

"Tell me," Noelle said firmly.

Sarah's flush deepened and her voice dropped to a whisper. "I do not know how to be a satisfactory wife."

Chapter Five

D o you mean . . . ?" Noelle pressed gently.
    Humiliated, Sarah wanted to die, here among the
fabric bolts. Clearly her flaming face gave Noelle clues.
When she'd said she did not know how to be a wife, she
wasn't talking about dinner table conversation or how to tie
his cravat.

"I should not have said anything." She turned away.
"My, isn't this blue silk just lovely?"

Noelle took her arm and gently spun her around. There
was no judgment in her expression, no humor, nothing at
all to indicate that she was anything but sympathetic to
Sarah's situation.

"Please. I insist you allow me to help," Noelle said. "I
grew up with Gabe. If anyone knows him, I do."

Having opened the door to this conversation, Sarah felt
that perhaps sharing her concerns might actually help.
She'd only just met Noelle, but she felt a kinship with her.

Glancing around, she assured herself that they were
alone, took a deep breath, and plunged ahead. "Our wedding night was a failure. I did not know what to expect. The

only information my aunt passed to me before she died was that a man pushed up your gown and put his male part inside of you."

Lud! Mortified over the confession, she said a silent prayer for a heart seizure. The prayer failed.

Thankfully, instead of laughing, Noelle took her hand.

"You truly *were* an innocent bride." Noelle blew out a breath through pursed lips. "I hope that Gabe was, er, patient?"

"He was." Sarah instinctively knew that the night had not gone well for him either. He'd tried to hide his disappointment but she'd felt his regret. "He was just so big, so . . . bearded, a stranger. He wanted to wait until I knew him better. I wanted it over. Thank goodness he had the good sense to end the evening before it went too far."

"Would waiting have changed things?" Noelle asked. "If he took you to bed now, would you feel calmer than you did then?"

Sarah thought about her handsome and confident husband and her stomach tightened. She shook her head. "He intimidates me in and out of bed. But the situation was far worse when—" She could not finish the sentence.

Noelle was kind enough not to giggle, snicker, or guffaw with Sarah's admission. Instead she worried her bottom lip between her teeth and her thoughts seemed to drift off for a moment, then two.

Finally, she nodded. "I will help you make things right between you and your husband, outside of bed, of course. We cannot let your marriage fail. I have seen enough miserable and loveless marriages. My parents included. Once there is affection between you, the rest will come easier.

The marriage could not fail for more reasons than Noelle knew, Sarah thought. She'd not yet had the chance to look into her father's death. In fact, she had no idea where to start.

"But what can we do?" Sarah said, refocusing her attention. She looked down at the borrowed gown and frowned as it hung on her thin frame. "Gabriel does not look at me like a man besotted. I think he was relieved to end the seduction so he'd not have to force desire where he does not feel it. Why would a man like him find a woman like me passion inspiring?"

Noelle's eyes narrowed. "You must not perceive your lack of polish or your thinness as shortcomings. Your neglect was not your doing. You were failed on many fronts, not the least by the men in your family. They were supposed to protect you."

She took Sarah's hand. "From this moment forward, you are not to make one negative comment about yourself in my presence, or I will never speak to you again." She looked straight into Sarah's eyes. "You are so much more than you see."

The harshness of Noelle's statement surprised Sarah. She swallowed deeply. "Are you always so outspoken?"

Noelle's smile flashed. "It is my best quality."

Sarah bit her lip. "I envy that in you," she admitted. "My aunt saw boldness in a woman as an unpleasant quality. She would have found you shocking."

Laughter followed. "I do love to shock." Noelle leaned in. "I married a man in trade and stunned the Ton. Thankfully, I care not what they think. I love Gavin madly."

A wistful sigh escaped Sarah. Now that she'd accepted her lot, she truly did want to be happy. She'd do anything to meet that goal. "Please tell me no more. Help me to acquire the happiness you have and I will be forever grateful."

"I shall make it my mission." Noclle rubbed her hands together. "I only have one question before we begin."

"And that is?"

"Do you find your husband handsome?"

"I do," Sarah admitted. "How could I not?"

Noelle nodded. "Then we shall start from there. It is hard to make a successful marriage when a wife finds her husband repulsive."

I could not know the depth of what I'd unleash when I agreed to allow you to teach me how to become a successful wife," Sarah groused. It started with a brisk walk around Hyde Park to bring some color to her cheeks and led to a visit to a pastry shop for a platter of sweet treats.

Lady Seymour had begged off after shopping, leaving the two alone to complete the first set of Noelle's instructions.

"Eat the last one," Noelle insisted, ignoring Sarah's scold. "We need to put at least a half stone on you."

Knowing it would be futile to argue, Sarah ate the final pastry. The flaky fig concoction was delicious. "With you in charge of my weight, I'll gain ten stone and Lord Seymour will need to widen the doorways."

"Posh. A half stone will bring you up just enough to keep a brisk breeze from blowing you down the street."

Minutes later, they left the shop and returned Sarah to Harrington House. After a quick hug, Noelle made Sarah promise to eat a hearty dinner and drove away in the Blackwell carriage.

"I do not know how I'll be able to eat anything after a platter of pastries," Sarah said under her breath.

After going to her room to freshen up her hair and remove her pelisse, Sarah returned downstairs and went to look for her husband. One of Noelle's notions was to keep herself within eyesight of him as often as possible. He could not overlook her if she was always underfoot.

A bit of searching found Gabriel in the library speaking with an older gentleman. "Oh, excuse me." She tried to withdraw. Gabriel called her back. He walked over and took her arm.

"Come, Sarah. My father is most interested in meeting you."

Her stomach twisted. As head of the Harrington clan, His Lordship's approval was vital. If he despised her, the rest of the family would follow suit. If he liked her, his acceptance would go far to ease her transition into his family.

Under Lord Seymour's scrutiny, she froze.

Lord Seymour walked over and Gabriel made the introductions. Sarah managed a decent curtsy. Up close, Lord Seymour was quite handsome. Aside from the few gray hairs at his temples, he and Gabriel looked much alike.

"So this is my new daughter?" He took her hand and bowed over it. His smile was wide. "My pleasure, Mrs. Harrington."

A slight nudge from Gabriel helped her find her voice. "S-Sarah. You must call me Sarah, Milord."

"Then Sarah it is." He looked down at his dusty riding clothes. "I am afraid we will have to wait until later to further acquaint ourselves. I need to have a bath and spend some time with my beautiful wife. Until dinner, then."

He left them. Sarah watched him go.

"Your father is an imposing man, yet kind," she said. Relieved to have somehow passed the first test to get into the earl's good graces, Sarah's stomach unclenched.

Gabriel nodded. "He was born to this life. My mother was penny poor when they met. Much like you." He gazed into her face. "If anyone can sympathize with our circumstance, it is my parents."

"How interesting that their story is similar to ours," she said. This certainly explained the lack of judgment displayed by Lady Seymour when they met yesterday. She should have demanded the marriage be set aside as any other noble mother would have. "Well, I'm sure they knew each other for more than an hour when they wed."

Gabe grinned. "My mother wanted nothing to do with my father. She thought he was a rogue out to charm and seduce her. Though that was his goal, he married her first."

Sarah laughed. "You Harrington men are shameless. Do you always get what you want?"

"Always," he said with a wink.

That bit of knowledge made her feel better. "Thank you for telling me. Though, it is impossible to believe that your perfect mother was once impoverished."

"When Father met her, she was barefoot and wearing cast-off clothing."

Sarah smiled. The image of Gabe's mother barefoot and in an old gown did not meld with the countess's current circumstance and perfection. Lady Seymour carried herself as if born into society. "Then I will take no insult when she looks aghast at my wardrobe."

Gabriel chuckled and looked her over. "There is something different about you today. I cannot place what, exactly."

She kept herself from smoothing her frock and dropping her gaze to the floor when he looked at her. Noelle insisted she show confidence with Gabriel, so she kept her gaze level on his, a difficult task indeed. When he peered at her with those green eyes, she was knock-kneed.

"Noelle took me walking in the park." She touched her cheek. "I think the sun burned me a bit."

"Your cheeks *are* pink," he agreed. "Whatever the change is, I like it." He pressed a quick kiss on her knuckles, smiled his devastating smile at her, and left her to sigh like a silly schoolgirl in his wake.

A brisk head shake snapped her from melting to the floor.

"Such foolishness," she mumbled. "Noelle is correct. Men enjoy a chase. I cannot be chased if I am trotting at his heels like a besotted ninny."

The image of her following him around with her tongue hanging out like a puppy did amuse.

At the moment there was little to tweak his interest. She was a stranger to him, too. And although he showed her friendly interest, he was not slavering to get back into her bed.

Nor had he once tried to kiss her again, the light brush of their wedding kiss aside.

What would his kiss feel like if she actually welcomed his attention? Would she like the press of his lips on hers? Or was she eternally doomed to frigidity?

"What a notion." Of course she was not frigid. Just the sight of Gabriel in tight breeches sent a warm flush over her skin. And there was nothing frigid about the tingles she felt in her most private parts whenever he kissed her knuckles.

No. She was just too innocent of the ways between men and women. Thankfully, Noelle knew what to do to change everything.

* * *

"Ouch." The dance instructor, Mister Robicheau, released Sarah and stepped back. He glared, lifted one skinny leg, and rubbed his long-suffering foot. He did a half hop and faced Lady Seymour. "Countess, she is hopeless."

Lady Seymour made a valiant attempt to hide her amusement behind a hand, and Noelle turned away to closely examine a painting of a fox and hounds.

Neither reaction gave Sarah encouragement. Her shoulders slumped. "I *am* the worst dancer in the history of dancing. It *is* hopeless."

"See, even Mrs. Harrington knows she cannot dance," Mister Robicheau continued unabated. His narrow frame was stiff and unyielding in his ire. "She has the grace of an ox."

"Now Robicheau, you must not insult Mrs. Harrington." Lady Seymour walked over from her place by the wall. "You know she has never danced before. You must have patience. Even a butterfly begins life as a graceless caterpillar."

The instructor began to list all the reasons why the lessons were a waste of time: her posture, her foot placement, her failure to learn even the most basic instructions.

Sarah looked up at the ceiling where candles flickered in the chandelier and tried not to take insult with his rant.

The seldom-used ballroom had been aired out for the lessons, and Sarah was wearing a new cream frock and slippers. Yet, not even pretty clothes could change the fact that she hadn't the expertise to pull off even a simple country dance with any sort of grace.

She *was* an ox.

Perplexed by all the steps required for dancing, she was about to beg off the rest of her lesson when a flash of blue by the door caught her eye. Her heart dropped. Gabriel, dressed in a deep blue coat, had a fist to his mouth, his eyes alight, watching his mother and the instructor arguing over whether Mister Robicheau could use his immense talents—Lady Seymour's words—to bring Sarah up to snuff.

When the man was ready to call the day a waste of time, Lady Seymour offered to double his fee, and his voice changed instantly from annoyed to compliant.

"Perhaps Mrs. Harrington could learn a simple dance," he said, albeit reluctantly. His pinched expression softened a bit.

Excellent. Her husband was witness to her failure.

She glanced at Noelle, who tapped a finger under her own chin. Sarah nodded, squelched the desire to run and hide, and jerked up her chin. Noelle indicated her approval.

"Shall we try again, Mrs. Harrington?" The dance master gingerly extended his hand.

"Please. Allow me." Gabriel pushed away from the doorjamb and strolled over. He waved a hand at the dance master. Mister Robicheau took a quick side step to avoid being trod upon by him. "I would like to dance with my wife."

Sarah's eyes widened. "I—I am not ready."

"Nonsense." He took her hand and his eye twinkled. "Even an ox can manage a few steps of the waltz." He looked over at the violinist brought by Robicheau and the music began again.

Lud. He *had* seen her disgrace. His teasing did nothing to settle her nerves. Damaging his toes would not further her efforts to make him see her as an acceptable wife.

Unfortunately, she was trapped. "Watch your feet, Husband," she said and let him lead her into the center of the floor. He took her into his strong arms. She shivered.

"How much have you learned about the waltz?" he asked.

"I understand the basic steps," she said, defeated. "The execution fails me."

Gabriel leaned down. His spicy scent warmed her. "Robicheau is an impatient toad," he whispered. "Now that you have a real partner, let us see what we can accomplish."

With that, Gabriel led her slowly through the steps while she clung to his shoulder for balance. There was toe trodding, though his suffering was not nearly as onerous as what she'd imposed on the instructor. After a half hour or so, Sarah realized she'd gone a full circle around the ballroom without faltering. She suspected it was his skill and the confident way he held her in his unyielding embrace that saved her from making a fool of herself.

"Excellent performance, Mrs. Harrington," Gabriel said. He twirled her around. She wobbled but kept upright.

Sarah beamed and curtsied. "Thank you, Mister Harrington." They took another turn around the room. This time she felt more relaxed and even managed to look into his smiling eyes while he led her and not at her clumsy feet.

Noelle and Lady Seymour clapped. Even Mister Robicheau appeared to concede that she'd done the impossible. It was difficult to read his thoughts when scowling was his expression of choice.

Just as her confidence welled, she stepped on his toe again, drawing laughter all around.

"You have done well, my dear," Gabriel said. "By the time you debut at your first ball, you shall be a fine dancer." He stopped her near his mother and bent into a sweeping bow. "Alas, I have a meeting that I'm already late for. I shall leave you to your lesson."

Sarah forced herself not to watch him leave the room.

Noelle walked over. "Well done, Cousin. Your husband was transfixed. This is a win."

"Of course he was transfixed. He was focused on saving his toes," Sarah teased, then, "It *was* wonderful to be held in his arms. He cuts a fine figure, my husband."

Mister Robicheau clapped his hands, ending further conversation, and Sarah spent the next hour despoiling the dance master's toes and suffering ear pain under the abuse of his complaints.

Gabe left the town house shaking his head. His wife, despite the shyness and awkwardness she displayed in his presence, had spirit. She did not let insults from that puffed-up buffoon, Robicheau, keep her from learning the steps of the waltz.

Though she'd shown little talent for dancing, he had a

feeling Sarah would eventually become quite competent, if not an expert, on the dance floor.

His wife was an interesting mix. While holding her in his arms, he'd noted the silky softness of her skin, her lovely violet eyes—the same eyes that often pointed toward the floor when he spoke to her—and the way the soft scent of orchids swirled around her.

He'd not gone to her bed since their wedding night, hoping to ease her fears with patience, giving them a chance for affection to grow between them. The next time he bedded her, she'd be as willing as he.

And this time, there would not be a frayed nightdress to come between him and her delightful breasts.

This thought surprised him. He'd spent years listening to Albert's stories, thinking of her almost as his own little sister. So vivid were the images of her with braids and scuffed knees painted in his mind that it was difficult to see her any other way.

Even now, with the braids gone, he continued to battle those images. The grown-up Sarah was winning the fight. Her breasts stirred him in a way that no sisterly Sarah could.

Replacing Albert's tales with new experiences was an effort he must make, if he was to treat her not as a child, but his wife.

With that thought in his mind, he whistled softly as he collected his horse and headed for White's. In the male-only club, he looked forward to renewing old friendships and making new acquaintances.

And to finding a bit of raucous fun.

Chapter Six

Gabriel missed dinner, so Lord Seymour filled in his absence with stories of his son's youth. Though amused by tales of the rambunctious lad, Sarah was miffed to be snubbed by her husband, without explanation, after Noelle had spent so much time getting her ready for the evening.

White lace lined the low bodice of the pale green gown, and sprigs of darker green flowers drew the eyes to where her bosom pressed precariously upward. It was a dress to entice Gabriel's attention; a wasted effort for all of Noelle's good work.

He was clearly not interested in spending time with her. Someplace, or someone else, held more appeal.

Was she wasting her time trying to improve her marriage? Maybe she *should* return to her original plan; a plan she'd all but forgotten while settling into her life here. She meant to discover the truth behind Father's death and return to the cottage with a comfortable allowance, if she could get Gabriel to agree she was entitled to an income. With Gabriel funding the venture, she could make the house livable, and live out her remaining years, alone, with her books.

Maybe she'd get several cats for company. They were less trouble than an unacceptable husband.

Was Gabriel unacceptable? Could she make that judgment with such a short acquaintance?

Suddenly, a return to the cottage no longer appealed as it once did. She was becoming used to the title of Mrs. Gabriel Harrington. More so, she liked the earl and countess and being part of their family. She liked London. She liked Flora. She liked pretty dresses. And she adored Noelle.

She liked not having the ominous presence of Mister Campbell lurking around her.

It was Gabriel she wasn't certain she liked.

Yanking her mind from her absent husband, she resisted the urge to tug up the fabric, trying to remain a picture of confidence in such a daring gown. Well, daring for her. Lady Seymour's ice blue gown was a touch lower and kept Lord Seymour's eyes occupied when he wasn't charming Sarah.

"Miss Ann Cunningham was not pleased to discover that Gabriel had stolen a kiss from her housemaid when he was supposed to be sharing tea with her," Lord Seymour was saying and drew Sarah's attention back to him. "She chased him out of her house with a broom and told him to never return."

Sarah's eyes widened. "Gabriel kissed a housemaid?" Her heart sank. Was he the sort of man who took advantage of his position to slake his needs with his female staff?

"It was not as it seems," Lady Seymour rushed to explain. "He was only thirteen, the scamp. After his father took a switch to his backside, he never again crossed that line."

Relief released the tightness in her chest. "Thank goodness," she blurted out, then her cheeks heated.

Lady Seymour smiled indulgently. "My son was never a saint, but neither was he a libertine. Still, no young man can resist a pretty face and well-turned ankle. Gabriel was no exception. I suspect he has settled with age."

Not even the countess's assurance soothed Sarah's concerns. Gabriel did not share her bed. Eventually, he'd want a bedmate. Where would he go? Whores? Widows? No matter which, he'd find a woman who'd overlook his marital status for a chance to take Sarah's strong, handsome husband to her bed.

Did she care what he did with other women? She puzzled on it and came to no solid conclusion. Another minute of pondering turned her ambivalence to annoyance. The idea of Gabriel shaming her with his sexual antics made her realize quickly that she'd not be happy with that one whit.

She was his wife. He needed to act like a doting husband. The only skirts he should be chasing were hers.

The next morning, Sarah awoke with renewed determination to follow Noelle's lessons to the letter. When the Lady arrived early in the afternoon, Sarah hurried to greet her.

"What is the matter, Sarah?" Noelle asked. "Did the dress and your fetching coiffure not attract Gabe's attention?"

"Gabriel did not come home last evening. I stayed up until nearly midnight and still he did not appear." She toyed with the fabric of her sunny yellow dress. "I fear he has found someone else."

Noelle snorted. "Nonsense. I saw the way he looked at you while you danced. He may not be blinded by passion, yet, but he cares for you. He'll not embarrass you by acting a cad when you are so newly wed." She looked Sarah over. "We may need desperate measures. I need to make a list."

The two women sought out paper and pen. "We have already covered dancing. I brought several recent newspapers so that you have current topics on which you and Gabe can converse. You can read them later. Today we will work on flirtatious fan waving and how to navigate your way through a formal dinner. The table settings alone can be daunting." Noelle scribbled everything down. "We shall add curtsying and delve deeper into titles; how to address dukes and earls and such."

Sarah peered at the notations. "I shall never remember it all."

"Posh." Noelle added a few more items. "I shall work each into your brain until you feel you were born to this. By the time you attend the Hollybrooks' ball at the end of the month, you will be this Season's incomparable."

Incomparable?

At Sarah's look, Noelle had to explain what an incomparable was. "Although this title is usually reserved for a young lady fresh from the schoolroom, I think you may, at the very least, be the belle of the Season."

Sarah scrunched up her face. "You believe my abilities well above my skill set. I will never be the most admired woman of the Ton."

Noelle shot her a scathing glare. "What did I say about belittling yourself? Do we have to cover the topic all over again?"

Sarah bit her lip to hide her smile and lifted her nose upward, to an extreme and snooty level. "I am to project confidence at all times, never speak—or think—badly about myself, ever, and always carry myself like a queen."

"Excellent." Noelle dropped the pen into the inkwell. "Now we must seek out the countess. First we will tackle the barons and move on from there." She cast Sarah a side-long look. "And I have an idea that should affirm to Gabriel that you deserve his attention."

"What is this idea?" Her curiosity warred with trepidation. The smug expression on Noelle's face gave her pause. There was no telling what the other woman had planned for her. She was certain not all of her friend's ideas would be agreeable.

"Later. Now off we go." Noelle stood and walked away, with Sarah close on her heels.

Sarah's worries came back to haunt her a few hours later, when Noelle's husband, Mister Blackwell, came to fetch his wife home. In his well-cut gray coat and trousers, he was almost as handsome as Gabriel. Almost. After a brief introduction and a few pleasantries, Noelle explained what she wanted from him. His surprise was only slightly lower than the level of mortification Sarah felt.

He darted a glance to Sarah, seated primly on the couch. "You cannot be serious, Noelle. It is entirely improper."

"Nonsense. I am positive Sarah has seen two people kiss." She glanced at Sarah, who shook her head. She frowned and tipped her head slightly to the side. "Never?"

"Not unless you count Gabriel's lips on my cheek to seal our vows and a few brushes of his mouth that night." Sarah entwined her fingers on her lap and twiddled her thumbs.

Noelle gaped. "That's all the kissing you've shared?"

"That is all."

Noelle shook her head.

"Did Gabriel steal her from a convent?" Mister Blackwell teased softly and was rewarded with a punch to the arm. "Ouch." He rubbed the spot and turned back to Sarah. "I do apologize, Mrs. Harrington, for my impertinent comment."

"Do not let him be rude, Sarah, or he will become insufferable," Noelle scolded and took his arm in a tight grip.

Unable to resist his charm, and remembering her earlier lesson, Sarah cast him a sidelong glance and flicked her lashes. "No apology needed, Mister Blackwell. I was indeed sheltered."

Mister Blackwell's grin widened. "It's Gavin. It would honor me if you called me by my given name."

Noelle laughed at Sarah's coquettish smile. "Brava, Sarah. You have just charmed my husband."

"Women throwing themselves at me is the curse of having a pleasing face," he said.

Noelle grunted. "See what you've done, my friend? It will take me weeks to deflate his puffed-up head."

Sarah laughed. She enjoyed watching them spar, their love evident in the way they looked at each other. She wondered if she and Gabriel would ever tease and laugh in that way.

Love between them seemed like such an unattainable concept.

"Now, about kissing." Noelle turned Gavin to her. "Since Gabriel has been lax in his duties, you need to get his attention. I think it time that you kissed him. With my husband's cooperation, I shall show you a simple kiss."

Mister Blackwell shrugged and dropped his hands on Noelle's waist. "If I must," he said warmly.

Heat crept up Sarah's neck. She was about to watch an intimate act between husband and wife. However, Noelle's rule about not staring down at the floor kept her from pressing her face into the pillow at her elbow.

Truthfully, she wanted to see the kiss, inasmuch as she wanted to look away. Drat her curiosity.

"Since Gavin is tall, I must stand on my tiptoes to kiss him." She pushed up. Even then, she was still a bit shorter. "You can either tangle your fingers in his hair, like this." She demonstrated. "Or you can cup the sides of his face, like this." Another example followed. "Lastly, if you want to hold his attention, you must keep his eyes locked on yours." Noelle looked into Mister Blackwell's eyes. He smiled. "Now, the kiss."

Noelle reached around his neck and pulled his mouth down to hers. What started as a simple press of lips changed as Mister Blackwell splayed his hands around his wife's waist and tipped his head sideways to deepen the kiss.

Oh my!

Sarah gaped. Her entire body flamed with embarrassment as her eyes held fast, fascinated by the moment.

The room warmed considerably.

When Mister Blackwell finally lifted his head, Noelle's face had a dreamy cast, her eyes soft. It took her a moment to bring herself upright and take a step back. She cleared her throat and smoothed the waistline of her dove gray gown.

Mister Blackwell chuckled and Noelle's eyes sparkled when she turned to Sarah. "That was a kiss."

The handsome Mister Blackwell winked at Sarah and her cheeks burned. "If you kiss Gabriel like that, he will follow you around like a lapdog."

With that, he took his wife by the hand, made some hurried excuse about needing to get home for some reason or another, and pulled Noelle from the room.

Noelle turned her head just before they vanished from sight to grin at Sarah. "Class dismissed."

Sarah groaned as she heard the door open and then close behind them. She slumped back on the cushioned settee.

"I cannot do that," she mumbled. "Or can I?" She lifted a hand to her forehead. The passion between the married couple still crackled in the room.

Unsettled, she snatched up the pillow and fanned her face.

It was an hour later when Gabriel arrived home. Sarah heard his footsteps clomp down the hallway and peered out her open bedroom door to see his condition.

His clothes were disheveled, his hair askew, and his carriage, not the confident upright posture she knew well. Truthfully, he looked as if he'd had an accident with a coach and four. And the coach and horses were victorious.

As he fumbled for the door handle, she hurried into the hallway, miffed and seeking answers. Though she did not want to sound like a shrewish wife, neither did she want him to think she'd accept rudeness. He should have sent around a note.

"I see you've finally managed to find your way home."

He turned and stared at her through red-streaked eyes. From the front, his appearance was worse. His coat was torn and his cravat, dirty.

"Did you roll about in the gutter last night?" She took in his dusty and crumpled clothing and the streak of what she assumed was blood on his shirt. After a quick perusal, it was clear that he'd suffered no injury. The blood belonged to someone else. Whose, she could only imagine.

"I am not in the mood to hear you prattle on, Wife." He turned back to the door, twisted the handle, and pushed the panel open. Sarah followed him in, finding some humor in his misery.

Once inside, he looked a bit unsure of his next step. Out of courtesy, she moved forward and helped him out of his coat.

"Thank you," he grumbled and reached for his cravat. The strong smell of port and unwashed body clung to him. Sarah lifted a finger to her nose as his valet, Benning, arrived.

"Please arrange for a bath for Mister Harrington," she said. The valet nodded and did her bidding.

Gabriel managed the cravat, as it was already loose, and she helped pull his shirt over his head. While they worked on shedding his clothing, a tub was carried in and water began to arrive for the bath. He dropped onto his bum on the bed.

Oddly enough, the sight of his bare chest did not strike childish fear in her as it once would have. In fact, his sun-kissed and muscled chest was pleasant to look at. If not for her annoyance, and her imagination working over the possibility that he'd spent the evening with one, or more, other women, she might have thoroughly admired the view.

Still, despite her annoyance, her heart did flutter . . . just a little . . . when she touched his skin.

Lud, more than a little. There was much to admire.

"It was very rude of you to worry me and your mother when you did not come home." Sarah wasn't sure Lady Seymour was worried about her wayward son, but she thought added guilt would be just punishment for his lack of consideration. "For all we knew, you were dead in an alley somewhere with your pockets picked and a knife protruding from your chest."

He lifted his face and stared at her through one open eye. "If I tell you about my evening, will you cease speaking so loudly? The shrillness of your voice is causing a headache."

Shrill? Her modulated tone was anything but. However, knowing he suffered for his evening of drinking and debauchery left her highly amused. "I promise."

The valet finished stripping him and helped him into

the bath while Sarah turned her eyes away. A bare chest she could manage. Anything hidden by breeches pushed the edge of what she could handle at the moment.

Benning handed Gabriel a brandy, which was gladly received. Sarah waited until Gabriel settled in the water before dismissing the valet and pulling a chair up beside the bath.

Gabriel groaned, leaned back, and closed his eyes.

"Your story, please," she said.

Thus began a tale of meeting old friends at White's followed by drinking, a trip down to the docks for more drinking, and a scuffle with a trio of merchants just arrived from Venice.

"I think Lord Pickering, Mister Crowell, and I slept the rest of the evening and most of today in the parlor at Collingwood House. How we got there, I do not know. I awoke an hour ago to the face of my very annoyed new cousin, the duchess, staring down at me. She ordered her footmen to drag us out, put us into her coach, and drop us off at our respective homes. Otherwise, I remember little after the scuffle with the merchants."

Merchants from Venice? She rubbed her temple. At least there was no mention of women in this tale of woe.

Sarah sighed and slipped off the chair. She collected the soap and moved behind him. He did not protest when she ran her hands through his silky, albeit dirty, hair. She picked out and flicked away a piece of ash and a leaf from the tangles.

His hair was very soft.

"If you expect sympathy from me, you have none." Lifting a pitcher, she poured the water over his head. He rubbed his eyes. "However, I cannot fault you for an evening of mischief with your friends. You've been gone from London for a very long time."

He groaned again. "You promised no speaking."

Sarah laughed softly. As silent as a mute, she pushed up her sleeves, washed his hair, and scrubbed his shoulders and upper back, leaving anything below the waterline to him.

The intimacy of the bath made her feel closer to him. Every part of her was aware of his nakedness, mostly her private areas. Despite her innocent mind, her body reacted to him in an ancient and primitive way.

How she managed this simple wifely duty, she wasn't certain. Her eyes were preoccupied by a spattering of faint freckles on his broad and sun-kissed shoulders and the way his warm and supple skin felt beneath her hands.

Her husband *was* a magnificent male specimen. Her mind drifted to Noelle and Mister Blackwell's kiss, and a bit of naughtiness welled inside her.

How could one not be naughty with a man like Gabriel naked in the tub at her knees? Now, their wedding vows made taking liberties acceptable.

There was no time like now to try her latest lesson.

"I shall leave you to your bath." She moved to his side, leaned down, cupped his chin in her hand, and gave him a somewhat chaste, yet lingering kiss on his firm mouth.

Tingles spilled over her skin. He tasted of brandy and maleness, a most pleasing combination. When she lifted her head, his eyes were wide and puzzled. She smiled and straightened, having given him something to ponder. "Sleep well."

Without a glance back to gage his reaction to her boldness, she left him to finish his bath.

Gabriel's cock jerked to attention beneath the sudsy water. Well, from attentive to steely hard. Her hands on his bare skin had aroused him. The kiss had snapped him to attention. Sarah, his country mouse, had kissed him full on the mouth; a surprising turn, indeed.

What had Noelle done to his timid wife? He suspected she was the culprit, as it was her that Sarah most admired.

No matter the source of the change. He reached up to touch a wet fingertip to his lips. After a night of male companionship and too much cheap ale, he'd found that he enjoyed the sweet taste of her lips mixed with her ever-present orchid scent. Had she not left him in a stunned state, he would have enjoyed tasting other parts of her, starting at her perfect breasts.

Painfully aroused now, he leaned back and examined the ceiling. Had he waited too long to attempt to seduce his wife again? Was her kiss an invitation to come to her bed, or only the curiosity of a sheltered virgin?

Certainly she would not have kissed him had she not wanted his attention. Correct? His ale-soaked brain was certain she was ripe for seduction. His body agreed.

Intrigued, he hurried through his bath and donned a robe. He peered into the empty hallway and padded bare-foot to her door. Without knocking, he pushed inside . . . to find the room empty.

Disappointment was his reward. She wasn't waiting for him wearing nothing but a sheet and a welcoming smile. In fact, there was no indication that she wanted him to ravish her at all. The minx had left him to suffer.

Damn. The kiss had been merely a kiss.

His cock was equally disappointed at the downward turn of events. With a frustrated groan, he padded back to his room, climbed into bed, and fell into a restless sleep.

Sarah stepped from the shadows, having seen Gabriel exit her room. She took satisfaction that her drunken husband had not had the chance to seduce her. As if she'd allow it! Despite the sweet kiss, she was still annoyed. She was not yet his cherished wife, but she was not to be dismissed as inconsequential either.

Clearly, her attempt to use the kiss lesson had stirred him enough to seek her out; a success by all accounts.

Thankfully, she'd gone downstairs to collect a book and he'd missed his opportunity. The oaf. When—and if—they finally shared intimacies, it would not be while he was under the lingering effects of ale.

Sarah could not wait to tell Noelle of her coup. She'd

won a battle for her husband's attention and had herself found some pleasure in the kiss.

If kissing was pleasurable, as she'd glimpsed twice now, then perhaps she'd find other aspects of her marriage pleasurable, too. Could she grow to love Gabriel and he love her in return? The idea of being loved by such a man made her heart beat a little faster.

Noelle's lesson about confidence worked its way into her thoughts. With the right information and her lessons, she *could* entice her husband, and perhaps make him love her; if only just a little bit.

Yes, she could do this. Away from the cottage, she was changing, growing confident. Although she still had much to learn, her future no longer looked dismal.

A slow smile crossed her lips. With Noelle to coach her on the ways of men, she might actually win some affection from her husband, perhaps more. Gabriel wouldn't realize he was hooked until it was too late.

Chapter Seven

Through dinner that evening, Sarah was cool and polite to her husband, as if she'd already forgotten the kiss. He should not get too confident in his charms, she thought. Let him believe she'd not been enticed by his lips in the least.

Gabriel, on the other hand, appeared to struggle with a headache. His red eyes bespoke his misery better than words, and his surly grumbling was tempered only by his mother's frown. The countess, knowing of his adventure, avoided pressing him to join the conversation and allowed him to suffer in peace.

Sarah found his condition both pitying and amusing. She ate her dinner while covertly watching Gabriel from under her lashes.

She'd hoped he'd notice her new green frock. Her hope fell flat. He was too unhappy to notice much of anything. She bit back a sigh. Gabriel himself was proving to be the largest barrier to her attempts to make a success of their marriage.

"Please bring my son a glass of brandy and a headache

powder," Lord Seymour finally said, after Gabriel growled at a maid. The nearest servant went off to do his bidding. "Next time you're in this state, we will have a tray sent to your room."

"Next time I am in this state, shoot and bury me."

The countess brushed her napkin over her lips. "The headache is your curse for imbibing too much. Perhaps next time you will find another way to celebrate with friends."

"I understand eating ground glass is all the rage," Sarah snipped. "Or dosing oneself with poison."

The dark glare he showed was not amused. "If my family wasn't so disagreeable, I would not have to drink." His focus was on Sarah. She refused to flinch at his angry tone.

"You worried her," Lady Seymour snapped. "You worried me."

"I should have stayed in America," he grumbled. "The women there are less querulous."

A hand slammed down on the table. Lord Seymour pushed halfway up from the chair. "I'll not have you take out your sour mood on your mother and wife. Apologize to them."

Gabriel winced under his father's thunderous tone. "I apologize, Mother, Sarah."

Lord Seymour settled back in his seat. Silence fell but for the clink of silver against plates. After a few minutes, the earl turned to Sarah.

"You've been spending a fair amount of time with Noelle of late," Lord Seymour said. He lifted his wineglass and peered over the rim.

"I have." Sarah nodded. "We've become friends and she is an excellent teacher. I will have her, and Lady Seymour, to thank if I make my debut into society without tripping over my hem while dancing or insulting a duchess by calling her merely 'My Lady.'"

She shared a smile with the countess.

"You must take care, Wife," Gabriel broke in. "Noelle is a mischief-maker and prankster. She may get you into trouble with her 'lessons.'"

"Noelle is very kind," Sarah countered sharply. She'd had enough of his surly disposition for one day. "She has been nothing but generous with her time and experience. It is not easy changing a country mouse into a swan. You should be grateful for her assistance." She dropped her napkin on the table. She smiled at Lord and Lady Seymour. "If you will excuse me, I feel my own headache coming on."

A bolt of pain shot a path behind his eyes. He grimaced as he watched his wife stalk from the room. He'd not meant to ruffle Sarah's feathers, and he'd done so twice. Nor did he mean to insult his cousin.

Well, yes to insulting Noelle.

To his defense, Noelle *was* troublesome, though it was not entirely negative. Of his many cousins, she'd been the most fun. If there'd been mischief to be made, she was always at the center of the whirl.

"I just wanted to warn Sarah lest she be at the receiving end of a prank," he muttered under his mother's scathing frown.

"You might consider the work Sarah is putting into becoming a wife you can be proud of, and compliment her a time or two, instead of grumbling over her friendship with Noelle," Father said. "Though, I think she needs no polishing. I find your wife an excellent addition to the family."

Mother glared. "How you managed to find such a jewel, and convince her to marry you in a rush, is beyond comprehension. And clearly you've lost your manners while you were away. Perhaps Noelle should take *you* under her wing and teach you how to be a better husband."

Gabe stared from one parent to the other and held up his hands, palms open. "You needn't defend Sarah to me. I, too, find her of the first order." He sighed. "As for Noelle, I adore the termagant, and appreciate her friendship with my wife."

"Then perhaps you should spend more time with Sarah and less time chasing your own interests," Mother scolded. "She deserves your full attention."

"I agree," Father said. "She is withering for the lack of sun, holed up in this town house as she's been. You need to take her out, lavish some attentiveness upon her, and be an engaged husband."

Scowling, Gabe nodded. It felt like a vise squeezed his head. "I will do my duties by my wife. Now can we please end this verbal battering? I will apologize, again, to Sarah."

With their lecture twisting through his pained head, he excused himself and went to seek out his wife. He found her curled up on the settee, in her sitting room, with a book clutched in her hands.

She made a pretty picture in the flickering lamplight, though she could use some color on her cheeks.

His parents were correct. There *was* a bit of withering. He *had* been neglectful. He'd spent more time getting soused with his friends last evening than he'd spent with her during the entirety of their marriage. It *was* time to court his wife, outside of his plans to seduce her.

"Is there something you require, Gabriel?" she asked, lowering the book. She clutched it tightly to her chest. Perhaps she was considering throwing it at his head.

"I believe I owe you a more heartfelt apology. I was a dreadful dinner companion."

"On that, we agree."

"Rather than subject you all to my condition, I should have stayed in my room and wallowed in my self-pity alone."

"Again, I agree."

Despite his headache, she made him smile. There was much to like about his wife. His gaze flicked quickly to her modest bodice and back up again. The gentle swell of cleavage above lace caused him to falter slightly and forget why he'd sought her out. He cleared his throat to regain focus.

"Now that I've been forgiven, I'd like to ask you to go driving with me tomorrow morning," he said. "The park is lovely at sunrise."

He knew she was an early riser and would not be put off by the request. Whether she'd want to take an outing with him or not was another matter.

Her eyes narrowed slightly, as if she were pondering his request, or perhaps deciding if she wanted his company at all. He'd not blame her if she refused. He'd been a dreadful boor at dinner. Thankfully, a small smile appeared.

"I think a drive would be lovely." With that, she lifted her book and soundly dismissed him.

The image reminded him of the moment in the coach when he tossed her book out the window. He suspected that she was sharing the same memory. There was light in her eyes.

"Tomorrow, then." His headache began to ease, and he whistled as he left her to her reading. As he cleared the door to her bedroom and stepped into the hallway, he was almost certain he heard a hint of muffled laughter.

The streets were quiet as Gabriel and Sarah drove along, with only an occasional servant about her duties to witness their passage through Mayfair.

Rain from last evening still dotted the street with puddles and gave the air a damp feel. Fortunately, the clouds had dispersed and left the morning clear for their drive. By the time they reached Hyde Park the sun had already taken hold of the dawn and scattered pink and orange across the muted gray blue horizon.

"It's unfortunate the grass is still wet," Gabriel said. "We could walk by the river."

"Ladies are not to soil their hems by walking on wet grass or through rain puddles," Sarah said in her best and haughtiest voice. "Or so the countess said."

Gabriel chuckled. "My mother and Noelle have made it

their duty to teach you how to be a Lady, but I ask that you keep some of shy Sarah in you, too. I liked my country mouse."

Sarah warmed beneath her cloak with the compliment and did not take offense at his choice of words. The title of country mouse had been hers when speaking of herself. And she knew he meant no insult by its usage.

"Training will only polish my edges. My aunt did her best, but she never spent time in society either," she said. "I lived half my life in that little cottage. It is part of me."

"Good." He flicked the reins. "Too much polish ruins many an otherwise perfectly acceptable society miss."

They found a quiet path and weaved their way through the park. Sarah was surprised to find such an unspoiled sanctuary inside the bustling city.

She smiled and drew in a deep breath. "You were correct. It is beautiful here." She felt his attention on her and lifted her gaze. He was not admiring the sunrise but looking at her with something akin to curiosity in his eyes.

Under his attention, she clasped her gloved hands together to keep them from trembling as her confidence slipped away.

"London is home to several parks," he said softly. "We can visit them all if you'd like."

"I'd like that very much," she replied. Her charming husband had returned. "I cannot believe how much I miss open fields and cows grazing unfettered across the landscape."

He flicked the reins again. "I cannot promise you cows, but I hope you find London satisfactory. I know it can be crowded and loud, but it does have its amusements."

"I do enjoy the city, though it takes some getting used to." She watched a large bird fly across the path. "Remember, I was born here. London is part of my history."

Gabriel nodded. "Excellent. I want you to be happy, Sarah."

They fell into a companionable silence while she considered her answer. She was happy with some parts of her life and not so certain about others, Gabriel being first on that list. But she did have hope.

"I desire the same." She met his eyes. "For both of us."

Gabriel pulled the horse to a stop beneath a large oak tree. He set the brake and half turned in the seat to face her. Muted sunlight danced between the leaves.

He was so very close. So very handsome.

Had they been courting, Sarah might have found the moment romantic. Lud, it *was* romantic.

"Is that the Serpentine?" she asked, her voice husky as she glanced toward the river to collect herself.

"It is," Gabriel said, his leg shifting slightly until it brushed her thigh. The contact, whether intentional or accidental, caused her to tense. The uncertainty of her feelings for him warred with the puzzling way her body reacted to his touch. It was as if she were two Sarahs. Neither was entirely comfortable with this one husband.

"Have I told you how fetching you are this morning?" He did not look down at her cream cotton day dress nor her stylish new matching hat. No, he was staring at her mouth.

"You have not," she said, breathless. He leaned forward and she did the same. He was going to kiss her!

"Ho, Harrington!" The voice startled them apart. Both Gabriel and Sarah twisted to see a man and woman come up behind them on the path. The pair was seated atop a set of fine horses.

"Who is it?" Sarah whispered.

"The Duke and Duchess Stanfield."

Sarah had no time to register the names when the couple pulled to a stop beside the carriage. Up close, they were a handsome couple. The duchess's amber eyes bespoke her identity. She was somehow related to Noelle, and a Harrington.

"Your Graces." Gabriel tipped his hat to the duchess, before indicating the duke. "It has been a long time, Your Grace."

"It's been years, Harrington," His Grace replied. Both the duke and duchess glanced at Sarah. They were not surprised to see her with Gabriel. Noelle most likely had told them all about her and how she and Gabriel met and married.

Gabriel introduced them.

"My pleasure, Your Graces," Sarah said. She knew the pair were Harrington cousins, in some fashion, and that Noelle was particularly close to the duchess. How close, Noelle had yet to confide, but she suspected there was an interesting story behind their kinship. As a new member of the family, Sarah had yet to learn all their secrets.

"We have heard all about you, Mrs. Harrington," Her Grace said. Her hair framed her smiling face. She was beautiful, no less so than her husband. He was quite handsome. The Harrington women had excellent taste in spouses. "Noelle has spoken highly of you."

The duchess cast a narrowed glance at Gabriel. "I see you have recovered from your . . . illness, Mister Harrington. I hope your friends have done the same."

Sarah pressed a hand to her lips to hide a smile, while the duchess took Gabriel to task for his drunken and unwelcome arrival at her door.

Smiling sheepishly, Gabriel nodded. "Once again, I do apologize for my behavior. I truly have no idea how I ended up at Collingwood House."

"From what I understand," the duchess said, "you and your companions were singing a bawdy tune on our stoop sometime around six o'clock when our butler went to investigate the noise. Once he recognized you and your companions, he pulled you all inside so you'd not rouse the neighbors, and settled you in the parlor. That is where you were when my maid advised me a few hours later of your nocturnal visit. I found you snoring quite loudly in my new settee and your friends taking up space on my new rug."

"I must have been curious about my new duchess-cousin," Gabriel replied. Puzzled, he frowned. "I think I remember that sometime during the evening, while drinking copious amounts of cheap ale, I launched a plan to meet the infamous Duchess Stanfield. Unfortunately, my drunken condition did not allow me to consider the consequences of my behavior."

The duke leaned back in the saddle. "If you wanted to meet my wife, Harrington, you could have sent around a card. We would have invited you and Mrs. Harrington for tea."

"True that," Gabriel agreed. "But now the duchess will never forget our first meeting."

Her Grace shook her head. "Had you awoken the baby, I would have had you three dumped in the garden without ceremony. She is teething and I seldom get more than a few hours' rest."

Sarah and Gabriel congratulated the pair for their daughter. Sarah found the duke and duchess charming. She'd heard that the duke could be cross and overbearing, but she saw nothing of that side of his nature here. He and Gabriel carried the conversation easily, as old acquaintances, and the glances he sent his wife were warm and loving.

"Well, we must be off," Her Grace said. "Our daughter only allows us short rides in the mornings before she demands most of my attention for the rest of the day." She looked at her husband. "She has her father's nature."

The duke frowned and she smiled brightly. "Untrue," the duke said. "I believe she has her mother's stubborn demeanor." They said their good-byes, spun their horses about, and continued their good-natured bickering as they went up the path.

"It appears as if Eva has softened the duke," Gabriel said, turning back to Sarah. "He used to be a bear. I do not believe that I ever once saw the man smile."

"They do seem quite happy." Sarah watched the couple until they were out of sight. "How do you not know the duchess?"

Gabe shrugged. "She is a recent addition to the family. I will leave the story for Noelle to tell when she is ready."

Sarah let the matter rest. It pleased her to meet them, but

she regretted that their untimely arrival had interrupted a potentially romantic moment. Gabriel was going to kiss her, of this she was certain.

Gabriel clucked his tongue and the horse walked on. Despite her disappointment, he did not appear the least concerned over the missed chance to kiss her.

Insecurity filled her. Had she misread his intention? Perhaps the reason he leaned in was to brush an eyelash from her cheek, or a stray hair out of her face.

"It is nice to see a couple so happy in their marriage," Sarah said. "All couples should be so blessed."

He grunted. "Sadly, happiness in marriage is rare. My parents are an exception. It is best to enter into a union with low expectations so as not to be disappointed later."

Low expectations? Annoyance welled. How low were his expectations when they came to her? Very, very low, she suspected.

She seethed.

He did not notice.

"It looks like we'll have a fine day of clear weather. After two days of rain, sunshine will be a welcome relief." Gabriel eased the carriage past a fallen branch.

"Yes, it will be nice," Sarah mumbled.

"Winter is not far off," he continued, unabated. "I look forward to snow."

Snow? They were down to discussing the weather? Did he not notice her stiff posture or the tap of her fingertips on her thighs? No. He was too focused on the silly topic of snowfall.

Blast, she did not care if it snowed to the rooftops!

Defeated, her ire changed to frustration and a touch of sadness. With his attitude toward love and happiness, she feared that her marriage would forever be one of duty and not affection. Gabriel would never kiss her the way Mister Blackwell kissed Noelle, or look at her the way the duke and duchess looked at each other so lovingly, or touch her the way Lord and Lady Seymour touched when they thought no one was looking.

She was destined to be trapped in a loveless marriage, and there was nothing she could do to change her situation.

G abe passed beneath an arch made by two trees on each side of the path and silently cursed the duke and duchess for ruining his chance to steal a kiss from his wife.

He was certain he'd seen the invitation in the softening of her eyes as the colors of the sunrise played across her pretty features. It had been a missed opportunity to take a small advance forward in his courtship.

When his shy Sarah had kissed him while he bathed, he'd realized she no longer saw him as the unshaven beast that had carried her off and married her without giving her a moment to change her mind.

She was making an effort to be a good wife. It was he who had hesitated. Wavering in his commitment to be a better husband had become commonplace with each passing day.

One day he wanted to become personally acquainted with her breasts, and the next, he was not certain what to do with her. He'd lied to her about their engagement and betrayed his dead friend by marrying her under the cloud of those same lies. Forcing Albert's sister into an unwanted marriage, when he knew it was not what Albert wanted for her, still weighed heavily on him. The guilt of the betrayal was hard to forgive.

What would she think if she discovered their union was not the wish of her dying brother? Would she hate him? She should hate him.

He could have married her off to some pleasant fellow who would give her children and a comfortable life. But no, there had been something about her from their first meeting that drew him in and made him want to be the man who rescued her from her dismal existence.

It was the damnable need to prove he was more than the selfish and irresponsible rogue Albert thought he was. He wanted to be her knight, to prove to his friend, and himself, that Albert's trust had not been misplaced.

Still the guilt of his deception was an invisible wall between them, difficult to tear down. Even when he lusted after her, Albert's condemning face would come to mind . . . and between them.

"Will Noelle be visiting today?" he asked as silence strained between them.

"I suppose she will."

The horse gingerly stepped through a puddle. "What is her lesson for today?"

"We will be going through the invitations with your mother and choose which will be my first introduction to society."

"I thought we were launching you at the Hollybrooks' ball?"

Sarah tipped up her face. "Lady Seymour thought it best if she introduces me to some friends before the ball. That way, I will know a few ladies before I'm thrown into the societal mire."

"I see." This conversation was strained. He left it to die and turned the carriage toward home.

Lacking the skills needed to make a good English husband, he longed for his days of adventure when a grunt or wink was all that was needed to get a woman into bed, the days when his life was much less complicated.

Hell, he was barely out of short pants when he'd made a run for the first ship out of England. Before that, he'd been incorrigible—his mother's words—and unwilling to do much more than drink and chase women of loose morals. He'd had no pressure to beget an heir—that was Simon's job—so he planned to spend his life avoiding virgins and their marriage traps.

Instead he'd turned about and shackled himself to the primmest virgin in all of England.

Gabriel glanced down at Sarah, her hand clutched in her lap and her back stiff. He knew it would take more than a grunt to get his shy English wife to climb willingly into his bed.

Albert's last words knifed through his brain, and the image of Sarah naked vanished. He knew that the only way to assuage his guilt over betraying Albert, and to prove to his friend that he was worthy of Sarah, was to make her happy.

This was proving to be an insurmountable task. Was he up to the challenge? Did he want to win her?

On this, he was not entirely certain.

Chapter Eight

The street was filled with pedestrians when the hackney stopped in front of the *London Times* building and Sarah alighted. She paused on the walk and stared up at the façade, hoping within these walls she'd find some direction in which to start her search for answers.

A young man with closely cropped copper hair greeted her when she went inside and approached him. He introduced himself as Hiram Smart. "How may I help you, miss?"

Sarah straightened for courage. Once she began this investigation, she had to face whatever she found, without veering from her course, and no matter how terrible the information might be. Her father deserved justice.

"I am seeking information about a ten-year-old murder." His eyes widened. She didn't blink. "I do hope you can provide the information I need."

After his initial surprise, he settled. "This is an unusual request, and I cannot guarantee the result you are hoping for." He pulled off his spectacles and rubbed them on his coat. "We have many murders each year, and not everyone makes the *Times*. Do you have a name and date?"

Nodding, she reached into her purse, pulled out a small square of paper, and held it out. Written on the page was her father's name and the month and year of his murder. "The victim was Henry Palmer. I haven't the exact day of his death, but it was sometime between October second and the tenth of that year." She knew this because Father died the week after her birthday.

He took the information. "Do you know where he died?"

"I do not." She held out her hands, palms up. "My expectations are not great. I only hope you can provide me with somewhere to start my investigation." At his curious look, she added, "He was my father."

"I see." He stepped back around his desk and laid her note down. "Our archives are extensive, but I don't think it will take too long to find the issues from that week. Come back on Monday and I will have them pulled for you."

Sarah smiled. "I thank you very much Mister Smart. Any help is much appreciated."

With the task completed, her footsteps were lighter when she left the building. Mister Smart may not find anything for her, or there might be clues aplenty; anything mentioning her father's death or similar crimes could perhaps be linked to his case. At this point she'd be pleased for a place to start searching for answers, no matter how seemingly insignificant.

The driver helped her into the carriage. "To Bow Street, please." He nodded and they were off. Once there, she briefly met with a Runner who offered little about the case, nor seemed enthusiastic about digging into the past.

"It has been many years," he said. "I do remember the murder was unsolved."

"You remember the case?" How odd that the death of a secretary would stand out in anyone's mind.

He nodded. "There was a significant amount of interest in the murder. Your father was both connected to Lord Hampton and murdered in Mayfair. It was many months before anyone felt safe to walk the streets unprotected. And despite calls for an arrest, the killer remains a mystery. Thus, I can make you no promises. However, I can see what I can find."

"May I check with you on Monday?" she said. She could visit both the *Times* and Bow Street all in one day. Too many outings might rouse Gabriel's suspicions.

"You may. Do not, however, get your hopes high."

Disappointed but not completely off put, she thanked him and left. Though she'd not received anything useful, at least the two men promised to help. It was a place to start.

Until Monday, all she could do for now was to wait and try not to lift her hopes too high.

I have failed miserably," Sarah said and dropped onto the settee in a fluff of pink satin. "I could not entice my husband to kiss me even if I were wearing a necklace made of his favorite strawberry tarts."

Noelle took a seat beside her and took her hand. "It cannot be that grim. Tell me everything."

Sarah recounted yesterday morning's events, leaving nothing out. When she was finished with the sad tale, Noelle stood, went to the writing table, and scribbled a note.

"Have you finally given me up as lost?" Sarah said, jesting. "What are you writing?"

Noelle ignored her. She called for a maid and gave her low-voiced instructions. Puzzled, Sarah waited until the maid scurried off to level on Noelle a curious stare.

Noelle shrugged. "I believe drastic measures are in order. I have called for assistance."

Though Sarah pressed her for information, it was nearly an hour before the butler came to announce a visitor.

"Lady Har—"

An attractive woman, her sable hair twisted into a knot at the base of her neck, came hurrying in past the butler, as if she were being chased by snapping hounds.

"—rington." The butler frowned and withdrew.

"Noelle, what is the emergency? Is Kathleen ill? Lord Seymour? Do tell me nothing has happened to Brenna or the baby."

Noelle met her halfway. "Calm yourself, dearest. There is nothing so dire." She took her arms and gave her a small shake. "Do take a breath, Laura, before you faint dead away."

"But your note said there was an emergency and to come straightaway." She glanced around the room, spotted Sarah seated calmly on the settee, and looked back at Noelle. She settled slightly. "What is this about?"

"I apologize for the clipped note. I know you have just returned from your country estate, but I had to see you." Noelle led Laura to Sarah. "This is Sarah, Gabriel's wife."

Laura appeared curious, though not entirely surprised. She'd clearly already heard about the newest Mrs. Harrington.

The women exchanged pleasant greetings. Laura smiled. The smile tightened to a teeth-grit when she returned her attention back to Noelle. "Though I have been eager to meet both Gabriel and Sarah, Simon and I planned to call in a few days after we've had time to unpack and rest. Certainly introductions do not an emergency make?"

Noelle shook her head. "This is not about introductions; this is about fixing a troubled marriage."

Laura stared. "I think you should explain yourself."

For the next fifteen minutes, the clock ticked while Noelle quietly explained their predicament. After the tale was told, Noelle and Laura fell silent while the duo sat on the settee facing her and stared. Sarah, remembering the rule about not fidgeting in social settings, sat with her hands clasped primly in her lap while they took her measure.

Her burning cheeks refused to cooperate with her attempt to put forth a serene countenance.

Laura finally spoke first. "I do not understand your cousin, Gabriel. Sarah is everything a man looks for in a wife. She is pleasant, pretty, and intelligent. What else is he looking for?"

Noelle nodded. "I cannot agree more. I've been search-ing my mind trying to figure out why he is hesitant to pur-sue his marital rights. My only thought is that perhaps he is used to less, shall we say, innocent partners and is intimi-dated by her sweetness."

"Hmmm." Laura tapped her chin. "From what I've heard about Gabriel, I do not think intimidation is his problem." She paused. "Perhaps he sees her innocence as a barrier to his more robust attentions. Some men tread cautiously where their virginal wives are concerned."

"Yes. You could be correct," Noelle said. "I had not con-sidered that. And, do you think that for years his thoughts of her were sisterly, through the stories told by Albert in his letters? Those innocent images could certainly cool his ardor."

"But he married me," Sarah protested. "We had our wed-ding eve. Sort of." She blanched under the unbidden image of her nightgown being pushed up and then, nothing.

"She's blushing," Noelle said to Laura.

"Therein lies the problem," Laura agreed. "How can she play a seductress when she cannot even say 'wedding eve' without turning puce?"

They returned to staring at Sarah.

"Why do I need to be a seductress?" Sarah asked. She felt entirely lost in this conversation. "Are wives not taught to lie back and wait for their husbands to finish, then roll over and go to sleep?"

Two pairs of eyes widened. "Oh dear," Noelle said.

"Goodness," Laura uttered under her breath. "Noelle, you are correct to call for me. This is an emergency."

Sarah's comment had struck horror in the minds of the two women. Their faces made that clear. And she wasn't entirely sure why. Everyone knew that beddings were for the pleasure of men, didn't they?

Laura drew in a deep breath and rubbed her palms together. Her concerned expression matched that of Noelle.

"My dearest Sarah," she said. "From this moment for-ward, you must forget everything, and I do mean everything, that your aunt taught you about men. First and foremost, you must know that a woman can find pleasure in her marital bed, with a husband who is unselfish and loving."

Sarah flicked a glance at Noelle. "Is this true?"

"It is."

Sarah slumped back against the settee and thought of her aunt and all the dismal things she'd been told about marriage. And there were many. "I have been misled."

"Desperately," Laura agreed.

"By an aunt who clearly did not enjoy her own marriage," Noelle added. "Thankfully, you have us to give you a clearer picture of marital expectations. And they do not involve lying back and thinking about the weekly menu."

They shared a nod. Sarah leaned her head back and closed her eyes. "If only it was possible to go back to the beginning of my developing years. That would be easier than unlearning all of her teachings."

The chatter stopped. Then, "What a splendid idea!" Noelle exclaimed, and Sarah's eyelids snapped open. "We must start from the absolute beginning. We must treat Sarah's lessons as if she is making her debut into society not as a married woman but as a virginal miss. We will teach her how to entice a mate, watch for rakes, flirt and laugh and dance with men . . . not Gabriel."

Laura bit her bottom lip. "Of course. Gabriel had his wife fall into his lap while making no effort whatsoever to court her. He must court her and woo her if he wants to keep her."

"I completely agree," Lady Seymour said from the doorway. "I have said the same myself, although I could not come up with a way to make it work." She joined them. "My son needs to earn his wife to appreciate her."

Noelle's eyes lit up. Sarah braced herself.

"I have just the way to start this game." Noelle rubbed her palms together. "The plan was to launch Sarah into society at the Hollybrooks' ball. I propose that instead we bring her to the Coventry Masque this Saturday. I will introduce her as a childhood friend, come to visit. Masked, she will be free to practice flirting, speaking of current events with Members of Parliament, or just making mischief, whatever suits her."

"I am not ready," Sarah protested.

"It's an excellent idea," said Lady Seymour and Laura in unison, ignoring the protest entirely.

With that pronouncement, Sarah's fate was sealed.

I do not like lying to Gabriel," Sarah said Saturday evening as she got ready for the masque at Noelle's town house.

"Nonsense," Noelle said and instructed the maid to add a bit more powder to Sarah's face. "Lady Seymour gave her permission. There is nothing to do now but enjoy your first ball."

"And when Gabriel finds out that I went without him?"

"You may lay the blame entirely at my feet." Noelle stepped back and examined Sarah's costume. Dressed as Anne Boleyn, wife of Henry VIII and once the most scandalous woman in England, Sarah was as far from the late queen in both style and temperament as one could be.

"This is a terrible mistake." Sarah reached up to touch the headpiece covering her hair. "I should return home to my books."

Noelle let out a long-suffering sigh and took her by her arms. "When is the last time you felt youthful and carefree?"

Sarah grimaced. "Never."

"Then hush about books and going home to that neglectful husband of yours. First, Gavin and I will watch over you so that you'll be in no danger of being seduced by some rogue. Second, we will have you home by the time Gabriel notices you missing."

Meeting Noelle's eyes, Sarah realized her friend was correct about everything. "I've gone from sheltered innocent to wife while experiencing none of the fun and frivolity most young women enjoy when launched into society. Oh, how I wanted to be frivolous!" A flush crept over Sarah's face with her outburst.

Noelle laughed. "Tonight you will have both."

Her friend's confidence gave her courage. "Once my mask is in place, I will be anonymous, free to explore my first society ball without the impediment of doing so as Gabriel Harrington's new bride, watched by everyone."

"Brava, dearest," Noelle said. "That is the spirit I like to see from you."

"Then we must hurry or we will be late," Sarah said. She walked to the dressing table to collect her mask and flounced to the door before she lost her courage. "There are men to charm with my saucy witticisms and flirtatious banter."

The ball was in full whirl when Mister Blackwell led them into the house with his wife and Sarah on each arm. The house was lit with more candles than she would have been able to use for ten years in her cottage, Sarah thought, as she was whisked through the receiving line and into the ballroom.

Within a half hour she confirmed Noelle's assurance that in costume, and with being new to London, there was no chance of recognition. She even managed to return the smile of a passing man dressed as a glorified dandy.

"See," Noelle said in her ear as the man was whisked away by a woman dressed as a shepherdess. "You just flirted."

"Truly?"

"Truly," Noelle replied. "An innocent miss would look away, lowering her eyes to discourage him from approaching. You met his gaze and smiled back. If not for the shepherdess clinging to his arm, I believe he would have stopped for conversation."

"Who knew that a friendly smile could encourage a man's attention?" Sarah puzzled over this. "If I allow a gentleman to kiss my hand, does that mean we are engaged?" she teased.

"Not quite," Noelle said. "Though if a young woman allows herself to be taken into a darkened garden by a man, and is caught, no matter how innocent the encounter, she could very well be ruined. Unless her irate father can get the cad dragged before a parson before gossip spreads about her downfall from grace."

"Hmmm. There are too many rules in your society." Sarah glanced around the crowded room, taking care not to encourage any man to approach. "There should be a book for young ladies to carry in their pockets for guidance."

"Most women are taught the rules from birth," Mister Blackwell added. He nodded to a passing devil. "You'll need years to catch up."

With Noelle as her tutor, Sarah managed to laugh with the Blackwells' friends and even attempted to flirt a bit with a pair of unattached men. Though it was awkward in presentation, neither of the men seemed to mind. They were both determined to see her unmasked and made a game of guessing her identity.

"If I tell you who I am then you will lose interest and I will be left bereft of your company," Sarah said. She waved her fan. "You shall just have to wait for the unmasking."

She knew they'd be gone before then and had no fear of losing her anonymity.

"Then at least you should allow me a dance," the bolder of the two men pressed. "I do enjoy dancing."

"I am afraid that I am not a very good dancer," Sarah said with an exaggerated sigh. "The dance master has deemed me quite incompetent."

The man was not about to be put off. He took her gloved hand as his companion moved off to find a partner of his own. "They are lining up for a country dance. There is little fear of you damaging my toes."

With a nod from Mister Blackwell, Sarah accepted the invitation with a weak smile and was taken away to join the row of dancers.

What have you done with my wife, Noelle?" Gabriel said as he closed in on Noelle and Blackwell. He'd arrived in time to see his wife taken away by a man dressed as what he assumed was the great lover Casanova.

Noelle startled and spun about. "Gabriel?"

Gabe pushed his mask up and glared. "I thought she was spending a quiet evening at your home. Imagine my surprise when I discover her here, in costume, carrying on with a pair of dandies, and clearly doing so with your permission."

"She is not carrying on with anyone," Noelle said, her tone brittle. "She is having fun. And since you seem perfectly content to leave her at home while you appear here without her, I have taken it upon myself to see that she gets out and enjoys herself as a woman of her young age should."

"She has a point, Harrington," Blackwell said. "I assure you that your wife is perfectly safe."

Gabe stared at Sarah, who was smiling at her partner as he led her through the dance. Though she was not as polished as the other dancers, she did manage a respectable job of the steps.

"If she wanted to go out, she could have said so," Gabe grumbled. For some reason he could not fathom, it irked him to see her with another man. "I would have escorted her."

"As your duty, not because you wanted to," Noelle snapped, drawing his attention back to her. "You barely notice her. So as you can see, she does not have that problem with other men. They genuinely enjoy her company."

His eyes flicked back to his wife. Over the course of the last few weeks, she'd put on some weight and had lost some of her skittishness, though he suspected this evening's newfound confidence had less to do with a change in her personality and more to do with the mask covering her face. She did appear quite comfortable in this setting.

"How I treat my wife is none of your concern," he said. He'd not have Noelle interfering in his marriage.

"You are correct. It is *you* who needs to concern yourself with your wife." Noelle took her husband's arm. "Sarah gains confidence every day. Soon enough, it will be you who is standing in the background while she lives a life without you."

With that, the Blackwells drifted off.

Was he that much of a cad? He'd not mistreated Sarah, nor had he done anything to harm her. He'd fulfilled his promise to Albert, had·he not? Why then did Noelle's words send a sharp poker right into his gut?

Because she was correct, damn her. His parents had also said as much. They all thought him failing as a husband.

Though he'd planned to eventually seduce his wife, he'd not thought of how he'd treat her outside of bed. Damn his years away from society. He was most unprepared to act like a doting husband.

Truthfully, he *had* been neglectful.

Gabe knew there was much more to this marriage business than just what happened between the sheets. His parents had been the example of what a loving couple should be. However, he and Sarah were not a loving couple. They knew very little about each other and, well, he was not wildly mad for her like his father was for Mother.

She was little Sarah. Albert's sister. Why could he not move past thinking of her as such? Worse, from the moment they'd taken their vows, he'd considered himself shackled with an unwanted wife, as if she forced him into the marriage.

Shamed, he vowed again to do something to change his thinking. She was his wife after all. Guilt and regret had no place anymore. Sarah did not deserve an absent husband.

Glancing to where she'd last been, he saw Casanova escort her off the dance floor. Determined to remove Sarah from the clutches of the dandy, and to spend the rest of the evening dancing in attendance to her, he pulled his mask back down and went to stalk his wife.

Chapter Nine

❧

S arah smiled politely when her partner asked if he could bring her punch. "Thank you, no," she said and withdrew her hand from his arm. The man was already too eager to impress her with his wealth, properties, and connections to the royal family. It was his want to blather on about these things in hopes of impressing her. Instead, she struggled not to yawn behind her hand.

She wanted to return to Noelle and Gavin. They were much more interesting.

"Would you care to dance again?" Casanova pressed. The man certainly was not timid. If only she could admit to being a married woman and send him on his way.

"I fear my feet are tired." Annoyance welled. He was beginning to turn from eager to downright pushy. "I think I shall sit out the next dance."

"Then I shall escort you back," he said and reached for her arm. Sarah stepped back to avoid contact.

"That will not be necessary." She held up a hand and said firmly, "I am quite capable of finding my way around a ballroom."

"Yes, however—" His protest was cut off by the approach of a man in black. The stranger was not overly tall, and a mask covered most of his face. He carried himself with aplomb as he crossed toward them. When he drew close, Sarah felt a shiver crawl down her spine. His gray eyes were flat and cold, his thin lips curled into a smirk.

"Your Lordship." Casanova dipped into a bow.

"Brightman." The stranger greeted her partner, but his attention was on her. As with his eyes, his voice held no warmth. "You must introduce me to this enchanting young woman."

Casanova's, or rather, Brightman's, shoulders slumped.

Clearly, whatever this stranger's identity, he was at a level or two above her partner. Brightman took a half step back from her as if the more dominant wolf had arrived to lay claim on the choicest sheep.

"We have not been introduced, Your Lordship," Brightman said, his voice quavering. "It is a masque and the Lady's face is covered."

A pair of hard gray eyes skimmed over her, both insulting in unspoken tone and sending an unnerving feeling through Sarah. She took an instant dislike to the stranger.

"Indeed," said the man in black. He touched his tongue to his bottom lip. "She is a mystery."

Sarah wanted to slap the smug smirk off his face.

"And she has promised me the next dance," a gruff voice came from behind her, rising just above the din, and without a trace of politeness in the tone.

Sarah felt a hand close over her elbow. Before she could turn her head to see the source of the comment, she was rudely whisked off toward the dance floor. She had to all but run to keep up with his long strides.

"Sir, please!" She tried to dislodge her arm without drawing too much attention, but his grip held fast. It was when she was spun about and pulled into a pair of strong arms, and she caught his spicy scent, that she realized that it was Gabriel who'd spirited her away.

Exasperated over the rough handling, she gritted her

teeth and spat out, "Must you be rude? I was having a perfectly pleasant conversation with the man in black."

The lie soured in her mouth, but she wasn't about to tell her overbearing husband that she was relieved with the rescue.

Gabriel's grip tightened as the orchestra struck up a waltz. "The man in black is Lord Pembrook, the worst sort of scoundrel. He is not the sort with whom my wife should associate."

Was there a touch of jealousy in his words? Likely not. He'd have to care in order to feel that emotion.

She dragged her gaze over him and admired what she saw. It was impossible not to. Dressed in black himself, but for an azure blue waistcoat, Gabriel was drawing more than a few feminine stares; not just hers.

Despite the mask, his handsome face was hard to hide completely, and his fine form was enough to set several fans fluttering as eyes followed him everywhere.

The proprietary envy was her curse, not his. She did not like the attention he was getting.

"If left up to you, husband, I would associate with no one outside of your family," she snapped. Her patience was at an end. "I may have lived a mostly solitary life in my cottage, but I did occasionally manage to see a friendly face in the village." He whirled her around the floor. When she trod upon his toes, drawing a masculine grunt, the misstep was not entirely accidental. "If my social interactions were left up to you, I'd be spending many hours counting the clock ticktocks while staring at the ceiling."

Gabriel's jaw tightened. "Mother promised to introduce you to a few friends, and you will be formally launched at the Hollybrooks' ball. After, you will not have a moment to yourself. The invitations will come at an alarming rate."

"The ball is two weeks away and I am still fearful of being thrown into such a large crowd for my first foray into society," Sarah countered. "Noelle, Laura, and I thought it best for me to try out my lessons under the protection of a disguise."

He expelled a harsh breath between gritted teeth. "And neither you nor your conspirators thought to ask my opinion before you snuck off like a thief in the darkness?"

Her spine tingled. "I did not sneak off. You were informed that I was spending the evening with Noelle, and I am."

"You left me believing that you were having a quiet visit at home," he said tightly.

"I certainly did not," she said. "You assumed as much."

For a moment, they fell silent. Gabriel expertly managed the waltz, despite years of little practice. Sarah's second and third toe-trod *were* accidental. Still, she offered no apology.

They did not speak again until the dance ended. His glare kept another potential partner at bay. The poor man took one look at her angry partner and scurried away.

"You have not explained your presence here, Gabriel," she said. "Are you seeking out a new mistress?"

Before their argument drew attention, Gabriel led her to the patio and into a quiet corner. He ignored her accusation. This did not reassure her.

"From now forward, if you wish to go out, I will escort you. I'll not have you wandering loose without supervision. You have only recently become my wife and your lessons are incomplete. We'll not risk your reputation on your ill-conceived whims. Mistakes will embarrass both you and my family."

Ill-conceived whims? Embarrass the Harringtons? Fire burned through her. She faced him squarely and tapped her toe.

"I am not a slobbering idiot," she ground out. "I can make polite conversation, manage proper fan waving, and am well-schooled in how to use the correct spoon . . . though I do loudly slurp my soup and wipe my mouth on my sleeve. Thank goodness they are not serving soup at this ball or I *would* shame the Harringtons down to their collective toes."

Was that a smile beneath his mask?

Sarah wanted to slap it from his face.

"Now you are being silly," he said. "I have never seen you slobber."

"Silly, impulsive, and an embarrassment?" Her voice rose. She crossed her arms. "You forgot plain, dull, improper, and impertinent. Is there anything I missed?"

"Sarah."

"No." She held her palms up and open. "You have not spent enough time with me since our wedding to dare make an opinion about my nature. However, I certainly know you. You are arrogant, boorish, and rude. You think only of yourself and nothing about the feelings of others."

"You have discovered all this about me in a matter of days, have you?"

"I have," she snapped. "Given another week, I should have a full list of your faults by which to confirm my conclusion."

Full of fire, she wanted to continue the argument but thought the location less than ideal. Instead she turned on her heel with the intention to leave him cooling his toes alone on the patio with her sarcasm ringing in his ears.

He had another idea. With a quick grasp of her arm, Gabriel spun her about and jerked her into his arms. She gasped as his mouth slammed down over hers.

Heat rushed into her body as he forced apart her lips and plunged his tongue into her mouth. Her shock turned to passion with a moan, and then shifted quickly to anger. How dare he give her a first real kiss after insulting her with his cutting words? How dare her body respond with interest when her mind was so outraged?

With a shove, she pushed back. He released her. "Do not ever kiss me again," she said through gritted teeth and stalked away.

Gabe waited until Sarah was out of hearing range and chuckled. Not ever kiss her again? Ha. Their kiss, as brief as it was, had been delightful. Her passion, peaked in part by her outrage, had certainly made his body take notice.

When had his wife become such a termagant? This had to be Noelle's influence. Yet, he found that despite her newly discovered desire to ruffle him up, there was something intriguing about having a wife who looked him squarely in the eyes and spoke her mind.

And Sarah had spoken her mind, quite elegantly in fact; without stammering, blushing, or looking at the floor. Who knew she was such a perceptive young woman. He *was* arrogant, boorish at times, and the other things she cast at his head.

He'd proven them all tonight. For good reason.

Finding his wife at the ball had raised his ire. Seeing her speaking with Lord Pembrook had both angered and alarmed him. Sarah was far too innocent and trusting to see through to the black heart of a man like Pembrook. Too many innocents had fallen to ruin in his bed.

Then, another thought came to mind. Perhaps he'd misjudged Sarah. She'd discovered courage, or perhaps she'd had it all along and just needed to bring it to the fore. And she *was* intriguing in her costume. The weight she'd gained suited her. She no longer looked like a starved chicken.

There was no reason for her not to draw male interest. She was both lovely and interesting. Despite her accusation, he'd never found her dull or anything else she'd claimed.

He truly needed to pay closer attention to his bride or he would lose her to another man. Fire burned in his stomach at the idea of another man kissing, and bedding, his wife.

The taste of her lips had stirred him. What other interesting things might he discover in his blossoming rose?

Gabe grinned. He should take her home and work some of the sass out of her, in his bed. However, he wasn't quite ready to press the issue. He wanted to give her more time to gain solid footing, for although she'd set him in his place and did not flinch away from his touch, he suspected that she was not quite ready for the intimacies of marriage. If he pressed her now, it might be a repeat of their wedding night.

The best he could do was to tempt her, tease her, and wait for her to come to him. She had kissed him in his bath.

It was the first sign of affection that she'd shown him. He wondered how long it might take her to find her own way to his bedroom.

Noelle's face was concerned when Sarah returned to the ballroom. She took Sarah's hand. "Was Gabe cross with you?"

Sarah nodded. "He was." She peered over her shoulder. Gabriel was not in sight. "He was not pleased with my presence here and told me so."

"What did you say?" Noelle asked. Mister Blackwell stood nearby, talking to a tall man in a red coat.

"I told him that I was not about to sit inside Harrington House and collect dust. I should be allowed to test my wings in this setting and did not need his permission to do so. I also called him rude and arrogant."

Noelle rubbed her palms together. "Brava, country mouse!" she exclaimed then lowered her voice when several pairs of eyes turned in their direction. She pressed her gloved hand over her mouth, her eyes amused. "I am certain that your husband was not pleased to have his wife argue for her freedom . . . and insult him, too."

Sarah scanned the crowd and caught a brief glimpse of Gabriel entering the room. Just as quickly, he vanished again in the crush. "Truthfully, I am not sure what he is thinking. We argued and then he kissed me. Hard. It was no chaste kiss."

Amber eyes widened. "He kissed you?" She reached out and drew Sarah back to the wall and out of earshot of a group of women lingering nearby. "He really kissed you?"

A slow smile tugged up the corners of Sarah's mouth. "He did." She flushed as heat crept up her body. "It was no innocent kiss. My body still hums from it."

"What then did you do?"

"I told him to never kiss me again."

Bubbling laughter spilled from Noelle. "You did not?"

"I did." A moment of worry overcame her and her smile

faded. "Did I do the right thing? What if he takes my words to heart and never tries another kiss?"

"Nonsense," Noelle interjected. "You have just issued him a challenge that he, as a man, will not be able to ignore. He will be driven to kiss you again and again."

"Truly?" This was an intriguing turn.

"Yes, truly. As I explained before, men do love to chase women for sport. They are hunters. It's in their blood. If we make it too easy for them then they get bored and turn to more challenging prey."

Prey? "You make it sound calculating."

Noelle patted her arm. "Not in the least." She glanced over at Mister Blackwell. "I did not like Gavin when we first met. I wanted no part of him, but he was a bold man. He would not accept my indifference. Now we cannot be apart."

As if feeling their eyes on him, Mister Blackwell turned, and seeing their stares, he winked at Noelle. It was a simple gesture, yet enough to draw a smile from his wife.

Sarah let her gaze drift over the crush. Gabriel was taking a very long time to return to her.

Could he be angry still? She *had* rebuffed him. What if he went off in search of more amiable female company?

It took a minute to finally spot him near the dance floor. Her fear was confirmed. Clinging to his arm was a woman dressed in a scandalous ice-blue dress, cut obscenely low. She wore the mask of a cat covering the upper half of her face.

Gabriel bent to speak intimately to her and she laughed, leaning forward to give him what Sarah suspected was a fully unencumbered view of her large breasts.

Heat crept up the back of her neck.

"Rest easy, dearest," Noelle said, tightening her grip on Sarah's arm. "He knows you are watching. Ignore the display. If he is like the rest of the Harrington men, he will not find the brazen offering of her wares enticing when he has a wife who holds his interest."

While doing her best to follow her friend's advice, Sarah pretended disinterest. After a few minutes, Gabriel dislodged the tart from his arm, sending her into a pout. He glanced toward Sarah, and she quickly looked away before he could see her staring.

This business of enticing her husband was headache inducing. Why could he not adore her madly and end this game?

She hated that she was not naturally passion inspiring. That she was just ordinary. No expensive gown or fashionable coiffure would turn her from mouse to swan.

"Stop that at once, Sarah," Noelle snapped. "I can see your wavering confidence on your face. You are letting your insecurities take over your mind." She darted her eyes about. "Smile at the man in the gray coat."

"What?"

"Smile at him," Noelle commanded. "Now."

Sarah smiled at the stranger. He stopped abruptly and was almost hit from behind by a matronly woman in a pink gown. Within minutes, Sarah was squired out onto the dance floor, the stranger's compliments on her beauty filling her ears.

How he found her beautiful when she was masked was beyond comprehension. Still, it did lift her spirits to be considered so, even if it was nothing but empty charm.

With Noelle's encouragement, Sarah danced for the next hour with several partners. Occasionally, she noticed Gabriel watching her from his place near the wall, his eyes drifting over the heads of several changing companions as he seemed more interested in her than whatever conversation was going on around him. When she partnered with a young man so handsome that he made her eyes ache, Gabriel glowered. Yet he did not approach.

She managed to hide her satisfied smile. She stepped forward to her partner and was twirled about.

Gabriel had not danced. She was certain that it was not from lack of effort from the women of the company. Every woman, from young misses newly launched from the schoolroom, to women well past the blush of youth, paraded past him in a steady line of fluff and satin.

Not that he'd noticed.

Politely, he had rebuffed them all, appearing content to sip spirits and watch her.

She shivered under the intense heat in his eyes. She felt hunted, just as Noelle predicted.

And she was content to be the subject of his attention, though she tried not to find so much pleasure in such. Perhaps Noelle was right. She held his interest. For now.

The night grew late when Noelle was no longer able to hide her yawns behind her fan and Mister Blackwell pronounced it time to get his wife home to bed.

They left the ballroom to collect their wraps when Gabriel appeared. "I think I can manage to get my wife home safely, Blackwell," he said. Gavin nodded. Noelle and Sarah quickly exchanged kisses on both cheeks and said their good-byes.

"I will see you tomorrow," Noelle said.

Sarah nodded and they exchanged a pair of satisfied smiles. She whispered, "I still have much to learn."

Gabriel took her elbow and ushered her out into the night. He said nothing, leaving the sounds of chatter from the departing guests to fill the quiet between them. After she was settled into the Harrington coach, she leaned back against the squabs and shook out her skirt.

The weight of his gaze drew her eyes up to his. She could not read his mood from his expression.

"Did you enjoy your first ball, Wife?"

"I did," she said. "Very much."

He rested his chin on his bent hand and let his eyes drift over her. "You managed to snag several admirers."

Her brows went up. "Did I? I did not notice."

Teeth flashed in the dim light as they passed slowly down the street. "You not only noticed, my dear Sarah, but took pleasure in flaunting the attention."

"I think you misread my politeness for something more," she replied, lifting her chin. Inside she was pleased he'd noticed. "Though, I cannot speak for the men."

"They were besotted," Gabriel assured her. "I must take

comfort in knowing that you were in masque. Had your identity been discovered, the Harrington town house would be besieged by eager bucks on the morrow."

Heat crept into her cheeks. "You speak nonsense."

"Do I?"

"I am not the sort of woman with whom men become 'besotted,'" she said. "I believe men are easily taken by a new face; even one that is masked. Had they a chance to meet me in another setting, the outcome would have been different."

He watched her for a moment before speaking. "You see yourself as plain?"

She shook her head. "I am practical. I do not consider myself plain. I consider myself as average, not above other women. Were I not Albert's sister, and we had met at a society event, you would never have noticed me."

Chapter Ten

Gabriel wanted to argue her point but knew she was correct, and he felt like a cad for being so superficial. Had they been introduced at a ball or party, he would have politely spoken to her for a few minutes then excused himself and gone off to find a stunning beauty to spend the rest of the evening dancing attendance to.

"See, I am correct," she said, a touch of hurt filling her expression. She turned toward the window.

"You are not correct," he replied. A soft lock of hair brushed the curve of her jaw, hiding her expression. "Perhaps once, a pretty face was enough to hold my interest, but not anymore. Now I find myself entranced by a woman with both beauty *and* intelligence."

How odd then that as he sat in the coach, the lamplight illuminating her face in a silvery glow, he discovered there was nowhere else he wanted to be.

"Hmmm. Someday you will have to introduce me to this perfect creature."

The comment took him aback. Despite Noelle's best efforts to build her confidence, she was still unsure of herself.

From her elegant neck, to her full mouth, to her trim, yet enticing, figure, it was clear why men sought her out.

His wife underestimated her power over his sex. "True, you are not the kind of woman who'd bring men to their knees the moment you walked into the room, because you are shy and do not seek to draw attention to yourself. However, when you choose to bestow one of your smiles on a man, his attention is all yours."

And she *was* lovely. A fact largely unnoticed by him until this evening. She had filled out a bit, his wife, and her cheeks no longer held a deathly pallor.

It was easy to see why men were drawn to her. By the time they attended the Hollybrooks' ball, Sarah would be in the full blush of her youthful prettiness, making it harder for him to run off men like Lord Pembrook.

"How kind of you to say so, but I know my limitations."

He wanted to shake her. "I think you do not see yourself as others do." He stretched out a leg and placed an arm casually across the back of the seat. As he stared, he could see her struggle not to fidget. "I shall have your mirrors polished so that you may observe yourself clearly."

Her pretty mouth parted slightly and an impatient sigh escaped. "I see now why women have been casting themselves at your feet since you were a lad. You do have a full measure of charm."

The tart comment brought his grin. "I thought you were immune to me and my devastating handsomeness and appeal."

Sarah's body tensed. She was clearly not of a mind to accept his teasing banter; lingering effects of their earlier argument, most likely.

"It is impossible to see around your inflated sense of worth to determine if your face is indeed handsome, Mister Harrington."

His laughter filled the coach. "Who knew your tongue had such a painful bite, Wife."

Despite the dim light, he saw a flash of embarrassment in her eyes. His outspoken wife still had a measure of sweetness in her. He liked knowing that had not been "les-soned" out of her.

Even now, he felt her struggle not to look down at her toes. Her confidence had its limits. "I think you should let me kiss you again, dearest Sarah."

Her eyes widened. "You would not."

"You are my wife. It is my right."

Before she could summon up a scathing reply, he stood, pivoted, and dropped onto the seat beside her. He knew that they were seconds from arriving at the town house. If he was to torment her, it was now.

Emboldened by her scent and her full mouth, he realized rather quickly that she'd not fight him. Her hand gripped his waistcoat, and she gave no sign that she intended to scream for help or knock him off the seat.

He cupped her face, held her gaze, and breathed against her mouth, "Kiss me, Sarah."

Her lips quivered, her eyes darkened, and her lashes fluttered closed. He pressed forward, closer, until he could almost taste her mouth. He wanted to kiss her; yearned for it, eagerly.

How easy it would be to kiss her. But not yet.

Thankfully, the coach rolled to a stop. He fought the urge to smile when her eyes popped open and she appeared a bit rattled at the near-kiss. He drew back.

"Damn. We missed our opportunity."

The coachmen opened the door and Gabe alighted. He turned to help Sarah down and felt her hand quiver. The chit was not as off put by him as she wanted him to believe. And he wondered how long she'd lie in her bed tonight, thinking about the kiss that did not happen.

They went inside, removed their coat and cape, and he led her up the staircase. Her hand trembled throughout.

He knew it was wicked to tease her so. Yet, he could not resist. He wanted her to want him. Passionately.

The only way to accomplish this goal was to make her eager for his touch, his kisses. He could seduce her, yes. She might even enjoy his touch. But he wanted her to feel passion for him, and passion was the one lesson Noelle could not teach her. It was something she had to discover inside herself.

"There we are." He pulled her to a stop before her bedroom door and took her hand. He kissed her gloved knuckles and stared deeply into her violet eyes. "Until tomorrow, then."

Sarah watched him enter his room, which he did without once turning back to see her standing there, waiting for him to notice the hunger and longing she felt to her toes; the kind of emotion that both frightened and intrigued her.

Lud, she wanted his kiss.

When he'd touched her in the coach, she'd been unable to push him away, her bold husband. When he'd brushed against her body in the close confines, her hand had involuntarily gone up to touch his chest.

When he'd leaned in to kiss her, his lips so very close to hers, she'd ached in anticipation. If not for the untimely arrival at Harrington House, she would have melted against him and allowed him to have his way with her eager mouth.

Drat. She told him not to kiss her anymore. If only there was bite behind the sentiment. She was just as befuddled by his charms as any other woman. So much for leading him on a merry chase.

Slowly, she turned to open the door and slipped into her room. Leaning back on the panel, she looked at the ceiling, confused at the new emotions he'd invoked in her. These were yearnings she knew would only be satisfied by his touch and experience . . . but how? How could she explain the happenings inside her body, when she did not fully understand them herself?

All she knew was she wanted him to kiss her. That was easy enough to put words to. Why then did her breasts ache when he kissed her? Why did she feel tingles between her legs?

Pushing away from the door, she walked over to sit on the bed and wait for the maid to come to her.

How shocked would Gabriel be if she rapped on his door and begged him to kiss her the way Noelle had kissed her Mister Blackwell? Extremely shocked, if she were to guess.

Would he think her forward? Too forward?

With a groan, she dropped back on the bed. "What to do?"

Any decisions were set aside when the young lady's maid in training, Ivy, arrived, stifling a yawn behind clenched teeth. The girl worked with quiet efficiency to strip her to the skin and draw a soft cotton nightdress over her head. By the time her toilet was completed, all thoughts of kisses were pushed aside for the desire for sleep. She crawled into bed and buried her face in the pillow.

The next afternoon, Gabriel called Sarah into the parlor. When she arrived, a man of medium height, nearing fifty if he was a day, stood near the sideboard with Gabriel, watching the door for her arrival. The man wore a hooded expression.

Gabriel was clearly not happy. When he spotted her, he walked over and spoke to her in a low voice. "Why did you not tell me you'd gone to the *London Times* building and asked for papers pulled, during the time of your father's death?"

Her lips parted and no sound came out. Then she said quietly, "I did not think it a matter needing discussion. I can do as I wish, without your permission. I also visited Bow Street, if you must know."

"You did not think." He crossed his arms. "Apparently your visit brought you to the attention of the Bow Street Runners." He glanced over his shoulder. "Mister Brown, do come and meet my wife."

Bow Street Runners? Here? Sarah didn't have time to

process this tidbit when the man joined them. He was not entirely imposing, but carried himself with confidence.

"Mister Brown, this is Mrs. Harrington, the former Miss Sarah Palmer."

The man bowed. "A pleasure, Mrs. Harrington."

Sarah brushed aside any further pleasantries. "I cannot fathom why my visit to the *Times* or your offices would be of interest to the Runners. Surely my search for a few articles about my father's death is of no interest to anyone but me, and the Runner I spoke to discovered no helpful information to share."

Mister Brown seemed bemused by her abrupt tone. "Perhaps we should sit, Mrs. Harrington."

The Runner took a chair and Sarah the settee. She waited, her apprehension rising by the heartbeat. "I've done nothing wrong."

"This is about more than your search for answers in your father's death," Mister Brown said. "The mystery of his murder, and your curiosity, has kicked open a wasp nest."

"I do not understand." She frowned. "A wasp nest? I did nothing but ask to read a few articles. Please explain."

He nodded. "Two days ago, your cottage was partially destroyed by a fire. We suspect it was started by the same person who searched the building before setting the flame."

Sarah went cold, quickly changing from alarmed to confused. "Why would anyone do such a thing? The cottage contained no valuables."

Gabriel stepped forward, ignoring her question. "Why are the Runners involved in a cottage fire? Surely the vandalism, and Sarah's visit to the *Times*, is not enough to garner your attention?"

Mister Brown refused tea from a maid and Gabriel shooed her off. He looked from Gabriel to Sarah and back. "Might we speak privately, Mister Harrington?"

Gabriel shook his head. "Whatever news you have can be said in front of my wife. The cottage was her home and it's her interest in her father's death that led to your visit."

Grateful she'd not have to assert her right not to be excluded from the conversation, she waited for Mister Brown to continue. The man appeared somewhat hesitant to begin. Whatever his reason for coming, it was about more than the hunt for the vandal who damaged her cottage.

It took a moment before he nodded and spoke.

"We think that the fire has something to do with the death of Mrs. Harrington's father," he said bluntly. "That is why your interest in the articles drew our interest."

Sarah gasped. Gabriel walked to her and placed a hand on her shoulder. Her heart raced. "My father has been dead for more than ten years. This case was left to gather dust a long time ago."

After giving her shoulder a squeeze, Gabriel walked around the settee and took a seat beside her. She took comfort in his nearness.

Mister Brown continued, "What I am about to tell you must be kept secret." Sarah and Gabriel nodded and he rubbed his hand over his chin. "For almost twenty years, your father was a spy for the Crown. We've confirmed that his death was not the act of a footpad, as we were led to believe. He was targeted for something he was investigating."

"That cannot be." Sarah's mind went back to her memories of her kind and bookish father. "He worked as a secretary for Lord Hampton. He was not a spy."

"Indeed he was, I assure you." Mister Brown leaned forward. "He was one of our best. He had the ability to move within certain circles without drawing notice. I deeply regret his loss. He was a friend."

The weight of this news was almost more than Sarah could carry. She stood and walked to the fireplace. Everything she thought she knew about her father was taken from her. He lived a life of which she and Albert had no part.

How could he keep this secret? From her, yes, she was just a child then. But Albert? How much did he know?

"I thought his travels were part of his duties to Lord

Hampton," she said softly. "I cannot believe this is true. There must be a mistake."

Mister Brown joined her. "I know this is a shock, but I assure you that your father *was* the man you knew, with this one exception. His information saved many, many lives early in Napoleon's reign."

Sarah looked into his kind eyes. If nothing else was true, they shared a great loss in the murder. "You must tell me everything."

For the next hour, Mister Brown told her tales of her father's adventures, times they worked dangerous missions in faraway places together, and of a secret friendship built on a shared desire to help king and country.

"He once spent a week with the emperor's mistress, right beneath his haughty French nose."

Sarah shook her head. She remembered her father's handsome face. He would certainly attract women from all levels.

The tale was not so hard to believe. Yet, the picture did not entirely fit. "My bookish father dallied with Napoleon's consort?"

"He did." Brown chuckled. "Your father cuckolded the emperor."

Pride welled, not for the affair but for knowing her father was admired for his ability and heroism.

Brown continued, eyes filling with grief when he spoke of learning of the murder. "When I heard he'd been killed, I went to find you and your brother, hoping I could offer guidance, but someone had gotten to Albert first. Your brother had packed you up and vanished."

"I well remember that night," Sarah said. "Albert came into my room and took me from my bed. Our nanny sobbed as she packed my valise. We said a brief good-bye to Nanny, and Albert rode away with me into the night. I never saw her, or my home, again." She touched her brow and fought to keep her emotions controlled.

Mister Brown nodded. "I suspect that your brother became privy to enough information about your father's activities to realize the danger. He hid you to keep you safe."

"He left her destitute," Gabriel said, his voice tight. "I found her living in desperate conditions. I would not call that keeping her safe."

The Runner shook his head. "Your father had funds. I know that as your father's heir, Albert was able to get access to some of the funds. I was able to discover as much after you vanished, though I could not find you."

"There is an inheritance?" she asked.

"We believe so. Your father secreted away most of his assets. We know not where. Albert took what he could find in a few days and set up an account, through your aunt, for your upkeep. This much I was able to learn from your nanny, Mrs. Fielding, before she, too, vanished. I tried to trace you through the account, but Albert hid it well."

"Her pension," Sarah said. "I thought it was a settlement from her late husband." Albert *had* taken care of her in a fashion. "He did not know that her death would cut off the payments."

A headache pulsed behind her eyes. There was too much information to process. "How did you find me?"

"In addition to your visit to Bow Street, one of our contacts recognized you when you arrived at the *Times* building. Though he had not seen you in ten years, he was almost certain it was you. Mister Smart confirmed your identity. I took the information and traced you back to the cottage and the village. The parson informed me of the marriage. However, it was your eyes that convinced me. Your father shared your violet eyes."

Sarah smiled at this. She remembered Father's eyes. They were deep violet with little flecks of gold at the irises, nearly unnoticeable unless he was out in the sunshine. Hers were the same.

"How does this all link to the cottage?" Gabriel said, bringing the conversation back to the present.

The Runner expelled a breath. "We believe Henry had found information about a high-ranking traitor in our government. That is why he was killed. I also believe that when you asked Smart to dig up old articles about the case, our traitor realized that it was possible that you might be in possession of your father's papers. If I found you, others could, too."

She glanced to the window and smiled ruefully. Someone at the *Times* had alerted both the Runners and an arsonist to her whereabouts. "There are spies everywhere."

"Worse, my dear Sarah," Mister Brown said. "Your life may be in danger."

Chapter Eleven

Danger? A cool shiver spread across her skin. "Why would anyone want to harm me? I was a child when my father died and Albert went away. I knew nothing about any of this spying until you arrived today. I am not a threat to anyone."

Gabriel rubbed his eyes with his palms. "I believe that Albert's death, and your query, may pose a threat to the person behind your father's death." He walked to the sideboard and poured a brandy. "Albert and I traveled extensively, never staying long in one place. He'd given me enough information to know he was fearful of discovery. After he died, I no longer felt the need to keep his true identity secret."

"It is possible," Mister Brown said. "If whomever your father was investigating is as powerful as I suspect, they would have contacts in America. It would not be difficult to keep watch over the passenger lists of outgoing ships."

"For ten years?" Sarah said. "And that would mean they'd have to know you were traveling with my brother." She found this all too much to believe.

"Albert's first stop when he fled was New York," Mister

Brown said. "That was easy enough to discover, when I searched for you after you went missing. He vanished from there."

"We met in New York," Gabriel said. "I'd just arrived in America and he was passing through on his way to St Louis. We spent several days there, causing mischief and becoming friends before moving westward. If someone was looking for him, New York is the best place to catch a ship to anywhere. That is where a person would look first."

"This still does not explain how someone would connect you two," Sarah pressed.

"I may have raised a few toasts in Albert's honor," Gabe said. He looked sidelong at Sarah then admitted, "More than a few. I spent a week in New York, waiting for the ship to London; most of my time in taverns. I missed your brother. I lamented his passing to anyone who'd listen. I may have spoken to the wrong person while waiting for the ship."

Sarah frowned. "I cannot believe anyone would search for Albert for ten years."

"If your father's information is connected to someone powerful enough to kill for it, then ten years is not that long to wait." He sighed. "Or this may not have anything at all to do with Albert, or America, and everything to do with you. It is possible they learned of his death and the focus turned in your direction."

"All of this is neither here nor there now," Mister Brown broke in. "This mystery brewed for a decade. We will probably never have all the answers." He walked over to reclaim his hat, which he'd left on the table by the door. "I wanted to see that Sarah was well, express my condolences for your losses, and warn you to keep vigilant." He nodded to her. "As soon as I discover anything further, I will send word."

He left them.

Her strength fled her body. There was so much information to pick through. Add the news that she might be in danger and her emotions were raw.

"This puzzle is far-reaching." Gabriel tossed back his

brandy and poured another. "My promise to your brother may have led a killer to your cottage."

"None of this is your fault. My visit to the *Times* and Bow Street lit the fuse," Sarah said and met his eyes. There were so many troubling questions. "My father had many secrets."

"That he did," Gabriel said.

"How much had I really known my father, or brother? Both men had strived to keep me safe, yet in doing so had possibly put me in danger." Her world had upended in a matter of minutes. Every childhood memory became a question, a matter of what was truth and what was an illusion. "If only Albert had left a note, something to explain his absence. Maybe then I might be better prepared for this new twist in my life."

"I should have pressed him to divulge his secret," Gabriel said. "Despite his fears, never did I think this would come back to endanger you."

"How could you? I was the sister in braids you'd heard about in stories, and Albert's ramblings about danger could've been from the unreasonable fears of an overwrought mind. His father was dead and his sister a sea away, living under the shadow of secrets. I'm surprised he did not go mad."

"I never saw anything in Albert that led me to believe he was anything but level minded," Gabriel assured her. "He truly worried about you every day. He thought he was doing what was best."

"Then that leads me to wonder what Father was hiding and how much Albert knew? If my father was a spy, it's acceptable to think his killer was also a spy."

"From what Brown said, nothing has surfaced about the case since your father's death, or they would have caught the killer. One would think the matter was put to rest."

"The war is long over and Napoleon exiled," Sarah agreed. "Unless there is another reason the traitor wants to see this case buried."

Gabriel shrugged. "Although you have no information

about the killer's identity, he does not know that. His fears will make him dangerous."

Sarah worried her thumbnail between her teeth. She hoped Mister Brown's prediction was just speculation. She did not want to spend her days watching over her shoulder for a knife-wielding thug.

"We could look at this in another way," Gabriel said. "The cottage had a few items that might attract thieves were they desperate enough." At her skeptical stare, he held up a hand. "Or, there are people who just like to set fires. An abandoned cottage would be ideal in that regard. They'd search for valuables then set it ablaze to watch it burn."

She pondered his thoughts for a moment. "True. The fire could be the work of a miscreant bent on mischief." She wanted to think so. "We have not seen any indication that I am in danger, despite Mister Brown's warning."

"Then we shall keep vigilant and hope this matter comes to naught." He walked to her and drew her up from the settee. He placed a kiss atop her head. "Until then, I think I will do some investigating on my own. I, too, have friends in highly placed positions." He smiled. "Stay inside until I return."

Sarah watched him go, feeling a bit warm from his casual show of affection.

Her husband certainly knew how to make her knees knock.

Noelle arrived minutes later to find Sarah standing at the window, her mind filled with thoughts of her father and his secret life. Father had been a spy against France, and a hero. But to her, he was just the man who teased and taught and made her laugh. With Mister Brown's visit, he'd brought with him a renewed grief over the loss of the man she'd adored.

"There you are," Noelle said as she swept into the room, her arms weighted down with books. "I have brought books about furniture and house plans. When you and Gabe purchase a home of your own, you must know how to decorate it properly for entertaining. We Harringtons have a standard to set."

Sarah watched her in the reflection in the glass. She brushed a hand over her damp cheek and turned.

"Unless the house is fully furnished," Sarah said. "Then I will hope the previous mistress had acceptable decorating talent."

Noelle placed the books on the table and frowned as Sarah walked to her. "You've been crying."

"It is nothing," Sarah assured her. Her voice caught, ruining her attempt to keep her tone light. Noelle took her hand and drew her down onto the settee.

"Dearest, tell me what is the matter."

Tears began anew. Noelle handed her a handkerchief. Sarah sniffed and began, "I received some news about my father." She proceeded to share the information gleaned from Mister Brown, and against his wishes. She trusted Noelle with her secrets.

"What a puzzle."

"Gabriel also had his trunk stolen upon his departure from New York. The theft of the trunk and the cottage burning may be nothing more than unconnected incidences. Neither may be related to my father's work. Or they could be clues. We do not know."

Noelle screwed up her face. "Men do love their secrets and spy games." She watched the maid arrive with tea. Once the girl left, she sipped from her cup. "This is a muddle."

"That, my dear Noelle, is understating the situation." Sarah folded the handkerchief and tucked it into her bodice. "Gabriel has gone off to see what he can learn. Until then, I am to stay in the house, for my safety."

"Gabriel is protective. Harrington men are."

Sarah remembered Gabriel's tight face when Mister Brown was telling his story. Anger had flashed in those green eyes when the Runner spoke of danger.

"I cannot say I will not be pleased if he stays protectively close." As soon as the words were out, Sarah flicked

her gaze to Noelle and touched her fingertips to her mouth.
"I have looked for a way to get my husband's attention.
Now I have one. He will not let me come to harm."

Noelle nodded slowly, a dawning washing over her
face. "Lud, you are correct. And what is superior to a bit of
danger directed at his wife to get a Harrington man's blood
fired up? And when his blood is heated, he will seek out his
passionate wife."

Although still apprehensive at the thought of Gabriel
taking her to bed, Sarah knew Noelle had a point. "We
cannot be certain there is no threat until the Runners conclude their investigation." A shy smile crossed her face.
"Perhaps my husband and I should shackle ourselves
together lest I am snatched off the street."

"Perhaps we should forgo furniture in favor of teaching
you about perfumes and silk stockings and lacy corsets,"
Noelle said. "The correct placement of perfume can drive
a man mad."

The smile faded. Sarah's thoughts turned from spies to
her husband. "Sadly, I know nothing of what maddens a
man like Gabriel. He may prefer a drab cotton nightdress
to lacy corsets."

Noelle nodded and scrunched up her nose. "I have an
idea. It is terribly scandalous and you cannot tell anyone
about this." She stood and called for the maid. When the girl
appeared at the door, she asked for their bonnets and cloaks
and the footman to hail a hackney. She turned back to Sarah.
"Come, we cannot linger. The day is growing long. We need
to return before Gabriel realizes you are missing."

Sarah tried to question Noelle, but the woman stub-
bornly refused to answer her queries. They climbed into
the waiting hackney. Noelle gave him the address and they
were off.

"This is our secret," Noelle said, repeating her earlier
warning. "Not a whisper."

Dire warning aside, Sarah was intensely curious. She'd
only known Noelle for a few weeks and already would follow her anywhere, if just to see what sort of mischief her

friend could get them into. Never having had a close female friend, she was enjoying the experience immensely.

"I will not speak a word."

The ancient hackney rattled along for a bit while Sarah and Noelle speculated on whether they'd conclude their journey without the wheels falling off or the roof collapsing in on them. Finally the coach drew to a shuddering halt.

Sarah looked out the window and saw a three-story building, weighted with decorative trim. In the yard, a full dozen or so children played. The mass of tangled bodies screamed and dashed about after a hapless puppy.

"I cannot imagine why you have brought me here," she said. The pup managed to escape under a bush.

Noelle took her arm. "Not that house." She pointed out the window on her side. "That one."

The town house was not large or interesting. The façade was uninteresting, simple of design, as if all of the good trim had been used up on the house across the street.

"It is all clearer to me now," she muttered, unimpressed.

Sighing, Noelle let the driver assist her down and paid him after he assisted Sarah to the street. "Do I detect a touch of sarcasm, Cousin?"

Sarah shrugged. "I admit to a measure of disappointment. With your mysterious behavior and dire warning, I expected an adventure. Pirates. Smugglers." She squinted up at the house. "Not this."

A tsk-tsk followed. "You cannot always judge with your eyes only. I am about to give you an adventure the likes of which will keep you awake for many nights to come."

Within minutes of entering the house, Sarah was overtaken by the first of many blushes that she knew would continue for the rest of the visit when Noelle introduced her to Miss Sophie.

"Sophie runs the courtesan school."

Miss Sophie welcomed her, shot a questioning look at Noelle, and went off to the kitchen to order refreshments.

"A courtesan school?" Sarah whispered, her voice tinged

with mortification. "You have brought me to a school that teaches women how to be courtesans?"

Noelle took their bonnets and cloaks and hung them on hooks by the door. "Absolutely not." She led Sarah down the narrow hallway to a small parlor. "The courtesans come here to escape their profession and to learn how to be proper wives."

Relief filled Sarah's bones. "Thank goodness." She paused, and then said acerbically, "I'm comforted by this knowledge."

Noelle countered, "You must learn to be open to new adventures no matter the form in which they come. Sometimes it is best to close your eyes and leap into the abyss."

Sarah ignored the comment. "Why are we here, Noelle?"

"I thought you might want to ask questions of the women about what interests men. These young ladies know how to attract and keep men slavering at their heels. If anyone can give advice about men, it is a courtesan."

"Former courtesan," Sophie scolded. She'd returned bearing a tea tray and cakes. "We are no longer courtesans once we pass through these doors."

Sarah stared at Sophie. She was a courtesan, too? The woman did not look like what Sarah thought a courtesan would. She was positively proper in her brown dress and hair primly knotted at her nape.

Under her curious look, Sophie shrugged. "Except for Cook and Miss Eva, all the remaining women living here were once courtesans, or mistresses, if you prefer that term. We have six women currently taking lessons, though all but Mary are out shopping with Miss Eva. Mary has a sniffle."

As if hearing her name spoken, a small blond woman with a bright red nose, dressed in gray wool, stepped into the open doorway. A handkerchief was clutched in her fingertips.

"You called for me, Miss Sophie?"

Miss Sophie frowned. "Why are you not abed?"

"I am weary of staring at the ceiling," Mary said softly,

chastised. "I have been sequestered for a week. If I did not flee my room, I feared I would soon succumb to the desire to leap from my bedroom window headfirst onto the bush below."

"Oh dear. Miss Eva would be most displeased," Noelle said, her lips twitching. "She adores that bush."

Her jest deepened Miss Sophie's frown. The woman leveled a glare on Noelle and turned back to Mary. "You may join us for tea, then off to bed."

"Thank you, Miss Sophie." She scurried over and took a seat on the settee next to the older woman who poured fragrant tea for everyone.

After they settled down with their cups, Sophie turned back to Noelle. "We have not seen you in several weeks, Miss Noelle. I thought that perhaps you were ill." She glanced at Sarah. "Clearly you have returned with a purpose in mind. Perhaps you should explain what it is?"

Three pairs of eyes turned to Noelle. Somehow, Sarah was not surprised that Noelle knew the school well. Her friend was not above doing shocking things. Spending time in the company of former courtesans confirmed that belief.

Noelle fingered the lace on her sleeve and glanced sidelong at Sarah. Sarah braced herself for embarrassment.

"I have an, er, friend who is having difficulties in her marriage and requires some advice," Noelle began, and Sarah's face blazed. "You see, she is shy and does not know how to enchant her husband. He sees her as a duty, not as a lover."

Sarah was certain she was as red as a baboon's backside. And she'd seen enough paintings of the odd-looking primates to know the similarity.

"Do they sleep in the same bed?" Mary asked. She nibbled on a sugared oat cake.

"They do not."

With her free hand, Mary rubbed her nose with the handkerchief. "I suppose that is to be expected if she is noble. Is she noble?"

"Her husband is. She was not before they married, although

my friend is of a certain class above, not a washerwoman or maid. Her father was a secretary to a lord."

Sophie leaned forward. "Do they get on well enough otherwise?"

"They do," Noelle said. "There is some affection there. The union was made by her deceased brother and was not a love match. My friend would like it to be so."

Sarah stopped herself in mid-nod. She did not want the two former courtesans to suspect her in this tale. It was difficult enough to have her privacy spread out for all to examine.

"Hmmm. This may prove to be a challenge," Mary said and dabbed her watery eyes. "Men usually feel passion the instant they see a desirable face or figure. It is difficult to build on what is not immediately present."

"Then it's hopeless?" Sarah exclaimed. When she realized her outburst, she put her hands over her mouth.

This time three pairs of eyes were on her. Her throat closed up. In a moment, she would collapse dead on the floor from shame. "Oh dear," she whispered.

Mary smiled before turning back to Noelle. "It is not hopeless. A glimpse of an ankle, the curve of her neck, a hint of perfume will all do well to tweak his attention." She reached for a second cake. "If those choices prove unsuccessful, she can always bend over to pick up her stocking from the floor, wearing her lowest-cut corset, or wriggle her bottom while clad in nothing but a sheer chemise."

"Excellent points," Noelle agreed.

Sarah was just pleased to see the women had decided to ignore the obvious proof that she was the unhappy wife and continue on as if she'd not called out.

The idea of strangers knowing her troubles mortified her. Still, there were things Mary said that gave her hope. Perhaps this little adventure *was* the solution to her troubles.

The former courtesan spent the next fifteen minutes explaining other ways to entice men. "Men are a simple lot," Mary teased. "A low neckline and a pushed-up bosom can offer them hours of salacious entertainment."

The young woman had a point. Mary continued, "The wife could greet him abed in nothing but a smile and her husband would be happy indeed. But if she wants to drive him mad, she must subtly tempt him. Once he is hooked, he'll never understand why he ever saw her as a 'duty' to her brother."

Mary's words made sense. Whether Sarah could put her advice to application was the question. She was no seductress.

"Of course, there are things a woman can do in bed to leave a man panting," Mary added. Sarah's attention snapped back to the former courtesan. "Would you like for me to list them?"

"No!" Sophie and Noelle said in unison.

Mary giggled, sneezed, and giggled again. She looked at Sarah. "If you ever want my list, you will find me here for the next few weeks. I will be happy to teach you everything I know."

Despite Noelle's lesson, her eyes turned downward and she stared at the faded rug.

Noelle saved her. "I think it time for us to go. It is growing late." They all stood. Noelle took Sarah's hand, thanked Sophie and Mary, and led her from the room and out of the house. They stood on the stoop while the butler called for a carriage to be brought around.

"Did I not tell you this would be an adventure?" Noelle said as the waiting hackney driver climbed down.

Sarah's nose went up. "You are a horrible friend. I think I shall never speak to you again."

Laughter followed her pronouncement. The driver helped them into the carriage. "Posh. You might be off put now but in a week you will be thanking me after you try some of Mary's suggestions. You will soon have Gabe slavering at your heels."

Struggling to hold on to her annoyance, Sarah bit her lip at the image. "Gabriel is not the sort to slaver."

"Oh, he will slaver," Noelle said. She glanced at the driver and whispered to Sarah, "Try the 'bending over in a low-cut corset' trick. Once your bosom is displayed for his viewing, he will never again think of you as Albert's drab little sister."

Sarah returned to Harrington House, hugged Noelle farewell, and walked inside. "Mrs. Harrington, Lady Seymour would like to see you in the parlor."

"Thank you, Busby."

As she walked down the hallway, the sound of feminine laughter caught her attention. Her steps slowed and she stopped just outside the door, peeking around the jamb to see several ladies seated together on the pair of settees. Before she could flee, the countess glimpsed her there.

"Sarah, do join us." Sarah forced herself forward and inwardly groaned. Minutes ago she was partaking in a discussion about seduction with former courtesans. Now she was expected to share tea with women of the Ton and chat about the weather?

She bit back a wicked grin. What would they think if she skipped past the weather or the theater and instead brought up the topic of pushed-up bosoms and bare bottoms?

Chapter Twelve

Lady Seymour walked over to Sarah and took her hand. Sarah was introduced to Mrs. Hathaway and daughter Dora; Lady Stanwood and her daughter Alice; and Mrs. Dubury. Only Mrs. Dubury was rude enough to openly stare. The rest were unfailingly polite. Sarah sat next to Lady Seymour, hoping the countess's close proximity would limit the barbs cast in her direction.

"Sarah has become my closest companion," the countess said after a few minutes of casual chatter. "I have missed Brenna very much. Now I have two new daughters to fill my time. Simon and Gabriel made excellent matches."

"How did you meet your husband, Mrs. Harrington?" Mrs. Dubury asked with her hawkish eyes boring into Sarah. "It must have been very soon after his return."

"It was," Sarah responded kindly. "The day he stepped back onto English soil, he came to my cottage to inform me of my brother's death—a fact of which I was already aware—and we were both instantly smitten. It was as if my late brother had a hand in our match."

Miss Hathaway sighed. "How delightful." Her round face took on a wistful cast. "And he begged for your hand?"

Sarah nodded. "He did. We rushed off to the parson and wed." It was partially true. He did whisk her off on his horse. The smitten part was a lie. The truth was not to be shared outside of the family. She'd not be made fodder for gossip.

"Proper young women would wait for an appropriate period before accepting a proposal," Mrs. Dubury said.

The insult cut. Sarah felt Lady Seymour tense beside her. Before the countess could rise to her aid, Sarah swept up both young women into her gaze.

"Have you seen my husband?" She smiled benignly at the old crow. "If Gabriel Harrington dropped to one knee and asked you to marry him, would you hesitate?"

Miss Alice and Miss Dora vigorously shook their heads. "He is most handsome," Alice said.

Dora flushed. "I envy your good fortune."

The countess gave Sarah an approving nod. She'd defused Mrs. Dubury's sting without showing a bit of temper.

For the rest of the hour-long visit, the ladies talked of many things, while Mrs. Dubury stewed. At the end of the hour, the women took their leave, with Alice and Dora promising to call sometime soon.

Though Sarah did not expect the two to become close friends, they were pleasant young women and she welcomed both for tea and conversation.

When the door closed, Lady Seymour took her arm, as pleased as a cat with a mouse. "I admit I was worried about Mrs. Dubury when she arrived with Lady Stanwood. The old witch is known for ripping unsuspecting young ladies apart with her talons." She took a deep breath. "You took her down a peg without drawing blood. Well done."

That evening, the countess spoke of Sarah to Lord Seymour and Gabriel with pride in her voice. The two men laughed over Sarah's triumph.

Gabriel escorted her to her room after brandy, tea, and chess. "I wish I'd been there when you deflated that biddy,

Mrs. Dubury. I saw her last week in Hyde Park dressing down her maid. The poor young woman was in tears."

"She should be flogged for mistreating a servant," Sarah groused. Gabriel chuckled.

"Next time she visits I will get a whip and you can hold her down," he said. She laughed softly.

They stopped before her door. He took her hand. Sarah waited, her nerves taut, wondering if he'd attempt a kiss.

"You tiptoed through your first official introduction into society with grace and humor in the face of a formidable adversary." He leaned and brushed his lips on her cheek. "I am proud, Wife."

With a wink he walked back down the hallway and vanished down the staircase. Thankfully, he did not look back, for the smile on her face was anything but casual and the sigh a bit too filled with longing.

She sincerely needed to work on feigning indifference.

Despite Mister Brown's warning not to travel out alone, Sarah managed to slip away from Harrington House—claiming a headache—and retrieved the newspapers from Mister Smart. Although he did not appear to be a spy, she could not be certain he wasn't.

Paranoia had fully set in. After Mister Brown's visit and confirmation of someone at the newspaper gleaning information about her, she was convinced spies were everywhere in the *London Times*' office.

"I cannot allow you to take them out, but I do have a room where you can read them," he said and led her to the indicated space. The room was small with a table and two chairs. "I pulled papers from several weeks until the story was no longer mentioned. I hope you find what you need."

The stack was large and already sitting on the table. Her heart squeezed painfully. She was about to learn the details of her father's murder. She wasn't at all certain she was ready.

"Thank you," she said. "I do appreciate all you've done."

She smiled and he nodded. "When you've finished, leave the papers there and I'll return them."

After the door closed, she took a seat and reached for the first paper. Shockingly, the story of the murder was on the front page, in the lower left corner. She jerked her hand back.

An unidentified man had been found on the walk outside of a bookstore, in the early morning of October seventh, stabbed to death and robbed of his purse.

He was four streets over from their house, almost to safety, and his children.

A sob escaped her and the words blurred. She'd long ago come to terms with her father's death. To read about it as though it had just happened proved to be emotionally jarring. Tears flowed freely down her face and she sat for a few minutes crying quietly over the loss of the man she'd loved so deeply.

"Papa." She remembered his face, his laughter, the scent of tobacco on his coat. She remembered how he took them out of London and taught her and Albert how to ride and enjoy the beauty of the countryside. She cried for her brother and how she had no one left to share those wonderful memories.

All that was left of her childhood, her family, was locked forever in her mind.

When grief threatened to overwhelm her, footsteps in the hallway brought her upright. Now was not the time for grieving. She had to collect herself and find answers.

Swiping her handkerchief over her face, she took a deep breath and forced herself to focus.

She collected her valise and pulled out paper, a pen, and an inkwell. She reclaimed the paper and began to read. It took a day for Bow Street to confirm his identity after his servants reported him missing. Once the newspapers had his name and that of his employer, the frenzy to solve the crime began.

An hour and a half passed as she meticulously read each article several times and took notes. The clues to the crime were thin, though there was plenty of speculation. She was thankful that Father had enough status in his job as secretary to warrant a fair amount of interest in his death.

As expected, his spying was not mentioned.

When she finally finished, she arched her tired back and scanned her notes. Clues took only half a page. Still, she knew where he died and when, how, and a few other minor details.

Emotionally drained, yet invigorated to continue her quest, she knew she had to look at this case intellectually. With Gabriel's and Mister Brown's help, and that of the other Bow Street Runners, a new clue would eventually be unearthed to solve this case. She had faith. The killer had ten years of freedom. He would not get another ten if she had her way.

When she left the *Times* she went to Bow Street. Mister Brown was away for the afternoon, so she decided to return to Harrington House. She thought of asking the driver to take her past the spot where Father died but was not yet emotionally strong enough to do so. Instead, she leaned back against the squabs and let memories flood her mind.

Upon returning home, Sarah slipped unnoticed up the stairs and tucked her notes away. There was nothing she could do at the moment about the case. She might as well work on her marriage.

Unfortunately, there would be no bosom displayed most scandalously to entice her husband in the days before the Hollybrooks' ball. Gabriel was busy with his father and catching up on his life and responsibilities. Sarah was trapped in a whirl of lessons, lessons, and more lessons.

They saw each other over shared meals, though those were infrequent, too, and in the company of his parents. Sarah struggled with wanting to try her courtesan lessons to please her husband and was not entirely disappointed with the delay. She was an innocent still.

Was she ready for the intimacies of a true marriage?

"Let me look at you. Turn around," Lady Seymour ordered and Sarah spun for her inspection. "Perfect."

Sarah smiled into the mirror. "It is perfect, isn't it?"

The ball gown was lavender, cut low, and skimmed down her body to show a hint of the curves she'd gained since her marriage and forced dining. Though she would never be considered buxom, her breasts were nicely rounded out— from Noelle badgering her to eat—and her waist trim and hips slender but shapely. She no longer looked like a starved chicken.

"Gabe will be pleased," Lady Seymour said and walked off to finish her own toilet.

Taking one of Mary's suggestions, Sarah had earlier dotted some orchid perfume on her neck and décolletage before dressing. Also included were areas covered by her undergarments; places she was shamefully certain Gabriel would never sniff.

"You look beautiful, Mrs. Harrington," Flora said. She took one last opportunity to examine the gown for imperfections and settled a shawl over Sarah's shoulders. "There will be no one lovelier at the ball."

Flora helped her with her white satin gloves then left. Sarah turned once again back to the mirror.

She thought the maid's comment an exaggeration but was pleased anyway. She did look nice.

"I cannot believe this is my country mouse," Gabriel said from the doorway where he leaned on the doorframe. He was dressed in charcoal gray with a gray-and-white-striped waistcoat. As always, he looked magnificent.

Sarah turned slowly and met his smile. She swished her skirt back and forth. "Your mother and Noelle helped me choose the gown. I have never worn anything so pretty."

Gabriel pushed off and walked to her. "I wasn't admiring the gown, darling Sarah." He touched her face. "You've changed these last weeks, grown confident. I like this new Sarah. She meets my eyes when we speak."

His teasing widened her smile. "You were intimidating

when we first met. You frightened me. I thought you were half bear."

"I know. You wanted to stab me with a hatpin." Her jaw dropped. He chuckled. "Did you think I did not notice when you reached for your weapon? I lived for five years among men who would as easily shoot you as invite you to eat with them at their campfire." He replaced his proper English tone with an odd-sounding drawl and winked. "One small, skinny gal was nothing more than a buzzing gnat by comparison."

Her teeth clacked closed and she spun back to the mirror with a sniff. "Had I known what a bothersome sort you'd turn out to be, I may well have chosen to try the hatpin anyway and been done with you."

He leaned to put his face next to hers. "Then you would never have gotten the gift I have for you."

Her heart flipped. "You brought me a gift?"

"I did." He drew a box from behind his back and reached around to put it in her hands. "A few days ago I realized that I'd not bought you a wedding gift. I apologize for the delay and hope you'll forgive me when you see it."

Sarah slid the white ribbon off the box and opened the lid. Inside was a diamond necklace with tiny amethyst stones scattered among the white. It flashed in the lamplight like dozens of white and lavender stars. A pair of matching earbobs completed the set.

Her breath caught. "Oh, Gabriel. They're beautiful."

Taking the box from her hands, he removed the necklace. "Mother told me about the dress and I chose this to match." He lowered it around her throat and fumbled a bit with the clasp. Frowning, he grumbled, "They make clasps too small."

Sarah smiled as he finally finished the task. She drew her hand over the row of stones then added the earbobs to the picture. "I never dreamed of owning something as stunning as this. I will cherish them always."

Gabriel grinned and leaned to press a kiss on her shoulder. Sarah shivered. Her gloved hand moved involuntarily up along his neck, and he smiled against her skin, moving his lips to the spot where her shoulder and neck met.

"Did I ever tell you that I love orchids?" he whispered.

"You did not," she said, though not entirely certain. Was that breathless voice hers? He weaved a seductive spell around her with his warm mouth.

Encouraged, he ran his mouth up to her ear and nipped her lobe. She sighed. "They are my favorite flower."

Her lips parted. "Do tell."

A clearing throat at the door broke the moment. Gabriel groaned and lifted his head. Lady Seymour stood in the opening, clad in a gown of deep red, a hint of amusement in her eyes.

"I see that you approve of the necklace, Mrs. Harrington," Lady Seymour said. She took a step into the room. Sarah did a half twirl so the countess could better see the necklace and dress together.

"Very much so, Lady Seymour." She beamed.

Gabriel tucked her hand under his arm. When they passed his mother, the countess winked at Sarah and stepped in behind them. He escorted the women downstairs.

Lord Seymour waited in the entryway. He wore black, and when his wife joined him, they made a stunning pair.

The servants helped the women into their cloaks, as the evening had turned cool.

"Shall we?" Lord Seymour led them to the waiting coach.

Hollybrook Hall was festively lit as coaches lined the circular drive. The coachman pulled into the row that spilled into the street. They waited a full quarter hour until they arrived at the head of the line. The minutes waiting were filled with speculation of who might be attending while Sarah spent the time holding a hand over her quavering stomach.

Gabriel noticed her anxiety when the door opened and Lord and Lady Seymour alighted. He took her hand.

"Have courage, love," he said. "You have already attended your first ball."

"In masque," she said as he helped her down. "You know well how difficult it was for me to be brave when no one knew who I was. Out of disguise, I'm terrified. Perhaps I should have brought the mask."

"And cover your lovely face?" he said. "I think not."

Voices filled the hall when they stepped inside, which only served to raise Sarah's unease. There were people everywhere, slowly filing into the grand ballroom and bedecked in their expensive finery.

The country mouse returned with a vengeance.

They joined the receiving line. "I feel a headache coming on," she said. "We should return home."

Gabriel expelled a breath. "Nonsense." He met her eyes. "Are you my shy Sarah Palmer, or Mrs. Gabriel Harrington, a fierce warrior who stands up to all foes and ferocious dance masters alike?"

She shook her head when Mister Robicheau's pinched face flashed across her mind. "He is the devil."

"And you survived his lessons largely unscathed." He drew her gloved hand up and pressed his mouth to her knuckles. "If you endured the company of that feral French fox, you will easily survive the claws of judgmental society matrons."

"Hmmm." Truthfully, there was no way to flee without causing a scene. Gabriel had her hand in his firm grip, and Lord and Lady Seymour were already exchanging pleasantries with their host and hostess. They were next. So she forced a smile as Lord Seymour turned to introduce her and Gabriel to the couple.

"Of course, I do remember your Gabriel, though he was barely out of the schoolroom when he left," Lady Hollybrook said happily. Her plump cheeks flushed pink when Gabriel bowed over her hand. The middle-aged woman tittered girlishly. "He's grown so handsome, he has."

Sarah squelched a snicker. Women of all ages were not immune to Gabriel's charms. Lord and Lady Seymour wandered off to greet friends, leaving Sarah to navigate her entry into society on her own. Was she ready?

"What a delight to see you again, Lady Hollybrook, Lord Hollybrook." He released her and turned to Sarah. "This is my wife, Sarah, Mrs. Harrington."

Sarah bowed to her hosts.

The Lady took both of Sarah's hands while her tall and lanky husband looked on. Clearly His Lordship allowed his wife to speak for both of them. "Mrs. Harrington, I am delighted that you have chosen our little party to make your societal debut. Your husband's reappearance and your marriage have been all the gossips have spoken of since your arrival in town."

"I do hope the news has been favorable?" Sarah said with an exaggerated sober mien. "We'd hate to disappoint."

Lady Hollybrook clapped her hands and laughed. "Why, you are a delight, Mrs. Harrington. Of course, the information was speculation and servant gossip until now. I expect that by the end of the night, the old crows will have something truly scandalous to twitter about you tomorrow."

Sarah reclaimed Gabriel's arm. "Then let us be about setting tongues to wagging."

Gabe chuckled as Lady Hollybrook's laughter followed them off to the ballroom. "Well done, Wife. We have barely removed our coats and you have already made one successful conquest."

The hand on his arm gripped tightly and confirmed she was not as confident as her banter portrayed. In fact, he suspected that she was considering a bolt for the door.

"I thought I might faint. Thankfully, Lady Hollybrook is easily charmed, or my attempt to be witty may have fallen flat."

He looked down, his eyes enough above her to have a full view of the delightful swell of her breasts. His lower extremities took notice, too. If not for the crush eliminating any chance of privacy, he might have dragged her behind a screen and made free with his hands over, and inside, her bodice.

If the night went as he hoped, he might turn his comfortable marriage in an entirely different direction.

"The Lady will spend the rest of the evening championing you to anyone who will listen and boasting about what a coup it was for her to officially launch you into society."

"Noelle will be pleased if I become celebrated." Sarah wrinkled her nose. "She will consider that *her* coup."

Gabe led her in a turn around the room. Curious eyes followed them. He thought he recognized several faces, but years had faded some names in his mind. He needed to find his parents before he insulted someone with a wrong name or title.

"You do not want to be top-notch?" he teased, well knowing the answer was no.

She placed a hand on her stomach. "I want to get through the evening without casting up my accounts in our hostess's expensive Chinese vases."

Grimacing, he nodded. "You would not be incomparable but you would certainly be memorable. However, I think it would not be the kind of infamy for which you'd want to aspire."

Sarah's violet eyes softened. "Your family has been so kind to me. I'd rather not do anything to ruin their good name."

Gabe snorted. "You think a few minutes publicly bent over a vase would ruin the Harringtons' good name? We have an entire family history filled with blackguards and ne'er-do-wells who've done far worse. And if family tales hold true, we've even had a pirate or two. My dear, you must reach higher than a queasy stomach if you desire to be remembered as a scandalous Harrington."

A gloved hand went to her mouth to hide a smile. "I now understand where you inherited your roguish nature. It has been bred into you through many generations."

The light dancing in her eyes made him grin. His wife was becoming a delightful companion.

She leaned in. Her neckline gaped open just enough to draw his attention to her cleavage. "I suspect that no amount of scolding will keep our sons from following in your scandalous boot steps. I can only pray our daughters will have more sedate temperaments."

Sons? Daughters? The idea of having children with Sarah, or rather making children with her, left him eager to push forward with the courtship of his wife. By the time he bedded her he would have her full participation.

"There is only one way to make children," he said, after bending to her ear. "If you'd like I can call for the coach to take us home and we can start making our family tonight."

A flush started at her neckline and quickly spread up to her cheeks. Her left eye twitched, she stopped breathing, and her gaze dropped to the floor.

Disappointment welled. It was as he expected. Though she'd suffered his attentions on their wedding eve, and she flirted with him, shamelessly, his wife was still apprehensive of joining him in his bed. He had to be patient, even if it was growing more difficult every day.

He lifted her chin and held her gaze. "Shall we dance?"

Relief flooded her face. "I would love to dance."

Gabe led her onto the dance floor, and within minutes the tension left her body and she laughed lightly at her attempts not to tread upon his toes. After the cotillion ended, they found his parents and began the arduous process of meeting what he was sure was everyone in attendance at the ball.

Noelle and Mister Blackwell and Eva and the duke arrived shortly after, with a tale about a broken wheel causing their delay, and the party truly began in earnest.

Although Gabe enjoyed renewing old acquaintances and greeting friends and family, his eyes were on his wife. She was largely unpolished and entirely without guile; and she was utterly charming. Her occasional shyness was not a detriment in the least. Her honest nature drew people to her. By the time the first hour passed, he was certain that Noelle was right. Despite his wife's protests to the contrary, he realized she was, and always would be . . . incomparable.

Chapter Thirteen

❦

I cannot believe I danced the entire evening without damaging any feet," Sarah said, wriggling her tired toes inside her slippers. Her back ached and her face was tight from smiling. All in all, the night had been great fun.

The coach rambled back toward Harrington House amid quiet conversation and squelched yawns.

"You did well, my dear," Lady Seymour said. "I heard no complaints about your dancing prowess."

"Everyone, save Mrs. Spaulding and Mrs. Dubury, were so kind," Sarah said and glanced at Gabriel. "I understand from Noelle that Mrs. Spaulding desired a match between you and her daughter, Minerva, and kept the poor girl refusing other suitors these last five years while waiting for your return."

Gabriel frowned.

"Mrs. Spaulding is an overbearing witch who hoped to snag Gabriel for no other reason than our wealth," Lady Seymour groused. "When not plotting a wedding between her daughter and our son, she says horrible things about our family."

"She does know how to wield her saberlike tongue," Gabriel said, still frowning over Sarah's comment. "Never would I have considered taking Minerva as my wife. Her laugh is like a braying donkey, poor girl."

Lord Seymour placed his hand over his wife's. "When we first married, she called Lady Seymour a grasping milkmaid who had no business in society and should keep to chasing cows."

"Oh, how horrible," Sarah said, aghast. She glanced at Gabriel, who fought to keep from laughing.

It was Lord Seymour who chuckled first. The countess glared at her husband.

"Lady Seymour responded by agreeing that she knew all about cows. She then informed Mrs. Spaulding that her own sour disposition was the direct result of spending too much time in the field eating grass and not enough milking."

Sarah lost her composure. She, Gabriel, and His Lordship laughed wholeheartedly while Lady Seymour briskly fanned herself and fidgeted in the seat.

"It was not my proudest moment," she said as her lips twitched. "Truthfully, I truly think she hoped to marry her daughter into my family so she could torment me into an early grave, for likening her to a bovine."

The rest of the coach ride was filled with laughter and teasing Lady Seymour about her lack of control over her temper.

When they arrived and said their goodnights, Gabriel took Sarah's hand and led her up the stairs. Her feet silently begged for relief. The night had been long.

"Did you enjoy your first official ball?" he asked and rubbed the back of her hand with his thumb.

"Very much so." She enjoyed the feel of their fingers linked together. His hands were warm through her gloves. "I thank you for staying by my side all evening when I wasn't dancing. I think your presence kept the gossipy matrons from shredding me apart."

Gabriel drew her to a stop outside of her door. He turned her and took both her hands. "I had to stay close lest another

man spirit you away. There were several men who were
smitten. I'm quite certain Lancelot Cameron will be
perched on our doorstep tomorrow spouting poetry and
begging you to run off with him."

Sarah scanned his face and a shiver went through her.
He was so close and she ached to touch him. "You jest.
There were many beautiful women in attendance who had
men chasing them around the ballroom. I was just one in
the crowd."

He smiled in the dim light from a nearby sconce. "Then
perhaps it was only me who was smitten."

Realizing his intention, Sarah's lips parted as he slowly
lowered his face, her heart quickening. When his lips
brushed against hers, she leaned in. He released her hands
to span her waist and pull her against him.

Lifting his head, he smiled into her eyes and lowered
his mouth again. What had begun with a mere brush of his
warm lips deepened when he reclaimed her mouth for a second time. He tipped his head slightly and teased her with the
tip of his tongue. She eagerly opened up for him.

The effect of his invasion into her mouth was breathtaking. He pulled her to his chest, overwhelming her with his
embrace, this powerful male. She reached to put her arms
around his neck and melted against his hard body.

She kissed him back with the innocent enthusiasm of
her curiosity, learning from his lead. He groaned, taking
her closer until they were one. The kiss went on until footsteps were heard on the staircase.

Gabriel lifted his head and stared into her eyes. He
blinked to clear his mind.

"Good night, Sarah," he said and reluctantly released her.
With one last touch to the side of her face, he waited while
she entered her room and closed the door. She heard his
valet's voice through the closed panel.

With a soft smile, she leaned against the doorframe and
touched her mouth. In that moment, with that incredible
kiss, Sarah knew her life, and her marriage, had changed
forever.

* * *

Benning undressed him with quiet efficiency. Gabe's thoughts lingered on the image of Sarah's face when he'd broken the kiss. The sweet innocence of her expression and the softness of her eyes belied her passionate and heated response to the simple and incomplete seduction.

"Will there be anything else, sir?"

"No. Thank you, Benning."

When he was alone, Gabe stretched out on the bed, fighting everything within him not to walk across the hall and take his wife to bed. He'd just knocked down a large part of her protective wall. Soon enough, he would finish the job and she would be fully his.

He grinned. Gabe truly never expected such passion from his wife. After their dismal first attempted coupling, he'd thought the best he could expect in bed was perhaps some moderate affection. What happened in the hallway had been a surprise, probably for both of them. He'd certainly not seen a hint of her passionate nature until then, and he'd been taken aback by the moment.

The kiss at the masque had been more about power than passion. Tonight it was about seduction.

Sarah had more than enjoyed his kisses. He felt her desire through every part of her body. She'd discovered a side of herself she did not know or understand. He would teach her to command control of her desires and enjoy the fruits of her awakening.

Still, one question remained. How long would it take before she unleashed her newfound passion?

Morning came when Flora opened the drapes and offered her a cheerful greeting. "I thought to let you sleep but knew you'd want to join your husband for breakfast."

Sarah stretched from her fingertips to her toes. "I do." The desire for laziness fled. She wanted to see Gabriel's face.

Flora turned from the wardrobe with a pale green day dress in hand as Sarah scrambled from the bed, padded barefoot to the dressing table, and dropped onto the stool. She dabbed a bit of perfume behind her ears and between her breasts.

"We must hurry," she said. At the maid's curious look, she shrugged. "I am famished."

Dressing quickly, her toilet was completed before the clock hand made a quarter turn. Sarah lifted her hem and rushed from the room and down the staircase, only slowing as she arrived outside the breakfast room.

She took a few deep breaths for calm and walked in as if she had not hurried. Thankfully, Gabriel had not left for the day. He was reading the newspaper with Lord Seymour. She barely noticed the earl. Her husband appeared to have suffered the same sleepless night she had. He appeared a bit weary around his eyes.

Her gaze hungrily scanned his face.

"Good morning, Lord Seymour, Gabriel." She walked to the sideboard, casting a glance over her shoulder at her husband. He peered at her over the paper, his eyes crinkling at the corners. Her stomach fluttered.

"Good morning, Sarah," Lord Seymour replied. Sarah filled her plate and joined them. She looked across the table to the empty seat.

"Lady Seymour will not be joining us?"

"My wife threatened beheading for the first person who awakened her this morning. The maids, and I, were too afraid to tempt fate. We will leave her to her rest."

Taking a few minutes to eat, Sarah watched Gabriel read the paper, catching his occasional glance in her direction. She did not need to see his smile to know it was there when he looked at her. The crinkles gave him away.

"What are your plans for the day, Son?"

Gabriel put down the paper. "Sarah and I are going out. We have some business to attend to."

"We do?" She put down her fork. "Where are we going?"

"It is a surprise." He pushed aside the paper and finished his coffee. "As soon as you are ready, we will be off."

Sarah took a few last bites and washed them down with a generous swallow of tea. "I will get my boots."

Gabriel met her in the entryway a few minutes later and helped her into her pelisse. "Will you give me a hint of our destination?" she asked.

"I will not." He led her out and helped her into a waiting carriage. The day was cool but Sarah barely noticed. Her curiosity kept her mind occupied.

The ride took them to a quiet street some distance from the Harrington manor house, in a modest neighborhood on the edge of Mayfair. Gabriel pulled up in front of a three-story town house and set the brake. She scanned the brick façade with her gaze and felt a tug in the back of her mind.

"There is something familiar about this house." Her eyes narrowed. She looked up to the second floor and saw the pale pink of a faded curtain in the window. Her stomach lurched. "I was born here."

"You were." Gabriel climbed from the carriage and helped her down. "I did some investigation into your father's financial dealings and discovered that with Albert's passing, this town house now belongs to you."

Her eyes widened. "Truly?"

"Yes, truly." He took her hand. "I am certain the old place needs attention. The house has stood empty for ten years. However, with a thorough cleaning and airing out, it will soon be fit for habitation."

Gabriel pulled a key from his pocket and handed it to her. She happily opened the door and they went inside. She paused in the foyer as memories tugged. "Albert used to chase me up those stairs with a jar full of spiders, or a beetle, or whatever scary creature he could find in the garden."

"Albert enjoyed a good prank," Gabriel agreed. They crossed the foyer, kicking up dust as they went. "He once stole my horse and left me to walk five miles to town."

"He was horrible," Sarah said, smiling. "I miss him."

Grime covered everything, and the stale scent of neglect filled her senses. She wrinkled her nose. "It will take a full dozen maids a week to clean up the dust alone."

"They will arrive soon."

Sarah peered up. Gabriel shrugged. "The sooner the work gets started, the sooner you can decide what is to be done with this town house. It should not sit empty forever."

Frowning, Sarah said, "As my husband, this house is yours. I have no right to make decisions regarding its future."

He shook his head. "This house, your father's pension, and whatever accounts he left behind belong to you."

The kindness warmed her. She lifted to her toes and kissed him. "Thank you." With a happy sound, she hurried into the first room. Someone, likely the servants, had covered the furniture with sheets before they closed up the house. From there, she raced from room to room, floor to floor, drawing together snippets of happy memories as she went.

"I used to hide in there when I wanted to spy on Albert," she said, indicating a small closet across from his bedroom.

"This was my room," she said, pushing the door open to a pink and white bedroom that overlooked the street. "The bed is so tiny."

A hint of rising melancholia remained acceptably tamped down by her happiness until they walked into the master's bedroom. Then her exploration came to a halt and sadness forced its way forth. A painting of her parents hung over the large bed. "They looked very much in love. I wonder if it was painted soon after their wedding."

"They do look very young," Gabriel said.

Tears sprang into her eyes. "I used to scramble onto the bed with my father and stare up at this painting. I spent many hours asking him about my mother. She died giving birth to me."

Gabriel came up behind her and circled his arms around her waist. She leaned back into him. His spicy scent eased the smell of dust and decline.

"She was beautiful," he said.

"She was. Father used to say she was the most beautiful woman he'd ever seen. He knew the day he spotted her at a fair that he would marry her. Within six weeks they were wed and Albert came a year after."

They stood for a quiet moment. "You look much alike," he said. "She lives in you."

Sarah took a long look at her mother. They had the same hair, chin, and nose. This renewed the ache over never having known her. "I never noticed the resemblance. I do favor her. What other likenesses would we have discovered together about each other had she lived?"

"Probably many things. You were a little girl the last time you saw the painting, love," he reminded her. "I'm certain you've grown and changed a bit since then and the resemblance has sharpened with age."

Standing in her parents' former bedroom, staring at their painting, and seeing the affection between them—captured brilliantly by the artist—Sarah's spirits lifted. She wanted to be in this house. She wanted to make new memories under this roof.

"I think we should live here," she said. Without turning from the painting, she continued, "I want to live here. I want to have a family in this house."

There was a short pause while she waited for Gabriel's refusal. Instead, he said, "I think it's an excellent idea."

Her head snapped around. "Are you jesting?"

He shrugged. "Why would I jest? We cannot live with my parents forever. This house is large enough for the two dozen children we'll have. The address is in Mayfair, so we will be close to the rest of the Harringtons." He scanned the room. "Besides, this a very nice house. Once it's cleaned, you can decorate to your liking and it will be our home."

Sarah let out a whoop and launched herself at him. He caught her up in his arms. "Thank you! Thank you! I will feel close to my family here."

She kissed his cheek, his chin, his mouth. Gabriel deepened the kiss and Sarah eagerly kissed him back. The joy of the moment made her forget everything but him.

Shivers tingled through her body with his expert kissing and she moaned deep in her throat. Without dropping her or breaking the kiss, Gabriel spun around and lowered her onto the bed. Dust puffed up around them, but Sarah hardly noticed. His hand moved down her body, not quite salacious but not entirely innocent either. He skimmed her waist, the side of her breast, and upward to cup her face. It was voices from below that broke the moment.

When he lifted his head, Sarah released a small sound of disappointment. "The maids have arrived," he said.

"I despise maids."

He looked up. "Had it not been them, the painting would have eventually cooled my ardor. I cannot properly love my wife with her parents staring down at me."

Sarah followed the path of his eyes. It *was* as if they were being watched. She kissed the underside of his chin. "We shall move it to the drawing room first thing in the morning."

Sarah offered instructions for the maids while Gabriel wandered the house with a critical eye. There was more to his agreement to move into the town house than just the desire to make Sarah happy. He suspected that whatever her father had been hiding might be secreted within these walls. The disturbances in the dust confirmed his suspicions that he was not the only person to believe this.

Boot prints in the grime of several rooms were not his. He suspected that whoever had searched and burned the cottage had also come here. Since there was no sign of anything more than footprints wandering the rooms, they probably did not find what they sought. There was a good chance they'd be back. He wanted to be in residence when it happened. He'd do whatever it took to solve the death of Henry Palmer.

"What do you think of pink?" Sarah said. She looked up at the rows of books on the library shelves. "I was thinking we could decorate the entire house in pink."

He grimaced. "You may do what you wish, but I'll be staying with my parents. I cannot stomach pink."

She laughed and he realized she'd been teasing him. "Well, then. We shall make it comfortable for both of us. I will not be pleased with the speculation about why my husband refuses to live with me." She joined him by the desk. "If I have to give up pink, you will have to give up the notion of twenty-four children, unless you plan to take a second wife."

His brows went up. Fire flashed in her chest. "Do not consider it, Gabriel Harrington. I'll not share you with any woman." She crossed her arms and turned away.

"You are enough trouble without me adding a second wife to my life." He walked past her and swatted her backside.

"Oh!"

"Let us go." He grinned. "I have business with my father before lunch."

Sarah grumbled behind him and they left the house to the maids. As he helped her into the carriage, he took one last look up at the brick façade.

The question most foremost in his thoughts was not two dozen children or pink drapes; it was whether this town house hid a critical clue to the identity of a killer.

Chapter Fourteen

With her investigation stalled, Sarah sent around a note to Mister Brown asking him to visit at his convenience and hoping he'd have some news to share. Investigating a crime was more difficult than she'd imagined, and her growing frustration left her with headaches and restless sleep.

"Dearest, the investigation is ten years old without any new information," Noelle said. "You cannot expect to solve the matter in a few days."

"And why not?" Sarah shoved aside her notes and leaned her elbows on the desk. She rubbed her temples. "I thought that I might learn something the Runners missed. So far, there is nothing. What information Mister Brown provided has gotten me no further. The killer is a ghost."

"You should talk to Gabriel."

"I cannot," Sarah said. "He'll think I am putting myself in danger and forbid me to continue."

"Forbid? And that would stop you?"

Sarah leaned back in the chair. "Absolutely not. That is the issue. Gabriel and I are growing closer. I do not want to risk our newfound affection by fighting over my obsession."

"You deserve to have answers," Noelle said.

"And I will. The case continues whether I am directly involved or not. I will just keep my investigation quiet. For now."

As a day passed, and then two, without word from Mister Brown, Sarah—requiring a distraction from the case— fell into the task of readying the town house for the future residence of Mister and Mrs. Gabriel Harrington. She left early each morning, usually with Noelle in tow, and spent the day choosing fabrics and carpets and whatnot to turn the empty house into a home.

"I think it should go a bit to the left." She waited as a pair of footmen adjusted her parents' painting as instructed. The canvas slid across the space. "Not too much. Back the other way just a touch. Perfect."

Over the drawing room fireplace was the perfect spot for the painting. She smiled as the footmen marked the spot, lowered the item onto the mantel, and reached for a hammer and nail.

Noelle tilted her head. "I can understand how Gabriel would find them peering down at him while he's bedding their daughter . . . unsettling," she said softly.

Sarah sighed. "He still has not come to my bed," she whispered back. "I have not had time to make use of my lessons."

The banging of the hammer caused Noelle to scowl. She pulled Sarah across the room to a quieter corner. "If you do not do something to hook Gabe's interest soon, you'll become dried up like an old, dead rat."

"Thank you for that unfortunate image," Sarah scolded. "We have been busy. I have a house to ready and he is working with *your* husband on some new venture. By the time we get within a few feet of each other, we are both too weary to stand, much less attempt anything more vigorous."

"No man is *that* tired."

Her friend was right. It wasn't Gabriel with the hesitation.

It was she. Her concern came not from the actual bedding, but rather of finding out that she was indeed frigid and would never find lovemaking pleasurable. The thought of disappointing her husband made her stomach ache.

"I see something in your eyes, Sarah. Tell me."

Sarah hesitated. She waited until the footman finished banging and reached for the painting before confessing her true fear. "I worry that I will disappoint Gabriel. He is used to women of experience."

Noelle's expression softened. "You will be naked. Gabe will not be disappointed."

Warmth crept over Sarah's face. "What if I am frigid?"

"You are not frigid," Noelle said. "You enjoy his kisses? Did you not tell me your body hummed from his caresses?" Sarah nodded. "You should not see Gabe's experience with women as a detriment. He is exactly the sort of man who can teach you pleasure in lovemaking."

"I know you are correct." She placed her hands on her cheeks. "The first step is difficult to take when you are walking in the darkness."

Noelle touched her arm. "The fact that we are having this conversation at all, without you perishing from embarrassment, is a huge leap forward from the shy girl you were. If you give your husband even a modicum of encouragement, he will do the rest."

Noelle's advice rang in her ears later that evening when she excused herself after dinner and a game of chess with Gabriel and called for a bath. He always came to her room before retiring to say good night. If any time was perfect to present herself as open for his seduction, it was now.

Flora pinned up her hair and she stepped into the bath. The hot water soothed her frayed nerves. Well, as much as her nerves could be soothed when she thought of Gabriel naked.

"Would you like me to wash your back, miss?" Flora reached for the washing cloth.

"No, thank you, Flora. I believe I would like to be alone."

The maid nodded and left. Sarah lay back in the tub and closed her eyes. The scent of lavender whirled around her.

Gabriel. She smiled. While they'd played chess, he'd loosened his cravat and removed his coat, baring a small measure of his chest for her viewing. She'd thoroughly enjoyed watching him as he moved the pieces, hungry not to win but for his touches.

"Ah, what a muddle," she said softly to herself. "I want him. I don't want him. What to do?"

Her thoughts drifted to their kiss on her parents' bed, when his hand skimmed up the side of her body, to her breast, causing curious sensations inside her. Even now, she could feel an ache begin between her legs with the recollection.

Her body heated beneath the water and a realization came to her in that moment. Noelle was correct. If she longed for his hands on her and his kisses, she was not frigid.

With this new information, she wanted him to come to her. It was time to banish her fears and succumb to her curiosity.

Every part of her anticipated the night ahead. Gabriel was all a woman could desire. And he was hers. It was time to close her eyes and leap.

She quickly washed then leaned back again to wait for his arrival.

Nearly a half hour passed and she began to worry he wouldn't come. She almost abandoned the cooling tub when his knock finally sounded on her door.

Excitement danced in her stomach. "Enter."

Gabriel came in. As if anticipating her usual position on the stool at the dressing table, it took him a moment to find her as he scanned the room. His bland expression changed to interest when he saw her reclining in her bath.

"I did not expect to find you bathing, Wife."

His voice dipped low. She hid a satisfied smile. Naked

was the only requirement to entice her husband. How easy men were to entice when it came to such things!

"I spent a better part of the day chasing cobwebs and dust motes with the maids and thought a bath appropriate before bed." She shifted slightly until the curves of her breasts bobbed to the surface. "If this makes you uncomfortable, you may return later when I'm dressed."

His eye took on a wicked glint. "I am certainly *not* uncomfortable." He walked over and let his eyes drift over her. The soapy water hid just enough to leave most of her body to his imagination. "I could use a bath myself."

With a few jerks, he removed his cravat and tossed it aside. The cloth fluttered to the floor.

Panic lurched in her chest. "You wouldn't dare." Yes, he would. A lingering bit of alarm filled her. She fought past the feeling. This was what she wanted, was it not? She forced herself to remain calm.

The white shirt followed and joined the cravat on the floor. Sarah shoved her hands to her sides to keep them from shaking. His boots came off in an awkward dance-hop as he worked to remain upright during their removal.

When he was down to his trousers, he reached for the waistband and paused. "Ready?"

She bit her lower lip and nodded. Slowly, and with a grin on his handsome face, he slid the trousers down his legs and kicked them aside.

Sarah gasped, convinced she was about to die of embarrassment. There he was, naked and fully aroused as he stepped over the rim of the tub. She pulled her legs to her chest and slid as far back in the tub as manageable to avoid any contact with his large man part.

The space was entirely too small. "Perfect," he said. "I finally have you trapped where I want you." He reached for her feet and pulled her legs to his chest. The crisp hair tickled her toes. He then slid his own legs along the sides of her. She *was* trapped, fully and completely trapped!

"There is not enough room," she protested. Water spilled over the rim and onto the floor. "You must get out."

"The space fits us perfectly." He examined her feet. "Relax and enjoy the moment." He ran his fingers over her toes. "You have excellent toes."

Both exasperated and intrigued as well, she slumped back. "How can I relax when you have taken up most of the tub?"

Grinning, he leaned and nipped her left biggest toe. "Oh!" She tried to pull free. He held tight. "You are the devil." He sucked the same toe into his mouth. A tingle ran up her leg.

Her lips parted. He kneaded the foot, pressing his thumbs into the arch and moving up and down. She moaned and closed her eyes.

"Have you never had your feet rubbed?" he asked.

She shook her head. "Do not stop."

Gabriel chuckled. He gave her foot his complete attention until she nearly forgot that they were both naked in the bath. Then he moved to the other foot and worked that one over with his expert hands.

"Women would pay you to do this," she said, sighing. "You have a talent with feet."

"So I've been told. And with other things, too."

One eye popped open. "Such arrogance," she grumbled. She did not want to hear about his former lovers. She was too entranced with his attention.

"Alas, arrogance is the Harrington curse." He let go of the second foot and rubbed her ankles. Her eye closed again. "We Harrington men have always held a mysterious power over women. They cannot resist us."

Sarah shook her head on the rim. He *did* hold a power over her. But she'd die before admitting the truth. His confidence was already beyond measure. "I do not care if you are the most arrogant beast ever born. Just keep with what you are doing and I will forgive your lapse in humility."

The chuckle sounded again. "Yes, My Lady." He kneaded from her ankles to her calves to the backs of her knees. Sarah moaned, the feeling of intense sensuality washing through her bones, over her skin. He moved up to her thighs and she knew he could do anything to her now and she'd not fight him. Her body had melted in his hands.

"If you enjoy this, I have something more pleasurable to show you." He slid his fingertips between her legs. She tensed slightly but he gave her no time to give in to her fears. His thumb brushed the bud of her femininity and she gasped and nearly came out of the tub.

"Do not fight me," he said and began to move his thumb. Her legs dropped against the sides of the tub. He teased her while she moaned, reaching for an escape from the torment. Just when she thought she was on the edge of something wondrous, he pulled back, stood, and stepped out of the bath.

Before she could find the words to demand an explanation, he slid fully wet into his trousers and vanished out the bedroom door.

Sarah gaped. Stunned by the turn, she could find no reason for his departure. Had she done something wrong? She was certain she had not. The only idea that made sense was that he intended to torture her and leave her wanting. But why?

Outrage like she'd never felt before grew hot in her breast. She stood and reached for the towel. Drawing it around her body, she walked to the door, jerked it open, scanned the hallway, then stomped to his door and entered without the courtesy of knocking.

Gabriel stood near the bed, dripping wet, his sodden trousers opened at the waist. "How dare you leave me so callously when it was you who came into my bath?"

A wicked grin etched his mouth. "I knew the only way to assuage your virginal fears was for you to come to my bed. This had to be your choice." He walked over and jerked the towel off her body. "Let us finish what we started, shall we?"

He gently pushed her down on the mattress and spread her thighs. Sarah gasped again as he lowered his mouth to the still-lingering pulse between her legs. He lathed the bud until she could no longer breathe. The pleasure was intense. When she finally cried out and slumped back on the bed, she was spent.

"I did not know—" she said over her pounding heart. He gave her no time to collect her thoughts. He peeled off his trousers, covered her with his body, and kissed her soundly. After she relaxed again, he lifted his head. "This may hurt a bit."

"It cannot be helped," she replied. Knowing the first time had its challenges for a woman, she forced herself to calm. She did not want a retelling of their wedding night. She wanted Gabriel madly.

He nuzzled her neck, then without further preliminaries, he gently buried his erection inside her until she feared she'd break apart. Sarah tensed for only a second when he began to move with long, gentle strokes. A deep kiss helped to distract her from the discomfort. His sweet, comforting words, as he moved to nip her earlobe, further eased her tension.

He gave her no time to puzzle over her lost innocence or worry if she was a satisfactory wife. His rough hands caressed the most scandalous places on her body as his lips tormented her with his attention to her mouth until she was fully engaged in their lovemaking. Within minutes, her body happily accepted his seductive intrusion and she moaned deep in her throat.

"Damn, you drive me to madness, sweet." Gabriel leaned to nibble her breasts, teasing the nipples with his tongue and eliciting happy whimpers from her. He eased in and out, rubbing against the tender bud with a fingertip, until she was ready to peak again. When she cried out for a second time his thrusts became more fervent. Within moments he found his own release.

Sarah ran her hands down his back to the ridge of his buttocks. Whether he'd consider her too bold, she did not care. She'd wanted to touch him for weeks. Now she was in his bed and would not hold back.

He held himself up on his elbows so as not to crush her.

She kissed his throat. "I cannot believe the difference a passage of weeks makes," she said. "I thought you did not find me appealing."

Lifting his head, he met her eyes. "We were both unsure about the marriage. My hesitation had nothing to do with your appeal. I find you immensely desirable." He rolled over onto his back and pulled her close. "At first I thought of you as Albert's little sister and thought myself traitorous for wanting to bed you."

"You found me desirable?"

He snorted. "What an innocent you are. Did my kisses not show you my interest? I've been plotting your seduction for weeks. Tonight you gave me my opportunity."

No matter how much Noelle claimed she saw Gabriel's interest, Sarah refused to believe it was anything more than a man starved of feminine attention. Any woman would do. His comment proved her incorrect. He did not want just any woman. He wanted her.

"Why then did you wait?"

"Our wedding night was abysmal. You were not ready. I felt trapped. I thought our failed coupling was my punishment for pushing you into a marriage."

"I recall it was I pushing you." She swirled a curl on his chest with a fingertip. "I feared you. I thought you a savage. Tonight you proved me correct."

He kissed her. She smiled beneath his mouth.

"That night I did not know how to be a husband, how to properly seduce a virgin. Even now, I could use some lessons," he teased and pressed his mouth to her forehead. "Until you refused my rescue, I did not plan to be your husband."

It took a moment for the words to sink in. "What do you mean, 'I did not plan to be your husband?' We were betrothed."

Gabriel lay back and stared up at the ceiling. Sarah pushed onto her elbow and scanned his face. "Gabriel?"

He expelled a breath. "We were never betrothed. Albert only asked that I watch over you. When you refused my help, I took it upon myself to coerce the marriage. To do so was impulsive and deceitful. However, I was certain without the betrothal, you would refuse to come with me to London and I would fail Albert. Fail you. I thought I had no other choice."

Scrambling onto her knees, she pulled the sheet up to cover her nakedness. "You lied to me? You used my dead brother to force me to wed you?"

"Sarah—" He reached for her.

"Noooo." She scrambled off the bed. "Do not touch me." She tucked the sheet around her and struggled with the overwhelming sense of betrayal.

"Sarah, I'm sorry."

She met his eyes and felt the last hour of happiness rip out from under her. "You led me to believe our marriage was my brother's last wish. How could you?" She did not wait for his answer. With a sob caught in her throat, she whirled around and fled with her heart shattering.

Gabe winced at the sound of her door slam and the lock click into place behind her. He swore, rolled from the bed, and padded across to close his own door, lest a hapless maid stumble across him bare assed and half erect.

He wanted to go to Sarah and try to explain his reasons, try to make her understand the duty he felt to her brother, who was like a brother to him, to protect her even if he sacrificed his own freedom. He wanted to kiss away her anger and spend the rest of the night proving he was not the bastard she thought he was. He wanted to remove the hurt from her eyes.

Taking a step forward, he reached the door then stopped. His attempts to make things right would not be welcome. She was hurt and angry. No words would soothe her.

Damn! This was not the way he wanted the evening to end!

Worse, he'd betrayed his wife in the most callous of ways, by making her believe a lie, rather than offering her a choice; come with him to London and hand her over to his mother's care or marriage to him.

Why had he not given her that choice?

Gabe retrieved her discarded towel and wrapped the damp cloth around his waist. He went to the window and peered out, past his reflection to the garden and the street beyond. A misty rain fell, dampening the street, forming puddles that reflected the dim light of the streetlamps.

Guilt wedged into his twisting gut. He'd made a mess of nearly everything since he'd shown up on her doorstep. And when their marriage finally came together, he'd ruined their first loving moment with his badly timed confession.

Sarah hated him now and he hadn't a clue how to fix the damage.

Chapter Fifteen

W hy?" Sarah jerked on her nightdress and paced. She thought of the days since their marriage and the growing bond between them, forged by a brother who wanted the union between his closest friend and sister. Or so she'd been led to believe.

"A lie," she cried. "All lies."

Their match had not been made by Albert. He'd never asked Gabriel to marry her. Why, when drawing his last breaths, had he not asked the man he trusted most to accept the ultimate favor? Marriage to his sister.

"Doubtless, he'd seen something in Gabriel's character and warned him away from me. And tonight—" She could not finish the thought. She could still feel his mouth, his hands, smell his scent on her skin. She'd gone willingly into the bed of Albert's betrayer and shared the most intimate acts, all while living in a place of ignorance.

What a fool she'd been.

Sarah ripped off the nightdress, climbed into the cool water of the tub, and scrubbed Gabriel from her body.

* * *

That night, sleep gave her no relief. Sarah rose the next morning and splashed some tepid water over her face. She followed up with a bit of powder, hoping to hide the last vestiges of the devastating end to a most perfect evening.

Gabriel had betrayed both her and Albert. What sort of man would do such a thing? Had she been wrong about him from the first? Had she missed seeing darkness inside the true Gabriel, hidden behind his handsome face?

"Will you be going to the town house today, miss?" Flora held up a pair of serviceable stockings for her inspection.

"I will." Sarah took a seat at the dressing table. "I think the brown dress should serve. The new drapes arrive today. Dust will swirl when the old drapes come down."

She let her mind drift back to her traitorous husband while Flora readied her for the day.

Truthfully, Gabriel's betrayal had less to do with her than her brother. He'd had no loyalty to her, a stranger, when he'd come to her cottage. To know he could use a dead friend to get his way showed a flaw in his character.

How could she ever trust his word?

With her toilet complete, she joined the family for breakfast. "Good morning, Lord and Lady Seymour. Gabriel."

If he heard ice in her voice, he did not acknowledge the chill. She received a reserved good morning in return.

The countess looked through a stack of invitations. "You were quite a success at the ball, Sarah. Everyone wants you at their soirees."

"Hmmm." Sarah filled her plate and sat as far from Gabriel as possible without drawing the curiosity of his parents.

The food had to be forced down.

"What are your plans for the day?" Lady Seymour asked.

"We have new drapes arriving as well as fabric to replace

the worn covers on two of the settees. After today, only the floors will be left to polish, the windows washed, and the house will be ready to move into."

"Excellent. I cannot wait to visit your new home," Lady Seymour said. "Though I will miss your company, I understand the desire for a newly married couple to want their privacy."

Privacy with Gabriel was the last thing Sarah wanted. When Lady Seymour looked away, she took a bite of ham and cast a shaming glance at her husband. Unfortunately, he seemed lost in the newspaper and missed her glare.

Still, she could not change her mind about moving without rousing suspicion. "Of course you may come anytime," she said. "Gabriel and I look forward to having a home of our own."

Gabriel lowered the paper and was rewarded with a curt dismissal. She turned pointedly away.

If he hadn't felt the strength of her ire last evening, her actions showed she was not in a forgiving mood.

"All those rooms will not be empty long. Soon you'll fill them with my grandchildren," the countess continued, unaware of the storm brewing inside Sarah.

The hopefulness in her eyes made Sarah wince inwardly. She could not tolerate her husband. How could she bear his offspring?

"Kathleen," Lord Seymour interjected. "Leave the children alone. Let them settle in before you push that issue."

Lady Seymour shrugged. "Can I help that I want more grandchildren? I have one grandson who lives too far away to visit often, and Simon and Laura have not yet given us that happy news. Is it wrong to long to fill this house with grandchildren?"

Sarah put her hands in her lap and closed them into fists for patience. She wanted to tell the Lord and Lady that she had no intention of adding to the Harrington brood. Ever. She hated their son to the deepest part of her and would never again share his bed while there was still life in her body.

Instead, she forced a smile. "Children come on their own time. They will not be rushed."

The topic was allowed to fade as Lady Seymour questioned Sarah more about the town house. After the meal ended, Sarah called for a carriage and driver and fled. She did not want to risk a private encounter with Gabriel while her anger still sizzled through her, out of fear she might break something over his head.

The household bustled with activity an hour later when the new drapes arrived. As she'd expected, the old ones, having been neglected for ten years, were covered with dust. Sarah insisted on opening the windows, despite the inclement weather, to keep the servants and herself from falling into coughing fits.

"What shall we do with the old drapes?" the maid, Merrie, asked, her arms weighted with soiled fabric.

"When it stops raining, beat them out and donate them," Sarah said. "I am certain that a children's charity can put the fabric to good use."

Noelle and Laura arrived in short order. They stood with Sarah in the doorway of the parlor as the workers removed the faded flower coverings of the two settees and replaced them with fabric in a pretty blue-and-gold-striped pattern.

"I love the colors," Laura exclaimed. "They match perfectly with your new blue drapes."

Sarah agreed. The fabric was well chosen. "I wanted to decorate in a way that Gabriel would be comfortable with." She'd made the selection before their fight. She should have gone with a pink floral pattern on every available surface . . . and the walls as well, just to spite him.

At the moment, she did not care if he lived the rest of his days with his parents, or how many tongues wagged about their rift!

"I may just make over my parlor in these colors, too," Noelle jested. "We can have matching rooms."

A loud bang sounded from above. "Oh dear." The three women hurried from the room. When they arrived in the upstairs parlor, they discovered that part of the fireplace mantel had ripped away from the wall. Broken pieces of wood were scattered across the floor.

Two footmen and a maid stood nearby gaping at the wreckage. Sarah placed a hand to her chest. "What happened here?"

The maid wrung her hands. "I was polishing the mantel and it broke. It was an accident, Mrs. Harrington!"

One of the footmen picked up a piece of oak. "The wood is rotted." He pointed up to a stain on the ceiling. "I think rainwater leaked through the ceiling and down the wall." He broke off another chunk and brought it to Sarah. "The damage is long-standing. Years is my guess."

The piece all but crumbled in her hands. Sarah had not previously noticed the damage when inspecting the premises. The well-built structure had hidden its abuse.

"I see your point." The plaster ceiling was slightly bowed where he indicated. "It appears that we may need repairs to the fireplace, the ceiling, and the roof. We should see what the floor above looks like."

Sarah, Noelle, and Laura climbed the stairs to the fourth-floor attic and found similar damage to the ceiling there. The rain had leaked down two levels and seeped through the wood floor above the parlor. She pushed down on it with her foot. The floor moved.

"This floor will have to be pulled up and replaced." Sarah frowned. "The repairs will be costly."

"You should be pleased the damage was not worse," Laura said, trying to be helpful. "Ten years of neglect and a roof leak and damaged floor is the worst of it. Thankfully, the house is not overrun with rats."

Noelle shuddered. "Yes, rats would be worse."

Nodding in agreement, Sarah went off to speak with the men Gabriel hired to do repairs. Once the work order was completed, she returned to the ladies. Knowing everything was moving smoothly, Sarah allowed herself to be talked into a brief sojourn out for ices. When they arrived back at the house, Noelle and Laura left her to her work.

To her surprise, she found Gabriel alone in the library, his coat removed, moving books around and tapping the walls behind the shelves with his knuckles. She crossed her arms and watched him for a moment. Then she asked, "Are you checking for mice?"

He didn't bother to turn around. "I am searching a secret panel where your father may have hidden his private papers."

She stepped into the room. He had her interest. She walked over to him. Curiosity overcame the desire to snub him. "So you do believe there is something to Mister Brown's story?"

"Don't you?"

"Truthfully, I have not thought much about the reason for his murder, outside of wanting his killer caught," she admitted. "I assumed Mister Brown would come to us if he found further information. Since he hasn't, I concluded that there is nothing to worry myself over."

Gabriel slid a pair of books back into place. "I would not be so quick to dismiss his thoughts about your father's secrets. Someone was in the house before we took possession. I found boot prints in the grime."

Beneath her gown, her stomach tightened. "You think the trespasser might be the same person who burned the cottage?"

"I cannot say." He pulled a handful of books out and set them on a nearby table. "But someone was curious enough to break into the house and have a look around."

The tapping began again. A new thought came to mind. "Is this why you agreed to move in here? Not because you wanted to live here with me but because you wanted the freedom to freely search the house?"

Was his quick capitulation another manipulation? Was this all about solving the case and being a hero?

He glanced back at her. "Partially," he admitted. "I also think we need a home of our own."

"I am rethinking the move," she said, her voice tight. "Perhaps we should sell the house and stay with your parents."

A deep sigh followed. "Am I ever to be forgiven?"

"Do you deserve forgiveness?"

Gabriel put the books back and turned. "I admit to making a mistake in judgment. I thought marriage the best way to protect you. After you tried to run me off, I took a desperate path. I could not leave you there and risk your neck."

"And you lied to achieve your goal on the words of my dead brother." He had the good sense to grimace. "How am I to trust you will not lie to or betray me again?"

"I explained my reasons. I cannot do more to convince you to trust or forgive me." He straightened the books. "The fire proved that Albert had a reason to worry. Had I left you there, you may have perished. Certainly that is enough to earn some forgiveness."

The point was taken. Still. "At the time you pushed the marriage, any danger was speculative at best. That argument is only true when looking backward through the lens of recent events." She paused. "Can I trust when you say you are with friends and not seeking out other women? Can I trust when you say you are not gambling away your fortune when you go to a club, or that you are not participating in illegal activities . . . like smuggling? I truly do not know you at all."

"You are being unreasonable," he grumbled.

"Am I?" She crossed her arms again.

His body tensed. He reached up and swept out his arm, knocking an entire row of books to the floor. Sarah winced but held fast.

"Albert *was* my friend. I would have given my life for him." He spun and closed the distance between them. "Do you think I wanted to marry you? I did not. But I sacrificed my freedom to fulfill my promise to protect you. Had you not been so stubborn, willing to starve to death to keep your pride, I'd not have lied to you and pressed the matter." He took a deep breath. "I would marry you again if only out of loyalty to your brother."

Sacrificed his freedom? He'd only marry her again out of loyalty to her brother? Deep in her chest, her heart squeezed. She *was* a duty. His cold words confirmed her fear.

"I did not want to marry you either," she whispered. "Though, I would not marry you again given the choice." With that, she turned and walked stiffly from the room.

Once in the hallway, she stomped up the stairs and slammed the door to the master bedroom. Childish, she knew, but it felt good to hear the sound rattle through the house. Then, just as quickly, her eyes tipped up. Thankfully, there was no sign that the ceiling was about to fall on her head.

The damage seemed limited to the upstairs parlor.

She sat on the bed. "What a tangle my life has become."

Everything Gabriel said was true. Well, most anyway. She'd not have married him any other way. Her hurt came from his lack of feeling for her after weeks together. Any affection she'd thought she felt growing between them came from her hope for it to be so and not from any confirmation on his part.

"Last evening was no different to him than bedding any other woman." Sarah fell back on the bed and stared at the ceiling.

The sound of her footsteps pounded into his ears as she fled upstairs. He grimaced when the door slammed overhead. Her bitter and somewhat truthful accusations had finally caused him to lash out in frustration. It had pained him to see the hurt in her eyes. The lies he'd battered her with left bitterness on his tongue. Albert was no longer any part of the reason he wanted the marriage.

He would marry her for no more reason than affection for his shy mouse.

"Damn!" He raked his hands over his head. He turned and kicked the discarded books aside. Determined to find a secret panel, and wanting to take his frustration out in a productive way, he rapped his knuckles along the back of the shelves for the next hour until his hands ached.

No luck. He'd gone as far as he could reach. Tomorrow, he'd come back with a ladder.

In no particular order, he retrieved and shelved the books. Though his aching hands were some penance for hurting his wife, he still felt like a cad. It would take actions, not words, to prove he was worthy of her trust.

She'd had every right to berate him for his actions. He should have taken it stoically as a man would and then explained that given the chance, he'd choose her all over again.

Chapter Sixteen

Sarah slipped from the town house and took the carriage back to the Harringtons'. She was still angry and hurt over Gabriel's comment and unwilling to make polite conversation over dinner with him. She feigned a headache and closed herself in her room for the rest of the evening.

"I brought you a tray, Mrs. Harrington," Flora said. She laid it out on the table next to the bed.

"Thank you, Flora." Sarah didn't move from the bed after the maid left. The tray remained untouched.

She wasn't angry with him for marrying her out of duty, or knowing he hadn't wanted to marry her. She'd felt the same. What hurt was the implication that had he the chance to choose again, he'd change the outcome and not marry her at all.

After loving her so tenderly last evening, he still felt weighted down with the chains of their marriage?

Biting her lip, she vowed not to cry. She'd accept her fate, as it was, with stoicism.

As Lady Seymour and Noelle predicted, invitations had come in by the dozens since the night of the ball. Every morning, Sarah and the countess went through them all, choosing which to accept with careful consideration.

The idea of attending fetes left her cold. She'd be required to feign affection for Gabriel.

Now as Sarah stood and walked to the window, pondering the fight with Gabriel, she wondered how she would get through what remained of the Season on his arm.

Worse yet, how could she get through the next fifty years knowing Gabriel felt trapped?

The next morning dawned with no clear solutions. She had to make the best of her life, but how? Then she remembered one of her lessons. A Lady must keep her emotions in check when in public. If she wanted to rail at her husband or throw a book at his head, it must be done in private. Otherwise, she'd present the façade of calm.

Sarah hated calm. Book throwing sounded much more fun.

Noelle begged off the next few days, sending around a note that she and Mister Blackwell would be visiting Bath for a short holiday. Sarah and Gabriel, accompanied by his parents, attended a play and a soiree. The effort to come across as carefree left her head splitting.

After the countess sighed through breakfast one too many times over missing James, and the desire to see her grandson, Lord Seymour dropped his napkin on the table and ordered packing to commence immediately.

"It is better to go with her whims than to listen to her sigh over how James is growing up without the love of his grandmother," Lord Seymour teased. He was rewarded with a buss on his cheek. His happy wife hurried off to supervise packing. "We should not be gone for more than a few weeks. When we return, we want a full tour of your town house."

"Yes, My Lord." Sarah hated to see them go but understood their desire to see Lady Brenna and her son. Though Sarah had not yet met the family, she'd heard many, many stories about the smart and handsome little James.

The earl passed Gabriel at the door and told him of their plans. Gabriel nodded and entered the room. Sarah reached for the paper and pretended to read the headlines while her husband collected breakfast. He sat across from her.

"Anything interesting in the news today?" he asked. Sarah continued to read.

"The Duke of Boyton has bought a new coach and four," she said. "The horses are a matched set of grays. They are noted to be an excellent purchase and quite costly."

"Fascinating," Gabriel said. "Boyton does like to show off his wealth in flashy ways."

"Hmmm." Sarah perused the paper for a few minutes and ignored Gabriel. Most of the stories were about Parliament. She did not discover anything interesting there. No matter how hard she tried, she found politics tedious.

"Anything else of note?" Gabriel took a bite of eggs.

Sarah sighed. He was clearly determined to mend the rift. It was impossible to consider throwing something at him while he was so unfailingly polite. "There is a mention about one Lady Tewksbury who left her husband and ran off with his secretary. Rumors say the couple was last seen boarding a ship to America."

"Lord Tewksbury is a buffoon." He chuckled. "How long did he think his wife would accept him tupping his mistress under her roof without either killing him or finding her own lover? I am pleased to see the bastard get his comeuppance."

"His mistress lived with them?" Sarah asked, before remembering that she was speaking only to be polite and not for general conversation.

"He met the woman at a courtesan ball and secretly set her up as an upstairs maid. It took the shamed Lady Tewksbury about a month to hear rumors about the affair and realize she'd been duped. Over the last few months, she tried to get the woman ejected, but Tewksbury ignored her protests. Now he is without a wife, and the scandal should keep him from society functions for many months to come."

"Then I shall hope for a joyous life for the Lady and her lover, and pray her husband is miserable in his banishment."

Gabriel nodded. "He will not be missed. The man was not well liked. He's a pompous toad."

Sarah wondered how many Lady Tewksburys there were out there, forced to suffer the indignities of husbands who openly flaunted lovers without regard for their humiliated wives?

"Lest you get your mind fixed on how long it will take until I begin the hunt for a mistress, know that I am committed to you and this marriage." Gabriel leaned back in his chair. "I know you don't trust me now, but you will never have to suffer Lady Tewksbury's fate."

"Is that a promise?" she said bitterly.

His eyes narrowed. "I will choose to ignore your tone and instead urge you to ready yourself for a trip to the town house. I plan to search all day for your father's papers, and every day thereafter, until we find a resolution to the mystery of his death."

If she wasn't so put out by him at the moment, she'd be pleased with his determination to see her father's murder avenged. In this, they were of a like mind.

"I shall say farewell to your parents and meet you in the foyer in a half hour. I trust that will be sufficient?"

"I'll be waiting."

T he town house was largely quiet when they arrived but for the workers on the roof. After a week of long hours scrubbing and dusting, Sarah had given the maids and footmen a much earned day off. When Gabriel had hired them for cleanup the post was meant to be temporary. After spending several days in their company, Sarah had gone and hired them on permanently.

Today, she'd not planned to return to help Gabriel search the house, so there was no reason for the staff to be present.

It unsettled her to be alone with him.

"I covered these shelves here. If you'd like to search behind the lower three on those two walls we should be able to get this done by this afternoon." Gabriel set a ladder against the bookcase. "Check the books, too. He may have hidden clues inside the volumes."

"How clandestine." She flipped through a book on horticulture and found nothing but drawings of plants. "I still cannot grasp my father as a spy. He was so . . . ordinary."

"Ordinary makes the best spies."

Sarah pulled out an armful of books and flipped through them, then tapped the wall behind and found nothing. She had a feeling that this search would be less about finding secret panels and more about tedium.

She decided to give up her ban on conversation. If she had to spend the next several hours in silence, she'd go mad.

"Do you think my father ever met Napoleon? Or do you think he slipped in and out of the Palace of Versailles without ever passing the emperor in the hallway?"

"It is possible, if the mistress was secreted in the palace." He descended the ladder and slid it over. "Would he dare flaunt her under the nose of Marie Louise? Was your father gone long enough to have spent time at Versailles?"

"I'm not certain." She picked through her memory. "I do remember him being away two or three times for several weeks. I thought it was for his position as secretary. I missed him terribly when he was gone."

Her mind went back to the mistress. "I try to imagine this mysterious mistress. Did my father care for her? How many secrets may he have discovered in her bed?"

"It depends on how loose-tongued Napoleon was, and the same for the mistress. If she felt affection for your father during their brief affair, he may have learned many useful things."

"Enough information to have helped lead our army to victory?" She pondered the thought. "No, he was gone before then. Still, we will never know what he accomplished in those years before his death."

"Maybe the missing papers will hold some information," Gabriel said. He tapped the wall.

"True. I never suspected he was in danger."

Dark alleys, meetings with killers, political intrigue; it was impossible to fit her father into those settings.

"Spying was a noble thing."

Sarah hugged the book against her chest and watched him climb the ladder. "I know. However, the selfish part of me wishes he had been merely a secretary."

They spent the next few minutes searching.

"There are times when, if not for the painting, I have difficulty recalling Father's face. Ten years have passed since Father, Albert, and I were all together. Each day also further fades my brother's face from my memories. Thank goodness for the small painting of him at eighteen. I hate to think only a pair of paintings will refresh them all in my mind."

"At least you have the paintings."

She stared wistfully at her husband's back. The Harringtons were her family now. Gabriel was her family. Eventually, they'd make a truce and have children, as was expected of men of Gabriel's ilk. He might never love her, but he'd do his part to continue the Harrington name.

What a maudlin idea.

A moment of despondency swept through her. She slid the book back on the shelf and let her gaze drift around the room. This was one of several rooms she'd keep intact.

"I think we should not change anything in this room," she said. "I can picture my father here, slumped over his papers, a brandy always nearby."

"Do what you wish." Gabe paused from tapping. He pressed his fingertips against the panel. A small door swung open.

Sarah froze. He probed the space. "Damn. It is empty."

Her shoulders slumped. "How disappointing. However, if there is one hidden door, there may be others."

A movement at the window caught her eye. She was startled to see a strange face peering in, shadowed beneath a wide-brimmed hat. Just as quickly, the face vanished. "Gabriel, someone was at the window! He's fleeing!"

"Are you certain?" He quickly climbed off the ladder

and bounded after Sarah. She ran from the room, down the hallway and across the foyer.

"I am!" Sarah jerked open the front door. She made it down the steps and around the corner of the house in time to see a figure in black jump the hedge and race into the mews.

Gabriel's longer legs took him past her. He slowed slightly, enough to spot the retreating figure, and raced off in his wake. Sarah lifted her skirts and chased after the pair.

With the disadvantage of her gown hindering her progress, she had to limit her pursuit to the narrow alley and glimpses of the men running between the stables. She did her best to keep an eye on the stranger, a difficult task, as the window peeper possessed extreme speed and surprising agility.

"Over there!" she called out as the man disappeared between two stables. Gabriel headed in the direction she pointed.

Unfortunately, the peeper widened the gap between himself and Gabriel. He darted away, weaving in and out of the buildings and climbing over fences. Gabriel tried to keep up, but the wily man could not be caught. He soon vanished over a wall and was gone.

Sarah caught up to her husband at the end of the alley.

"Damn. He must have secreted a horse nearby," Gabriel said. He leaned to put his hands on his knees to catch his breath. She brushed a damp lock out of her eye.

"He is a ghost," she replied. "I have never seen anyone with such speed. The man is inhuman."

Gabriel tipped his head to peer up at her. "You are incorrect, love. The spy was female and definitely human."

Sarah gaped, incredulous. A woman? "This cannot be. He was dressed in breeches."

"I assure you that he was a she." He straightened. "Years carefully studying the female form have given me the expertise to tell the difference between the two."

He did have a point. Still, she found the idea of a female peeper befuddling. "I did not see his—her—face clearly in the window," she conceded. "But why would she want to sneak around my town house . . . unless she is the one whose boot prints you found in the dust?"

"That is entirely possible. The prints were not large." Gabriel led her back down the alley toward the town house. "Up until now, I thought the housebreaker just possessed small feet."

There were so many new things to consider. "This means it's possible that my father was investigating a female spy."

"Or a nest of spies," Gabriel said. They entered the back gate. "We will contact Mister Brown and give him this new clue. He might know of the woman in black."

Despite Gabriel's urgent note, Mister Brown did not respond to his plea for a meeting. Impatient, Gabriel traveled to the Runner's offices on Bow Street. He returned to find her pacing the library. "Mister Brown is out of the city. According to a man there, Brown will not return for several days."

"This is discouraging news," Sarah said. "We shall never find the killer with all these delays."

"Have heart, Sarah. Ten years have passed and the case has only recently drawn new attention, thanks to your interest," Gabriel said. "You must also resign yourself to the possibility of the murder never being solved. The killer may be dead."

This was the first time he'd put her own fears into words.

"I understand your point but cannot think negatively." She had to cling to hope. "I think I shall travel to where Father was found. I would like to see if the area holds any clues."

She walked from the parlor and retrieved her cloak. Gabriel followed. "I shall go with you. Two people are better than one for clue searching."

Any other time she might have welcomed his presence. However, she was not feeling up to spending another couple of hours with him, when her heart still stung. Still, his set face told her that arguing over the matter would not change his mind.

And he thought her stubborn. "If you insist."

"I do." He helped her into her cloak. "Besides, it will give me time to charm my way back into your good graces."

Her nose went up. "I would not expect such an outcome. You have done nothing since we met but lie to me." She left out the part about not wanting her as his wife. "You cannot expect a swift resolution to this matter. I may never forgive you."

Gabe wanted to argue that he'd only lied to her to save her from harm; however, it was a big lie and he thought it best to let her win this one. She'd only dig in her heels if he pressed the issue and tried to defend himself. When she had her hackles up, there was no soothing her with charm.

"Then perhaps we should focus on your father and leave our squabble for another time."

Sarah sighed. "I'll await the carriage."

They spoke very little on the short ride. Sarah sat stiffly on the seat and left him free to examine her profile. Her delicate cheekbones and thickly lashed violet eyes held him fascinated. Letting his mind drift to their lovemaking, he felt a stirring in his trousers.

Hell. His wife knew how to both exasperate . . . and fire him up. Even with annoyance still obvious on her face, he wanted her naked and moaning beneath him.

Just when he thought she was softening toward him today, her temper flared again and all politeness vanished.

Damn his bungled confession!

Truthfully, despite her anger, the admission had assuaged some guilt. Albert would never have given him his blessing to marry Sarah, but he would have admired Gabe for taking Sarah's verbal battering as his due and found some humor in his current suffering.

"We are almost there," he said through gritted teeth. "Turn to the left and follow, almost to the end of the street."

Sarah sat straighter on the seat. He knew she'd tried to be brave, but her quivering hands bespoke her anxiety.

The carriage turned and pulled to a stop before a tidy little bookstore on a tree-lined street. There was nothing evident to show a murder had taken place in this spot. It was all very ordinary.

"I thought I'd see something of note," Sarah said softly, echoing his thoughts. "A mark on the walk . . . something. There is no sign of the violence committed here. Not that I'd expect there would be." She expelled a breath. "Truthfully, I did not know what to expect."

Greenery spilled from window boxes, and a colorful sign over the door said, FARNESS AND SON'S BOOKS.

"I agree." He helped her from the carriage. "I cannot imagine your father meeting his end on this quiet street. Whitechapel or the wharf, perhaps, but not here."

Sarah stood on the walk, looking down at the stone beneath her feet, up at the store, scanning her eyes over everything in sight. She clasped her hands together and touched them to her chin. All was quiet for a few minutes.

"There is something about this place I cannot put to words," she said finally. "I feel an odd sense of peace here, almost as if my father is watching us."

"I believe he is," Gabriel said. He was rewarded with a small smile. "He loved you very much."

The smile slowly faded and her face turned pensive. "I miss him terribly."

"I know, sweet." A lively group of a dozen or so men and women appeared from around the corner. They chatted and laughed, their voices upraised. "We should go," Gabe said.

Sarah nodded and he helped her back into the carriage. The driver clucked his tongue and they were off.

"Do you think I am doing right by wanting to find his killer?" Sarah asked. "My father is at peace. Should that not be enough to satisfy me?"

"What do you think?" Gabriel faced her. "Will you be able to accept that the killer never meets justice?"

She stared off at the passing buildings. "I would not be pleased with that outcome. From the time I was around twelve years old, I wanted to come to London and solve the case. It was in your arrival at my door that I saw my chance."

The admittance raised his brows. "I thought my lie was the only reason for the marriage. You had another reason for your quick acceptance?"

Her jaw tightened. "Albert's wish was the most important reason. But as I considered the betrothal, I knew you were likely my only and last chance to get to London. I thought our marriage a worthy price for the chance to avenge my father."

The admission stunned him. "What a calculating woman you've proven to be. I've underestimated you time and again."

"Not calculating. Practical." She adjusted her hood against the wind. "As you said, I was starving and facing certain death. You offered me a chance to live a better life and to serve my father. What would you have done?"

"The same," he admitted. "Your fortitude is one of the reasons I admire you." Despite the hood, he saw her smile. The compliment was well timed and genuine. "There are many."

Slowly, he felt her relax beside him. It was a small but significant victory.

"Thank you for coming today," she said and glanced up at him. "Though I hate to admit this, I think my father would have liked you."

He chuckled at her sour expression. The admittance cost her much, his spirited wife. "A man without sense, your father."

Her mouth twitched. He placed his hand on the seat beside hers, their smallest gloved fingers touching, and she did not snatch her hand away. Another victory.

"None of us Palmers ever had any sense," she groused and accepted his touch.

Chapter Seventeen

I suspect the woman you speak of is a French spy called The Widow," Mister Brown said three days later when he arrived at Harrington House unannounced. With a grave expression, he continued, "She always dresses as a male, in black, and is shrouded in mystery. No one knows her true identity. However, it has been seven years since anyone has heard from her or seen signs of her work. Many Runners thought she was dead."

The description fit their peeper. This worried Sarah.

"If this is The Widow, then something has drawn her from hiding," she said. "Could it be Albert's death?"

"It's possible," Mister Brown said. "Your brother hid you well. When you arrived in London and started looking into your father's death, you not only drew our attention but hers. As long as Albert was out of England and you were not a threat, she was content. Your curiosity has piqued their interest."

"Who are they?" she asked. "We only saw her."

"The Widow would not work alone," Mister Brown

said. "Doubtless, someone is paying her to come out of hiding."

Sarah glanced at Gabriel and saw his concern as he met her eyes. "I assume from her title that The Widow is dangerous," he said. "How dangerous?"

Mister Brown went silent for a moment. "You would not want her as your enemy."

A burn flamed in Sarah's belly. "Excellent news, that," she said. Worry turned to fear. The spy's appearance outside the town house did not bode well for her. "I'm innocent of any wrongdoing and pose no threat to anyone. Yet, I may be in the path of a killer."

The Runner nodded. "I will give this new information to my colleagues. Hopefully, we can find and stop her."

Gabriel stepped forward. "Pardon me if I am not convinced that Bow Street will succeed in capturing The Widow. You've had ten years since Palmer's murder to flush out and arrest any French spies who remained after Napoleon's exile. And if this woman was a spy during the war, then she's had many years before and after the murder to hone her skills. She will not be caught easily."

"This is a complicated matter," Mister Brown said defensively. He puffed up his chest. He obviously didn't like his failings pointed out. "Palmer was a master spy and made many enemies. It's near to impossible to whittle the suspects to one."

"Then we shall continue our own investigation," Gabriel replied. "We have our entire town house to search. I plan to leave no hidden panels uncovered."

Sarah led the Runner out. Without speaking, they gathered his coat and her pelisse and drove to the town house. She went off to see if any work had begun inside; it had not, and she returned to find her husband back to the shelves. "Mister Brown is not pleased with you."

"Mister Brown needs to find The Widow and her nest. It is not my job to coddle him."

They were in agreement there. "It was easy to dismiss Mister Brown's warning of danger when there was nothing on which to base his conclusion. With her arrival here, she has confirmed his worries. I am in danger."

Gabriel did not immediately answer. "Not necessarily. As long as we do not have what they want, they will not harm you."

"They want access to this house," she said. "If they kill me, the house will be overrun with Runners tearing the house apart looking for evidence. Our spy will not want the Runners to find the papers before we do . . . or she does."

"That is why we need to keep searching."

"Do you truly think my father hid his important papers here, in this house?" She wrinkled her brow and looked up at the immense collection of books. The shelves went from floor to ceiling on three walls. "Wouldn't it have brought danger to our family?"

He rubbed his forehead with his hand. "I do not know what to think. But I do know that until your father's papers, journals, or whatever documents he used in his cases are found, you will not be free."

"What a muddle." She inhaled deeply and walked to the shelves. Thankfully there was only a small section left to search. They finished within an hour.

"Damn." Gabriel raked both hands over his head. "I was certain we'd find something here."

The disappointment was not only his. "I agree." She returned the last books to the shelves and straightened them to line up in a perfect row. "This was the obvious place to hide secrets."

Gabriel slumped into the desk chair. The desk had been emptied before they ever arrived on the first day. "Too obvious, perhaps? Still, we had to start somewhere." He tapped his fingertips on the desk and glanced around. "Where did you hide your mysteries, Palmer?"

Sarah walked around the room, tapping on the walls, unwilling to accept defeat. "We have many rooms left to search. Do not give up quite yet."

The next two days began and ended in much the same way. Rise, eat, travel to the town house, search the rooms, return home, eat, and sleep. Sarah and Gabriel developed a routine of sorts, pointedly ignoring the lingering tension between them. They were painfully polite, though Sarah found her dreams not at all in that vein.

There was nothing polite about dreams of his mouth on her breasts and his hand between her legs.

"Lud," she mumbled on the morning of the third day after another night of restless and heated sleep. "I wish he'd never taken me to bed."

"Mrs. Harrington?" Flora queried from the wardrobe.

"It's nothing, Flora." She rose and stretched her arms overhead. "I think I shall wear the gray today."

She ate alone and met Gabriel in the foyer for the trip to the town house. An hour later, the last of the rooms on the lower floor were thoroughly examined. Gabriel stood back and scanned the wood-paneled walls of the dining room.

"Hell. This is becoming a futile effort."

Sarah joined him. They stood side by side. "Many hours of work and no more hiding places are to be discovered in here. What a time waste."

"Not a waste, for we have cleared several rooms," Gabriel said. "If not for our spy confirming that your father possesses damning information, and the presence of The Widow, I'd think this matter nothing but the paranoia of one Mister Brown."

"What about the cottage fire?"

"It could be nothing more than vandals."

"Your missing trunk?"

"Thieves."

"You believe this?" she pressed.

He rubbed his neck. "At this point, I do not know what to believe. All I know is that we don't really know anything except at least one woman is curious enough to peep in our window. She could be nothing more than a common housebreaker."

"Without proof she is The Widow, you might be correct."

The maid arrived with tea and sandwiches. She laid the

tray out on the desk. If the servants thought their new employers' behavior was odd, they were well trained not to let it show on their faces. All were unfailingly efficient.

"Thank you, Franny." The maid left.

Sarah sat behind the desk and reached for a sandwich. "How long before rumors abound through the Ton about the mad Mister and Mrs. Harrington, the couple obsessed with moving their books around and banging on walls?"

Gabriel pulled a chair over and sat. "It depends entirely on the discretion of our servants." He took a bite of sandwich. "They have not been in our employ long enough to build loyalty. I'd say the whispers have already begun."

Her mouth quirked. He grinned. Her bones turned to mush.

Drat! She tried, and failed, to turn away. Instead, her eyes roamed over his face, his unruly hair, the way his muscles moved under his shirtsleeves. If only he were not so frustratingly attractive!

"By the time we finish all the rooms, the servants will petition to have us committed to Bedlam," she managed, just.

Green eyes lit with humor . . . and something a bit more scandalous. "As long as we can share a cell, I will accept my confinement with grace."

Warmth prickled through her as she stared at his mouth. He had an excellent mouth. "I despise you. I do not trust you."

"I know. Do you need trust to share a bed?"

"Hmmm." She reached for and sipped her tea. Every part of her wanted every part of him, naked. Could she accept the sensual parts of her marriage while still angry with him? Could she bed him while knowing their marriage was nothing more than a matter of convenience?

Marriages were built on much less. And she wanted him so desperately. Her sleepless nights demanded a resolution.

"The master bedroom is ready for occupancy," she said tartly and stood. Her body flushed with anticipation of a lusty romp. "I think I shall test the worthiness of the mattress."

Hurrying from the room, she heard the chair scrape behind her. She smiled as she went up the stairs. The sound of hurried boot steps pounded up behind her. Sarah laughed as she reached the top, lifted her hem, and raced for the bedroom door.

She managed to close a hand over the door handle when Gabriel caught her around the waist and swung her about. He slammed his mouth over hers in a delicious and heated kiss.

"Mmmm," Sarah moaned. He pushed her against the wall and then molded her body to his. Gabriel overwhelmed her and she was lost in his heat.

The door somehow opened behind her and she was spun around and nudged into the room. Gabriel kicked the door closed and rattled a lamp on a table nearby. He reached for her. Locked together, with his mouth eagerly mating with hers, they stumbled to the bed. The advancement halted when the backs of her legs hit the mattress.

Sarah tore at his cravat and shirt until his chest was bare. Her hands greedily explored the muscled expanse. He turned her around long enough to unfasten her gown then twirled her back to reclaim her mouth.

"I want you," she said beneath his lips.

"Then let us get you undressed. He removed her gown, her undergarments, everything down to her garters and stockings. Then he ran his gaze over the feminine items and grinned. "I think we shall keep those on."

Sarah laughed and he removed his boots and trousers. "How wicked you are, Mister Harrington."

His hands slid, open palmed, up her thighs. "Do not forget insane. With you, I would spend a lifetime in Bedlam."

Her laughter deepened as he nudged her back on the bed. Her body ached and her heart lightened with the knowledge that he cared for her enough to be committed to a place for the insane with her. Even in jest.

"I shall take that as a compliment, though I'd rather limit our romps to a comfortable bed."

". . . or the floor, the tub, under the bushes in the garden . . ." he quipped and leered. "Of course, there are always coaches."

"Scandalous, scandalous man."

Without pause, he joined her on the mattress and into her waiting arms. Sarah pushed him onto his back and rose over him. He groaned when she closed her hand around his erection and nipped his chest.

"You smell spicy," she said, trailing kisses down to his taut belly. She placed a kiss on the tip of his erection, then back to his stomach, still too shy to attempt anything more. The sounds Gabriel made during her exploration assured her he was fully engaged.

Fingers worked on the knot at the back of her head, and her hair tumbled about her in a mass of brown and light. "I once thought your hair uninteresting," he admitted. "I was mistaken."

She lifted her head and peered through the strands. "I once feared you," she replied. "I was right in that belief. You are a dangerous draw that I cannot resist."

Laughing, he pulled her up and kissed her. "You are a minx."

Sarah climbed atop him and straddled his thighs. His hardness brushed her core. She wriggled to find a better fit then rubbed against him. "You are an infuriating cad and I refuse to forgive you for lying to me. However, I feel that withholding my body from you will only cause me extreme physical discomfort, so I will allow you to take me whenever I see fit."

Two hands fondled her breasts. She sighed.

"Someday I will earn back your trust." He rolled her onto her back and settled between her legs. "Until then, I am your devoted slave."

In a swift motion, he pushed inside her. Sarah emitted a breathless sound. He slid in and out of her, slowly at first then faster as their passion grew. He kissed her, kissed her breasts, and made free with his hand until Sarah was ready for her release. As if sensing the moment, he reached between them and used his fingertips to push her over the edge, following quickly with a shudder as he spilled himself inside her.

"Lud I missed you, this," he groaned.

With a sigh, Sarah pulled him down and played with his damp hair, weaving her fingertips in the dark locks. "It is *I* who am your slave," she whispered, and he lifted his head. His expression was serious. "We are a pair, you and I."

He slid up to kiss her. "Despite my cutting words to the contrary, I have, and never will, regret marrying you, Mrs. Harrington. Never."

Tears sprung to her eyes. The tenderness in his voice rocked her emotions. She had no appropriate response, not when disappointment still simmered deep inside her. For now, all he'd get from her was her body. Nothing more.

Instead of speaking, she eased him off her and snuggled up to his side. His hand caressed her back.

For a time they dozed. When Sarah awoke, an idea had taken root in her mind. "Gabriel, wake up." One green eye opened. "I know how we can find the secret panel." She waited for him to rouse completely. "If anyone knows this house from cellar to attic, it's my nanny."

Both eyes opened. She had his full attention. "You have not seen her in ten years. She could be anywhere," he said, and added gently, "or deceased."

"No matter the outcome, we have to try and find her." She scrambled onto her knees and ignored the last comment. She refused to believe Nanny was dead. "If nothing more, I would like to see if she is well and happy. She raised me from birth and was like a mother to me."

Gabriel put a hand on her knee. "Then we shall scour all of London to find her if it pleases you."

With a happy cry, she pounced on him and kissed his chin. "Thank you. Thank you."

He cupped her bare bottom. "You are certainly effusive with your thank-yous, sweet."

"Only when deserved," she said and showed him her appreciation.

S arah, this is Mister Crawford, the investigator I hired to find your nanny," Gabriel said, a long and vexing four days later when Sarah was becoming convinced Nanny would never be found, and was likely deceased.

She looked up from placing new pillows on the settee to see Gabriel standing in the doorway with a man of middle years and graying hair.

"A pleasure to meet you, Mrs. Harrington," Mister Crawford said. He walked to her, limping slightly.

"Likewise," Sarah replied and took his hand. He was a pleasant-looking man with a charming smile. The confidence in his carriage renewed her optimism. "I hope you have found my nanny?"

"I have."

Hope lifted her heart, despite his tone giving no indication of whether the news was good or bad. Sarah indicated a chair and he sat. Gabriel joined her on the settee.

Mister Crawford spoke. "After several days of futile searching for a woman of a similar name, it was not difficult to find the correct Mrs. Fielding. She is living just outside the city with her widowed daughter and the daughter's eight children."

"Oh my." Sarah's brows went up. "Eight children?"

Crawford chuckled. "It is a harried household."

It wasn't impossible to imagine Nanny helping with her many grandchildren. She'd always been patient with Sarah and Albert. "I did not know she was a mother. I don't remember her being away, caring for her own family."

"Her daughter was already grown when you were a child. Mrs. Fielding took employment with your family after her much older husband died and left her with no support."

Nanny, married and widowed, with a daughter?

"This is another thing I didn't know about someone close to me," Sarah said tartly. "Was our tutor a highwayman?"

"You were a child," Gabriel interjected. "You weren't expected to be privy to the secrets of the adults. How would you know her history unless she spoke of it to you?"

"Hmmm." His insight did not make her any less put out.

Crawford cleared his throat, returning the attention back to him. He stood. "I must be off. I have another appointment." He pulled a square of paper from his pocket and handed it to Sarah. "Here is the address. Good luck, Mrs. Harrington."

"Thank you, Mister Crawford," she said. Gabriel stood and showed him out.

Raw excitement welled in her for the first time in many months . . . years, truly. She looked forward to seeing her beloved Nanny again. In her grief, she'd forgotten there *was* someone to share with her all those childhood memories. Nanny had been there through everything in her first nine years of life.

Gabriel returned and she clasped her hand around the paper. She was just a step below giddy. He stared at her face and shook his head.

"You want to leave now, I suspect?" At her eager nod, he said, "I shall get my coat."

Within a quarter hour, they were in the carriage and on their way out of London. Though the horse stepped lively, he was not quick enough for her. Anticipation would not keep her firmly planted on the seat.

"Do not fidget so or you'll fall from the carriage and be crushed by the wheels," Gabriel warned lightly.

"I cannot help my enthusiasm," she replied. "Will the horse go faster?"

Truthfully, Sarah did not have to wait long. The address was only a half hour outside of the city proper and down a narrow and pitted road. She screwed up her face when she saw the ramshackle condition of the house.

Gabriel turned the horse up the short drive.

"Are you certain this is the correct address?" she said.

"I'm afraid it is. Crawford spoke to her himself. There is no mistake."

Chickens roamed freely about the overgrown yard, and children's voices could be heard in the distance. The roof sagged in the middle and a thin dog lay on the stoop, rousting only to peek at them through narrowed lids. Clearly uninterested in what he saw, the mutt laid his head back on his paws.

"It appears Nanny and I both suffered a fall in circumstance when Father died." Her heart grew heavy.

"It is grim," Gabriel agreed. He drew to a stop and helped her alight. They scattered the chickens as they walked toward the door. Before they could conclude whether the lazy dog was a friendly sort, the door opened and a familiar face peered out.

Gladness filled Sarah to her bones. "Nanny!"

The old and weathered face went from wariness to happiness as the door flung wide and the elderly woman stepped onto the stoop. She shooed the dog out of her path.

"Sarah!" She wobbled down the steps, arms flung wide. "My baby, my precious baby, Sarah!"

Sarah ran to her and wrapped Nanny in her embrace. The familiar comfort of being held in her nanny's arms brought joy and chased away everything else. Tears ran down both their faces. "Nanny, I've missed you so."

They hugged for a long stretch, Nanny rocking her gently. "You have grown." She pulled back and cupped Sarah's chin. Her eyes scanned tear-stained cheeks. "And you're so beautiful."

Sarah smiled and brushed her tears away with her sleeve. "I cannot believe it's been ten years. You look as I remembered."

"Posh." Nanny linked an arm through Sarah's. "I am a very old woman now, with many wrinkles."

"I see no wrinkles," Sarah teased. They hugged again. The warmth of Nanny's hug, the familiar scent of cinnamon, from her love of baking, took Sarah back to her childhood. She never wanted those memories of that time of innocence to end.

A moment passed before she remembered Gabriel standing near the carriage. "I have someone I want you to meet."

She led Nanny to Gabriel. "Nanny, this is my husband, Gabriel Harrington. Gabriel, this is Mrs. Fielding, my nanny."

Gabriel smiled, took her hand, and bowed over it. "My wife has spoken fondly of you."

Nanny's eyes narrowed. "My Sarah has married a charmer." She took his measure. Gabriel stood quietly while she gave him a thorough perusal. After a minute she locked onto his eyes and warned, "You had better treat her well, Mister Harrington, or you will feel my wrath."

Chapter Eighteen

※※※

Gabe resisted the urge to smile. Though slightly stooped, and old enough to be his grandmother, Nanny would be a daunting foe even at her advanced age. She clearly loved Sarah.

Thankfully for him and his continued good health, he intended to make his wife happy.

"Yes, Mrs. Fielding."

The old woman nodded. "I shall take you at your word, sir. Now, come inside and I will make tea."

The inside of the house was clean and neat. The furniture was shopworn, and everything else looked as if it had seen centuries of ill use. But it was the sadness in Sarah's eyes, as she realized just how low in circumstance the woman who'd raised and loved her had fallen, that set his mind to work. He knew he had to correct this situation.

Immediately.

Nanny looked away from Sarah when they took their seats on the faded settee, her discomfort clear. "The landlord will not pay for repairs. He claims our rent is not substantial enough to cover more than to keep the roof from caving in. What redeems the property is that my daughter can walk the distance to the cemetery where her husband is buried."

"The man should be arrested and forced to serve a sentence of hard labor," Sarah said, her hands closing to fists. "To allow women and children to live this way is appalling."

Gabe's mind flashed to the condition of Sarah's cottage and how similar the circumstances of both women had become. When he returned home he'd see about purchasing the place and make arrangements for workers to tend to the house and grounds.

"I shall worry for his safety if your paths ever intersect. You were always my tiny warrior," Nanny said. "For now, tea."

While Nanny fixed a small repast, a woman arrived burdened with a group of young children, one in her arms, and several others on her heels. She was worn, her obviously once pretty features faded with age and her grim circumstance. She briefly greeted them and went on her way, the children staring in the doorway at Gabe and Sarah until their mother returned and shooed them off.

"My daughter lost her husband two years ago," Nanny said, passing the departing family as she returned to the parlor. "He left her very little money to care for herself and the children. Between us, we have just enough to pay for this house and little more."

Sarah sent a silent plea to Gabe, who nodded. She smiled.

"You have a lovely daughter and grandchildren," Gabe said and took a cake from the tray. The biscuit was simple but good.

"Thank you. I cherish them all."

Once the tea was poured and Nanny took her seat, she and Sarah spent the better part of two hours sharing how they spent their time apart and stories about the first nine years of Sarah's life. Gabe watched Sarah, more animated then he'd ever seen her, and laughed when Nanny told amusing anecdotes about his wife. The pair was truly as close as mother and daughter.

When the visit came to a close, the women hugged and Sarah promised to return often. "I shall come again and again until you've tired of tripping over me."

"Never, dearest," Nanny said. "This door will never be closed to you."

He watched them and finally remembered the original reason for the visit. He interrupted their farewell. "Before we go, I have a question to ask. There is renewed interest in solving Henry Palmer's murder. We were wondering if you know where he kept his important papers."

"Yes, it is very critical that we find them," Sarah said. "They may include clues of his last days."

The woman frowned. "Will it help catch his killer?"

"We aren't sure," Gabe admitted. "But we think we might find information to lead us in that direction."

Nanny clasped her hands in front of her mouth and stood quietly in thought. "Henry had many secrets." She met Sarah's eyes. "There are things about your father of which you are not aware."

Sarah nodded. "We know he spied for the Crown."

The older woman's eyes widened, then she nodded. "Then you are privy to everything I know. He only confided in me once when you were very young, because he knew I would protect you should something happen to him. Instead it was Albert who took that role after his death. Your brother knew that if I remained with you, your chance of discovery was higher than if we lived apart. Our connection was no secret." She cupped Sarah's chin. "It broke my heart to lose you."

"Mine, too," Sarah said softly.

Gabe's hope rose. "Then you know where he hid his papers?"

After a moment, Nanny shook her head. "I cannot say. He never divulged information about his work. I thought he kept his files in his desk. If they are not there, then I can give no answers. I'm sorry."

Disappointed, Gabe took her hand. "Don't fret. The chance was small that he'd confide all his secrets. We will find another way to get what we need."

Sarah kissed Nanny on the cheek. "I will see you soon."

The ride back to London was reflective as Gabe made a list in his head of what he needed to assist Nanny. Although she did not complain about her plight, he could not leave the woman, who loved and raised Sarah, to such a dismal existence. Hell, *no* woman deserved that fate.

"We have to help them," Sarah said finally.

"We will, love. We will."

Sarah laid a hand on his leg. "You are a good man."

He snorted. "Please do not tell anyone. I much prefer cad, bounder, and ne'er-do-well."

When she looked up at him, her eyes were soft. "It matters not what all of London thinks, as long as I know the truth."

Gabe could almost see a fissure in her protective wall. It was another step to earning back her trust. She'd given him her body. He selfishly wanted her heart, too.

It took a day to discover who owned Mrs. Fielding's house—a weasel of a fellow named Beasley—and offer him more than the value of the property. With a scribbled signature on vellum, Gabe became the new owner of twenty acres of swale and a house needing expensive repairs.

But it was the joy in Sarah when he handed her the deed that made everything worth the bad investment.

"What is this?" she'd said, looking over the contract. It was weighted with wordy gibberish, making sense only to the barrister who wrote it out.

"You now own the property Nanny and her family live on. Workers have been dispatched to begin repairs, and servants and food have been sent out. Make a list of anything else you think she'll need and I'll see that it's made available to her."

Her eyes went wide, and a squeal—the volume of which he'd never previously believed could exist in such a small woman—broke from his wife. She jumped into his arms and hugged his neck in a strangle-inducing grip. Then she led him to the bed and did all sorts of things that made him the happiest of men.

That small patch of swamp and rot was the best investment he'd ever made.

I was thinking sometime next week I would like to visit Nanny and see how the repairs are coming." Sarah walked into the library and over to the desk where he was working. Since the day they'd made love upstairs, they hadn't spent another night at the Harrington town house. They'd packed up their personal belongings, and Flora and Benning, and moved in. The rest of their possessions had followed over the next few days.

Gabriel hired a butler named Harris, and Sarah settled into her role as mistress of the house.

"I think that is an excellent idea." He scanned the investment sheet from Gavin Blackwell. He'd sunk a large chunk of coin into Blackwell's shipyard, and thus far, all was well. Blackwell could turn a rock into gold. "I shall go with you. With The Widow loose, we cannot have you wandering about alone."

"I can take care of myself," she protested.

"Give me this, love." He flipped a page aside. "We Harrington men come from a long line of knights and highwaymen. I am just arrogant enough to believe you need my sword and shield to protect you. My manliness requires your agreement."

She leaned a hip on the desk and kissed his temple. "Then I shall pick a day to visit. You can bring your sword to bed, later, if you'd like."

"I will put it on my calendar," he replied, distracted. "Or once I hire a secretary, he can update my calendar." It took a blink for her words to cut past the columns of investment figures in his mind. He sent her a sidelong look. "My sword?"

"Sword? Staff? Manroot? Whichever you prefer."

He grinned. "What a temptress you've become, Wife." He leaned to kiss her. "This pleases me."

"I do enjoy pleasing you," she said.

"Later," he promised and turned back to business.

Sarah got up and began pacing in front of the desk. "I wonder what Nanny thought when the workers descended upon the house. I hope they did not frighten the children."

"You will have to ask her, next week." More pacing.

"I think I will have new drapes made in Nanny's favorite colors. What do you think? I think new drapes are an excellent start. Don't you?"

"Anything you wish, love. It is your house."

The pacing continued. "And she needs a new rug in the parlor; something that can withstand little feet."

He finally lifted his head, giving her his full attention. "This endless pacing cannot all be over concern for your nanny. Is there something else you need, love?"

Sarah sighed deeply. "I'm bored."

This explained her restlessness of late. "Can you go shopping with Noelle?"

"She has not felt well since returning from Bath."

"What about Laura?"

"She had an appointment today." She ran her hand over the edge of the desk. "And lest you ask, I did check the parlor and pantry for hidden doors."

"There has to be something for you to do," he pressed. "Perhaps you can help at a charity for orphans or attend a meeting of the Ladies of Something or Other? I know you've been invited to many functions. I've seen the mail."

"We do have a ball and a musicale to attend this week," she said and cast a glance askance at him. "There is one place where I think I can be of assistance. It's a charity that helps women who are . . . mistreated. Noelle said the Duchess Eva is a proprietress of the school."

"Are you speaking of the courtesan school?" Sarah visibly tensed. He hid a smile. The minx actually believed he was unaware she'd been taking tea with former courtesans. "Did you think I did not know about the trip you took there with Noelle?"

She frowned. "Do you spy on me?"

"My mother told me, with a bit of torture on the rack in the attic. She did not want to break your confidence. However, the courtesan school is not well hidden in our family. I would have discovered its existence eventually."

"And I suppose you forbid me to go again?"

He stood and leaned over the desk, placing his hands flat on the surface. "Indeed I do not. If it will keep you busy and away from this desk, so that I can make certain my investments will not fail and leave us destitute, I will gladly call a footman to find a hackney to take you." Her face brightened. "Now give me a kiss and be off. I've work to do."

As requested, Sarah kissed him, swirling him into her web of orchid perfume. "I shall be home before dinner."

For a moment he thought of taking her on the desk, but he *did* have to make certain they could pay for decorating two houses, her gowns, and future children. Plus, his family had recently grown by ten with the addition of Nanny and her family. The investments with Blackwell were part of that. He had to focus on financial matters and not on his seductive wife. So he watched her swaying backside as she left him and returned to his chair.

Damn, if moving out from under his father's long shadow, and taking a wife, hadn't given him new challenges and responsibilities.

He desperately needed a secretary, if for nothing more than giving him the freedom to seduce his wife whenever and wherever the mood arose.

Thus, he left her to go off to assist former courtesans, and he, regretfully, turned his attention back to the paper stack.

* * *

I did not think you'd return, Mrs. Harrington," Sophie said as she joined Sarah in the foyer. "This is a pleasant surprise."

"I thought I might help with . . . something." She wasn't certain her presence was needed. But after her last visit, she felt drawn to return. "I know Noelle is ill and the duchess is busy with Catherine." She shifted her feet. "Perhaps I should go."

"Nonsense." Sophie smiled. "You came all this way. We are nearing our matching party and the ladies could use assistance with planning what to wear and with topics of conversation. They are obviously anxious to make positive impressions."

Sarah nodded. "It would please me to stay." She followed Sophie into the parlor. To her surprise, she found not only the room covered with gowns of many colors, but Laura in the center of the group of women, laughing as they fussed around her.

"Sarah!" Laura gingerly made her way across the room, careful not to trip over scattered boxes on the floor.

They embraced and Laura whispered, "I am surprised to see you here. Does Gabriel know?"

"He does." Sarah pulled back. "I came once with Noelle. I cannot explain it, but I had to come back."

Laura nodded. "I feel the same, though my reasons are quite different. I will tell you all about my story later." She tugged Sarah into the room. "First, we choose gowns for the ladies."

Within minutes, Sarah was swept into the midst of a whirl of women. Mary welcomed her warmly. "Has your friend made progress in her marriage?" she asked softly.

"She has," Sarah said with her face warming. "She is very happy."

"Excellent. Now help me choose between the green and the burgundy." Mary led her to the two gowns and they quickly chose the latter. What followed were choices of lace or plain gloves, shoes with laces or without; whether one should talk about Parliament or keep to the weather.

"Parliament can lead to a very dull conversation about political matters," Sarah said with a grimace. "I suggest sticking to the weather or how well he knots his cravat. Men do like to discuss their achievements."

This brought giggles. One of the women, the lovely Beatrice, said, "Lord Broughton liked to boast about his prowess, convincing me to accept his protection, for a chance to be the luckiest woman in all of England. Thankfully, his wealth was vast, for it was the only reason I did not run him off after our first night together, the lying beast."

Cecily stepped forward. "They all think they are better endowed than the entirety of all other men. I wonder what instrument they use to measure. It is certainly flawed."

More giggles. Thankfully, the arrival of Sophie ended the scandalous conversation. Sarah's cheeks could not take much more. She met Laura's eyes and they both fought back laughter.

The hour grew late as Sarah and Laura took their leave, chatting as they climbed aboard the hackney. "The courtesan school gives many women new lives," Laura said as she leaned her head back on the squabs. "Me included."

Sarah startled. "You were a courtesan?"

"For a while, I thought I was." She spent the rest of the ride telling her tale. It was both shocking and heartening. By the end, Sarah saw her friend in an entirely different light.

The sound of a screeching cat with its tail ablaze filled the room as Tildy Cloverton slaughtered her second song of the evening. If not for the sweetness of Tildy's mother, and the way the entire company stared at her as if to gage her reaction to the performance, Sarah would have placed her hands over her ears and fled from the room.

Thankfully, the song was not long and Tildy was replaced by her younger sister, Tempe, who did have a voice straight from heaven. The sweet sound soothed Sarah's abused ears . . . and nerves.

"What do you think of your first musicale?" Gabriel leaned over to whisper. "And how large will the dowry need to be for some poor dupe to take the lovely Tildy off her father's hands?"

Sarah placed a finger to her mouth to squelch a laugh. "You are horrible. I am certain Tildy has other delightful attributes." She made a quick glance around them. "And quite a large dowry, I would say."

Gabriel chuckled low. "I think twenty thousand pounds should about cover the cotton fluff for her husband's pained ears." He frowned. "No, make it thirty."

"Hush."

By the time Tildy's turn came back around, Gabriel had taken her by the hand and they'd escaped from the drawing room.

Refreshments were laid out and they nibbled cakes and sipped punch while the off-key warbling continued; thankfully at a distance, though still not far enough.

"Tomorrow we shall send around an anonymous note to Mrs. Cloverton," Gabriel said. "The woman needs to be told that to make Tildy sing forever damages the prospects of the poor girl ever marrying."

"No note. But sadly, I agree," Sarah replied. "The poor dear needs to find another talent."

A rustle of skirts turned them around. Noelle and Mister Blackwell joined them. Noelle was still pale from her illness and dark smudges rimmed her bottom eyelids. She grimaced when she looked at the cake Sarah was eating. "I fear we should not have come. I'm still feeling a bit weak."

"I'm taking her home," Mister Blackwell said and called for their coach. His concern was evident.

Sarah took her hand. Noelle's skin was clammy to the touch. "Would it be acceptable if I visit tomorrow?" Worry furrowed her brow. Noelle had been sick all week and did not seem on the mend. In fact, she appeared worse.

Noelle managed a shaky smile. "Please do visit. I am

weary of keeping my own company while Gavin is working."

Saying their good-byes, the Blackwells left.

"I'm troubled by her condition," Sarah said and pressed her clasped hands to her mouth. "She does not look well."

Gabriel took her arm. "Noelle is tough. Whatever is causing this will pass and she will be back to her high-spirited self."

They stayed for another hour until a reasonable time to flee. Mrs. Cloverton thanked them effusively for coming, and Gabriel hurried Sarah out of the house and into the coach.

"Thank goodness that is over," Gabriel groused and took a seat beside her. She snuggled under his arm. "I think my left ear is permanently damaged."

"Then I shall only whisper naughty things in your right," she said, and they shared a sweet kiss. A light rain fell as they drove through the darkened streets, adding a chill to the evening. Fall continued to press forward with crisp air and rainy days and nights. Sarah hated to see gray skies become the norm. She enjoyed sunlight over endless cloudy days.

"The weather cannot be helping with Noelle's recovery," she said while listening to the tap of raindrops on the roof. "She needs dry air and sunshine."

"London seldom has dry air, sweet." He rubbed her shoulder. "Blackwell told me about a specialist who is coming tomorrow morning to have a look at her. By the time you visit, she should have a diagnosis of her condition."

Sarah took comfort in his presence. "I do hope so. I hate to see her suffering."

The Blackwell town house was quiet when Sarah arrived the next afternoon. Her worry did not abate when the maid led her to Noelle's room and she saw her friend abed, her face white and taut. Gavin held her hand and spoke softly to her. He lifted his gaze when he saw Sarah there.

There was deep worry in his eyes.

Sarah's stomach turned to stone.

"I will leave the two of you alone," Gavin said. He kissed his wife on the forehead and exited the room.

Sarah crossed over and took the chair he'd vacated. She leaned her elbows on the mattress and scanned Noelle's face.

"You look better today," she said, stumbling over the words. "Your cheeks have color."

"There is no need to lie to me," Noelle said and touched her pink-flushed cheek. There were dark smudges under her eyes. "I look like death."

"Do not say such a thing," Sarah scolded. She reached for Noelle's hand and braced herself for terrible news. "You must tell me what the physician said and leave nothing out."

Noelle closed her eyes for a moment then began. "I am suffering from a lung ailment he believes I caught from someone in Bath. He is convinced I will recover, though it may take weeks to do so."

"That is good news." Relief filled Sarah.

Noelle nodded and bit her quivering lip. "There is more. I am with child."

The unhappiness on her face kept Sarah from expressing joy. She knew how much Noelle wanted children. Why then was her expression grim? "You should be pleased, no?"

Noelle's eyes flooded with tears. "The illness has weakened me and the physician fears I may lose the babe."

"Oh, Noelle." Sarah pushed up from the chair and climbed onto the bed beside her. She took her friend into her arms. Noelle trembled and tears fell.

"I cannot bear losing the baby." Noelle sobbed. "Gavin and I have struggled to conceive. This may be our only chance to have a child, to give him his heir."

"Shhh." Sarah blinked back tears of her own. "You must keep positive thoughts for your recovery and for this babe. I will not let you fall into despair. No looking down at your shoes. You must show confidence at all times."

With her familiar scold turned back on her, Noelle

sniffed and lifted her head. She rubbed her hand over her eyes. It took a moment for her to collect herself. When she did, she frowned.

"When did you become so bossy and strong-willed?" Noelle asked. "You used to be reserved and polite."

Sarah smiled and gave her a pointed look. "I started the moment we met outside the dress shop and I quickly realized you were both wonderful and temperamental. I realized instantly that I wanted to be like you."

Noelle laughed lightly. "You poor dear," she said, and then the tears began anew.

Chapter Nineteen

Over the next two weeks, Sarah went to the Blackwell town house every day and returned home weary in both mind and body. She'd often drop face-first on the bed, where Gabriel would rub her back then turn the massage into something more . . . stimulating.

"You know what I need," she'd say and he'd flip her over and love her passionately until she'd forget anything but him.

"I have not thought about the case for nearly a week," she'd said after one such exhausting day. Her eyes drooped and her sated body lay liquid on the bed. Guilt stepped in and ruined a perfectly romantic moment. "I am a horrible daughter."

Gabriel had tucked her to his side. "Nonsense. You've been a loyal friend and the case will keep until Noelle is well. Care for her and Brown will keep hunting The Widow."

Thankfully, in the middle of the third week, Noelle made an upward turn in health, and the pregnancy continued.

As Sarah returned home today, on the afternoon of the seventeenth day, a sudden feeling of unease caused tension between her shoulder blades. The house was very quiet, too quiet.

Listening silently, she finally heard laughter coming from the direction of the kitchen, a mixture of male and female voices. Smiling at her foolishness, she glanced through the mail, discovering a note with no obvious signs of the sender.

"Odd." Most likely, some doddering Lady or Mrs. forgot to leave her mark on another invitation. It had happened a few times previously.

Too exhausted to assuage her immediate curiosity, she tucked it into her pocket, lifted her damp green hem, and walked wearily up the staircase.

Gabriel was off at White's with a friend, and they had no plans for the evening. When she crossed over the threshold into the upstairs parlor to check the ceiling for further rain damage, the unsettled feeling returned in a rush.

Something *was* amiss.

The evidence came in an inhaled whiff of rose perfume. Expensive perfume, she knew, from one of her lessons.

She stopped and her body tensed.

A slight flutter of the drapes caught her attention.

The rain came down in sheets and a small fire flickered in the damaged hearth, just enough to cut the chill. There was no reason for the window to be open.

No reason she could fathom with reasonable clarity, anyway.

With caution, she looked for boots or slippered toes peeking out beneath the hem of the drape. Nothing obvious caused alarm. She stepped cautiously toward the window. The sound of the footman talking below gave her courage.

If she screamed, help was near.

Reaching out her hands, with her heart pounding at a furious clip, she swept the drapes open. Much to her relief, no housebreaker jumped out after her.

Her body slumped as the tension fled. Still, she said, "I know I did not imagine the rose perfume." And the window *was* opened slightly. Someone had been in her house, a woman who could afford costly perfume.

The Widow? Could that be?

She walked to the bell cord and waited. The butler came to the door. "Harris, did a woman call for me today?"

He shook his head. "No, Mrs. Harrington. We received no callers."

"Thank you, Harris." She dismissed him and turned back to the window. She pushed it open and leaned out. Though having the potential for bone-breaking if one fell, the height of two stories was not enough to deter someone like The Widow, if she were inclined to make the climb up the ivy.

A shiver went down her spine. She'd been so focused on Noelle that she'd all but forgotten the danger around her. If The Widow had breached these walls to commit mischief, she was becoming more brazen. And more dangerous.

Gabriel would not be pleased. He already worried that her search for Father's killer put her at risk. Now their home had been breached, again. Searching before they took possession of the town house had not satisfied their thief. He, or she, had returned here and would continue to be a threat as long as there was no solution to this mystery.

"Harris said you were up here," Gabriel said a few minutes later when he arrived home. He joined her at the window and looked out at the rain. She leaned back against his deep blue coat. "We can take a walk if you'd like fresh air. Then, it is a bit damp for strolling."

Sarah wanted to lie to ward off his worry about her safety, but she could not. Gabriel easily read her expressions, so he'd know she was untruthful.

"I think The Widow was in the house. I smelled roses in this room, and the window was left partially open. With the cold, it is unlikely the maids would have done so. I can find no other conclusion that makes sense."

His jaw tightened. "You are sure?"

"I cannot be. However, I am convinced someone broke

in, and a man would not wear perfume. The Widow is my best guess, be it one made without proof."

Gabriel inhaled deeply and closed his eyes for a few seconds. Then, "Let us assume you are correct. For her to break in here during daylight, and with a house full of servants, leads me to believe the woman and her companions are desperate. I think it best if we send you off to live with Brenna where you will be safe"

Anger stiffened her spine. She stepped away from him and spun around. "I will not go. I've made too many sacrifices to not see this to its conclusion. I'll not be chased off by my father's killers."

"And I'll not risk your life."

The level of his protectiveness both comforted and frustrated her. "Mine is not your life to risk," she stated. "I kicked the wasp nest and will not be scared off by the stings." She met his stare and refused to blink. "My father deserves justice. If you send me away, I'll move in with Nanny and not return."

The look in his eyes told her he was mulling both taking the chance of angering her further by sending her off and wondering how serious was the threat. Finally, acceptance slipped over his face. "How did I ever think you an amiable wench? Had I known Noelle would turn your temperament from shy to fearless, I would have forbid her instructions."

Sarah's lids narrowed. "You cannot blame her for the change. I always had a spark of fierceness in me. It was my aunt who squelched the flame with her stern rules. By Noelle's example, and my own desire, I discovered my strength again."

Gabriel placed his hands on her shoulders. "I do not like the danger you face. These people are killers. They will not hesitate to eliminate us both, if we threatened them to exposure to arrest."

She closed her hand over his. He cared for her; of this, there was no question. "I know. However, with you at my side, we are a fearsome pair. The Widow will not win."

His mouth twitched. "The Widow had best run and
hide. My wife is on her tail."

Smiling, Sarah rose onto her toes and kissed him. He slid
his hands up her back and locked them together. How she
loved his kisses and hands on her body. There were so many
differences between them, so many reasons why their marriage shouldn't work, but not because of this.

Once the kiss ended, Sarah reluctantly released his
neck. It was then that she remembered the note and withdrew it from her pocket. "This came today." She held it up.
"The sender is a mystery."

"I hope it is not an invitation to another musicale,"
Gabriel groaned. "My ears have not yet recovered from the
last."

"Hush. If it is such an event, then I shall refuse with
some reasonable excuse." She ripped open the note and
realized immediately it was not an invitation. She read it
aloud:

> *I have discovered some new information about the case.*
> *Meet me at the Black Bess tomorrow afternoon at three.*

"It is signed by Mister Brown." She handed the cryptic
missive to Gabriel. He scanned the page and frowned.

"The Black Bess is in a squalid area near the wharf." He
turned the note over. "There is nothing else to indicate why
the Runner would want to meet us there. His news must be
of grave importance for him to choose the Black Bess."

"Perhaps he's found where The Widow is hiding?"
Sarah said, hopeful. "A woman spy wouldn't hide in fancy
drawing rooms."

He rubbed the back of his neck. "You'd be surprised
where spies hide. It's rumored that Lord Hayman was once
a spy, though it has never been confirmed. He is all of
eighty now."

"His is a story I'd like to hear," she replied. "What tales
the octogenarian could tell if the rumors are true."

"Let us focus on one spy at a time." He folded the note

and tucked it in his coat. "First, I will have additional locks installed on all the windows immediately. We cannot have our spy breaking in whenever she wishes, and I'll not have her standing over our bed while we sleep."

The notion made her shiver.

"Second, I do not like the idea of taking you to the pub. The area is not for ladies of quality." He held up a finger before she could protest. "However, we have already had this argument once today. We will figure out a way to keep you safe."

"I do appreciate your acceptance of my part in this drama, though I did not seek your permission," she said tartly. "However, I do prefer you accepting what you cannot change over arguing until I get my way, anyway."

The area around the Black Bess *was* squalid. The fetid smell of rotten fish and seawater burned her throat. The streets were not swept, and the buildings had the over-all look of disrepair.

This was the sort of place a woman of quality would not want to wander alone, or risk more than her body. She could lose her life.

Keeping her hands in her pockets proved challenging. However, if she wanted to be a believable chimney sweep or one who delivered coal, she could not put her finger under her nose to block the smell. Only a young woman with weak sensibilities would.

Similarly dressed as Gabriel in ash-covered clothing and a smudged face, with her hair tucked under her hat, she was still thin enough to resemble a boy. No one would ever recognize her as a lady without stripping her to the skin first.

The final item to complete her disguise was a knife tucked into her waistband and hidden under her coat. Gabriel had insisted she carry a weapon, and the pistols were dismissed as too bulky to hide under her boy-sized coat.

"I do not understand how Mister Blackwell works under

such conditions every day," she whispered. They passed a pair of rough-looking sailors leaning against a wall. "The smells are offensive and the people, worrisome. How can he not fear cutthroats and thieves?"

"His business is farther down in a place not as disreputable as this," Gabriel muttered back. "Though, I'd rather you limit your travels to more fashionable districts."

It didn't take much to agree. The idea of wandering here alone, day or night, sent an icy shiver through her. She'd be a perfect target for the worst in men.

"You do not need to press the issue," she said, pulled her hat lower over her eyes, and stepped lively, determined to stay close on his heels.

The Black Bess was nearly empty when they arrived. A serving woman, well-worn and well-endowed, brought two tankards of ale and clunked them down on the table.

"Would ye like stew?" Gabriel looked at Sarah and she shook her head. "Suit yerself." She ambled off, large hips swaying.

"I fear anything cooked here," Sarah said and sniffed the ale. Feeling a bit mischievous, she took a sip, shuddered, and pushed the tankard away.

Gabriel chuckled. "It takes a while to develop a taste for ale." He lifted the heavy cup and took a large swallow. He grimaced. "Especially when drinking this cow piss."

Time ticked by for a half hour and then for another and Mister Brown failed to appear. They waited nearly two hours before Gabriel lost patience and rose. "He is not coming."

"I hope he did not get robbed on his way here," Sarah said. "In this area, one has to hold tightly to one's purse."

"Brown would know the dangers. He'd be cautious."

The comment did not assuage her. "Wherever Mister Brown is, he missed our appointment. I fear something's gone awry."

"You may be correct." Gabriel tossed a handful of coins on the table and led her out of the inn. "However, there is nothing to do now but return home and await his next contact."

A breeze hit her face and her throat closed, leaving her unable to reply. Odd that she found the air less foul inside the shabby inn than outside where the unforgiving wind brought the unmerciful stench.

She tucked her face into her shoulder and drew in a few deep gasps, accepting that she could not hold her breath indefinitely. "I need a bath," Sarah said after a moment. "With heavy lye soap."

A grunt was his reply. He was keenly watching a ship unload several dozen sailors, who whooped and stumbled down the gangway, headed straight for the inn. Several doxies stepped out of the shadows, wearing dresses that covered very little.

"Let us go before the fighting and wenching begins." Gabriel hurried off with Sarah close behind. They weaved their way back toward the street where a hired hackney driver was promised a generous fee to wait. Sarah was thrilled with the thought of putting the wharf well behind them.

They were about halfway there when a man stepped out from beside a warehouse and into their path. Gabriel stopped and reached out to push Sarah behind him.

"We have nothing for you here, sir," he warned. "Move on."

The man grinned, his mouth possessing very few teeth. "Ye are Gabriel 'arrington?"

Sarah felt Gabriel tense. His body was whipcord tight. Danger rippled off him. She fingered her knife.

"Who's asking?"

The man peered at Sarah. The look he gave her was anything but simple curiosity. Either he had a penchant for boys, or he knew she was female. No matter his predilection, his interest did not bode well for her.

"Brown sent me to fetch ye. Said ye'd be looking for 'im at the Bess. Come." He turned and ambled away.

"I do not like this," Gabriel said. He appeared torn between continuing toward home and meeting Mister Brown. "We might be led into a trap."

Sarah nodded. His concern was not for himself, but for her. She had to show strength. "True, that. However, if this toothless man knew of our meeting with the Runner, then Mister Brown may have either discovered important information or be in danger. We have to find out. He may need our help."

Gabriel expelled a breath. "Stay close."

The stranger waited impatiently near the side of the largest warehouse in the row. There was something feral in the man's eyes, a warning of danger to come.

Gabriel stopped. He reached for the pistol in his waistband. "This is a mistake. Turn back!" he called out to Sarah, but it was too late.

A trio of men burst from the building and were upon them before she could pull the knife free. A fourth man came up behind Gabriel as he lifted his pistol and clubbed him on the back of the head.

He staggered. They fell upon Gabriel, who fought mightily against the men. He managed to damage two faces before he was overpowered by their sheer numbers. In the melee, the toothless stranger grabbed for her. He shoved her face-first against the building and pinned her arms behind her.

"Let me go! Gabriel!"

Despite a valiant effort, Gabriel could not overcome his adversaries. They forced him down and took his pistols. "The bloke broke me nose," one of the men said, clutching his nose. He stumbled to his feet. Blood trickled down his face to drip on his stained white shirt.

"It is no less than you deserve," Sarah snarled. The bloodied man took an angry step toward her. Her captor swung her out of reach.

"Leave 'er be," he commanded. "We need 'em alive."

Broken Nose met her defiant eyes, turned, and kicked Gabriel in the ribs. He grunted but remained stoic. She refused to flinch as they pulled Gabriel to his feet. She could not show weakness.

Once their captives were secure, they dragged Sarah

and Gabriel into the warehouse and shoved them into the darkness. Then, without further comment, they backed out of the warehouse, slammed the door shut, and threw the bolt home.

Sarah dropped to her knees beside her husband. "Gabriel?" She pushed his hair back from his battered face and leaned close. "Can you hear me?"

He groaned and raised a hand to his head. "Have I died?" He blinked several times and then focused on her face. She smiled softly into his eyes.

"No, love, you are not dead."

"Damn." He rubbed his temple and rolled up onto his knees. "Were I dead, my head would not hurt so dreadfully."

Sarah helped him to his feet. He wobbled slightly but quickly found his balance. She touched a cut on his forehead. "Thankfully the blow confirmed what I have long suspected; you have a thick skull."

Another groan broke the moment. Sarah glanced up at Gabriel then into the shadows. In the dim light she spotted what looked like someone seated on a chair in a corner.

She released Gabriel. He leaned on a crate and kept to his feet. "Careful, sweet," he urged. She walked into the shadows.

Sarah closed the distance to the man, certain now, from the way he listed to the side on the chair, that he was no threat. Ropes at his ankles confirmed her assessment.

Eyes adjusting to the darkness, the battered man became clearer to her view. She leaned down and peered into his swollen face. Her stomach flipped.

"Mister Brown?" She reached out to touch his shoulder. "Mister Brown. Can you hear me?"

An almost imperceptible nod followed. "Mister Brown, I want to help you." She searched him for serious injuries and discovered when she moved behind him that his hands were also tied. She made use of her knife and cut him free. It took her assistance for him to lift his hands to the chair arms.

"Thank you," he rasped out. She freed his legs.

"Can you stand?" she asked.

"I cannot."

With Gabriel unsteady on his feet and Mister Brown injured, she knew their escape was up to her. She hadn't had a chance to formulate a plan when the door screeched open and fading daylight spilled through the opening to illuminate part of the warehouse.

A rat ran off with a squeak.

Their attackers had returned, with one addition to their band of thugs.

A woman dressed all in black.

Chapter Twenty

꧁꧂

The woman was much as Sarah remembered. As before, she was wearing black breeches, coat, and shirt, though this time her long dark hair was braided. The heavy plait fell forward over her shoulder and almost to her waist.

She stood in shadow with her face not clearly visible. However, Sarah could see enough to watch her gaze encompass the room, pausing in her perusal on Mister Brown.

A sharp whisper followed as she spoke to her men. She was clearly displeased. Why? The answer came when one of the thugs walked to a nearby table and collected a bottle. He walked to the Runner and lifted the rim to his swollen lips. Mister Brown eagerly drank.

"See, we are not monsters," The Widow said and took a step closer. She managed to stay in shadow. For a woman of her profession, keeping her identity secret was prudent.

"I would say not." Gabriel's voice was dripping with sarcasm. He touched the corner of his bruised eye. "Beating men bloody is a sign of good breeding."

Her laughter filled the space. "Mister Harrington, you are a delight."

Beside her, Sarah felt Gabriel on the ready should he need to fight. He'd been taken by surprise the first time, likely distracted by her presence and his need to protect her. He'd not make that mistake again.

Unfortunately, the men were heavily armed. Still, Sarah knew her husband and felt danger ripple off him. If the need arose, he'd fight to the death for her, weapons be damned.

"What do you want?" Gabriel bit out. "You have not killed us, so you must have another purpose."

The woman tapped her riding crop against her boot. "You know what I seek." All humor fled her voice. "Palmer hid papers worth a good deal to some very powerful people. You have them. I propose we trade the information . . . for your wife."

The only sign of tension Sarah saw in Gabriel was a tightening of his jaw. The Widow underestimated her noble-born husband. "Why don't I kill you and end this today?" His voice was low and razor-sharp.

The tone sent a chill through Sarah. In that moment, she realized her husband was more dangerous than any spy. She did not have to see The Widow's face clearly to know the woman felt it, too. Her hand tightened on the crop.

The woman shuffled her feet, her confidence, and smile, wavering. "Such violent talk from such a spoiled English boy. Your years abroad left a mark on your disposition."

"You do not know what I am capable of," Gabriel said, his voice low.

The Widow took another step forward and shadow and light played across her face. Sarah could see that she was not as young as first thought. She had to be somewhere well past thirty, if she spied for at least the last twenty or so years, as Mister Brown claimed. Still, she was stunning.

She met Gabriel's eyes. "I know more about you than you think." She tapped her boot. "Now enough of this prattle. I want those papers, you have them, and we will trade for them. If we keep this civilized then no one needs to die."

"We do not know where the papers are," Sarah protested.

"You know this. You've been in my house. Did you see any evidence we were hiding my father's papers?"

No denial followed the accusation. It confirmed Sarah's suspicion. She was their housebreaker.

"Then you will find them."

Sarah slowly shook her head. "I will not allow Gabriel to trade me, and he will not help you if you harm me. I think we are at an impasse."

"I could kill you."

"Then you gain nothing," Sarah said. "You have already had ten years to find your evidence. You've failed. I believe the reason we are still alive is your hope that we will succeed where you've failed."

The woman said nothing. Then, "I do not need to kidnap you today to get my way. I can take you anytime I wish. Your husband should keep this in mind should he dare defy me." She nodded to her men. "I will be in touch." The group turned and filed out.

Sarah looked up at Gabriel. "When she gets what she wants, she will kill us."

"She will try." He rubbed his bruised chin. "Once we are in possession of the damaging information, we are a danger to the man, or men, she protects."

"I will not accept this as our fate. She wins, unless we use the information first. Once the truth is out, there will be no reason for anyone to want us dead. We will possess no secrets."

"True, but first we need to find the papers." He sighed. "We are having a bit of trouble with that."

He walked over to Mister Brown. "The Widow is everything you said. She is a bloodthirsty bitch."

The Runner slowly lifted his head. One eye was swollen shut and blackened. "I told you she was dangerous."

Gabriel reached to help him from the chair. "She is." He slid under the Runner's arm. Sarah slid under the other. Between them, they kept the battered man upright.

"You know The Widow well, Mister Brown," Sarah said. "You described her quite accurately."

Mister Brown grimaced and took a step. His legs struggled to bear his weight. "I should know her. She is my wife."

Sarah's feet faltered. She scrambled not to lose her grip on Mister Brown. "Your wife?"

Gabriel steadied them both and glanced into her wide eyes. He was equally stunned by the pronouncement.

The Runner set his jaw and said nothing more.

They walked away from the warehouse and covered some distance before hailing the hackney. The driver's brows lifted at the sight of them stumbling across the street, but he held his tongue. He opened the door and they climbed inside. The Runner settled in the hard seat and groaned.

Her patience strained, Sarah sat next to a scowling Gabriel and stared at Mister Brown. "You are married to The Widow? You put us in greater danger by keeping this secret. I think you owe us an explanation, sir."

The coach jolted forward and the Runner spoke. "I do. As you might suspect, this news is not something I often share. The Runners do not know of our connection. I thought it best."

"This is not the time for excuses," Sarah snapped. "Tell us everything or I will have you unceremoniously dumped into the Thames, without suffering a moment's regret."

Gabriel's lips twitched.

Mister Brown sighed. "I met Solange in France, early on in Napoleon's rise to power and long before Waterloo. He was bullying his way throughout the Continent and our government worried we would be next. Spies were installed to watch over him. I was one of the first to take the assignment. I moved to a house just outside Paris, in the shadow of the Palace of Versailles." He turned to the window. "Solange worked in the palace kitchen. I met her in the village. She was very young, barely eighteen, and very beautiful. I was twelve years older. We fell in love."

"Did you know she was a spy?" Gabriel asked.

"I did not, although I admit I did have my suspicions. Her hands were not those of a woman in the laboring class. However, I did not want the truth. I wanted her."

"How did you discover she was spying for Napoleon?" Sarah said. "That had to be a difficult secret to keep."

"She was guarded from the first, and I told her I was a sea captain." He stretched out his legs. "We were together for almost a year when Henry came to me with disturbing information. Solange was suspected of passing intercepted missives to Napoleon that got three British spies killed. I did not want to believe her guilty of such a deed."

"My father discovered who she really was?"

He glanced back at Sarah. "Yes. I hated Henry for forcing me to see the truth. My marriage was forever tainted with that information. I could not look at her without seeing those dead men. I had worked with two of them."

"She was guilty?" Sarah said.

"She was." Even now, his pain was evident. "I knew this was about war and I was equally guilty of passing French secrets to my own government. But she was my wife. I did not want to see her as a danger to me, my friends, and my country."

"What did you do?" Gabriel asked.

Mister Brown turned back to the window. "Instead of arresting her, I told her she was dead to me. I left her there, in the cottage we'd shared, and never saw her again, until today. I almost did not recognize her."

The clop of hooves and rattle of the hackney filled the quiet. Then, "Leaving her alive was a mistake. She changed from a simple spy to The Widow, the most notorious agent in Napoleon's army. I knew from the moment I heard tales of her exploits that she was my Solange. Her name, and attire, revealed that I was dead to her, too."

While the Runner struggled between anger for what Solange had become and his memories of the beloved young woman she'd once been, Sarah was empathetic for Mister Brown, who'd given up everything out of love for king and country.

Gabriel leaned forward. "By keeping this secret, you may have jeopardized the safety of *my* wife. Give me a reason not to expose your secret to Bow Street."

In that moment, the Runner aged before her eyes. He slumped against the squabs. "I will not try and convince you to keep my confidence. You owe me nothing."

"We do not," Gabriel said. Yet, Sarah could see her husband's inward struggle. "What about now? She clearly carries no lingering affection for you."

Pain crossed his face. "Despite the years and the darkness in her, I still love her." He paused. "I ask only one favor. If anyone is to take her life, it will be me."

Shocked by his bluntness, Sarah glanced at Gabriel. He appeared relaxed, far more than she, but there was something dark in his eyes.

She suspected that he was still angry about the lie and wasn't certain he could trust Mister Brown. She felt the same. She knew the Runner was Father's friend and loyal to their country, yet he'd kept his link to Solange a secret from everyone. She was a weakness that he could not overcome.

How loyal was he, really? If it came down to Solange's life or that of Sarah and Gabriel, what choice would he make?

Mister Brown hated The Widow but loved his wife.

The rest of the ride passed in silence. When they arrived home, Sarah had Mister Brown settled in a guest room and his wounds tended to. Once she was certain he was set up with food and brandy, she joined Gabriel in their bedroom.

She found him at the window. Their eyes met in the reflection. She softened and brushed a fingertip over the bruises that marked his face, then moved onto his cut lip.

"You should let me tend that."

He took her hand and kissed her fingers. "I am fine, love." He turned back to the glass and crossed his arms. "We can no longer trust Brown."

"I know." She hooked an arm through his. "I do not

think he will harm us, but neither do I think he will follow through with his vow to kill her. He is torn."

Gabriel nodded. "Agreed. He will continue to investigate and we will keep his secret. For now. However, we must remain guarded against Solange and her companions. Doubtless, she will follow through with her threat against you if cornered."

The notion unsettled her. She went to the window to stand beside him and peered out. There was nothing visible to cause concern; no obvious sign of spies watching the town house, no black-clad figures hiding behind hedges, no large thugs waiting to kidnap her while she slept. Still . . .

Reaching out, Gabriel pulled her against him. She snuggled in his embrace. "I will not let harm come to you," he said and kissed the top of her head.

"I know." She spun and wrapped her arms around his waist. "And I will not allow anything to happen to you."

He snorted. "Do you know how to shoot a pistol or fight with a sword?"

"I do not," she admitted. "However, I think I can manage quite well with a candlestick or pot."

He leaned to kiss her and said, against her mouth, "Remind me to watch for flying pots if ever I get your ire up. I'd like to keep my skull intact." He nipped the corner of her mouth then reclaimed her lips.

Sarah snuggled closer and welcomed a full exploration. Lud, how she loved his kisses.

When his hands made free with her breasts, she broke the kiss and placed a hand on his chest, and he slid his hands down to cup her buttocks. "Mrs. Channing will expect us down to dinner soon."

He reached for the lacings of her dress. "Our housekeeper can wait. I have a wife to ravish."

Where are we going?" Sarah asked the next morning. Gabriel had roused her from sleep with a swat on the bottom then all but dragged her limp form from the bed.

Once she was upright and grumbling about his inconsiderate behavior, he gently nudged her toward Flora, who stood at the wardrobe awaiting instructions.

"Out," he said. He turned to the maid. "Dress her in something serviceable."

"Out?" She put her hands on her hips, her hair falling in tangles around her face. "You wake me before the roosters and that is all the explanation I get?"

"There is no time for questions. If you are not dressed and ready for breakfast in a half hour, I will take you as you are." He scanned the nightdress with a salacious expression. The thin fabric did not hide much to his gaze. "I think the gentlemen of London will be highly intrigued."

Flora leaned into the wardrobe to hide her smile. Sarah huffed and took a seat at the dressing table. Gabriel called for Benning and walked through the sitting room to the chamber beyond. Although he slept with Sarah, he preferred to keep his clothes and toiletries separate from hers, away from her perfumes and fripperies.

"That man tests the limits of my sanity," Sarah said and stared at her sleep-reddened eyes in the mirror. The bed called for her return, but her curiosity—and the idea of parading about London in only her nightdress—kept her from crawling back beneath the coverlet.

Flora laid a simple blue frock on the bed and walked over to collect a brush. The process of detangling her waist-length hair began. "He adores you."

Sarah stilled. Unlike the maid, she wasn't sure what he felt. He enjoyed her body and company. This she knew. But he'd never spoken of his feelings for her.

Of course, Gabriel was not the sort of man to spout poetic nonsense anyway. If he ever did fall in love with her, he'd probably tell Benning first, after a night of drink and mischief-making with his friends.

With expert hands, Flora made quick work of her hair, tying it back with a simple black ribbon. The dress finished her toilet and she was downstairs a mere thirty-five minutes later.

Gabriel made a show of checking the clock. "You now have twenty-five minutes to eat."

She held his eyes with a glare and regally crossed to the sideboard and filled her plate. "You, Mister Harrington, are a bully. I should be allowed another two hours of sleep before being dragged from my bed."

He reached for the newspaper. "We have no time to dawdle. There is much to accomplish today."

"Where is Mister Brown?" she asked and sought out evidence the Runner was joining them for breakfast. "We cannot leave him. It would be rude."

"He rose early and left."

"I see." She had no further excuses to stay in today. "Was he in a reasonable condition?"

"After suggesting he spend the day here, to rest, he assured me he was well enough to go. Who am I to disagree?"

"Hmmm. Men." She would have had Mister Brown tied down for his own good. He had been badly beaten. "What about you? Your face is a fright."

"A dull ache is all," he said. "A few bruises will not keep us from our mission. You have nineteen minutes."

Sarah ate, silently amused by the entire matter. Yes, she was put off by the early hour—after he'd kept her up until after midnight with his delicious attentions—but she had to admit she wanted to spend the day with her husband. She found she liked being with him more than being without him.

Enamored was understating her feelings for him. She was heading off a cliff toward love and could do nothing except brace for impact on the rocks below.

Did she trust him? Not fully. Was he earning her trust? He was, a little more each day. Still, there was a tiny part of her that needed more time to examine the deepest part of his character. It wasn't easy to move past Gabriel's betrayal of her brother. Yet, she was trying.

She placed her napkin aside and rose. "I am ready."

The sun shone brightly outside the windows, so Sarah

chose a gray pelisse and a bonnet with a wide rim. Gabriel decided to drive them himself, and they left London behind in an open carriage.

"Are we visiting Nanny today?"

Gabriel snapped the reins when the gelding slowed. "Perhaps later, if we have the time. First we have a pressing matter needing attention."

They drove for an hour past field and dale until Gabriel eased the horse off the road and onto a narrow path. The path led into an empty field that was choked with weeds and briars.

"Where are we?" Sarah asked, her eyes drifting around the unplowed plot then behind the seat. There was nothing of note but a rolled-up blanket. "If you planned a picnic, you should have brought a basket."

"No picnic." He helped her down and claimed the blanket. Leading the way, he crossed the field and found a place where the ground was largely cleared and grassy. He put the blanket down and carefully unrolled the item. Tucked inside were a scabbard and sword and a knife. He pulled a pistol from under his coat and added the weapon to the rest.

Her brows went up. "Do you plan to run me through and bury me here? There are certainly less bloody ways to rid oneself of an unwanted wife."

Ignoring her, he took off his coat and reached for the knife. "This property is owned by the Marquess Terwilloby. He offered its use, as there are no houses nearby to disturb the citizenry."

"Then you *do* plan to rid yourself of me." She looked down at her serviceable dress. "At least you could have allowed me my best gown. I will be the shabbiest-dressed woman in heaven."

He turned the knife around and held it out, handle first. "Enough prattle about murder. Take this."

Sarah removed her pelisse and bonnet and took the knife. She held it up to the light and ran a fingertip over the polished steel. "The blade is dull."

"It is. For my protection." He reclaimed the item. "When we spoke last evening, I realized that you are desperately ill suited to protect yourself against spies and thugs. Although I am certain you can swing a pot with lethal accuracy, you cannot hide a pot under your gown. You need a weapon to tuck into your garter when you are outside the town house."

The scabbard was heavy when she crouched to claim it. She scrunched up her face and slid the blade partially out. Steel from the sword flickered in the sunlight. "I will need a bigger garter," she joked.

Gabriel glanced skyward. "I brought that, as your father had no other weapons in the house. It is American and I believe it dates back to the Revolution."

"I wonder where Father found this."

He took the sword and handed her the knife. "Pay attention. First. When under attack, you must keep your head. As an unskilled fighter, you'll want to slash about, hoping to hit some part of your attacker." He showed her by example. The blade went this way and that with no control. "This will give him opportunities to hit you here, here, and here." He pointed to the vulnerable places under his arm, his stomach, and his neck.

"I see." Sarah touched her stomach. It curdled with the idea of a sword sticking out of the soft flesh.

"It is imperative to focus on those same places with your blade." He thrust with precision, careful not to touch her with the sword tip. Sarah struggled not to flinch. "Let us try this slowly."

Gabriel showed her how to stand, with her feet apart, one behind the other. Her blade was shorter than his, and less lethal, so he adjusted his stance accordingly.

"Now thrust." She did so and he spun away. "Good. Now try again. You will not hurt me."

Sarah pulled her bottom lip between her teeth and advanced. After a few weak attempts, and him mocking her for not trying hard enough, she began to find her feet and determination. She thrust with greater energy, forcing him back, and once narrowly missing his arm.

A grin followed the near-miss. "Excellent," he said. They went on that way for what seemed like hours until her arm was numb and sweat trickled between her breasts and down her spine.

"I think you have the basic tools for knife fighting," he said. "We will continue on."

She lowered the blade, somewhat—if not completely— satisfied with her performance. "I only hope my opponent is as green as I."

"We both pray for that," he teased.

Pride straightened her spine. She tightened her hand on the handle. "Hmmm. I take umbrage with that comment." The knife came up. Sarah circled him, hips swaying, her eyes locked onto his. "You are supposed to inspire confidence, Husband, not toss insults. I think you underestimate my skill."

She thrust. Caught off-guard, Gabriel did not have time to react. The knife hit him, the dull blade glancing off his waistcoat and skimming across his rib cage, causing no damage, but giving her extreme satisfaction to have gotten in a lick.

His eyes widened and his mouth gaped.

Satisfied, and a bit shocked by her good luck, Sarah pulled back and made a show of wiping invisible blood off on her skirt. "Perhaps I am not so green after all."

Chuckling, Gabriel reached out—gingerly—for the knife. "You, Mrs. Harrington, never fail to surprise me."

Avoiding his reach, she pointed the knife at him, her stance perfect and her eyes lethally mischievous. "Drop your trousers," she demanded. "I want to claim my winnings."

The pause was only long enough for him to see the direction of her thoughts. "As you command."

The trousers came off quickly.

"Lie on your back," she said. He stretched out on the blanket. She straddled his hips then tossed the blade away. Bunching up her skirts, she lowered herself awkwardly over his erection. He helped by pushing her underclothing aside. Once freed of all encumbrances, she slid onto the shaft with Gabriel guiding himself inside her.

He groaned. "I have never been taken by a lady pirate."

Her hips rocked forward and back, the pleasure intense. "I have never enjoyed the spoils of war."

She leaned to kiss him, thrusting her tongue past his lips. The kiss was hard and deep as she rode him, no tenderness between them. He put his hands between them and jerked down her bodice. Rough palms toyed with her nipples. She ended the kiss and arched back. Her mind went blank but for the feeling of his hard cock inside her and his hands rough, kneading her breasts.

Harder she thrust toward her release.

Gabriel said words that tweaked her proper sensibilities, raw and dirty words. Aching, seeking, hungry, she rode him like a wild thing until her body could take no more. With a final carnal cry, she shuddered through a violent release, taking Gabriel with her in his own pleasured cry.

"Good Lord," Gabriel said as she sprawled on his chest, the scent of sex and sweat swirling around them. "You've killed me as no knife could."

Chapter Twenty-one

Unable to lift her head, Sarah laughed softly against his waistcoat. A button scraped her cheek. He shoved his hands in the disheveled mass of her hair, locking her body to his.

"Kick some dirt over me and leave me here," he said and closed his eyes. "Please tell my parents I died in a carriage accident. Harrington men have never expired while in the throes of passion. It will shame me to be the first."

Sarah's laughter deepened a notch. "Oh no. If I am to find a new mate, and have my pick of preeminent males, I must parade your dead body through London, boasting that I killed you while riding your manly frame. Within hours, I should be the most sought-after widow in all of London."

A sharp growl rumbled from somewhere inside his muscled chest in response to her tart comment, and she was swiftly displaced as he rolled her beneath him.

"Oh!" she gasped.

His eyes locked on hers. "First you nearly kill me. Then you threaten to ruin my reputation as a man of great sexual prowess. Followed up by not having the courtesy of waiting until my body has chilled before searching for my replacement? You are a cold and heartless minx, Mrs. Harrington."

She lifted her head and kissed the tip of his nose. "A woman needs a man to take care of her. Why wait?"

Under no circumstances did Sarah need a man to give her orders and treat her as if she was a mindless toy. She had a house of her own, and if Gabriel was ever met with an early and unfortunate demise, she would not need money either. She could live her life as she pleased.

By the look he gave her, he knew she was making sport of him. "If you want to replace me, you will have to try harder to kill me." His hands slid up to cup her buttocks. His cock stirred again. "I have all afternoon if you'd like to try."

Sarah let out a surprised yelp when he dove back between her thighs.

The rest of the morning was broken up between Gabriel trying his level best to cause his untimely demise, while buried inside his wife, and teaching her how to use a pistol.

He much preferred the former. It was Sarah who finally threw up the flag of surrender. "Should you take me again, I fear you will have to carry me home." She nuzzled his neck and said, "Besides, I've discovered I do not want a new husband. I am partial to the one I have."

With her bare body nuzzled up to his, a flood of happiness rushed through Gabriel. Dammit if the chit had not wriggled her way into his heart. "Interesting, that. I am partial to my wife."

Partial? Hell, he loved her.

Gabe looked up at graying clouds. Somewhere above, Albert was laughing until his ghostly side ached. He might not have wanted Gabe to marry his sister, but he would have found Gabe's falling pell-mell for Sarah tremendously amusing.

They had both vowed to avoid the love trap. And somehow

Gabe wondered if falling for Sarah was Albert's ultimate revenge for Gabe breaking his promise to find her a bland and suitable husband.

"What are you thinking?" Sarah asked. She whirled her fingertips in the hair on his chest.

"Nothing important." He slid a hand up her bare back. Somehow, during the time between her demand that he take off his trousers and now, they'd both managed to lose every thread of outer clothing. It was fun to see Sarah firing a pistol wearing only her chemise. "I was just wondering what Albert would think of this."

Sarah lifted her head. "Of you having your way with me in this field? I think he would not want to ponder the notion."

He snorted and rubbed his chin. "Not . . . this. I know our marriage wasn't what he wanted, but would he have eventually approved, now that we have settled into this union?"

"He would want me to be content. I'd assume he'd want peace for you, too." She bit her bottom lip. "Well, after he beat you senseless for lying to me."

Gabe eased Sarah off and sat. He pulled her up and faced her. "Are you satisfied with your life?"

She reached to place an open hand on his leg. "I am."

Thunder rumbled as darkness gathered in the distance. They both looked up in surprise. "We need to get back to London before the storm. The open carriage will offer no shelter."

They scrambled up and into their clothing. The soft breeze no longer skimmed across the sunny meadow. A harder wind kicked up, leading in the storm.

"Quickly," Gabe urged. He rolled the weapons into the blanket, took her hand, and they ran to the waiting carriage. They had just reached the outskirts of London when rain lashed down upon them. But Gabe barely felt the rain or noticed water dripping off the brim of his hat.

Her contentment was not a declaration of love nor was it proof of trust. That would come eventually. He was certain of this. A woman like Sarah could not give herself with such enthusiasm to him without feeling something other than mere satisfaction with her lot.

"I am soaked," she said through her teeth-chattering laughter. She held up the brim of her sodden bonnet with one hand and clutched the seat with the other. Her pelisse could not save her completely from the deluge. The blue dress clung to her curves. She was wet to the skin.

To him, she never looked more beautiful. "I do apologize for not noticing the turn in the weather," he called out over the rain. Water dripped from her bonnet down the neckline of the dress and between her breasts. "I fear you might catch a chill."

Instead of outrage, her eyes glowed with impishness. "How could you notice anything? You were otherwise occupied."

All sorts of delicious memories followed her comment. "Most women would be upset to be caught in a storm, their coiffures and gowns ruined. Not my Sarah. You are unlike any other woman I've ever met."

"Thank goodness for that," she responded. "I do like to be incomparable."

His bark of laughter startled the horse. He leaned to kiss her hard on the mouth then snapped the reins. "Sarah Palmer, you are definitely a cut above."

The invitation came the next morning before the mail, having been hand delivered by a servant. Lord and Lady Ashwood, and little James, were coming to London for a few weeks, and Lady Seymour wanted her family all together, under one roof.

The excitement of the event spilled through the countess's elaborate scrawl. Lady Seymour had to be giddy with the news. She spoke endlessly about her grandson, and now she'd have him for an extended stay.

Sarah placed a hand over her tumbling stomach. "The entire family? All staying at Harrington House?"

"My mother does like to trip over us all," Gabriel replied from his seat at the breakfast table. He sipped his coffee. "I have not yet met my new nephew or seen my troublesome sister in five years. I wonder if age and motherhood have softened her."

Troublesome? Lud. "I know the Harringtons can be devilish. How difficult is your sister?"

Gabriel cocked a brow. "Very."

"Excellent." She was finally getting used to the whirl that was her new family. In a few days she'd meet Gabriel's sister. What if Brenna did not like her? It would certainly make for tense times around the Christmas goose.

"I see concern in your eyes," Gabriel interjected. He reached out, took her hand, and pulled her down onto his lap. The maid hastily set the teapot on the table and scurried out of the room. "Brenna was a tyrant as a girl, bossy, demanding, and she had Simon and me all tangled up. We adore her, even if our actions did not always confirm that. After all, boys are expected to use toads and mice to torment their little sisters."

Sarah wrapped her hands around his neck. "Come near me with a toad and I will never speak to you again. I cannot tolerate toads."

He leaned to nuzzle her neck. "Brenna is as warm as she is prickly. If Noelle and Laura love you, she will, too."

A short time later, in the privacy of their bedroom, Sarah still couldn't quell the butterflies in her stomach. She was used to keeping her own company. Meeting the family a few at a time was challenging enough. Now she'd have to socialize with them all in one place?

Uneasiness filled her bones. Thank goodness for Noelle's lessons. She would not shame her husband by calling Lord Ashwood Lord Ellerby, or by loudly slurping her soup.

She spent several hours tapping walls and finding no hidden panels. There were only a few rooms left unsearched. She decided to move to one of the guest bedrooms.

The workers were largely finished with the roof and

would soon start on the ruined plaster and flooring where the rain still dripped through. Before long, her house would be finished. Eventually children would come and fill these empty rooms.

When her knuckles cried out for mercy, she stopped and slumped into the nearest chair.

That was where Noelle found her. Joining her was a woman with dark hair and Gabriel's eyes. Her stomach dropped. Brenna.

Lady Seymour had not mentioned anything about the Ashwoods having already arrived in London!

"There you are," Noelle said. She walked over and pulled Sarah from the chair. "The butler said you were up here rapping on walls. You realize your staff thinks you and Gabriel are a few steps away from Bedlam."

Noelle hugged her. The color had returned to her cheeks, and although she was a bit thin, she was well on her way to full recovery. They pulled back.

"I care not what the staff believes as long as we find those documents," Sarah said. "As for you, I thought you were not allowed out of bed."

"The physician says I can go out twice a week for fresh air and a short carriage ride," Noelle said. "Of course, my first outing was here. I have missed our lessons and plotting the downfall of spies with you."

Tears pricked Sarah's eyes. "I'm so glad you're getting well." Her gaze dropped. "And the babe?"

"He, or she, is also thriving." Noelle placed a hand over her stomach. "I think those weeks of pampering by his father and you have served us both splendidly."

Sarah brushed away a tear. "I adore you both. I could not do anything less than see you recovered."

Noelle hugged her again. "We must stop this lovey stuff lest we both start crying." She turned Sarah around and led her to Brenna. "As you have probably presumed, this is Brenna, Lady Ashwood. Brenna, this is Sarah, beloved wife of your irrepressible brother."

Brenna took her hand. "Mrs. Harrington."

"Oh, please, it's Sarah, Lady Ashwood." Sarah drew back her hand and waited for the Lady to finish her perusal. "Only the servants call me Mrs. Harrington."

Green eyes flashed with amusement. "I cannot believe Gabriel married. He swore from the time he was old enough to consider anything other than sticking spiders in my hair that he'd never marry. There were too many women in need of his attentions and he could never settle with one."

On this, Sarah did not know how to respond. Annoyance flared. "All those women will have to live with their disappointment, for Gabriel is mine and will continue to be so until his last breath."

Brenna laughed and glanced at Noelle. "You told me she was an ideal match for Gabe. At first blush, you appear correct." She returned her attention to Sarah. "Welcome, Sister Sarah, and call me Brenna. May you always keep my brother hopping."

The annoyance slowly drained from Sarah. Brenna had pricked her temper to gage her response. The chit. "Gabriel calls you a termagant. I suspect there is some truth in his statement."

Eyes narrowing, Brenna shook her head. "With two older and horrid brothers, I had to learn to stick up for myself lest they tromp all over me."

There was love in her exasperated expression. That was one emotion the Harringtons did not lack. They were a loving bunch.

It was Sarah's turn to smile. "Gabriel can be difficult," she agreed. "It is part of his charm."

"I would appreciate you not rattling off my faults to my wife, Sister. It is difficult enough to keep her from discovering the truth beneath my outward perfection without your help."

"Gabe!" Brenna fairly flew across the space and launched herself at her brother. He swung her up and around, placing a kiss on her cheek. When he put her down, she punched him on the arm. "It's time you got yourself home." She hugged him again. Then, "Arguing with only Simon has become a dreadful bore. I need you to make the next three weeks lively."

He rubbed his arm and scowled. "I see you have not changed. You're just as ill-tempered as ever."

Brenna harrumphed and examined him thoroughly. "You have not avoided the sun, and you seem harder, older, no longer the pestering boy I remember." She met his eyes. "However, I can still see mischief in you. If you are hiding a snake in your pocket, I will shoot you."

"You are armed?" Gabriel asked, feigning fear.

"I am not, but I am certain Sarah can find me a pistol."

Sarah nodded. She grinned at her husband. Gabriel sent her a scathing, yet playful, glare. Her heart warmed.

Gabriel and Brenna chatted about baby James, Lord Ashwood, and her life at Beckwith Hall. Sarah saw the happiness in her husband at the reunion with his sister.

Watching him made her heart flutter. She'd worked so hard to keep her emotions in check, trying mightily not to fall in love with her husband, but drat if she hadn't done so.

Even her mistrust was waning. Thus far, he'd done nothing to show that he planned to take a mistress, gamble away his fortune, or become a drunken sot. Outside of that one first lie, and it was hurtful indeed, he'd been an excellent mate.

And if he continued along in this vein, she would be forever a happy wife. Yet . . .

As their marriage was only weeks long, she still had to get past that last niggling doubt that the current contentment they were experiencing wouldn't last. He'd become used to living an adventurous life. Would being a proper gentleman become dull? Would he seek excitement elsewhere?

Is that why Albert did not sanction the marriage? Had he known Gabriel was not the kind of man who could settle into an ordinary life?

How long could she hold his interest? He'd been with women from fascinating places, enticing women who had not grown up sheltered. What did she have to offer a man like Gabriel?

"Sarah? Sarah?" Noelle's voice cut in. "I think she is woolgathering."

Looking up to see the trio staring at her, Sarah smiled sheepishly. "I was. I apologize."

"I said I thought we should move to the parlor where we will be more comfortable," Gabriel said.

"Yes, of course." Sarah led the way down the hall. The mess from the broken mantel had been cleared away, but the ceiling still drooped. "We have a leak," she explained. "Once the roof is repaired the plaster will be fixed and the mantel replaced."

Gabriel frowned. "Our workers were stolen this morning by the Duke of Worthington. He had a small kitchen fire, and as he is a duke, he used his power to gain an advantage. Mister Rice assures me that his workers will return in a few days."

"You did not tell me of their departure," Sarah said. "I'd hoped to get the work finished before the snow."

"I only just heard myself."

Brenna walked over and looked up. "There is no one else in all of England that can make the repairs?"

"Mister Rice and his workmen are the best, or so we've been told. If they do not return soon, I will have words with the duke myself," Sarah said. "Tea, anyone?"

They spent a pleasant hour or so with Gabriel, Noelle, and Brenna telling tales of their childhood misadventures, and Sarah laughing at the images the trio conjured.

"What about the time you climbed the large oak in the pasture and you ripped your dress on the way down?" Brenna said to Noelle. "Your mother caught you sneaking back into the house with your backside exposed and that was the last of your tree-climbing experiences. She was livid." Brenna laughed. "Your mother has no sense of fun."

"My backside was not exposed," Noelle protested. "My undergarments were intact. And yes, my mother is quite sour. I do not ever remember her laughing about anything."

The three nodded. Then Brenna set down her teacup.

"I hate to end this reunion, but I must save James from his grandmother, lest she spoils him beyond repair."

They rose and walked Brenna and Noelle downstairs. At the door, Brenna turned to Sarah. "It was very nice to meet you, Sarah," she said. "I look forward to getting to know you better next week."

Sarah nodded. "I, as well. There are many stories you can share about my husband. I look forward to their telling."

Gabriel's lids narrowed. "Perhaps I should rethink Mother's invitation. I fear for my sanity with my wife, sister, and mother all in one house. The torment will be intense."

"Do not forget me, dear Cousin. Gavin and I are also part of the party. Aunt Kathleen issued the invitation last week."

"Lord save me," he grumbled.

Harris opened the door for the ladies, and Noelle and Brenna passed Mister Brown on the steps. He tipped his hat. "Ladies."

Brenna and Noelle looked back, clearly curious about the Runner's bruised face. Sarah shrugged slightly and they continued to their waiting carriage. She would inform them of the recent adventure at a later time.

Mister Brown walked up the steps to join Sarah and Gabriel in the open doorway. "I have news." Busby took his hat and coat. They settled into the downstairs parlor.

The Runner's face was grim. "There has been a murder."

"Oh dear." Sarah put her hand to her chest.

"The man was Horton Hughes," Brown continued. "He was a tenant in Westwood Park, Lord Avery's property. Hughes came to see me last week hoping I would be willing to buy some information he had about a secretive meeting that took place on a road just off the park. Late at night, three days ago, he was walking back from the local inn when he saw a group of six men on horseback congregating in the middle of the road. Curious about the lateness of the hour and that they were strangers, he darted off into the trees and crept closer. He couldn't clearly make out all of the conversation, and only spoke rudimentary French, but understood enough to figure out what they were plotting."

"And that was?" Gabriel asked.

"They were on their way to kill Lord Avery and his family."

Chapter Twenty-two

At Gabe's insistence, he and Sarah rode out to West-wood Park with Brown. If there was even a remote chance the plot was connected to Sarah's father, he wanted to be there when Brown spoke to Lord Avery. Anything to move their sluggish investigation forward would help.

"Horton contacted the Runners after rushing to warn Lord Avery about the assassination plot," Brown said, filling them in on the murder. "His Lordship managed to get his family to safety with friends who live nearby."

The weight of an alternate outcome to Avery's situation hit close to Gabriel and burned hot in his chest. He felt a kinship to His Lordship. His wife was also in the path of killers. Perhaps the same killers.

"They were fortunate Horton was out drinking that night and decided to be a hero," Gabriel said. "Avery has three children and a wife. Imagine the horror if the killers had gotten to the park before Horton."

Sarah shuddered. "How could anyone want to hurt children? They are truly evil men."

"Soulless bastards," Brown agreed.

"How did Horton die?" Gabe said before the topic took another path. They must remain focused.

"It appears as if someone knew of Horton's visit to Bow Street and killed him for his selfless act." The Runner scowled. "Returning home, he was about ten minutes from the park when he was attacked. They left him at the side of the road. A farmer found his body. The local constable knew him and contacted Lord Avery. His Lordship contacted us."

"How dreadful," Sarah said. "He gave his life to save others."

"He did indeed," Brown said. "He was a good man."

Gabriel crossed his arms. "Why would anyone want to hurt Avery and his family? I've heard he is a decent sort, and his wife, sweet natured and well liked."

Brown drew in a deep breath. "According to what we understand, Lord Avery was involved in the capture of a French spy during Napoleon's reign. Though he had no part in the hanging of that man, and his identity was kept secret, we suspect there is a traitor in our midst. The spy somehow became privy to some documents and passed them on. There is a furtive investigation under way at Bow Street."

"So the plot on Avery was to avenge the death of the spy?" Gabriel said. He glanced at his wife. She was pale, her eyes wide with worry. He hated that she was involved with this case. His protective nature wanted to shelter her. Sarah would not have it.

"We believe so." Brown scrubbed a hand on his bristled cheek. He appeared to have neglected his toilet over the last day or two. With the healing cuts on his face, shaving had to be painful. "Thus far we've found nothing to indicate a traitor at Bow Street. However, everything indicates there is something amiss there. How could the killers know about Avery and Horton otherwise?"

Sarah pushed back her hat. "How is all this connected to Father's case?"

"Lord Avery worked briefly with your father," he said. "Anyone connected to Henry has to be investigated.

Although I do not believe your father was involved with the arrest of the French spy, we do think a member of the same group these Frenchmen worked with also killed Henry."

With the news, Gabriel watched pain flicker through her eyes. Still, she remained outwardly stoic. She had remarkable strength, his wife.

"Then your Solange may have killed both Father and Horton?" she asked, her voice strong and unwavering.

Brown nodded, his face grave. "It is possible."

Gabriel wondered what it cost Brown to admit the culpability of his wife in such despicable acts. Gabriel wondered how he himself would feel if it were Sarah in her place and Sarah was a traitor.

Could he take her life if it meant saving others?

"You cannot blame yourself for her actions," Sarah said softly. "I do not find you culpable for my father's death. Solange is responsible for her own behavior."

"Thank you. However, if I'd had her arrested when I discovered she was spying for France, your father would still be alive."

Sarah leaned forward and laid her hand over his. "You do not know that Solange *was* his killer. As a spy, the French would have wanted Father dead. Or Napoleon might have found out about Father's connection with the mistress. There were many reasons he was endangered. Solange was not the only person who was capable of the murder."

Brown's expression softened. "You are kind, like your father." He patted her hand. "He would be proud of the woman you've become."

They fell silent. Gabriel was taken aback by her kindness. By all accounts Brown's wife had murdered her father, and yet, she showed him compassion that in all likelihood he did not deserve. Despite what she said, Solange had been his responsibility and he'd left her free to continue spying. For that, he should wallow in his guilt for eternity.

Sarah reclaimed her hand and sat back. Within the hour they were at Westwood Park. The house loomed large, unfettered by gilt and opulence. In fact, the plain stone façade signaled nothing to indicate Lord Avery's great wealth or position.

It was like a monastery in simple lines and form.

"I asked Lord Avery to meet us here," Brown said and climbed from the coach. "If His Lordship is being watched, we do not want to lead the killers to his family."

Gabriel followed and helped Sarah down. She lifted her chin to examine the five-story manor as Brown led the way across the stone drive to the front door.

Once inside, the interior was as simple as the outside. Clearly, Lord and Lady Avery were not the kind of nobility that liked vulgar displays of wealth.

The butler indicated they follow. "Mister Brown. This way, please. His Lordship is waiting in the drawing room."

As they walked down a long hallway into the bowels of the manor, Gabriel felt a growing sense of unease. Something was amiss in this house, in this case, in the murder plot. He felt it in his bones.

Tension pressed down on Sarah, weighted by the feeling that something was not right about this story, this killing of Mister Horton. Even the comforting presence of her husband could not dispel her concern. She'd once seen a spider wrap a moth in its deadly silken webbing, and she could not help but feel much like that hapless insect.

Her steps faltered as they reached the drawing room.

"Easy, love," Gabriel whispered as if reading her thoughts. He touched her arm. "I, too, am wary."

Relieved that they were of the same mind, they followed the butler in. A man of medium height, and somewhat younger than Sarah expected, stood waiting near the fireplace.

He had to be little more than twenty or so when the French spy had been captured. Still a boy in many regards. And now his life, and that of his family, were endangered because he wanted to serve his country against a foreign foe.

Lord Avery walked over to them. Mister Brown made the introductions. His Lordship greeted Sarah warmly then turned to Gabriel. "I have heard from your father of your adventures," Avery said, smiling. "He sometimes shared your letters over a glass of port. It is unfortunate we must finally meet under these circumstances."

"Knowing my father, he likely embellished some of my antics for the enjoyment of his audience." Gabe gave a slight bow. "Perhaps someday soon we will meet up at White's, when this case is settled and danger is no longer shadowing us both."

"Yes, let's do." Lord Avery offered seats and refreshments. Brown refused a brandy, but Gabriel accepted. Lord Avery turned to Sarah. "I understand the Runners believe the plot to kill me and your father's murder are linked."

"They do," Sarah said. "If there is anything you know that may help us, we'd be appreciative to hear your thoughts."

His Lordship sipped his drink. "There really is very little to tell. I was twenty-three when I ran away from home to join the army. My brother was heir presumptive, and I was a lad with dreams of adventure. As the son of a noble, and with a French mother, the government saw me as an asset and decided I'd be best used away from the battlefield."

"They made you a spy," Gabriel said.

"Fluent in French, I could move among French society without drawing much notice. Spying sounded like great fun."

Sarah wondered if her father had once felt the same.

"Spying was not as I imagined. Being young and brash, I did not like to follow rules. Ferreting out secrets was difficult, trust hard to gain, and my arrogance did nothing to aid me. In a year, I had little to offer. Then my brother broke his neck in a fall from his horse and I was called back to England. It was on my last night before my ship sailed that I attended a—" He darted a glance at Sarah. "—party as a final farewell to Paris. I was out in a darkened garden with a lovely young woman when I overheard a conversation between two men. The information I gleaned led to the arrest of the French spy in London and thus ended my life as an agent of the Crown."

Despite her best effort, Sarah couldn't hide her disappointment. "Did you see the faces of the two men?"

"I did not," he said regretfully. "The garden was dark, I was hidden behind a hedge, and their conversation was brief. They'd vanished into the night before I realized the importance of what I'd heard."

"Damn." Gabriel's fists closed on the chair arms. "We are thwarted at every turn."

Mister Brown pressed forward with questions, but nothing further was gained. His Lordship had been but a young man without the skills to undertake the job he was asked to do. An inexperienced spy made one contribution to his country then returned home to take his brother's place.

"I am truly sorry I cannot be of more help," Lord Avery said. The questioning came to an end. "I knew your father, not well, but enough to realize he was a good man."

"Thank you," Sarah replied, and they stood. Gabriel took her arm. Once the three were settled back into the coach, Sarah gripped Gabriel's hand. He squeezed her fingers as the coach rolled down the lane.

"Do not lose hope, love," he whispered. "We have avenues left to explore."

With the Runner seated across from them, Sarah did not want to express her concerns, which were many. Although Lord Avery appeared to be an excellent source of information, the trip to see him proved a waste of effort.

"Every time a path appears in front of us, it ends in disappointment," she said.

Suspicion grew. Could Mister Brown be trusted? Truly? Could he be the traitor inside Bow Street?

So many questions without answers whirled through her head. She looked forward to getting home and discussing the matter with Gabriel.

"I worry about Lord Avery's family," Sarah said. "I know what it feels like to be in danger."

"Runners have been posted to protect them, and they have also hired a man named Jace Jones and his employees for further protection," Mister Brown said. "It will be almost impossible for the killer or killers to attack him again."

"That gives some comfort," Sarah said. "I cannot fathom how my plan to discover information about my father's death has become so far-reaching. Why attack the Avery family now? They've had many years to exact revenge."

"Not unless the traitor at Bow Street was only recently turned," Gabriel said. "Enough gold will tempt even the most stalwart of men. If they have accessed the information into your father's death, then they could have access to other cases."

"Then Lord Avery may not be connected to Father's death, other than the killers may be the same French spies?"

"Spies, determined to right all wrongs." Gabriel turned to Mister Brown. "I suggest your employers contact all agents past and present to inform them that their lives may be at risk."

"I will see to it immediately."

A loud crack rang out and the coach lurched.

"What is happening?" Gabriel called out. The coach sped up, wobbling on its wheels for a short burst, then rolled to a stop. Gabriel peered out then carefully stuck his head out the window. He looked toward the horses.

"Something has happened to the coachman." He pushed the door open. A second crack sounded and a thump banged against the side of the coach. "Get down." He reached out and pushed Sarah to the floor.

"Someone is shooting at us!" she cried. A third bullet zipped through the open door, past her head, and hit the seat above her! "Gabriel, duck!"

Gabriel swung away from the opening and onto the seat, his back to the wall. Another shot exploded from outside. He pulled a pistol from inside his coat, thankful he'd taken to carrying one since The Widow threatened to kill Sarah.

"Keep away from the door," he said to Sarah. "Wedge yourself under the seat if you can."

Mister Brown was already halfway beneath the seat opposite. He held a pistol in his hand. "Can you see the shooter?"

"I cannot, though I believe he is waiting for us to alight so he can kill us all." Gabriel primed the pistol, knowing he had one shot. If his aim was true, it was all he'd need.

"What do we do?" Sarah said with her eyes wide.

"You are not armed. Stay inside." He looked over at Brown. "I will try to get out and see if I can find the shooter. You stay and protect Sarah."

The Runner did not protest. Gabe shot her a glance then held out his hat. No shots. The silence following the shooting offered no comfort. How could he get focused on the shooter if he did not know the direction in which he was hiding?

"Be careful," Sarah urged.

He dropped onto his hands and knees and peeked out. Emboldened by no further shots, he leaned out further.

"I cannot see anyone." Taking a chance, he stood and leaped out. He hit the ground and his knees buckled. A shot cracked and he rolled under the coach and out the other side.

"Gabe!" Sarah cried.

"I'm unhurt," he quickly assured her and scrambled behind the wheel. The coach was angled sideways across the road and the weeds along either side were uncut. It offered him some cover from flying bullets. At his back was a ditch.

Not enough protection for comfort. Still, now he knew the direction of the shooter. That would help.

Careful to keep low, he jerked off his coat, put the pistol in his waistband, and slid sideways and away from the coach. The horses shuffled restlessly as he moved past them. Without the firm hand of the coachman, they were uncertain, nervous.

His extensive experiences in America gave him an

advantage. He and Albert had gotten into many situations when he thought they'd breathed their last, and yet managed to survive.

This shooter paled against a party of Cherokee, or a band of bank robbers whose horses they'd just borrowed.

His mouth twitched and a feral gleam filled his eyes. No, he and Albert had faced worse. They'd learned to hunt food with the best trackers in Texas, how to move soundlessly through wooded mountains when looking for a kidnapped girl, and when to turn and ride away when the odds were against them.

Damn. His heart grew heavy. If only his friend were alive to share this one last danger.

Never had the stakes been higher for Gabe in all his years away. Sarah's life was endangered. He could not fail her.

Sliding on his belly, he pulled himself from the ditch and into the weeds, his mind focused, shutting out every sound, every thought, outside of finding the attacker.

Another shot, then two, hit the coach. The man was getting impatient. The coach walls weren't enough to keep the bullets from gaining entry inside. He had to hurry.

Gabe's stomach burned. Like a cat, he moved, careful and nearly soundless, until he reached the fence bordering the road. From there, he crawled beneath the wood planks into the pasture and followed the fence to the east where a small wood copse stretched along the fence. His heart pounded in his ears.

The distance narrowed. It took concentration to hear anything past the thud of his heartbeats in his ears.

Eventually, he heard a low-voiced conversation amid harsh whispers. He edged closer. He could see the backs of two armed men, one nearer the coach, the other behind a small tree and to the back side of the front man. He was loading pistols for the other.

Gabe stood. With care, he stepped forward to within reach of the second man. He waited until the stranger put down the loaded and primed piece.

"Where is 'arrington?" the man asked. His answer was a hand over his mouth and an arm around his neck. The stranger struggled. Gabe quickly cut off his breath. He applied pressure until the man went limp and then quietly eased the unconscious man to the ground.

"I cannot see him," replied the first man, oblivious to the goings-on behind him, clearly too focused on trying to kill Gabe. "He must be under the coach."

Gabe cleared his throat. The man spun around, his jaw open. Gabe released a feral grin and lifted his pistol. "Looking for me?"

Chapter Twenty-three

"Harrington." The man was medium height, balding, but built to fight. His pistol was raised halfway, not yet positioned to fire. Gabe intended to keep him from taking a shot.

"One and the same." Gabe's weapon *was* ready.

The stranger smiled, showing one missing tooth. "I should've known you would not be easily killed. I once got in a brawl with an American seaman. Those bastards can fight."

Although not American, Gabe nodded. Americans were a tough lot. "Then you know that I have no intention of allowing you to kill me, my wife, or Brown. The decision is yours. Put down the pistol, or sacrifice your life."

The man seemed to consider his options, his smile never wavering. It was his eyes that gave him away. In a blink, the pistol came up and Gabe shot him through the heart.

Muddy brown eyes widened. He stumbled back. "Bastard." The man went down and breathed his last.

Without a second glance, Gabe walked to the other man and reached for his coat, pulled him up, and tossed him over his shoulder.

"Don't shoot me. There is no danger," he called out to Brown and walked out of the small copse. Brown peered out the coach door and Sarah moved up beside him. Relief flooded her features. "I shot the other one."

He dropped his burden unceremoniously on the ground and went to check on the coachman. Blood soaked the servant's gray greatcoat. Gabe climbed up for a closer examination, surprised to find the man breathing, though struggling to do so.

"I need help," Gabe called out. Brown appeared at his feet. Between them, they got the coachman down from his seat and into the coach. Sarah helped remove Gabe's cravat and stanched the blood flow.

"He needs a physician, and quickly," Sarah said. She pressed the cravat down with both hands.

"I will do my best."

Gabe left the coachman to her care and joined Brown outside. "You stay with our prisoner and I will go for help." He climbed into the driver's box and claimed the reins. Without another word, they were off.

It took fifteen minutes to return to Westwood Park and dispatch a pair of Runners back to Brown. Another half hour passed while hunting down a surgeon, and another hour for the coachman to succumb to his injury, despite a valiant effort to save him.

Sarah was bereft. She'd been certain her fight to keep him alive would save him. "I tried. I tried," she said as Gabe pulled her against his chest. Her weary body trembled. He wanted to take away the pain, but he could do nothing but comfort her.

"I know you did, love." He kissed her head and breathed in the scent of orchids. "The bullet nicked his lung. There was nothing anyone could do."

She lifted her head. There were no tears, just deep sadness. "I am pleased one of the shooters is dead. I only wish the other had a similar fate."

The coldness in her voice chilled him.

Recent events had changed his country mouse, and he hated the bitterness that now occupied his sweet Sarah.

"I wish the same. Unfortunately, we need him alive. He is our connection to The Widow and her merry band of killers." He took her hand, led her from the house, and they returned to the coach. His Lordship had offered his coachman to drive them back, and Gabe accepted. "Let us see what Brown has discovered."

If they intended to receive information about the shooter and his companion when they returned, they were disappointed. The man was still too befuddled by Gabe's attack to do more than babble incoherently before lapsing back into a stupor.

"He said nothing of use?" Gabe asked while they loaded the stranger into the coach.

"Nothing yet," Brown replied. He, Gabe, and the borrowed coachman loaded the body into the boot. "Although I did get enough to conclude that he and the dead man were brothers."

They rolled him onto the seat, and Gabe, Sarah, and Brown sat opposite him. They all stared. "He is not at all what I thought a spy would look like," Sarah said. "I expected more . . . polish."

"He is not a spy," Gabe explained. "I think they were hired for the purpose of following through with Solange's threat. They planned to kill Brown, injure me, and kidnap you. The Widow's employer is tired of waiting for your father's papers. If they have you, they know I'd do anything to get you back."

Her expression softened. Absent privacy, she did not need to speak to express her appreciation. She took his hand.

Lud, he loved her. Once this case was settled, he'd hand her the heavens if it meant never again seeing hurt in her eyes or hearing bitterness in her voice.

After dropping off Mister Brown, the body, and the prisoner, Sarah and Gabriel returned to the town house. Gabe hoped that by morning the stranger would be recovered enough to give them something to lead them to The Widow and her employer.

Sarah called for a bath and groaned as she slipped into the steaming water. Having been hunched over the coachman for the ride to Westwood Park in an effort to stanch his blood loss, her back ached dreadfully.

"I think I shall stay in here until morning."

Gabriel removed his soiled waistcoat. "The water will be icy in twelve hours."

"Then I shall instruct the maids to remove and replace the water as needed." She stretched her arms over her head. "I do not think that is too much to expect after the day we've had."

Placing her arms on the edge of the tub, she rested her chin on the back of one hand. "You are the handsomest man in all of England. No, the entire world."

He chuckled. "You are biased, sweet."

"I certainly am not." Her gaze drifted down his body, eagerly watching as he unbuttoned and slipped his pants off his hips and perfect buttocks. She touched her tongue to her bottom lip as his already rising erection sprang into view. She wondered if she'd ever think of him as anything but magnificent, even when he was old and stooped. "No man will ever challenge you for my attention."

For a time, they forgot dead men, and spies, and murder cases, and just enjoyed their bath. After, they dried off and snuggled together in bed.

Fire crackled in the fireplace while Sarah lay on his chest, listening to his heart beat strong in his chest. She wanted to stay this way forever, in his arms, and shut out all of the darkness outside of these protective walls.

"I love you, Sarah Harrington."

Her head popped up. "What?"

Gabriel toyed with her damp hair, brushing it from her face so he could look into her eyes. A smile tugged at his mouth. "I love you, Sarah."

All her strength left her, her bones turning to pudding.

The surprise of the unexpected statement left her unable to speak. She always hoped for affection between them. She never expected his love.

"Truly?" she asked, finally.

"I do."

She found the ability to push forward and kissed him. She laughed against his mouth. Her heart welled with happiness. "I love you, too. Lord knows why, but I do."

Chuckling, Gabriel kissed her long and passionately. They spent the next hour abed then went down for dinner, when Sarah begged for food. "I am famished. Getting fired upon taxes one's body. If you do not feed me soon, I will expire."

Over pigeon pie and pease pudding, they spoke of nothing about the case, murder, or thugs with pistols.

They loved each other. That was enough.

Harris found them there, relaxing over tea and port. "A pair of footmen sent by Lord Seymour left a trunk on the stoop for you, sir. They said it was shipped to Ireland by mistake."

"Ireland?" Gabriel rose and Sarah followed him out. Sitting just inside the doorway was a battered brown trunk.

"Is it yours?" Sarah asked.

"It is."

Gabriel popped open the lid and examined the contents. He frowned. "It appears that everything is here. To be certain, have the footmen carry it upstairs and I will look through it thoroughly."

Once the trunk was placed by their bed, Sarah and Gabriel took everything out, piece by piece, until the contents were all laid out on the mattress.

The items consisted largely of clothing, some letters, and a few trinkets he'd picked up from foreign places. In the stack was a cloth-wrapped package tied with string. He handed it to Sarah. "I could not pack Albert's clothing, so this is all that's left of his personal things. There are letters and some items he'd want you to have."

She took the package and caressed the surface. "Twenty-eight years of life all wrapped up in faded cloth and string." She'd open it later, when she was alone.

"Yes. However, they are the things he cherished most."

She set it on her lap and examined the scattered items. "Was anything taken?" she asked.

"I see nothing missing but for a pouch of coins and a musket that I bought from the son of an American soldier." He sat on the bed. "My trunk was not stolen by spies after all. It was sent on the wrong ship. A thief took advantage and stole a few things from it, nothing more. Thankfully, my name and my parents' address were written on the outside. I reported it missing when I arrived in London."

"At least it was returned." She caught Albert's package up against her. "I am grateful to have something of my brother's."

The clothing was sent off for cleaning. "I suspect you will not be wearing most of this here," Sarah said as she handed the maid a cowhide vest. She waited for the girl to scurry off before cocking a brow at her husband. "I had all but forgotten the fringed trousers. I was too fearful of you to appreciate how well they fit and how wicked you looked in them. I'd like to see you wear them again; when we are alone, of course."

A glint appeared in his eyes. "Yes, My Lady."

Flora arrived, ending any further talk about fringed trousers. In her arms was a box. "Your gown came for the party tomorrow tonight. You might want to check to make certain the alterations are correct."

"Drat. I'd forgotten about the Sherwood party."

Gabriel kissed her cheek. "I'll leave you to it, then." He slipped out. Flora stripped Sarah out of her day dress and pulled the deep blue silk gown over her head. The dress skimmed over her body. She turned this way and that in front of the mirror. "It fits perfectly."

The maid nodded. "I shall have it pressed."

Once they finished picking out fripperies to go with the gown, Sarah went in search of Gabriel. She found him in the library. He clutched a sheet of paper and did not acknowledge her arrival.

She cleared her throat. "A farthing for your thoughts."

He glanced up. "I've been pondering the case; going back to the beginning and working forward. There is one person we have not yet spoken to. Lord Hampton. He would be the man who directly supervised your father's activities."

"I had not considered him." Sarah sat in the chair before the desk. "I thought Father's job as a secretary was a cover for his spying."

"Perhaps. Even so, Hampton had to know your father's profession. A secretary is expected to be available at all times. Lengthy absences would be unacceptable and cause for dismissal. That your father kept his job over many years leads me to conclude that Hampton was the man whom your father reported to."

"Hmmm." She considered the idea. "Lord Hampton might be the one person who can give us the clues we seek. Whatever Father knew, Lord Hampton was privy to."

"I agree. I've sent around a note asking for an audience tomorrow."

Sarah left him to continue his reflections on the case and went back to their room. The trunk and contents had been moved into the connecting bedroom for Gabriel's dispersal, so she sat on the bed and opened Albert's package. Inside was a book by Charles Brockden Brown. Some of the corners were bent to mark his page, and the spine and cover were worn. She closed her eyes and imagined Albert reading the book by firelight.

Her throat constricted. "I shall have to see what you found so intriguing about this book, Brother." She set the book aside.

There was a small painting of a pretty young woman with black hair. *Hester* was written on the back of the frame.

"Who were you? What did you mean to my brother?" Sarah peered into blue eyes. "I must ask Gabriel."

Beneath the painting was a colorful beadwork cloth

with a dog or wolf embedded in the center, a white and black feather, and several small pieces of gold. A necklace made up the last of the trinkets. It was a small braided rope that passed through a round hole in a stone shaped like a crude arrowhead. She held it up to the light.

"Albert found the arrowhead in Mexico," Gabriel said from the doorway. "He fashioned it into the necklace. He wanted to give it to you when he came home."

Tears sprang to her eyes as she slipped it over her head and settled it between her breasts. "I will treasure it always."

With one hand on the stone, she reached for the painting and held it up. "Can you tell me who Hester is?"

Gabe smiled. "A few years ago, Albert and I rode for four weeks with a wagon train heading west from St. Louis. He fell madly in love with Hester. She was a beauty. Sadly, she was already married. When she turned him away, he claimed a broken heart."

"Unrequited love," Sarah said wistfully. "How did he procure the painting?"

"He stole it from her wagon. He spent many nights staring at her picture and claiming one day he'd go back for her."

"She probably has several children now."

"Yes, but I suspect she still thinks of your brother. I believe she was in love with him, too."

Gabriel left her to finish looking through the package.

There was nothing remaining but several letters addressed to her. Most contained news of his travels and some of the people and things he saw. He wrote of Gabriel and their friendship and some of their misadventures. Her mind filled with his wonderful descriptions, and she felt as if she'd shared the experiences with them.

The longest letter was dated earlier than the others. He pondered life and spoke of memories of their childhood, his despair over leaving her, an apology for the same. Finally, he wanted her to know of his love should anything ever happen to him, and his wish to be reunited with her one day. By the time she read his scrawling signature at the bottom of the last page, tears fell unchecked down her face.

The party the following evening was interesting only because Laura and Brenna, with spouses, were in attendance. Sarah found she liked the somewhat reserved Lord Ashwood, finding him the opposite of his vivacious wife. Oddly enough, she also actually enjoyed the bickering between Gabriel, Brenna, and Simon. It was quite entertaining.

"I do not know how Lord and Lady Seymour ever had peace with the three of you always squabbling," Sarah said, laughing, after an argument about the weather. They could argue about nearly everything.

"They did not," Brenna said, frowning at her brothers. "Mother claims she got her first gray hair the day Simon pushed me in the duck pond and I nearly drowned."

"I did not almost drown you," Simon cut in with a scowl. He pointed a finger at her. "You knew how to swim."

"True. However, I was wearing that horrid orange dress Aunt Frances gave me for my birthday. The weight of the bows alone sank me into the muck. If it had not been for Gabriel, I would not have survived."

Gabriel nodded. "I dragged her out by her feet." He smiled wickedly. "The good that came from the incident was that the atrocious gown was ruined."

"It was abominable," Simon agreed.

"The poor dear meant well, but Aunt Frances did choose the worst gifts," Brenna added. Gabriel and Simon concurred.

Lord Ashwood turned to Sarah and said dryly, "Did they all just agree on something?"

Sarah placed a hand over her mouth, her eyes wide with false surprise. "I think they did. Hurry, we must tell Lord and Lady Seymour so they may celebrate the occasion."

The three Harrington siblings stared.

"I never knew my husband possessed such a quick wit," Brenna said, frowning. "He could play a court jester."

"There was a time when Sarah did not know how to jest. Now she is ready for the stage," Gabriel remarked and winked at Sarah. Her eyes narrowed. "Take the lead in a farce, perhaps."

"Simon always possessed good humor," Laura added. "But never in the presence of his sister. She only hears his cross words. This is indeed a remarkable moment in Harrington history."

Sarah, Laura, and Lord Ashwood laughed. Then His Lordship held out an arm to both Sarah and Laura. "I think we should go for punch before the bickering begins anew."

With that, they walked off into the crowd.

Gabe was the first to recover. "There was a time when my wife barely spoke to me without looking down at her shoes. Now she is not one to hold back her opinions."

"She is your ideal match," Brenna said.

"I like her," Simon said. "She suits you."

"She does suit," Gabe agreed. "I never thought I'd find contentment in marriage."

Brenna stiffened then sighed. "Did we just agree again?"

Simon snorted. "I believe we did."

"Take shelter, siblings," Gabe said drolly. "The sky is about to fall in."

Chapter Twenty-four

"Mister and Mrs. Harrington, My Lord," the elderly butler said as he led them into a drawing room. "Would you like tea, Your Lordship?"

"Yes, Simpson." Lord Hampton held out a hand, indicating the settee, and Sarah and Gabriel sat. "Guests should always have tea."

The room was stifling hot. A huge fire blazed. Sarah wondered if an entire load of wood and coal had been dumped into the fireplace and set ablaze. She wanted to open a window straightaway, or three, but was too polite to ask to do so. Darn all those social rules! Instead, she sat politely and prayed she'd not expire into a puddle on the floor.

"Welcome to my home, Mister and Mrs. Harrington," he said. "I admit to my curiosity when I received your note. More so some weeks past when discovering that Sarah was alive and married." He smiled. "After you vanished with Albert, and we heard nothing more, I assumed the worst. I'm pleased to be wrong. You appear in excellent health."

"Thank you, Your Lordship," Sarah said. "It was a trying ten years. I lost my father, brother, and aunt."

"Tragic," he said. "Just tragic."

Lord Hampton sat in the chair next to the drawing room window, a blanket spread over his lap, sunlight streaming across his legs. A band of white hair circled his head, and bushy brows topped a pair of blue eyes.

Sarah was surprised at how frail His Lordship looked, as if he suffered from an unknown malady. This would certainly explain the blanket and the slight hint of yellow on his skin. He was about the same age as Lord Seymour, though Gabriel's father was robust and youthful.

Gabriel leaned in. "The death of Henry Palmer is why we're here. Recent events have led us to deduce that not only was Palmer's death connected to his government work, but that there are hidden documents that his enemies are desperate to discover."

A shadow passed over Lord Hampton's face. "I know nothing about any documents or that he worked for the government. He was my secretary. I would know if he had another profession."

Sarah and Gabriel shared a glance. "Lord Hampton, my father was a British spy."

He placed a hand on top of his head. His grizzled face grew puzzled. "A spy?"

"Yes," Gabriel said slowly. "We think you were his contact. Certainly you knew this?"

His Lordship fell silent. "I cannot remember anything about spies." He rested his chin on his chest. He muttered something about spies, and wine, and an actress with a French name. It was all nonsensical.

A sheen of perspiration covered Gabe's skin. He leaned close and whispered in Sarah's ear, "I think his memories are fading."

Her stomach sank. A feeling of dread washed over her. She whispered back, "Lord Hampton is the last link to my father, traceable back to those years of his service. If the earl cannot help, and the spies remain elusive, then the case is over."

This time, Gabriel said nothing to assuage her fears. There was nothing to say. She was correct.

"The French have not put out a decent wine since the Revolution," Lord Hampton said. "It is very disappointing."

"Your Lordship," Gabriel interjected. "Try and focus on Henry Palmer. Can you remember anything about his death?"

Fearing they'd hit another disappointing end, Sarah wanted to beat her fists on the table at her knees. Unfortunately, it would serve no purpose.

"Henry is dead?" Sadness etched his face. Then, "Of course, Henry is dead. He was murdered."

"He was." Sarah leaned forward. "Can you tell us what you know about his death?"

"It happened not far from here," His Lordship said. "He lived not far from here, with you and Albert. It was a sad day, that, when a good man cannot walk through Mayfair without being accosted and murdered."

He slipped back into muttering about footpads and the state of London where pickpockets roamed free.

"We will learn nothing here." Gabriel stood. Sarah followed. "I need some air."

As they readied themselves to leave, Lord Hampton lifted his head. "Wait. I do remember something. There was a woman who asked after Henry. She came here a few years ago. My son spoke to her. She was angry."

Sarah and Gabriel shared a startled glance. "Do you know what she was angry about?" Sarah asked. Finally something!

"She thought we had something of hers." He paused. "A journal. Then she mentioned the name of a Bow Street Runner. A Mister, Mister . . . Bloombush." He frowned. "No, wait, it was some sort of bush. Rosebush, I think. Oh dear, I cannot remember anything more."

"Mister Rosebush?" Gabriel grumbled. "I fear his memory is worse than I suspected."

"Father." A stout and sullen man entered the room. He crossed to His Lordship and placed a hand on one narrow shoulder. Together, the pair shared a strong resemblance. The viscount glared at Sarah and Gabriel. "You are not supposed to have visitors."

"Geoffrey, this is Sarah, Henry Palmer's girl. You remember Henry? He was my secretary."

Geoffrey patted his father's shoulder. "I do remember Henry." He tucked the blanket tighter around his father then faced them. "What is this visit about?"

"They said Henry was a spy," Lord Hampton said. "I am trying to help them solve his murder."

The Viscount Kilmer sighed. "We know nothing about spies or murder. I apologize for my rudeness, but I must ask you to leave. My father needs his rest."

"Of course," Sarah said. She could not fault the viscount's protectiveness. "Thank you for your assistance, Lord Hampton. I'm certain your information will be of great help to our investigation."

"You're welcome, Sarah." He gave a wave. "Do come and visit again. We can talk about Henry."

"I will," she said.

The viscount escorted them into the hallway. "I hope you do not put much weight on Father's ramblings. His mind is fractured. On some days, he struggles to remember my name." He led them to the door and jerked the panel open. "Please do not come again."

His forceful tone brooked no argument. He closed the door tightly behind them. When they reached the walkway, Sarah's frustration bubbled over.

"Will we ever find a solid clue and settle this case?" she groused. "It appears my father will never have justice."

Gabriel took her arm and led her to the waiting carriage. "Do not give up quite yet, love. All is not lost."

"It's as if my father's death was not meant to be avenged," she said, defeated. "How can I not give up?"

He grinned. "Because we still have a Rosebush to uncover."

Sarah waited until they were seated and Gabriel took up the reins. "I have never heard the surname 'Rosebush.' You cannot think it's a real person?"

"I do not," Gabriel replied. "I do, however, think that there is some truth to this name. Lord Hampton did possess some lucidity. That is why we are going to Bow Street. If anyone knows this 'Rosebush,' it is Brown. And hopefully he's discovered some information from our shooter. Between the two, we might have new clues."

For the first time in weeks, Gabe felt a rush of optimism, although, obviously Sarah did not share the view.

"I once had an aunt who'd also suffered from a fractured mind. Her moments of lucidity, though few, were there," he said. "With Lord Hampton, I suspect there is some form of truth in those moments. The name may not be entirely correct, but there is a chance it will lead us to the Bow Street traitor."

"I hope you are correct. However, we've had too many disappointments. I think I shall keep my giddiness in check until we are clear about the validity of the clue."

Gabe snorted. "I have never seen you giddy."

She tucked her hands on her lap. "I've been saving it for the time when the case is concluded and my father's killers have been convicted of the crime. Then I will be absolutely giddy."

A short time later, they pulled up in front of No. Four Bow Street. "Think positively, love," he said. "I sense we are about to see our luck change."

"Hmmm."

They went inside and were directed to the whereabouts of Mister Brown. He was seated behind a desk in a cluttered office. Upon their arrival, he stood. His cravat was askew and his coat rumpled. The Runner appeared to have had little sleep. The case was taking a toll on him, too.

"Mister and Mrs. Harrington. I was expecting a visit. Come. Sit." He indicated a pair of chairs. "We've unearthed a new clue."

"Did the shooter give up his companions?" Gabe asked.

"Sadly, no. Mister Chumley and his brother did not have the name of the man who hired them to shoot you." Brown sat. "The matter was all very clandestine. Their faces were covered when they were taken to an old farm a distance from London and given their instructions. However, his brother managed to overhear the name of the nearby village. That, and the description of the house, has given us a place to start looking. We have sent men to glean information from the local constable."

"This is excellent new information," Sarah said. Gabe heard hope in her voice.

"We also have information," Gabe said. "We spoke to Lord Hampton. His memory has faded, but he did have the name he believes is that of a Runner that The Widow asked his son about some years ago. Mister Rosebush."

Brown's eyebrows knitted over his eyes. "We have no one here with that name," he said, then paused, and his face went white. "No, it cannot be."

"You know him?" Sarah said.

"*Rosebush* must be *Abercrombie Bushnell!* He's a clerk here and that's the only name that fits. Excuse me." Brown got to his feet, rounded the desk, and vanished out the door. After a minute, muffled voices sounded from the hallway. Several men hurried past, including Mister Brown.

"We may have found our traitor," Gabe said as he stared out the open door.

"Found with help from the confused mind of Lord Hampton." She rubbed her hands together. "I feel a flush of giddiness bubbling up."

Gabe grinned. They shared some hushed speculation about Mister Bushnell. Minutes later, Brown reappeared, followed by a pair of Runners, dragging a weeping man between them.

The previously mentioned Mister Bushnell was short and stout, his hair white and his face mottled. It was nearly impossible to understand his hysterical stammering. However, Gabe understood enough to gather that he'd never meant to turn traitor. That he had a wife who spent more than he made as a clerk. And he did not think his actions would endanger anyone.

"You caused the death of Henry Palmer and maybe others," Brown said, and caught Bushnell by the throat. "You will tell me everything you know, or I will send you off to Newgate and make certain the inmates know you are a French spy."

"Please, no," the man sobbed. "They will kill me."

Sarah rose to her feet. Rage burned through her. She moved close to Bushnell. "Henry Palmer left behind children, you pitiful man. My brother and I lost our only parent when you gave his name to the French."

"I'm sorry," he wailed. Sarah was having none of his excuses. She drew back her fist and hit him square in the nose.

Bushnell's nose cracked and blood poured out. He made a strangled gasp as Sarah turned on her heels and fled the room.

Gabe hurried after her. He found her leaning against a wall, rubbing her hand, tears streaming down her face.

"The bastard," she said and held up her hand. "I think I broke my fingers."

Gabe took a look. There was some swelling. "Perhaps one or two bones," he agreed and pulled her close. "But Bushnell fared much worse. I am very proud of you."

Sniffing, she reached into his pocket, drew out his handkerchief, and wiped her eyes. "I wanted to kill him. I do want to kill him."

"I know." He kissed her forehead. "The web is closing in around our spies, and Bushnell may be able to save his pathetic life if he helps us catch them. Otherwise, he will hang with the others."

"Hanging is what he deserves."

"He does. However, if we can capture The Widow and those she works with, his life might be a fair trade. He will never be released from Newgate. There is some solace in that. It will be its own death sentence."

She grumbled under her breath and nodded. "I am exhausted. Can you take me home lest I change my mind and commit murder?"

Thunder rumbled, almost drowning out the sound of the door knocker. The normally wet London had seen more than its share of rain this week. Just when it appeared there might be a reprieve, the clouds would gather again and start another deluge.

Gabe had gone off to meet with Mister Brown, and Sarah was expecting no visitors. The emotional upheaval from yesterday left her drained, and she planned to spend a quiet afternoon at home. It was not to be.

She peered at her wrapped fingers and awaited the butler.

Harris announced visitors. "Lady Seymour, Lady Ashwood, Mrs. Blackwell, and Lady Harrington are here to see you, Mrs. Harrington." He appeared slightly winded after having managed to get through the list of titles.

"Thank you, Harris. You may send them up." Sarah stood and smoothed down her simple rose-patterned day dress. Having not expected visitors, she was decidedly underdressed.

"There you are." Lady Seymour breezed in like a mother goose, followed by her colorful chicks. "Gabe came by the house and told me about your unsettling day yesterday. So I decided to round up my daughters and Noelle and make a visit. Oh dear. Look at your hand. Gabe said you were involved in a brawl."

"It was hardly that." She wriggled her swollen fingers. "It was one horrid little nose." Sarah kissed cheeks. "I cannot imagine you all traveling in the storm." Wind lashed the house and rattled the windows. "Goodness." She peered up at her ceiling. Neither the roof nor the plaster had yet been repaired. "Do not stand over by the fireplace or risk the ceiling collapsing on your heads."

"You have been too kind to your workers," Brenna said,

frowning as a raindrop dripped from the crack onto a towel spread out on the floor. "I would have taken the men by their scruffs and marched them back to finish the job."

"Perhaps we should move downstairs to the drawing room," Sarah said as a second drip followed the first. "I've been sitting here imagining how I will decorate once my new mantel has been built. We really should go elsewhere."

"Nonsense," Noelle replied. "We are perfectly safe over here." She took a seat on the settee that had been pushed to one side of the room with the chairs, out from beneath the bowed ceiling. The other women followed. "Besides I have never seen it rain inside a house. It will be entertaining."

"Hmmm. I am not so sure how entertaining a flood in my parlor will be."

Lady Seymour changed the topic. "I am looking forward to your arrival next week," she said to Sarah and Noelle. "My household is in turmoil. It has been ma y years since we filled the rooms to brimming. I want eve '- thing to be ready for the festivities."

Lightning cracked. Sarah winced. More water dripped down. A maid, Edwina, can into the room, rushed back out, and returned a few minutes later with a bucket.

Noelle snickered. "I should have brought an umbrella."

"Let us go downstairs," Sarah insisted. "It has stormed hard all week and I'd really hate to have plaster fall atop our heads."

"Sarah does have a point," Laura interjected. "I prefer to keep my skull intact."

A maid arrived with tea. "Too late," Brenna said. Both she and Noelle clearly enjoyed the leaking ceiling.

Soon Sarah's concerns were set aside when the conversation turned to the list of parties and balls over the next week.

"There has been a change to the list. Mrs. Symonds has informed me that *her* sister, the duchess, is throwing the last ball of the year instead of Lady Ware," Lady Seymour said. "There will be an actual waterfall in the ballroom, with ducks and swans swimming about, and everyone will be required to wear something pink."

Noelle snorted. "Men in pink evening wear? How dreadful."

"I cannot imagine my manly husband wearing pink," Sarah said. "Pink boots, pink trousers, pink coat." She mock-shuddered. "What an unpleasant image."

The countess's mouth turned down. "Men are not required to don pink trousers and coat. She only expects some pink in their waistcoats."

"As the sister is a duchess, we will all comply," Laura replied and sipped her tea. "Simon will not be pleased."

The ladies all smiled. "Harrington men are a higher level of male," Noelle said. "They do not mince, simper, or dress like dandies. They would much rather hunt stags, box for sport, and ravage their wives."

The indelicate comment brought giggles. "Please do not make such comments in front of my mother," Brenna scolded, laughing behind her hand. "She has delicate sensibilities."

Lady Seymour rolled her eyes up. "As if I do not know the ways of Harrington men."

Sarah flushed. Gabriel was a robust lover, as, it seemed, were the rest of the Harrington men, and Gavin, too. It explained the contentment of the ladies in their marriages.

The ceiling groaned. Brenna shot to her feet. "Look at the rain come down." She was not looking out the window. Sarah also stood, followed by Noelle, Laura, and the countess.

"We need to go now," Sarah begged. "Brenna, please come away from there." But Brenna walked over as rain poured through the crack and a few particles of plaster broke loose. Sarah ran to her, and pulled her back just as the put-upon ceiling broke free. Water and plaster crashed down onto the bucket and floor and scattered wide.

"Goodness," Lady Seymour cried. The noise brought several maids, a footman, and, finally, Gabriel—newly arrived home—running to see the damage.

Gabriel, after glancing over the ladies, stared at the scene before them. "Thankfully, no one was hurt. Lord, what a mess."

"I could throttle Mister Rice," Sarah said. "This is his doing. If he'd not gone off, the new roof would have shed the rain and we'd not have a pond in our parlor."

"Perhaps Mrs. Symonds can ask the duchess to borrow a few ducks," Brenna said and was rewarded with a frown from her mother. "Would you rather have a swan?"

"This is not funny," Lady Seymour said as the maids rushed in, their arms laden with towels. They stopped, unsure of where to start. Water spread across the wood floor in rivulets, settling into indentations and cracks.

"Spread the towels around the perimeter," Sarah instructed. "We should be able to contain most of the rain in the center."

"Thankfully, the rain is only trickling now," Laura offered. "I wonder how long it was collecting in the ceiling."

"It probably has not fully dried out since the leak began, and who knows when that was," Gabriel said. "Weeks? Months?" He took a step forward, his eyes on the pile of debris. He paused at the edge and bent forward.

"What in heaven is that?"

Chapter Twenty-five

✣

Gingerly, and in a mass of swishing skirts, the women followed Gabe across the room, stepping carefully over pieces of ceiling and wet towels, all eyes peering upward for signs of further collapse.

The remaining ceiling looked sound. For the moment.

"It appears as if the release of water has ended the danger, for now," Gabe said, though his eyes were not skyward but rather focused on the metal item half buried in the debris. The rectangular shape stood out among wood and plaster.

His stomach flipped.

Could it be? He swung around and faced the servants lingering in the nearby doorway. "There is nothing more to see here. I need everyone to go back to your duties. We will worry about clearing the mess once the rain ends."

The staff filed out. Sarah sent him a curious glance. He responded with a nearly imperceptible head shake. She said nothing as the last maid exited the room.

Once only family remained, he turned his attention to his sister, standing closest to the hallway.

"Brenna, lock the door." She nodded, did his bidding, and hurried back. The women congregated together, waiting.

Sarah broke from the group and came up beside him. Her eyes narrowed. "You know something."

He grinned like a fool. "Look at the metal box." He pointed. "What do you suppose it is? A hint. It isn't part of the ceiling frame."

She braced a foot on a pile of plaster and leaned forward. Her eyes widened. "Good Lord. Could it be?"

"I think we have solved our mystery. I sent the servants off on the chance one of them may not be entirely loyal." He examined the floor for the best place to advance over broken plaster to retrieve the box where it lay next to the hearth.

"Oh dear," Noelle said, her eyes wide. "Surely this cannot be your father's hidden papers?"

"We will soon find out," Sarah said, her voice rising with her excitement. "Do be careful."

Gabe slipped slightly but kept his footing. He leaned to shove away the broken pieces and gripped the edges of the box. The item was heavier than he expected. He lifted it high, turned, and picked his way back to Sarah.

"Unless your father hid gold beneath the floorboards upstairs and this ceiling, this has to be his documents." He wore a silly grin. "What other explanation could there be?"

"We searched the walls, but not under the floor," Sarah said, awed. She watched him set the box down on a clean spot of floor. "I do not know if I'm pleased or apprehensive. If our spies learn of the discovery before we are able to determine the value of the find, we could be in graver danger than previously."

"That is why we cannot speak of this outside this room." Gabe rattled the lock. It held. "We'll lock ourselves in our bedroom before breaking this open."

He reached for the handles.

"Wait!" his mother called. She pointed up to the gaping hole above. "I think I see another box."

Tucked up in a portion of cracked ceiling, a corner of

another metal box perched on the edge of the opening. It appeared to be waiting for the plaster to break loose and send it tumbling.

"We have found more than one box of buried treasure." Sarah laughed. "And there was no X to mark the spot."

"The papers may be worth more than gold and jewels." Gabe crossed back over the rubble. The wood that made up the upstairs floor was stained darker where two boards met, attesting to where the raindrops had leaked through.

"Your father hid them under the floorboards above. Years of rain damaged both the attic, the room above us, and this ceiling. When the roof weakened with time, the water dripped down through all three floors."

"I suspect our workers tromping around on the rotted roof were also responsible for additional rain coming in," Sarah said. "Their abandonment of us for the duke has proved to be our good fortune. It may have taken weeks for the boxes to be discovered, once they finished the roof and tore down this ceiling."

Glancing around the mess, Gabe had an idea. He took off his coat, handed it to Sarah, and began shoving aside the wreckage. Once the space was relatively clear, he called for a chair. Laura obliged.

He climbed atop and realized the box was still out of reach. Sarah went to the fireplace and solved the problem. "Here, use this."

The fireplace poker had a hook on the end. She passed it up. "Thank you, love."

"You could go in from above," Mother suggested.

"I fear the floor may no longer hold weight." He stretched up an arm and tapped the box. It was as solid as the first. Chipping away a bit of the ceiling around it helped him expose a handle. Then it took several tries to hook the loop and slide it further out of the opening.

"Stand back." The women all moved back several steps. He pulled hard and the box dropped with a loud crash to the floor below. The lid popped open. A handful of papers fluttered out.

"Gabe!" Sarah cried. "Watch out!"

He scrambled off the chair as a huge chunk of ceiling broke loose over his head.

Sarah's heart stopped as Gabriel leaped off the chair and disappeared in the waterfall of soaked plaster and debris.

She coughed. "Gabriel?" When the dust cleared from her vision, she saw him still standing. She sagged with relief.

Her husband had missed the brunt of the deluge but was covered in white and small chunks of ceiling.

He swiped his hand over his already battered face and brushed off his shirt and waistcoat. "I hope that is the last of the collapse or we will have to replace this floor, too."

"Then get away from there before the floorboards above fall, too," she scolded, and reached for his arm as he stumbled over the growing mess. With the help of Lady Seymour, they brushed damp dust from his hair and off his shoulders.

"You are quite covered, Son," the countess said.

Once his face was clear, he retrieved the second box and shoved the escaped, and now soiled, papers back inside. Sarah and Brenna retrieved the other box, each clutching a handle.

"I think we should find other accommodations," Gabe said. Water droplets continued to dampen the wreckage. "I do not know if I should thank Mister Rice for his inconsideration or strangle him for ruining my house."

"If these boxes contain what we think they do, then I shall kiss him, hard, on the mouth," Sarah jested as they walked into the hallway. "We may never have found these, if not for his lack of loyalty."

"If this solves your father's murder, we'll all kiss Mister Rice," Brenna said, then grimaced. "I hope his breath isn't foul."

Laughter added to the anticipation of opening the boxes and picking through the contents.

"My stomach is fluttering," Sarah said. "A ten-year journey for justice may be at an end."

"We all pray for that," Laura said and touched her shoulder. "A killer has been free too long."

Gabe led the women to their bedroom. Once inside, they set the boxes on the floor. He then called for Benning to send some of the footmen to clear away enough of the debris to put down buckets. "We need to keep the third floor from becoming the second floor."

"Yes, sir." The valet stepped away.

"Oh, and Benning, please bring me a hammer."

"Yes, sir." Within minutes the valet returned. He handed Gabe the hammer and withdrew again.

Gabe turned to face Sarah. "Shall we see what we have here?" He walked to the first box, lowered onto his knees, and pried open the rusted lid. Sarah sank down beside him. The ladies gathered around and leaned in.

A black leather journal, cracked and faded with age, lay atop some pages. There were no markings on the cover to indicate what was within. All five women stared at the book as if it held all the secrets of the world.

Sarah was the first to move. "Open it, please," she urged.

Gabe did as she asked. He thumbed through the pages, scanning the words. "There is much about his early years as an agent of the Crown, some of his first cases and what life was like far away from home." Gabe flipped quickly through to the end. "It appears as if most of this was before he met and married your mother. It's unlikely we will find useful clues here."

At the moment, Sarah did not care one whit about the case. These journals held her father's history, penned in his own hand. They were very valuable. To her.

"To the case, perhaps, but there was so much I did not know about my father." She reached out and Gabriel handed her the book. "I look forward to learning more about him as a young man."

"Please continue," Noelle urged. Brenna poked her with

an elbow. "Can I help my impatience? This is a fascinating mystery."

Buried under a few loose pages were several more journals. Gabriel sat back on his heels. "It may take us weeks to read through these, and the papers, too."

"Not without help," Laura agreed.

"I would be willing to assist," Brenna said. "I'll take a journal and see what I can find."

"As will I," Noelle offered. "I am still not allowed more than short trips out. I'm bored and would love to have a part in this case."

"One for me, too," Laura said, smiling. "Anything to help Sarah find peace."

Tears sprang to Sarah's eyes as Lady Seymour also volunteered her time. "Then everything is set," the countess said. She put an arm around Sarah's shoulder. "Between Gabe and we five, there will be no stone left to flip over."

"No spies will be safe once we have uncovered proof of their dastardly deeds," Noelle added.

"The Widow could not know she'd unleashed a vengeful band of Harrington women upon her head when she sent her thugs to kill my brother and kidnap my new sister," Brenna said. She reached into the box and pulled out a journal. "We will all be present when justice is handed out."

Sarah sniffed. "You are all so wonderful." When she'd married Gabe, she'd not known what it meant to be a Harrington or how amazing it was to be part of such a big and loving family. "If The Widow knew what was best for her, she'd run off to the farthest corner of the earth and hide beneath a very big rock."

Lady Seymour squeezed her shoulder. "Enough tears." She reached into the box. "We all must get home and begin our investigations."

"Remember," Gabe said, "we must keep this secret."

Amid excited chatter, each woman took a journal and left husband and wife to the remains of the boxes. "There are still many pages and books to go through," Gabriel said.

"Let us hope that The Widow and her thugs do not hear about our discovery. I think a surprise attack will best serve our case."

Sarah opened the cover of her journal. Her father's thoughts and experiences were spread out in lines across the page, penned in his careful hand. Though eager to begin reading, she knew the later journals probably had the most useful information. She set the book aside.

"I will take what is left in this box and you can take the other," Gabriel said. "If you see anything you think is pertinent, set it aside. Anytime a name is mentioned, note it on paper and set it aside, too. We will not know who is friend or foe until the entire puzzle is laid out."

"What about Mister Brown?" Sarah said. "Should we inform him of our find?"

"Until we can confirm his loyalty, I think it best if we keep this discovery to ourselves."

Sarah rubbed her eyes and stretched her back. The words on the pages had begun to blur. "I cannot read anymore." She dragged herself onto the bed and dropped back on the coverlet. Having sat cross-legged on the floor for several hours, even taking dinner from a tray, her entire body ached. "This is like looking for a pin in a field of grass."

Gabriel returned a handful of unread pages to the box, moved it off the bed, and joined her. "Not once have you complained. I admire your fortitude, love."

She turned her head and rubbed his arm. "The tedium of the search has its rewards. I have learned much about my father and his work. He was a meticulous man who wrote nearly everything down. He enjoyed spying and also confirmed that he did work for Lord Hampton. Either the man was lying or he truly cannot remember those years."

"I saw no deceit in him and suspect the latter." Gabriel rolled onto his side and propped his head on his palm. "Between us, we have several names to investigate. I will get Crawford on them in the morning."

Sarah sat up. "Why Mister Crawford?" She rubbed her lower back and bit back a groan.

"At the moment we do not trust Brown. His Grace gave me Crawford's name and trusts him completely. If anyone can find a connection between those men and your father's death, he can."

Gabriel stood and pulled her off the bed. "I think you need a reward for your service." He tugged at the laces of her dress and removed it. He undressed her down to her chemise. "Lie on your stomach."

"Gladly." Sarah complied. Gabriel removed his boots and climbed in bed, sitting over the tops of her thighs. "This should help your back."

With careful movements, he pressed along her spine, kneading his way up her back, drawing soft pleasured sounds from her. "I am in heaven," she said into the pillow. "Never stop."

He chuckled. "My hands would eventually cramp and become useless."

"Then do not stop until the first cramp comes. Then you may stop. Until then, proceed as you are." He did so for a long time, moving from her back, down her legs, to her feet, and back again. "Where did you learn to do this?"

"From a young woman in San Francisco. She was trained in the art of healing with her hands. Albert and I both proposed to her several times, but she only laughed. She had a lover who was highly placed in government there, and we were young and with only the coins in our pockets. She wasn't about to give up everything to wander the continent with one of us."

"Did you love her?"

"I loved her massages." He leaned to whisper in her ear. "I have only loved once, sweet."

She smiled into the pillow. "Only once?"

Gabriel slid off her. She rolled onto her back. "Yes, unless you count a housemaid when I was thirteen." He leaned to kiss her. "It took a country mouse with a sharp wit, a steel spine, and the body of an angel to finally claim my heart."

Smiling, she ran her hands down his body to toy with the buttons of his trousers. "I think you are so besotted that you cannot see my many flaws."

He tugged his shirt loose from his trousers and removed it. "If there are flaws, I do not see them. Perhaps I should have a closer look."

Once naked, he leaned to examine her feet. "You do have one toe that is slightly crooked and another that is somewhat clubbed."

Sarah pushed to her elbows. "I do not have a clubbed or crooked toe," she exclaimed. He moved to her ankles.

"Your ankles are mannish, thick, and post-like."

"You are a horrible man." She peered at her trim ankles. "There is nothing mannish about them. They are perfectly acceptable."

"Hmmm." He ran his hands up to her knees. "Though knock-kneed, your legs will do. There is little we can change there. Perhaps if you learned to walk with a different gait . . ."

"Oh!" She pulled the pillow out from under her head and whacked him with it. "You are despicable! I shall never speak to you again!"

Laughing, Gabriel leaned to avoid another blow and they wrestled for the pillow as Sarah used skill to keep her weapon. Finally he wrenched it from her hands and tossed it away. He pushed her back on the bed and loomed over her.

She pushed against his shoulders when he made to steal a kiss. "If I had a sword, you would not mock me."

"If you were armed, I'd quiver in fear." He nuzzled the side of her neck. "I do have a sword and know very well how to wield it. Would you like a lesson?"

Her lips quirked. "I should say no."

"You will not."

Sarah tangled her hands in his hair. "You are arrogant beyond measure."

"And yet you love me still." He nipped her ear. Sarah sighed and pulled his head up for a kiss.

"That I do."

* * *

Gabe kissed her, tasting her sweet mouth, feeling her body become compliant beneath him. Half-closed lids and a fan of lashes all but hid her eyes from view.

She was warm and soft and lovely. Although he'd teased her for calling herself flawed, there was nothing about her he'd change, had he that power.

He ended the kiss and returned his attention to her neck.

"Have I ever told you that orchids are my favorite flower?" He skimmed his lips up to her ear. She wriggled.

"You have not." Perhaps he had, but at the moment all she could think about was his mouth on hers. Her hands moved over his shoulders, her touch featherlight.

"Until you, I never gave fragrances much notice." He trailed kisses across her skin, stopping at the neckline of her chemise.

"I see."

He took one end of the pink ribbon between his teeth. She smiled when he pulled the bow apart. "It is true. There are many things I've recently discovered that entice me; violet eyes, for example. Who could prefer brown or blue when you can have violet?"

"Go on." She watched him tug her chemise down to expose her breasts. Her nipples tightened.

"We must speak of nipples. There are many shades."

Her eyes narrowed. "I assume you learned this during your travels, with many examples on which to base this conclusion?"

"I tried to remain saintly, but your brother was a terrible influence." He shrugged. "If not for him, I would have married you largely untouched."

One brow cocked up. "Surely you do not expect me to believe such nonsense?"

"I cannot do anything more than tell my tale." He lathed a nipple. "I can, however, tell you with all certainty that I prefer rose nipples to brown or pink."

Sarah laughed. "You are indecent."

" 'Tis a curse." He teased her nipples, made free with his hands, and tempted her until they were both ready. When he slid his cock inside her, she was warm and eager, his seductive wife.

It was impossible to believe their marriage had begun with one disastrous wedding night.

He whispered naughty words in her ear, told her he loved her, and brought them both to release.

Later, when they were back to examining the boxes, Gabe grimaced. "Do we have to stay with my parents next week?"

"We do."

"Doesn't my mother realize what she is asking? Putting Brenna in the same house with Simon and me is like shooting a cannon into a crowded ballroom."

"Are you likening your sister to a cannonball?"

"She is explosive."

Sarah dropped a page into the growing pile. "One would think that you three would eventually get past your childish squabbling and make peace; if not for yourselves, then for your mother. She finally has her children all together again. Can you not set aside your differences for her happiness?"

"I will do my best."

Sarah reached for a journal. "I envy your family. I never knew my mother, and I had Father and Albert for such a short time. I would give anything for the chance to share confidences with Albert or have Father beg us not to quarrel."

"I can loan you Simon. He knows how to tweak my sister to maximize her ire. I'm certain he could do the same for you."

"It is not the same. But thank you." She fell silent. The clock ticked. "Although you are wary of the visit to Harrington House, I now look forward to it with great enthusiasm."

"Including the madness?"

"The madness is what I long for most," she said softly. "For so many years I lived with only my aunt for company, or alone. I cannot wait to give up quiet for a week or two of laughter, bickering, and late-night chats with my new sisters and cousin Noelle."

"Then I will go into the fray with you on my arm and my head high," he groused. "However, if there is bloodshed, do not say I did not warn you."

Chapter Twenty-six

Gabriel poked his head around the open parlor door where Sarah sat on a chair before the fireplace. "Crawford is here."

Sarah set sketches for the new mantel aside and hurried out of the room. She caught up to her husband halfway down the hallway. He moved along at a rapid clip.

"I hope he has news," she said. Banging sounded from overhead. After cleaning up the mess, and worried about further damage, Gabriel hunted down Mister Rice. Under threat of a pummeling, or worse, the workers arrived early yesterday to finish the roof. They were making excellent progress.

"As do I." His eyes were red. He'd spent the last three nights up to well after midnight, going through the boxes and organizing what they found that might prove helpful. Then he met with Mister Crawford each afternoon and gave the investigator his findings.

Lady Seymour, Brenna, Noelle, and Laura had returned yesterday, each with a page of names and notations they hoped might prove helpful. With their efforts and his, Gabriel winnowed the lists down to a couple of dozen names.

"He's only had a couple of days to investigate the men from my first and second lists," Gabriel said. "Do not expect substantial results."

"I will keep my expectations low," she assured him.

Sarah helped where she could while organizing for the repairs to the parlor and the temporary move to Harrington House. Between them, they were exhausted.

Crawford was waiting in the drawing room, a glass of port in his hand, looking rather fatigued himself.

"Good afternoon, Mister Crawford," Sarah said.

"Good afternoon, Mrs. Harrington." He waited for her to be seated and claimed a chair. His limp was more pronounced today. Likely it came from racing about London, chasing down clues.

She tried not to seem too eager, but with each visit, her hopes of finally solving the case grew. She struggled not to fidget. She braced herself for disappointment.

"I have information to share," he said. "I think I may have found where your spies have been hiding."

Sarah nearly leapt from the couch. "That is astonishing news! Where?"

"Summerdown Manor is just outside London. It belongs to one Mister Charles Downing. He is a merchant who spends much of his time traveling to the Orient and is rarely at home. From what I could gather, several men and a woman have let the property for six months. When I contacted his man of affairs, he had no information other than to say he knew nothing more than that they made their payment in full."

"What leads you to conclude they are our traitors?" Gabriel asked. He poured a drink and sat next to Sarah.

"The man you captured on the road was unwilling to talk under the worry he'd be killed. Once Brown promised to send him off to Scotland to serve his sentence, and the pain over losing his brother, he finally confessed the information his brother gave him. He did not know the exact location of the manor they were taken to. However, he did know the direction and an approximate distance from here to there. As you know, the Runners were already sent to the area. It was through my own investigating that we discovered the manor."

She rubbed her hands together. "I cannot believe we are making progress so quickly."

Crawford smiled. "The information came at a cost. I had to hire men to help me search. I know time is important to Mrs. Harrington." He paused. "One of my men spent an evening at an inn about halfway between London and Luton. He talked to several of the patrons and learned of Summerdown Manor and the strange happenings there. One man, a neighbor named Travers, was loose-tongued. He confided that he'd walked over to introduce himself to the lady of the house and was stopped at the edge of the forest by the sight of many heavily armed men walking the grounds. He turned and fled home."

"This does sound promising," Sarah said. She'd given up her plan not to raise her hopes. They could not be higher. "When do we leave for the manor?"

Gabriel started shaking his head even before the last words were out. "*We* are not going to the manor. Crawford and I are leaving in an hour and will be staying a day or two."

Sarah puffed up to argue, but Crawford spoke first.

"Please excuse my interference, but I have worked both for the Duchess Eva and your cousin Lady Noelle, as well as other members of your family. If your wife is anything like the rest of the Harrington women, you will spend much of this next hour arguing with her, and Mrs. Harrington will win ultimately. If you let her come, then you won't worry about her following us anyway or stumbling into mischief."

He sent Sarah an apologetic smile. She returned it.

Gabriel's jaw muscle pulsed. "I am not pleased to be outnumbered." He glared at Crawford. "If anything happens to my wife, I'll hold you responsible."

The investigator nodded. "I accept. I have spent enough time in the company of your family to know that a Harrington woman, bent on revenge, is to be feared. We will not have to worry about Mrs. Harrington."

Sarah did not take insult at the teasing words. She rather enjoyed being put into the same pot as the duchess and Noelle. Further, she was delighted to be allowed to travel along without wasting time arguing first.

Well, delighted was not the best choice of sentiment.

She stared down her husband. "I will not be left behind to spend my time sipping tea and staring at the hole in our ceiling, while fretting over what has become of the case . . . and you."

Gabriel said something under his breath that she assumed was not complimentary, but he nodded despite his misgivings. "You have fifty-five minutes to ready yourself of I'll leave you behind."

"I shall pack a valise." She stood and left them. Gabriel's grumbling voice followed her down the hallway.

With a full fifteen minutes to spare, she was at the front door, dressed in a simple black riding habit and matching hat with her valise clutched in her hand.

Gabriel's temper had not soothed in the time she'd spent preparing herself. She walked to him and put a gloved hand on his chest.

"I promise not to endanger myself," Sarah said. A snort was his response as he led her out. She shook her head. "Do you plan to grouse for the entire trip?"

"I've not decided."

"Then I am pleased to be traveling with the charming Mister Crawford. I'm certain he has many interesting stories to tell. We'll not need you to speak. We will amuse ourselves."

Crawford was already atop a gray mare. Gabriel helped Sarah mount and soon they were ready.

"I hope to make the village by nightfall, and we will stay at the inn nearby," Crawford said and kneed his horse. "I will acquire the rooms and you will enter through the back. As I am the only one of us three who is unknown to our spies, it will be best if we do not draw attention to you and Mrs. Harrington. The six men I hired will already be in place."

Gabriel moved up beside him. "Is six men enough?"

"We'll not know until we arrive."

On horseback, they did not press their mounts and still made good time. As the ride was not a great distance, they did not have to change horses. They reached Summerdown Manor, slowed to view only the top two floors of the house through the trees, and continued on into the village.

The inn stood just off the road, and the exterior appeared tidy through the curtain of dusk. They stabled their mounts and Sarah and Gabriel hastened around to the back. She'd pulled her hat low to disguise her face. Gabriel did the same. Once secreted beneath a low overhanging roof, they waited for Crawford to fetch them.

"Your modest skill with pistol and blade notwithstanding, I continue to have misgivings." Gabriel pulled her close.

"I know," she said. "I'll not do anything foolish."

"My worry is not that you will make mistakes," he assured her. "You are most competent. My worry is about these men. Given the opportunity, they will not hesitate to shoot you."

"Please do not fret, dear husband." Sarah cupped his face. "You will not lose me."

"How can I not worry, love?" He kissed her palm. "We may be desperately outmanned in the lair of killers."

"You'll not be outmanned."

Sarah turned to see Mister Brown walking toward them, trailed by a full dozen men. The group joined them in the shadows.

Relief flooded her. "I did not know if you'd receive my note or if it would be too late."

Gabriel released her. "Explain, Wife."

She took his arm and led him away from the group. She felt the tension in his body and saw the anger in the tightness of his jaw. "I sent a note with Flora to Bow Street," she whispered. "Although we are not entirely convinced Mister Brown is trustworthy, I knew we needed him. The Widow is his wife. He knows her best."

He glanced back at the Runner. After taking a moment

to reflect on her words, he sighed. "I had not considered using Brown. Your instincts were correct. Well done."

The door creaked open and Crawford stepped into the opening. He spotted the shadowed men and his hand went inside his jacket.

Gabriel stepped forward. "These men are Runners. Sarah called for additional assistance from Bow Street. Mister Brown and his companions are at the ready."

Crawford drew in a deep breath and dropped his hand. "I shall acquire a few more rooms."

Once everyone was settled in, they gathered in Gabriel and Sarah's room. Between Gabriel and her, Crawford and his men, and the Runners all together, the room was near bursting.

Several men eyed her curiously, but none protested her presence.

"I think the best time for launching an attack on the manor is after midnight," Gabriel said. "The people inside will be sleeping and the guards not as alert."

"I agree," Crawford said. "We must go in as quietly as possible and remove the guards, without an alarm being raised. My men are trained fighters. We will leave the guards to them and the occupants of the house to us."

Gabriel turned to Brown. "Sarah and I will enter the house with Crawford and make certain all is quiet. We'll open the front door to you and your men."

The Runner agreed. "They will not be taken easily."

"We do not expect so," Gabriel said. "If The Widow, as we suspect, is working with current or former spies, they will be well trained to fight. We cannot make mistakes."

Gabriel watched Brown's face and felt his inward struggle. Still, the man had not given any indication he was a traitor or that his presence was spurred by anything outside the desire to see the case come to its rightful conclusion.

Even so, he and Sarah had to remain alert to any possibility. They'd not be taken by surprise.

"Then we shall meet in the yard at one o'clock," Crawford said. Gabriel indicated he stay behind as the other men filed out. After the door closed, Gabe took Crawford into his confidence.

"I did not tell you of this earlier, but there is something you need to know. The Widow is Brown's wife, Solange."

Crawford's eyes widened. "You've chosen now to divulge this important piece of information?"

"I did not want this to prejudice your investigation," he said. "Brown was a friend of Sarah's father, and we do not believe him capable of harming her, or me. However, we both think he is still in love with his wife and do not know in what form that love may take if it comes to saving Solange's life, or ours."

The investigator ran both hands over his head. "What a puzzle. A Bow Street Runner is married to a notorious spy, who plans to kill you both, once the evidence against the French spies is unearthed. How many people know of their connection?"

"We are not privy to that," Sarah said. "However, I can only imagine there are few people he trusts with this secret." Sarah sat on the chair. "I wonder how much my father knew. If he was aware of the truth, would it have strained their friendship? If Solange *is* Father's killer, she was married to his friend. What did my father think when he saw her face right before he died?"

"We will never know, love," Gabe said. He expelled a breath. "We have another confession, Mister Crawford. We have not told Brown about the boxes of papers. Yet. We feared he might try to alert Solange so that she may flee."

Crawford stared, annoyed. "First Brown's connection and now this?"

"Once she has returned to France, my father will not be avenged. We did not intend to exclude you forever, merely for a few days until we put everything together." Sarah looked at Gabriel. "I have a confession for you also. If we do not return to London tomorrow as planned, Flora has been instructed to take the boxes to Lord Seymour."

"Why did you keep these plans from me?" Gabriel asked. His ire returned full force. "Did you not trust me?"

"This is *not* about trust," she said. "You decided, on your own, I might add, that I should stay home with my needlepoint like a good wife in the safety of our town house. To be perfectly honest, I was a bit insulted by your lack of faith."

How could he respond? She was right. His temper settled. "You do not needlepoint."

Glowering, she continued, "As such, I felt you left me free to do as I wished. While you were plotting with Mister Crawford without me, I made certain that not only did we have additional men to help keep us safe, but in the event that we do not come out of this caper unscathed, Lord Seymour will both know of our whereabouts and have the evidence needed to conclude my father's case."

"My mistake was not to want to keep you safe, but to underestimate my brilliant wife." He pulled her from the chair. "I promise I will not do it again."

His reward was her brilliant smile. "I have a feeling I will have many opportunities over the next fifty years to remind you of your promise," she said. "You are far too protective of me."

"I'll never apologize for that," Gabe replied.

"I did not expect you would." She stepped away with a grin and went to claim her valise. Gabe and the investigator talked of a few last details before deeming themselves ready for the night ahead.

Crawford excused himself, stating he would go below and have food sent up. Sarah changed out of her habit and into a pair of trousers she'd found in a trunk in Albert's old room.

"Thankfully, he was still a lad the last time he wore these," she said. "They are a bit long and loose at the waist, but Flora included a piece of twine in the valise for holding them up."

The dark brown trousers hugged her curves and caused

a stir in his breeches. "I have never seen anything so entic-ing." He cupped her rump. "I'll make you a trade. I will wear the buckskin breeches for you and you will wear these for me, once we return home."

Sarah chuckled and leaned back against his hands. "Who knew a pair of trousers could inspire such passion." She wriggled her bum. He went to full erection.

Enticed to madness, he removed his hands from the curved flesh and circled her waist. From there it was an easy shift to cover her breasts with his palms.

She moaned. "We do not have time to slake your needs, Husband. The maid will soon be up with food."

"Then we should hurry." He jerked down her trousers and kicked them away. His breeches followed. He lifted her up, carried her awkwardly to the bed, and dropped her down on the edge. With a fluid motion, he was buried inside her. With time limited, he pounded inside her to her pleasured gasps and toyed with her feminine bud until she cried out. A few more thrusts and he spilled himself inside her.

"I told you that we had time." Lying splayed out, her shirt in disarray and her hair a tumble of waves and hair-pins, she never looked more beautiful. He leaned in and nuzzled her neck.

"You did."

A knock sounded. She pushed him off and darted for her clothing. Gabe righted his trousers. "Coming."

She struggled to muffle a giggle. He chuckled at her rush to get the trousers up. She sat on the bed, pulled the shirt down over the gaping waistband, and settled a bland expression on her face.

Gabe jerked open the door, startling the maid. "I will take that. Thank you." He handed her a coin, took the tray, and closed the door.

Standing, the trousers pooled at her feet. Her laughter was infectious, but his eyes were on her shapely legs. "After we eat, I shall find that twine," she said. "I cannot sneak around Summerdown Manor with my trousers falling down."

"I like your trousers where they are."

"Scoundrel."

Sarah dozed on his chest. Just after midnight, he roused her with a kiss on the brow and a light shake. "Wake up, sweet."

The drug of sleep tried to drag her back with its murky coils. "Just another hour or two?" she protested, softly. He was so warm and the room was chilly on her exposed face. "Maybe three?"

"I would be happy to leave you here," he said against her skin. "However, I fear your wrath should I leave you behind."

"Erg." Sarah pushed her hair out of her eyes and sat up on the bed. It took a moment for her eyes to focus. "I've been waiting ten years for this case to come to its conclusion. I would be displeased to be left sleeping while the arrests are made."

"Then you had better ready yourself." He climbed from the bed and went to retrieve his coat. "We need to be downstairs soon."

Groaning, Sarah rose, quickly braided her hair, and retied the ribbon. She stuffed the whole up under a wool cap Flora had fetched for her. She tucked in the shirt and tied the twine tightly around her waist. Gabriel assisted by holding up the trousers for her, and stole a caress, or two.

"I cannot get ready, beast, with you taking liberties." She slapped his hand away. Inasmuch as she'd love to join him in the bed, they had no time to dawdle.

"Alas, you are correct." He helped her tighten the rope until she was certain her trousers would stay up.

A wrinkled black wool coat, too fine to wear to a housebreaking, finished her wardrobe. At Gabriel's look, she shrugged. "It was all I could find in Albert's trunk with big enough pockets for the pistols.

While she pulled on her boots, Gabriel readied their weapons and handed the smaller pair to her. She tucked the pistols into her pockets. "I'm ready."

When they walked downstairs at ten minutes to one, the taproom was already filled with men. A tired-looking tavern maid was seated in a corner, the only other person in the room. Clearly the owner had already sought out his bed. The woman did not bother to get up. She was already half asleep in the chair.

They all followed Crawford out.

Horses waited in the darkness. Several stable boys stood ready to assist. After each horse was claimed, Gabriel handed them each a coin and waved them off to bed.

"Tom made arrangements with the neighbor to stable the horses while we assault the manor," Crawford said, and they swung into the saddles. "There is a path through the forest. We'll follow it and spread out once we reach Summer-down. My men will have fifteen minutes to overtake the guards. After, we'll approach the house, hopefully with the occupants none the wiser."

The horses moved about as if sensing the tension of their riders. The yard fairly crackled with anticipation of the hours ahead. Sarah did not share the men's enthusiasm. To them, this was a dangerous game. To her it was the end of ten years of confusion and a ruined childhood.

"The goal is to capture The Widow," Gabriel said to the men. "We need her alive if we are to catch whomever she is working for."

In the darkness, it was impossible to see Mister Brown's reaction to Gabriel's order, but several heads nodded.

Beneath her ribs, Sarah's heart thumped. She was awash with both excitement and fear. Despite the comforting weight of the pistols, she'd had just one afternoon of training and wasn't completely confident in her skills. Still, she could not, would not, fail.

One mistake could mean her death, or the death of others.

Chapter Twenty-seven

The thought of potential deadly consequences, if she made any mistakes, strained Sarah's mind. For a brief moment she considered staying back at the inn with her head buried beneath a pillow. Then Father's face nudged into the forefront of her thoughts and she straightened in the saddle.

As the daughter of a spy, she had his blood, his courage in her veins. She'd not fail.

Staring up at a myriad of stars in the black sky, she hoped her father was watching, knowing how much she loved him.

She'd head confidently off into danger for him, for Albert, for the sacrifices they'd all been forced to make; a family destroyed, because of a killer.

"Sarah?" Gabriel said. "Are you well?"

Nodding, she lowered her eyes, tightened her hands on the reins, and swallowed past a lump in her throat. "I was thinking about my father. Would he be pleased with all this?"

Gabriel nudged his horse close and touched her knee. "He would be proud of you. I'm certain of it."

Crawford gave last instructions and they rode out. The

manor was just a short distance away, but with only the
moon to light the path, the horses had to move slowly or
risk injury on the pitted road. Silence, but for hoof steps on
packed earth and an occasional whispered word, followed
their progression.

Tension lingered between her shoulder blades, causing
an ache down her spine.

They turned up a drive and her heart skipped. Somewhere beyond her view were Summerdown Manor and its
nest of spies. Close. Sleeping. Unaware of what was about
to befall them.

The neighbor, Mister Travers, waited at his stable. His
eyes were feverish in the lamplight, his eagerness palatable. He stepped forward to grasp the bridle of Crawford's
horse. "I worried you weren't coming."

"We are not late," the investigator said and swung down.
"I thought you would be abed."

Several men began leading the horses into the stable.

"The trail is hard to find in the dark," Travers said. He
patted his ample belly. "I will lead you."

Crawford looked ready to argue. Instead he said, "As
you wish. However, I will not play nursemaid to you. When
bullets whiz past, you are responsible for your own head."

Travers swallowed deeply. "Perhaps I will keep watch
from the end of the trail. Should anyone try and flee, I can
alert you to their direction."

Even in the shadows, Sarah could see Mister Crawford's
amusement. She leaned into Gabriel as he helped her dis-
mount.

She whispered to him, "Mister Crawford clearly expects
Travers to flee with his tail tucked, at the first sign of
danger."

"We all think that, love."

The walk across the property to the trail took almost ten
minutes. The narrow path wound through the forest, giving
the trees an eerie feel. Sarah shivered, remembering a story
her father once told her of a headless horseman who rode

the countryside stealing hapless souls. She hoped the image was not an omen of things to come.

At a split in the path, Travers said, "This way."

Several more minutes passed and the trees thinned. From a distance, Sarah could see the outer shell of the large manor house looming. There was no light in the windows.

Crawford lifted a hand, halting their progression. In a low tone, he gave everyone their instructions, and his men walked off into the night. Almost immediately, their shadowed forms vanished from sight.

"This is your last chance to wait with Travers," Gabriel whispered in her ear. "No one will think less of you."

Sarah whispered back, "I will think less of me."

Warm breath caressed her cheek with his soft chuckle. "Murderous spies cannot frighten off my wife. The Widow beware."

Crawford snorted. "As I said about the Harrington women . . ." His voice trailed off. Sarah smiled.

The knot in her chest eased slightly. She was satisfied to have his support and confidence, and that of the investigator, in this endeavor. "How much longer?"

"About ten minutes by my calculation." Those ten minutes seemed to last forever. There was no sound of fighting, no lights blazing in the windows. But for an occasional nocturnal animal walking on leaves, there was only quiet.

Finally Crawford waved them forward. "It's time."

"We'll check the windows on the north and east sides and you the south and west. See you inside," Gabriel said.

Sarah kept one hand in her pocket, lest she need a weapon. Focused on not trodding on dried leaves and branches, she let Gabriel lead. He'd been trained to track in America and was skilled to get them to the house in a safe and timely manner.

Gabriel stopped abruptly, almost causing her to crash into his back. He stepped around a prone figure.

Was the man dead? *Have courage,* she repeated over and over in her head as they neared the house.

"Keep close to the walls," Gabriel whispered. They examined the doors and reachable windows as they moved forward. All were locked. Eventually, Gabriel found a small unlatched window at head level that he was able to push up. Further examination showed the opening was not large enough for him to crawl through.

"We have to keep searching," he said. He reached to pull it closed.

"No," she whispered. "Lift me up. I can fit."

He hesitated for only an instant then linked his hands together. His trust warmed her. She stepped into his palms and climbed through the tight space.

Carefully, she lowered to the floor, her boots making a soft scrape on wood. She turned to peer out. "Which way?"

He pointed. "Go toward the back and find a door to the terrace. And be careful."

Sarah flashed him a smile and lowered the window. Oddly, now that she was inside the house, her stomach settled. It was her heart that kicked up a notch. If she was caught, no one would know for several minutes; enough time to end her life.

Like a housebreaker, she moved stealthily across the room—the scullery, she thought from the condition of the space—her ears listening for any sound of movement, looked for any sign of human-shaped shadows.

Once she reached the door and entered the hallway, she headed for where she remembered the terrace being, and glanced in each room as she went. The right room proved easy to find, once her eyes adjusted to the darkness. A row of windows in a large parlor led her straight through to the terrace doors.

Her heart leapt when she pushed back the drapes to find Gabriel's face at the glass. She unlatched the door and he stepped inside.

"Did you see anything untoward?" he asked. They opened all four doors wide. Crawford arrived and took a position, facing out toward the grounds.

"I did not glimpse anyone. This floor is empty." Muted

footfalls on the flagstone announced the arrival of the Runners, with Brown leading. Crawford led them inside.

Gabriel found and lit a lamp. "With the guards outside either subdued or dead, there is no reason to stumble about in the dark."

"I'll look for candles," Sarah said. She searched through a nearby rosewood cabinet and found half a dozen candles. She lit one for herself and one each for Gabriel, Crawford, and Brown, then handed out the rest.

"Sarah and I will start on the second floor," Gabriel said. With Sarah at his side, they left the room. Once they were alone, he touched her arm and whispered, "If you suspect danger, do not hesitate to shoot. Our spies will not hesitate to kill you."

"I understand." She removed a pistol from her pocket. It shook slightly in her hand.

They found the staircase. The second floor housed only one wing of bedrooms; the other was taken up by a parlor, a library, and a huge gallery.

The first two bedrooms were empty. In the third they found a man snoring, naked, atop the coverlet. Gabriel nudged him with the pistol and hit him twice in the jaw before the man came fully awake. The man fell back and did not move again.

Sarah helped her husband roll the man in the coverlet and pushed him under the bed. "That should keep him," Sarah said and rubbed her hands together.

The next room yielded nothing. In the fourth bedroom, a man slept in a chair by the fireplace. With his back to them, his even breathing confirmed this conclusion. Gabriel clicked the door closed behind them. The man jerked awake, came to his feet, and spun around, a pistol clutched in his hand.

Sarah's mouth dropped open.

Lord Hampton's son stood bathed in firelight. Sarah blinked to confirm she was not imagining him. There was no mistake. He was the man she'd met a few days earlier.

"Lord Kilmer," Gabriel said and took a few steps forward. "How interesting to find you here. Did you take a wrong turn on the way to Luton?"

Clearly flummoxed by their surprise intrusion, Lord Kilmer said nothing but gripped the pistol at his side. With Gabriel's own pistol pointed at him, he dared not raise the weapon and attempt a shot and risk certain death.

"You bastard," Sarah hissed. "You knew where Solange was when we visited your father, because you were helping her. Traitor."

The man's eyes glinted. "Alas, it is all true."

"Is she paying you?" Gabriel asked. "Or is your connection more personal? She is years your elder, but still attractive enough to entice a man."

Before he could answer, the door pushed open and a woman stepped inside, wearing a dressing gown. "Geoffrey, there are men in the house! Hurry, we must flee!" She spotted Gabriel and stumbled to a stop. Her appearance confirmed the latter of Gabriel's two theories. They were lovers.

"Do not move," Sarah growled and brought her pistol up. Their gazes locked. Sarah held the item aimed at the ready lest The Widow dared to try to escape, or attack. Her mouth curved into a smirk. "You are not nearly so fierce when wearing only your nightclothes, Solange."

Solange's eyes hardened. "You should never underestimate me, Sarah. I do not need an arsenal to take down an enemy."

"Then we were both surprised tonight. Lord Kilmer was a completely unexpected gift, and you obviously never thought we would find you. You are not as intelligent as you let yourself believe."

Solange hissed under her breath. She said something in French that Sarah was certain was not complimentary.

Slowly, Gabriel moved sideways so he could face both Solange and the viscount. "Would you like to explain this, Your Lordship, or shall I guess why you've taken up with traitors? Well, other than the pleasure of sharing The Widow's bed."

The viscount held out a hand. "I would very much enjoy hearing your speculation."

Gabriel's eyes narrowed. "You were not much more than a boy at the time The Widow was coming into notoriety, so I assume you knew nothing about your father's traitorous activities. Yes, I fully believe he was a turncoat."

The viscount's face tightened. "You know nothing about my father."

"Oh, I think I do," Gabriel countered. "I assume his reasons fell into an easing of debts, seeking favor from someone, or a woman. It doesn't matter which. He turned against his country and cost the lives of his countrymen."

"And my father was murdered," Sarah snarled. "Somehow Father found out about Lord Hampton and confronted him. As they were friends, my father would want the truth. The Widow was sent to kill him to keep the secret."

"Is that what you think?" the viscount said. He chuckled. "Solange did not kill Palmer. I was the one who overheard the confrontation, found out about my father's activities, and realized that my life, and our family's reputation, would be ruined once Palmer shared the truth. I waited until Palmer was well away from the house before I shot him."

"Good Lord," Gabriel said. "You couldn't have been more than twenty then."

"I was eighteen," the viscount said. "When I realized Father would not kill his friend, even to save himself, I knew I had to do something to save him from his cowardice. To this day, Father knows nothing of my crime."

"Murderer!" Sarah cried. "I hope they hang you!"

All her life she'd waited for the moment when her father would be avenged. Never, even once during her imaginings, did she ever envision anything but an experienced thug as the murderer. And certainly not a boy barely into manhood.

His laughter rang through the room. "Foolish girl. I have done much worse than take your father's life since then. Still, I've escaped punishment. I will do so again."

Outraged, Sarah took a step toward him. "Never. I'll kill you myself."

With a smirk, Lord Kilmer lifted the pistol. Gabriel shot him through the heart. Gasping, he spun around and pitched to the floor with a thud. Gabriel lowered his pistol and stared, emotionless, at the fallen man. "It is done."

"You killed him," she said, breathless. Deep inside her relief flooded through her. She could have shot him, but could she have lived with taking his life? Perhaps. Now she did not have to find out.

"I could not let him harm you."

A flash of movement caught her eye. Before Sarah jerked her head back around to Solange, the woman was gone.

"Gabe!" she called out and darted from the room. She raced toward the staircase but the figure in a red robe had vanished. Mister Brown came running down the stairs from an upper floor. "Solange is getting away!"

Brown ran toward Sarah, veered off, and took the stairs down two at a time. Wind blew into the foyer as Brown bolted out the open door. Sarah got to the landing and raced after him. Several Runners and at least two of Crawford's men ran past her. She stopped and scanned the darkness. Solange was nowhere in sight.

"Find The Widow!" Brown yelled. Men separated, covering all directions as the night air wrapped them in a chilly cocoon.

Sarah stood frozen on the stoop, silently mouthing words a proper lady should not know. Even then, she realized that although Solange had not directly killed Father, she was guilty of other, just as grievous, crimes.

Someone came up behind her. She recognized the spicy scent.

"She is gone," Sarah said. "It was my mistake. Hopefully, it will not lead to further deaths."

"We both failed." Gabriel took her by the arms and eased her backward into his embrace. "She cannot get far dressed as she is. We will find her."

"And the viscount?"

"Dead."

Sarah sighed. "My father has been avenged. I should be pleased. Oddly, I feel nothing."

He turned her around and took her arms. "You will. Once the case has been closed and the spies arrested, you will be able to grieve for your father properly."

"I've not visited his grave." She leaned her forehead on his chest. "I wanted to wait until I was able to tell him that he may rest now peacefully with my mother. And Albert."

Gabriel hugged her tight. "We can go together."

The next hour was blurred as Sarah waited for news of Solange and answered questions from Mister Brown. Despite the presence of Lord Kilmer in the manor, and the pistol in his lifeless fingers, the Runner needed to conclude the shooting was justified before letting Gabriel go free.

"Gabriel shot the viscount to save my life," she said for about the tenth time. "The viscount killed my father and tried to kill me. There is nothing more I can add."

"And Solange?"

When I turned away from Solange, she vanished." Sarah's patience thinned. "I told you this many times already."

"Was she armed?" he pressed.

"I saw no weapon."

He stared then turned away to confer with one of the other Runners. Sarah sighed, long and deep. She was ignored for several minutes.

Finally, he rejoined her. "We are satisfied the shooting was a defensible act. Fetch Mister Harrington."

Although they'd kept Gabriel locked in the pantry during her questioning, so he'd not influence her answers, he was unharmed, albeit a bit put out. She went to him and slipped into his embrace.

Crawford returned. "Solange escaped. There is a woodcutter's cottage at the edge of the property. We found a horse and evidence of supplies, as if the cottage was prepared for the eventuality of a hurried escape. We've concluded that she took a second horse and fled. Several of the Runners have given chase, but I hold out no hope."

"Damn." Mister Brown slumped back in his chair. His

face seemed to have aged ten years since their first meeting. "Solange will return to France where we'll never find her."

Gabriel rubbed his chin. "Not if you post Runners at the shipyards. She may try to ride south to Brighton or Dover and cross the Channel there. She'll not be able to travel those distances at a fast pace without changing horses. Also, alert the posting inns to requests for horses from a woman of her description."

One of Crawford's men joined them. "There are three dead and three injured outside and four men arrested inside."

"Five," Sarah said, her voice weary. "There is one under the bed, in the third room on the left. We forgot him in the melee."

The investigator chuckled and went off with his man to fetch the prisoner. Gabriel took Sarah's hand. "It is nearly dawn. My wife and I are returning to the inn. If you have further need of us, you may speak to us this afternoon."

They walked hand and hand across the property, down the forest path, and reclaimed their horses.

Mister Travers peeked around the corner of the stable. "Has the matter been settled?" he asked.

Gabriel assisted Sarah into the saddle and handed her the reins. "The spies have been vanquished."

The portly man slumped. "Thank goodness." He puffed up. "I was not worried for myself, you understand. I was worried about my wife and children."

"Of course." Gabriel swung into the saddle. "You cannot be assured of your safety just yet. The Widow escaped. She may be hiding nearby."

Travers whimpered and rushed off toward his house like his breeches were ablaze.

"You are terrible. He will be looking for her under every bed," Sarah said with a light scold. "The poor man may suffer an apoplectic attack if the floor squeaks."

His wicked chuckle was her answer.

Chapter Twenty-eight

✦

"Pack the blue, the cream, and the rose silk," Sarah said. Flora pulled the gowns from the wardrobe and laid them on the bed. "Wait. And the green wool, too."

"We will have to retrieve another trunk, miss." The maid spun to encompass the room with her gaze. Every surface was covered with something that needed packing.

Sarah looked over at the last trunk. It was filled nearly to the top with gowns and fripperies, shoes and boots. And it was the second large trunk she'd filled. "Drat. Put the blue and the cream back."

"You will make yourself ill worrying so, love." Gabriel walked over and kissed her temple. "If you forget anything, you can send someone back for it."

She placed a hand over her fluttering stomach. "I cannot help but worry. I am perfectly fine with your mother, sisters, and cousin. However, being all together with the entire lot, and the ruckus that comes with such a large group, is what I am not so certain of."

"I thought you wanted the ruckus. I recall you saying so not long ago. In this very room, unless I'm mistaken."

"I do. It's just . . . wanting and actually doing are two different things." She dropped a stocking on the bed. "What if the duke or Simon or Gavin finds my conversation tedious? What if the children hate me and cry when I'm near."

He smiled. "The children will love you, and Blackwell has already shown his friendship. Simon and the duke will follow suit." He bent to catch her eyes. "You climbed through a window into a nest of spies without balking. You held a pistol on a dangerous and infamous spy, without your hand shaking. Surely the Harringtons will be relatively dull by comparison."

"Hmmm. Alas, my hand did shake just a wee bit. However, you do have a point." She did love his sensible nature. Still, she asked, "Do you think I should take the blue?"

Shaking his head, he chuckled and left her to fret.

Three hours later, Mister Brown arrived as the staff was loading the trunks onto the coach. He joined Sarah and Gabriel in the library. "The boxes of papers yielded several highly placed names, as you know. Two were men whom your father suspected might be spies, but were cleared by our investigation. This morning, we arrested Lord Pembrook, the Baron Greenwood, and several others. They will be tried for treason."

"Lord Pembrook? The man is a bounder, but he is also a traitor?" Gabriel crossed his arms. "The husbands and fathers of the Ton will feel a collective level of relief with his arrest."

"What about Lord Hampton?" Sarah asked. "His son is dead and his secrets exposed. Will he be tried for his crimes?"

"He will not," the Runner assured her. "He has been put under guard and in the care of a physician. He will live out whatever time he has left locked up in his home."

His Lordship, though a traitor, was in no condition to be exposed to the horrors of Newgate. "With his fractured mind and the death of his son, he is already suffering a deplorable fate," she said.

"What of your wife?" Gabriel continued. "Is there news?"

Mister Brown looked to the window. "We have sent men

to look for her, including two dozen soldiers. Thus far there is nothing to indicate where she's gone. It's possible she hired someone with a ship to take her to France. If so, we will never catch her. They will pension her off deep in the country and she'll live out her days as French gentry."

"That is unfortunate." Gabriel frowned and crossed his arms. "She should not be free."

"At least the men she worked with will face punishment," Sarah said. "Although I'm frustrated that Solange could remain free, at least the viscount is dead. Father is avenged. However, if she cannot escape to France, eventually she will be found. A woman like her would be hard to hide forever."

"Hard but not impossible," a voice interjected from the doorway. Gavin Blackwell stood in the space. "I think I know where your spy is hiding."

G abe came to his feet. "Where?"
"Three days ago, I noticed one of my ships appeared to have someone sleeping in the captain's berth. This is not entirely unusual, as sometimes a vagrant or soused sailor will go aboard for shelter and I have to run them off."

"What leads you to believe Solange is your mysterious guest?" Sarah said. She slid to the edge of the settee.

"A search turned up no one, so I put the matter out of my mind. Then last night, one of my watchmen thought he saw the figure of a woman on the deck of my schooner. It was dark and he could not be certain, but he did stand guard all night, in case of thievery. When he alerted me this morning, I checked again and found a stocking partially concealed under the bunk."

"Could one of your men have entertained a woman on board?" Brown asked. His face was tight.

Gavin grinned. "A woman of the trade would not own a silk stocking of such quality."

Sarah faced Gabriel. "It has to be her."

"How can we be certain she is still aboard?" Gabe said.

"I am fairly certain she is in the hold, the one place I did not think to check in my first brief search. When I realized she could not have escaped past my watchman, unless she jumped overboard, I locked her in."

Gabe chuckled. "She has to be frantic. How fitting. She fought to avoid arrest and now she's imprisoned anyway." The thought of Solange trapped like a rat did offer some satisfaction.

"We can either sit here all day, pondering her situation, or we can go catch a spy." Sarah stood, walked to the door, and called for a cloak.

Gabe collected a pistol from the desk, gave instructions for the servants and luggage to travel to Harrington House as scheduled, then he and the other men followed Sarah out.

They rode in Blackwell's carriage to the wharf where a man in worn clothing stood on the far end of the dock, looking over a schooner with a broken mast.

"It was waiting for repairs," Blackwell explained as they walked past the row of ships. "Your Widow likely saw it as a place to hide for a few days until the search waned. Had she not come on deck and drawn the attention of Fitch, she could have hidden for another week before the repairs began."

They came to a stop. "Have you seen a sign of her, Fitch?" Blackwell asked the watchman.

Fitch shivered. "I 'ave not see 'er, but I did 'ear screamin'. It were chilling, like from the grave."

Sarah smiled. Her eyes took on a wicked cast. Gabriel matched it with a satisfied smile of his own.

"Remind me to add a bonus to your pay this week." Blackwell thumped the man on his shoulder. "You may also be due a reward if this is the spy the Runners have been looking for."

A toothless smile followed. The man rubbed his hands together. "Thank you, sir."

Blackwell turned back to their group. "Shall we go aboard?" He walked away without waiting for an answer. Once inside they went below and he led them to a door with a lock dangling from the handle. He turned the key and removed the lock.

Gabe pulled out a pistol. "I'll go first."

The hold was cramped with a few crates along one side and a makeshift pallet of cloth and straw packing near the back wall. Chased away from the captain's cabin by Blackwell's presence above, she'd obviously been hiding in here since.

To his surprise a lamp flared and Solange stepped from the shadows, around a crate, and into the center of the space. She still wore her nightdress and red dressing gown.

"We've found our fugitive, gentlemen."

Her eyes grew wild and she sneered. Gabe instantly realized she was not looking at him but behind him. "I should have expected your disloyalty, Hubert. You could have allowed me to escape."

Brown stepped around Gabe. "You are no longer the girl I once loved, Solange. I cannot let you continue as you are. Good men have died because of you."

"We are at war!"

"Napoleon is in exile," Brown pressed. "Yet, you continue to play the game. Men are still vanishing, dying. You cannot hope for Napoleon's resurrection to power. The war is over."

Her voice dropped to a mere whisper. "The war will never be over, Husband."

Before Gabe understood her intention, she reached out and dashed the lamp to the floor.

The dry straw packing caught fire and spread quickly.

"Sarah!" Gabe spun, the flames already clawing at the crates and racing across the floor where bits of straw were scattered. Gray smoke rose to the ceiling, quickly filling the small area. He covered his mouth and coughed. Heat and smoke seared a path down his throat.

Thankfully, Sarah was closest to the stairs and safety. Blackwell spun her around. "Gabriel!" she screamed, fighting him. Blackwell forced her up. "Gabe!"

Terrified of being trapped in the fire, Gabe grabbed for Brown but the Runner shrugged him off. Desperate, he tried again.

Brown broke loose from his grip and ran toward Solange, his arms outstretched, calling for her. Even with her madness stealing the last vestiges of his Solange from him, Brown had to save her.

Gabe could not wait any longer; he hurried for the stairs, knowing he had to get out or would die.

In the billowing smoke, he stumbled, choking.

Suddenly Blackwell appeared with a cloth over his nose and mouth. He took Gabe by the lapel and dragged him forward and up the stairs until they reached the deck. They stumbled across the slick planks and landed on the dock as smoke billowed up from below.

"Gabe!" Sarah ran to him, sliding under his right arm as Blackwell took the left. They got to shore just as his legs gave out beneath him and his world went dark.

G abe, no!" Sarah cried. Pain ripped through her. His lifeless weight brought her to her knees. Gavin eased him onto his back and leaned to listen to his chest. It was the longest few seconds of her life.

"He breathes." He turned and called to Fitch. "Lift him up. We need to get him into the carriage." Between them, they half carried Gabe across the wharf to the carriage and settled him across the seat. Gavin helped Sarah up beside him and handed her the reins.

"Take him to Harrington House."

After giving her quick directions back to Mayfair, he slapped the horse on the rump, turned, and fled back toward his burning schooner.

The carriage raced through the streets, pitching and creaking from the speed, while Gabriel remained lifeless beside her. She sobbed, begging him to live. Once she found a familiar street, she turned toward Harrington House, crying out in relief when the familiar building finally came into view.

She dragged the horse to a stop, set the brake, and raced up the steps. She pushed the door open. "Lord Seymour!" she screamed. "Help me!"

People came from every direction. Lord Seymour appeared, his face blurred through her tears. "Sarah, what's wrong?"

"Gabe is hurt." She caught him by the arm and dragged him outside. Soon family and servants alike circled the carriage.

"He is dying," she wept. "There was so much smoke." Lady Seymour pulled her into her arms and her strength failed.

"Shhh, dearest," the countess said. "Be brave for Gabriel."

Lord Seymour climbed aboard the carriage and examined his son. "He's alive." He twisted around. "Step aside," Lord Seymour commanded. The servants parted to allow Simon and Benning through. The men took Gabriel from the carriage and carried him into the house.

Lady Seymour helped Sarah inside. "Abe, go quickly for the physician." The footman left and the countess and Brenna took the shaking Sarah upstairs to their old room.

Noelle met them at the door. "Sarah, where is Gavin?"

Her worried voice cut into Sarah's mind and brought her some clarity. "He is well," she assured her friend and walked into the bedroom. The room was full of trunks and people. She had to navigate the maze to get to where her unconscious husband lay on the mattress.

"Gabriel." Sarah rushed to his side and touched his soot-covered face. His skin was cool to the touch. She took solace in the rise and fall of his chest. As long as he breathed, there was hope.

Benning helped remove his clothing, and they pulled a sheet over him. Maids took the clothing away as Lord Seymour kneeled on the bed over his son.

"Gabe. You must fight this." His voice was low and hoarse. "How did this happen?" Lord Seymour asked.

"Gavin found Solange on his ship and came for us," Sarah said. "When confronted, she lit a fire. Gabriel tried to save Mister Brown and was caught in the smoke." Her voice caught. "I think Mister Brown and Solange are dead."

"How tragic," Brenna said softly and rubbed her arms.

"Although Solange was a French spy, I'd not want her to die so horribly. And Mister Brown . . ." Sarah brushed her hand over her damp face. "We never fully trusted his loyalty, and in the end, he chose his love for Solange over his life."

Lady Seymour brought over a washing cloth and bathed Gabriel's face. His breathing was uneven, and with every hitch, Sarah's heart flipped. She was certain each would be the last.

The physician, Mister Meath, arrived shortly thereafter. After Sarah explained the situation, he began his examination. He listened to Gabriel's chest, looked down his throat, and checked him over for burns. After ten minutes he straightened.

"I did not hear a rattle in his lungs, which is a common occurrence when someone breathes in a fatal amount of smoke. I did, however, discover soot in his throat, leading me to believe the throat was burned when he breathed in the hot air. It probably caused a restriction, rendering him unconscious."

"How serious is this burn?" Lord Seymour asked.

Mister Meath shrugged and collected his bag. "I cannot say. If he does not come around in the next few hours, his condition may be permanent." He walked to the door. "I shall return tomorrow morning to check on him."

Lord Seymour showed him out. Brenna and Lady Seymour sat on the other side of the bed. "He will not die," the countess said.

Brenna touched his shoulder. "We still have years of arguing ahead."

Laura and Noelle and Simon stood nearby. "I have not had time to know him well," Laura said. Simon put his hands on his wife's shoulders. She leaned back against him.

"When he is recovered, I will kill him for playing hero," Simon added, his voice heavy. "He always was reckless."

The door opened. Sarah lifted her eyes to Gavin's arrival. He was covered in soot. His clothing was ruined. She met his eyes. Hopefulness extinguished with his head shake.

Gavin crossed to Sarah. "Both Brown and Solange perished. Fitch saw no one escape. Their bodies will be retrieved once we can raise the ship." Noelle took his arm. "The schooner is lost. We managed to save the sloop docked beside it from the fire."

Sarah dropped her chin onto her hands where they clutched Gabriel's arm. She was so weary, so heartsick. She despaired over Gabriel's condition and the death of Mister Brown. He had proven to be a good and loyal friend to her father; to her. If only she'd realized it sooner.

Low voices hummed in the background as she watched Gabriel struggle for breath. "You have to fight this, love. I will not accept a life without you."

Gabriel coughed in his sleep. Over the next few hours, Sarah and Lady Seymour wiped bits of expelled soot from the corners of his mouth and prayed. Occasionally, there'd be a pause between breaths and Sarah would come out of her chair in fear.

The breath following came with her relieved sigh.

"I do not know how much of this waiting I can manage," she said to the countess. "I feel like I should do something more."

"Talking to him is a great help," Lady Seymour assured her. "He needs to know you are here at his side."

Sarah lifted her gaze. "I love him. I cannot lose him."

Lady Seymour smiled from across the bed. "I remember when we first met and I asked you if you loved my son. You said no. I admired your honesty then. Despite your situation, I had faith that you would grow to love my son."

Smiling softly, Sarah squeezed his hand. "I tried not to fall in love. He can be overbearing and protective. I am stubborn and guarded. In those respects, we are very different. But my heart would not listen."

"Do not let doubts into your marriage. Brenna and Lord Ashwood had a marriage of convenience. He was stoic; she, full of mischief. Now they have James and could not be happier."

Sarah watched the rise and fall of Gabriel's chest, willing him to fight, to open his eyes, to give some sign he was recovering. Sadly, he remained in his stupor.

And the clock ticked on.

Lady Seymour talked to her son, sharing her memories of times of joy in the family. She ordered a dinner tray brought up and forced Sarah to eat.

After a few bites, Sarah noticed the countess pushing her own food around her plate. "You must also keep up your strength, Lady Seymour."

The fork stopped. "I grow weary of you addressing me as 'Lady Seymour,' Sarah. It's too formal. I'd much prefer 'Kathleen.'" She averted her eyes. "Or 'Mother,' if you'd like."

Taken aback, Sarah's heart skipped. "I have never had a mother."

"I know." Lady Seymour glanced up. Their eyes met and held. "I would very much like to fill the position."

Raw emotion flooded Sarah's heart, and she blinked back tears. "I'd like that, too . . . Mother."

Brenna arrived and offered to watch over Gabe, but the countess shooed her off to care for James. Noelle, too, came to take a shift and was also sent away by Lady Seymour. "Your baby needs you to rest. Sarah and I will tend to Gabriel."

It was nearing ten o'clock when Gabriel started twitching. Sarah jumped to her feet. He arched back, made a gurgling sound, and went limp. "Gabriel?"

She felt his chest. There was no sound. "Gabriel!"

The countess rushed in from the sitting room with a handful of clean cloths in her hand. "Has something happened?"

Panic filled Sarah with its cold hand. "Gabriel is not breathing!"

Chapter Twenty-nine

Gabe." Lady Seymour shook him. Hard. "Gabe, darling, breathe."

Nothing.

A memory flashed through her mind and Sarah ran for the dressing table. She closed her hand around a hatpin and ran back to jerk the coverlet aside. She reached for his foot, lifted it off the mattress, and jabbed the pin into his heel.

He twitched.

"Thank goodness." The countess slumped on the bed. She placed her hand over her heart. "What a fright."

Sarah looked down at the hatpin. "If one pinprick is helpful, a second should be better." She gave his other foot a jab. He twitched again. She and Lady Seymour watched him.

"He does not look as lifeless as before," Sarah said.

"The pain roused him," Lady Seymour agreed.

After a few minutes, his body jerked. "Gabriel?" Sarah patted his hand. "Come now, wake up." A low groan welled from deep in his throat. His eyelids parted a tiny bit. "That's it," Sarah said. "Open your eyes or I will be forced to prick you a third time."

The countess clapped her hands together and mouthed a whispered prayer.

He blinked a few times then slowly appeared to gain focus. Sarah leaned over him and brought her face close to his. "Have I ever told you how much I love your green eyes?"

"Have I ever told you how shrill your voice is?" The words came out in a hoarse croak.

"My voice is not shrill." She smiled. Happiness filled her to bursting. "Once you are recovered, I'll be pleased to show you what a shrill voice truly sounds like. I intend to spend the rest of our lives being argumentative, and contrary, and stubborn. You deserve that and more for scaring the wits out of *Mother* and I."

Gabriel's brow went up. Sarah smiled brightly and nodded.

Lady Seymour sniffed, dabbed her eyes with her handkerchief, and stood. "I shall go tell the family that you'll live. All but Brenna will be pleased," she teased.

Gabriel frowned and rubbed his brow. "All I remember was Solange and a fire. Beyond is blank."

Sarah explained what happened. Then, "Mister Brown and Solange are dead."

"Pity, that." He lifted onto his elbows. Sarah placed a pair of pillows under his shoulders. "He was a good man. He deserved a better fate."

"I agree. However, I think that no matter Solange's crimes, he still loved her. He wanted to be with her at the end." She took his hand. "Sometimes a person cannot help who they love. His love just may have been misplaced."

"Perhaps." He knitted their fingers together. "Only he could make that judgment. I, on the other hand, think I have made an excellent choice in spouse."

"Despite my shrill voice and contrary nature?"

He pulled her arm and drew her down on the bed. She snuggled against him. He was warm and wonderful, despite the slightly smoky scent of his skin.

"Despite those, and more."

Sarah poked his side. He flinched. "I cannot figure out why I love you so. You are a hateful man. Any other husband would offer his wife compliments and kisses when he arises from near-death. But not my husband. He likes to prick my temper just to see my ire flare up."

He kissed her head and chuckled. "You are beautiful when you're angry." He eased her up so he could peer into her face. "Sarah, my love, you hold my heart. You will never fully understand the depth of my love or how much I cherish the day I appeared on your doorstep. You are the wife I always wanted."

She sniffed as tears welled and her eyes softened. "You did not want a wife."

"Can a man not change his mind?"

Gabriel spent that night and the next day abed, while Sarah and the ladies hovered and Lord Seymour threatened him with a whipping if he dared rise for more than brief clips. When the second evening came and they were alone, Gabriel did not need time to return to their more intimate activities. He was quite robust after a full night of rest.

The morning of the second day, the physician deemed him fit, but for a lingering sore throat, an occasional cough, and, of course, a pair of sore heels. The hoarse voice stayed for the better part of a week. Eventually, he was able to speak normally again. Sarah's favorite part of the return of his voice was when he whispered how much he loved her each night as she fell asleep in his arms.

While he recovered, Sarah spent her time getting acquainted with her new family. Eva, as she insisted Sarah call her, visited several times with her daughter. With two babies under her roof to spoil, Lady Seymour was joyous.

It was during one of those visits that Sarah's curiosity overcame politeness and she posed a question to Noelle and Eva.

"Please excuse my impertinence, but I cannot hold back my curiosity any longer. Why do the two of you have the same color eyes? I know that you are both related to

Gabriel, but what is your connection? That has never been explained to me."

Expecting a rebuke, Noelle glanced at Eva, who nodded, then answered, "We are sisters."

Sarah gaped. "Sisters?" This was highly unexpected. "Why is this kept secret?"

"We share a father," Eva said. "My mother was his courtesan. They fell in love. Then about two years ago, Noelle hunted me down. She'd discovered our connection and wanted to know me. I was not as eager, as my mother is fragile and I did not wish to put her under scrutiny. However, her persistence broke through my resistance and we are now very close."

"She can be pushy," Sarah said.

Noelle made a face. "Eva desires to keep our true connection secret for as long as we can. She doesn't want gossip to harm His Grace. She thinks the circumstances of her birth will hurt him politically."

"He is a duke," Lady Seymour interjected from where she played with James and Catherine on a rug by the window. "No one would dare snub him."

"And he loves Eva madly," Noelle said. "He cares not about her history. He is proud of his duchess."

"From what I understand, the duke has a bit of a temper," Laura added. She smiled sheepishly at the duchess. "He would pummel anyone who'd dare speak ill of his wife."

"This is my decision to make," Eva said, her voice firm, but with the tug of a smile. "I will decide when, and if, I ever disclose our relationship."

With that, the matter was settled. The women changed the topic and chatted about the upcoming Pink Ball. As the last event of the Season, the ball was expected to be quite a row.

"Many families are already packing for wintering in the country," Lady Seymour said. "This is the last chance this year for mamas to cast their daughters at unattached suitors."

"Thankfully we have years before Catherine will seek a

husband," Eva said. "I pity the young man who has to ask Nicholas for her hand."

The men joined them after a meeting at Bow Street.

"The investigation into the fire has been closed," Gabriel said and poured six brandies. "It was deemed an accident, so Brown and Solange may be buried together. Despite her crimes, he would have wanted her beside him."

The room briefly fell silent. Solange had paid for her wrongs by her horrible death. Sarah would not fuss over her burial with Mister Brown.

"Fitch received a generous reward," Gavin said, lightening the moment. He joined Noelle. "The bastard has quit my employment and decided to buy an inn. Damn, he was an excellent worker."

The duke and Lord Seymour chuckled.

Gabriel turned to Sarah. "Crawford was also in attendance. He gave me some news. He managed to find your father's accounts with the help of your nanny. Mrs. Fielding vaguely remembered him mentioning something about Scotland being the place to go if a person wanted to hide. All those hills. Crawford thought it worth checking. He contacted a banker he knew who then sent a note to a fellow banker in Scotland. The man, a Mister McBain, was able to discover an account in a bank in Glasgow."

"How could he find the information so quickly?" Sarah said.

"I'd asked Crawford to investigate the missing account weeks ago," Gabriel said. "I didn't want to tell you out of concern the search could come to naught. There is a hefty sum waiting for you."

"More gowns and fripperies for next Season," Lord Seymour said. "My wife will be eager to help you spend some of your newfound wealth."

Sarah shook her head and looked at Eva. "I'd enjoy doing something nice for your school. I also know of several charities where I'd like to make a donation in Father's name. Although I do love new things, I think the money would be better spent elsewhere."

There were several murmurs of agreement. "That is an excellent idea, love," Gabriel said. "Crawford also said that Nanny is thrilled with the repairs to the house, the allowance, and to scold you for not visiting over these last weeks. Once he informed her of the solving of the case, you were forgiven, for now."

"We will visit soon." Sarah grinned.

"I would not want Nanny unhappy," Gabriel said soberly.

The next morning, Gabriel drove Sarah to the cemetery. A haze covered London as the horse clopped through the quiet streets. When they arrived, the caretaker was just opening the gate. He nodded as they passed under the iron arch.

In Sarah's hand she clutched a small bunch of flowers with the roots intact.

Before they'd left Harrington House, she'd explained, "When I was little, I sometimes pulled up flowers from the garden and gifted them to him to keep on his desk. I thought the room too stark. He'd laugh as I trailed dirt across the polished floor, knowing Nanny, or our housekeeper, Mrs. Wallings, would scold me for the mess."

"Your father liked flowers?"

"He liked *my* flowers."

She deeply inhaled the damp air and pushed back tears as the two of them made their way to the grave site. Something odd caught her attention. Another stone was laid out beside her parents. When Father was buried, there were only two.

"How odd. There is a third stone."

As they closed the distance, she read the name, artfully chiseled in a perfect scroll on the face.

Albert Henry Palmer.

Tears sprang up and flowed unchecked down her cheeks. She looked up at Gabriel and saw his smile and the love for her reflected in his beautiful green eyes.

"Although Albert is buried in Texas, I thought you would want a place to visit them together."

She pressed a hand to her lips as a sob broke. He pulled her into his arms and she snuggled against his warmth. "I love you so much," she said through her tears. "This is perfect."

That evening the ball was in full whirl, and awash in pink, as Sarah danced with her wonderful husband and laughed with her new family. Her heart no longer ached with regrets. Her parents and Albert were together in spirit, and the murder case was closed. She was confident in Gabriel's love, and they were working on having a family. It was time to look forward to her future.

"Excuse me, Husband," she laughed as Noelle tugged at her hand, trying to draw her away from the men. "We are off to the retiring room to primp, share confidences, and grouse about our overbearing husbands."

He grinned, winked, and turned back to his father.

Lady Seymour, Laura, Eva, and Brenna were already tidying their hair and smoothing their gowns when Sarah and Noelle arrived. Resplendent in varied shades of pink, the ladies made a lovely picture. Sarah's heart warmed to be part of such a wonderful group of women.

"I have to find out where Martha Clairwood has her gowns made," the countess was saying. She tugged the puffed sleeve of her gown in place. "Although her pink confection offends the eyes, her seamstress is superb. I am filled with envy."

Noelle splayed her hand over her stomach. "Soon I will need to have my gowns made by a tentmaker." Despite her frown, her eyes were alight with happiness.

"Posh," the duchess said, smiling. "You'll have months before you'll waddle."

Sarah, Eva, and Laura laughed. Noelle sent them a quelling glare. This made them laugh harder. Noelle turned to Eva.

"Laugh all you will, Eva, for I remember when you

carried Catherine, your stomach made an entrance a full half hour before the rest of you. You were the empress of the waddle."

Eva nodded. "I thought I was having twins." She took Noelle's hands, her face filled with joy over her sister's condition. "As my sister, you will likely be just as large as I was, if not larger," she teased.

A gasp brought the private conversation to an end. Mrs. Dubury, obviously eavesdropping, stepped from behind a screen, her eyes wide as she stared at Noelle and Eva.

"You are sisters?" Her tone was pitched high, as if she'd been given the world's greatest Christmas gift. She did not wait for an answer. Their faces must have confirmed her suspicion. She snickered with uncontrolled glee and hurried off as fast as her stubby legs could carry her.

Eva's shoulders drooped. "Our secret is no more."

"By the time we return to the ballroom, the entire assembly will know the truth," Noelle agreed. "We knew it would come out eventually. Just not this way."

"I can ring her thick neck for you," Sarah offered. "She is a horrid woman. It would please me to do so."

Lady Seymour stepped forward. "No neck-wringing tonight, dearest." She peered one last time in the mirror then crossed to Eva and Brenna, took them each by an arm, and escorted them to the open door. "Come, darlings. We Harrington women will face the gossips together, and with dignity."

Brenna shot Sarah a glance over her shoulder. They both knew that despite the calm displayed by the countess, Mrs. Dubury would not end this evening unscathed dare she do anything to hurt Eva or Noelle.

Sarah smiled wickedly, hooked her arm through Noelle's, and followed their regal mother back to the ballroom. If there was blood to be shed, she'd be aggrieved to miss the moment. Once there, Sarah paused to scan the room. It was easy to find Gabriel in the crush. Her heart fluttered when his beautiful green eyes searched for and found her, too. She forgot all about Mrs. Dubury and gossip. He grinned and she pulled her bottom lip between her teeth. She knew her heart would never stop fluttering for him, no matter how long they lived.

"Who'd ever have suspected you two would be this ridiculously happy?" Noelle said as they walked across the room. "Even I envy the way he looks at you."

"I envy myself," Sarah teased, and they shared a smile.

Noelle released Sarah's arm. "Now where have Eva and Aunt Kathleen gone off to? I need to watch Eva's back lest she find a blade buried in it."

"What about you?" Sarah asked. "You are also at risk."

Noelle's eyes went dark and she covered her belly protectively. "Posh. No one would dare accost me or risk a slow and painful demise."

Sarah laughed as Noelle grinned evilly and went off to find her sister. Sarah turned back to Gabriel.

Gabriel excused himself from his father and took her hand. A shiver went up her arm. He lifted her gloved knuckles to his lips. The shiver spread through her body like a flame to dry tinder. Lud, she loved him so!

"Dance with me, Wife."

"Yes, my love." He led her to the floor and swept her into the waltz. Despite the whirl around them, his eyes never left hers. Sarah decided to keep Noelle and Eva's news until the dance was over. She wanted to dance without anything ruining the moment.

"Have I told you how beautiful you are tonight?" Gabriel said and pulled her closer. His scent teased through her senses as his hand tightened on her waist. Propriety kept her from demanding a kiss.

"I do not think you have," Sarah countered tartly. "You, my darling, are remiss in your husbandly compliments."

"Indeed?" He cocked a brow. "Then I shall have to correct the matter immediately." He glanced over her. "You are breathtaking in both face and form. The most beautiful butterfly weeps in despair when you are near, and flowers wilt as you steal from them the sun."

Sarah's laughter spilled free. "Truly?"

"I have heard and seen weeping and wilting," he assured her. His face was serious. "You are perfection in all things. A goddess, truly. Aphrodite is a dried-up old crone by comparison."

Her laughter deepened. "You are clearly a man besotted. No woman can live up to such a standard."

Gabriel slowed their steps and leaned to her ear. "I love you madly, Sarah. You will never be anything less than perfect in my eyes."

"I love you, too." She brushed her face against his. "Forever."

With that, he swept her across the floor. And as if to prove that his conclusion of her attributes came from love and not truth, Sarah's feet faltered and she stepped on his toes. He screwed up his face as he recovered the steps.

"Perfection? Me? I think not," she said laughing as the strains of the waltz slowly faded away.

3 2953 01171219 9